STAR CROSSED LOVERS

Leona succumbed to her desires, knowing she should have been more guarded, yet somehow it was all as if it had happened before, as if they had loved before. She felt faint in Philip's arms, overcome with a sense of deep passion.

He pushed the flimsy material of her dress still farther, and again his lips touched her skin, kissing her everywhere as his own breathing grew heavier with the excitement of the moment.

He lifted her and carried her to the bed in her inner sanctum, put her down gently, and stripped. Leona could not take her eyes off him. He fell down beside her and pushed away the top of her dress. Before she was even aware of it, she lay naked in his arms.

"I have known you for an eternity," he whispered.

Overcome with desire, Leona could only whisper one word. "Yes . . ."

Books by Joyce Carlow:

TIMESWEPT

A TIMELESS TREASURE

TIMESWEPT PASSION

SO SPEAKS THE HEART

Published by Zebra Books

So Speaks
the Heart

Joyce Carlow

Zebra Books
Kensington Publishing Corp.
http://www.zebrabooks.com

"Life is eternal; and love is immortal; and death is only a horizon; and a horizon is nothing save the limit of our sight."

—Rossiter Worthington Raymond
A Commendatory Prayer

Part I

One

A.D. *August 1, 497*
A Village in Persia

It was nearly high noon and the bazaar was filled with throngs of traders who congregated under their precariously pitched tents in order to escape the burning heat of the midday sun. Among them were merchants from the desert, draped from head to toe in loose-fitting sand-colored robes that were decorated with woven multicolored sashes. These were men who lived on their camels. They guided them across the endless sands to meet the golden-skinned dealers who traversed the very top of the world as they moved east to west, meeting here near the base of the snowcapped Elburz mountains. Here they bargained for bolts of silk as varied in their colors as the rainbow, or the flowers of Babylon's legendary Hanging Gardens, for gold and jewels, for spices, medicines, and all manner of household goods.

Traders who traveled from east to west were not the only ones in Rey's famed bazaar. Tall, elegant men—seemingly as slender as the reeds that grew along the edge of the Nile—also appeared now and again. These men were draped in pure white robes with knotted golden sashes; their skin was as black as coal and as smooth as a sea-washed rock. They came from the south, from barren deserts that lay across the top of Africa. They came from the land of the Mali and from the ancient Kingdom of Ethiopia. They came from Chad, the Kingdom of Kanem.

The Rey bazaar was the most fascinating of places. A hundred languages filled the air as bargaining reached a fevered pitch, a thousand smells mingled, fighting for olfactory prominence. The aroma of spices mixed with that of freshly baked bread just as the odor of human perspiration mingled with the reek of freshly dropped camel dung.

Noise, color, excitement, all blended in the bazaar, where scores came to buy cloth, lamps, pottery, food, and jewelry. Whatever one desired could be found in Rey's bazaar—even slaves.

Anstice was a silversmith whose tent was on the very edge of the bazaar. If he stepped through one flap, he found himself in a narrow aisle, one side of which was lined with smiths like himself, and the other side of which was lined with weavers. If he stepped out through the other flap, he was on the perimeter of the bazaar, beyond which lay the flat plain. The plain stretched out ten miles to the north, where the mountains rose to touch the sky. Beyond that first range of mountains lay Mount Damavand, which smoldered with internal discontent, and on occasion sent fire spitting from the center of the earth upward toward the heavens.

Four miles to the south, the village of Tehran was situated peacefully in the sun. Old men lay in doorways smoking, women hung their wash, children played in the sand. But it was Rey that was the center of commerce. It was here, in the year 330, that Alexander the Great had halted while pursuing Darius III, King of Persia, it was here that the great bazaar was located. It was to this place that Anstice had been directed. It was not *the* place, but merely the waiting place. The place where he would bear witness to the first sign.

To his distracted ear, the sounds of the bazaar resembled the drone of bees in their hive. Some voices were soft, others loud, some were angry, others pleading, calm, or agitated. But all blended together to create the din that hummed in the background of Anstice's thoughts. It did not matter that he was in the midst of a crowd. He was alone. It did not matter that to the attentive listener voices and conversations were distinct. To him it was all simply a droning sound; his thoughts blocked out all details.

Anstice wiped his brow, turned, and stepped out through the back flap of his tent. He wore a brown caftan with white stripes, leather sandals covered his feet, and a silver chain was tied around his waist. Anstice's skin was unusually pale, his eyes an intense blue, and he had a long white beard that fell nearly to his waist. The creases in his skin were deep, but his facial lines depicted kindness tinged with a distant sadness. Nevertheless, Anstice smiled often, though today he did not smile. This day he was intent on the coming events.

A look of concern covered his face, and he squinted his eyes against the bright light and ever-blowing dust to survey the heavens. He knew something was amiss, but even knowing did not quell the feeling of anxiety and anticipation that began to surge through him.

It began with a wind that swept across the plain and caused ripples on the Jajrud and Karaj rivers even as it shook the tents of the traders in the bazaar. It moved across the land in a single warm blast of air and was silently dashed against the Elburz mountains, where it curled about like a wave repelled by the shore, and again blew across the plain, this time in reverse. Though the wind was invisible, it was felt as surely as if it had been a hand upon the shoulder. The warm blast was repeated again and again, blowing first from the south and then from the north. The sounds of the bazaar were extinguished as people paused first in awe, then in fear. This was an unnatural wind.

Anstice again looked heavenward. The light cast by the sun was oddly muted as the wind suddenly ceased, and a stillness fell across the desert plain. It was as if a giant had exhaled and inhaled, and was now holding his breath. The next gust of wind was far stronger. The tents shuddered and then flapped wildly as they were liberated from their pegs.

Anstice shivered. His eyes fixed on a miniature tornado of swirling sand, his ears filled with the cries of angry vendors who pursued their airborne goods as well as their tents. This time the giant did not pause, he continued to blow, and as he blew, long shadows were cast across the sand as the noonday sun grew weaker and weaker. One moment it was high noon, the next second it was afternoon, then twilight flickered for an instant. And then there was darkness at noon! The sun had turned black though light surrounded the darkness with a halo so bright, he could not look at it. The earth seemed to shake, and Anstice's ears were filled with sounds of men and women screaming and shouting. Many fell praying to the earth, others hid their faces in their robes, still others ran, though there was no escaping the darkness.

"The end is here!" a woman screeched as she sank to her knees and looked upward.

"Don't look at it! Don't look at it!" an old man yelled. "It's a darkness that blinds the eyes!"

Many wailed, "It's the end of the world!"

The wind carried tents and merchandise swirling in all directions even as the owners of the scattered treasure screamed and prayed, shrieked and begged for forgiveness.

Anstice clung to a large rock, embracing it as if it were his mother, the woman who had given him his Greek name, a name which meant "resurrected one."

But he did not close his eyes or try to cover his ears. All his senses were alert. And though darkness covered the earth at high noon, Anstice was not afraid, for it had been foretold.

Then, just as the shadow had come, it began to move away, uncovering the sun as it passed, revealing to one and all that the sun still shined, that it was indeed noon. Then the wind gradually subsided.

Slowly, though still frightened, those who had been in the bazaar began to pick up their belongings and re-pitch their tents. Just as those in the city gathered up their children and returned to normal. It was not the end of the world. It was only a sign from the gods. Some would say it was a warning that preceded the Apocalypse, others would say it was a foretelling, still others would say it meant there should be a sacrifice.

Anstice straightened and looked heavenward. The sky was once again blue, the sun bright, the earth still. "She has been born," Anstice said under his breath. "She has returned."

Anstice went back to the site of his tent. It was in tatters. But the chest in which he kept his silver and his tools was intact, though it had been upended, having proved too heavy to have been blown away. Anstice retrieved the bits and pieces of his tent and put them together with his chest into the small donkey-drawn cart that was his own personal means of transportation. His donkey had also returned to normal, though it, too, had been terrified. Now it shook its ungainly ears to rid them of sand.

Anstice knew it was time to go. She had been born again, and as the intermediary, he would be led to her and instructed on how to prepare her. Now he had but to find her. Still, he was untroubled by the thought of his search. Dreams would guide him just as they had told him when she would be returned to the mortal world.

A thousand years! When last she came, it was as handmaiden to Aspasia, mistress of Pericles, who ruled Athenian society. Her coming marked the birth of a powerful female leader, a dramatic change, a new era.

Anstice was old, but he felt young, renewed somehow that the time of waiting had ended. He looked down at his feet and suspected they would have to carry him a long way. Yes, it was time to begin the quest, even though he knew not where to look. But he would be guided as he always was guided, by his vivid dreams. Visions sent by Zenobia.

A.D. July 27, 498
Near Antioch

Anstice inhaled deeply. How welcome was the sea breeze after the endless sands of the desert! He stood looking out on the ocean, still intrigued with its salty aroma, still rejuvenated from its trade winds. For a year he had traveled following his dreams, for a year he had moved through dusty towns and villages, pausing now and again to sell his silver goods so that he might travel on.

At this moment he stood on the shores of the Mediterranean in the seaport of Seleucia Piera, at the mouth of Orontes River in the land of the Assyrians, a few miles from the great city of Antioch.

This was a prosperous area. To the east of Antioch there were plantations of olive trees from which was produced a wonderful oil. These great estates were owned by the wealthy citizens of Antioch.

What a magnificent place this was! What an ideal locale to live in warmth and happiness, to dwell in peace! But alas, like all the cities Anstice had passed through, the citizens of Antioch were deeply involved in doctrinal and political disputes.

Christianity warred internally with itself as scholars argued about whether or not Christ's mortal life was entirely separate from his divine being. Those who believed he was entirely divine in spite of having assumed a human form were adherents to Chalcedonian doctrine, while those who believed otherwise were called Monophysites. The Monophysites, then, believed in the one nature of Christ, while the Council of Chalcedon had backed the Roman See and Pope Leo's view, called Dyophysitism. That view held that the two natures were perfect and perfectly distinct in the person of Christ.

But Anstice well knew that the theological arguments were important only because of their political uses. They gave excuse to the Syrians and the Egyptians who wished to resist the expanding power of Constantinople.

He was a traveler from an unknown land. In Rey, from whence he had come, in all of Persia, Zoroastrianism was still the most powerful religion. But it, too, was drowning in a sea of argument caused by schisms and cults that augmented the tenets of faith with rules of their own invention and particular interpretations. To Anstice it seemed that there was faith without enlightenment and argument without faith.

As an intermediary, he did not know what would happen to settle the troubling disputes that threatened peace and stability in Byzantium. But *she* who was born the day there was darkness at noon would be able to help settle the people by advising a leader. Not that she would know anything now, he reminded himself—now she was only a mortal child.

He sighed deeply. This would most certainly be her most difficult incarnation. As a mortal she would live a mortal life, but as an immortal this was the period of her young womanhood. And as in mortal life, it was a period of turbulence. It fell to him to set her on the right road during her mortal existence. It fell to him to teach her everything she would need to know in order to fulfill her destiny. Most important, it was he who would prepare her to face evil.

She would guide a leader toward the greater good, but the choice was always there, indeed it had to be there. Evil stalked the earth and found no shortage of followers.

Anstice had left the desert as directed by his night visions and come to this place. Now he had only to wait. He would dream and see reality through the mirror of that dream. He would be told what to do next.

A.D. July 30, 498
Seleucia Piera

Anstice tossed onto his side. He lay on a pile of straw, his precious trunk beside him, while a few feet away, his donkey also slept.

But the donkey slept soundly, dreamlessly, and without movement save for a twitch of his ears now and again. Anstice, on the other hand, moved restlessly, twitched, and on occasion spoke. Pictures, places, smells, and activity filled his mind and seemed to dance on his eyelids as a full-color spectacle of what was to come.

The street was dusty and filled with people, carts, wagons, and military men on horseback. Ugly-tempered camels pawed the dust, and throngs of people appeared from out of nowhere. They shook their fists, and angry expressions filled their faces.

Even in his dream, Anstice moved into the shadows, pressing himself against the side of a clay building as he sought safety from the mob.

Yet his eyes remained riveted on the riot. As the throng moved toward where he had been standing only moments before, it seemed to swallow up those who had been milling around there. Anstice searched the faces of the crowd, and his eyes fell on a woman dressed in a purple dress. She carried a child, a little girl no more than a year. His sleeping eyes sought the eyes of the child, and he knew instantly it was *she*. Her head was a mass of golden curls, her heavily lashed eyes were extraordinary. They were green—hypnotic, penetrating. In his dream their eyes locked on each other's—old man and child—yet even in this dream their minds melded, their thoughts became one.

Then Anstice felt his dreaming body stiffen. He heard the trumpeting call of the soldiers sent to quell the riot. Neither the cause of the riot nor the righteousness of the soldiers was of concern to Anstice. The cause was nothing, the result would be a bloody meeting of sword and flesh, of stampeding masses, of rearing horses. His was not to record or halt destiny—he had a single mission.

He moved quickly from where he stood, and even as he headed toward the woman and infant, the soldiers came. Dust and screams filled the air, horses trampled innocent victims, the soldiers slashed—order would be restored.

Though his eyes never left the eyes of the child, he knew the mother had been struck and had fallen to the ground dead. Not the victim of a horse or a soldier, but the victim of a huge rock hurled at the soldiers by someone in the crowd. A missile that missed its mark and hit another.

Anstice reached for the baby and, seizing her, ran again for the shelter of the building. He found it and also found the door open. He passed through it and out into a courtyard. He did not stop but hurried as fast as he could, holding her close. His wagon was where he had left it the night before. His chest was hidden in it. He was ready. He had the child, and together they would go to Constantinople. They would leave immediately without delay.

Anstice awoke and sat up. His whole body was bathed in perspiration. Yes, this was where he was to leave his chest and wagon.

Tomorrow he would return to Antioch.

Tomorrow there would be a terrible riot.

Tomorrow his dream would turn to reality and he would have his precious charge.

Dreams, Anstice had learned, were but foggy representations of reality. Those of most mortals were no more than past experiences mixed with hopes and fears. But his were special, they were a form of communication and instruction. Even so, they were a poor representation of reality, and for that reason Anstice searched out his shelter and checked his path of retreat, lest his vision led him to be overconfident. Anstice knew he was but an instrument of the fates, but sometimes he suspected that the fates played tricks on one another and that his dream might be an approximation of reality, lacking the exactness of reality.

A riot seemed a dangerous place in which to take possession of *she* who had been born during the darkness at noon. Could he not have found the child abandoned—hidden in the reeds by the water? Could she not have been delivered to him?

He shook his head. He should not question so much. Yet it could not hurt to check the locale, to make certain the dwelling he chose had a courtyard and a back door.

And so to satisfy himself, he took stock of all around him. The street was as it was in his dream. The building was the same, and the street was as crowded as in his dream. Still, no dream could produce the actual choking feeling that the dust brought to a man's throat, nor could it reproduce the smells and sounds of the crowd.

Yet everything was the same even though his memory of his dream had been static by comparison with this reality. He would not wake up, the truth was more dangerous than dreams.

He heard the racket of the rioters coming, whereas in his vision they had been silent, though no less menacing. He heard the clamor of the military and he felt, as he had not felt before, the onrush of people, the confusion, the actual pain of being shoved and prodded.

Then his eyes saw the woman and the child, and he moved toward them. It was all as it had been. He snatched the child and ran, the mother lying motionless in the street, felled by the rock.

The little girl clung to him, but she did not cry as others might have in similar circumstances. Instead, she was wonderfully calm, spellbound by the noise, the running, and no doubt curious about him.

He hurried, then, when he was far enough away, he stopped and sat down by the side of the road. She sat on his lap, their eyes locked. It was as if she could see through him, but she could not yet attest to this if it were so.

"Leandra," he whispered.

Her clear green eyes did not blink.

"I am your teacher," he said softly.

The little girl continued to stare at him. Finally he stood up. It was time he returned to his cart and his donkey.

It was time he and Leandra were on their way to Constantinople.

A.D. 500
Outside Constantinople

Anstice the silversmith was a student of history as well as a keen observer of human nature. He was in every sense a born tutor, a man whose unique insight enabled him to give meaning to events. He was a learned man, and in his profession scholarly men were unusual, since smithing was a craft. Nonetheless, the immortals had molded their intermediary well. Anstice spoke many tongues, read with agility, and knew what had passed before his own time. His dreams offered him a misty view of the future, thus giving his present a dimension few others could have.

For Anstice, life was a continuum—it was time unbroken and undivided. War and peace, health and disease, order and chaos, were all part of the continuum, and what had gone before would again occur, although perhaps it would not seem quite the same, since inevitably some part would be reordered. He saw the repetition of history like a bouquet of varied flowers. There were endless arrangements, but the flowers remained the same.

The Roman Empire established by Augustus had been far-sighted enough to govern a city, but it was unsuited to govern the far-flung empire. A short hundred and fifty years earlier, that great empire had been brought close to the breaking point. The misuse of authority, bureaucratic mistakes, civil wars, barbarian raids, and a chaotic economy all combined with the willful acts of men too ambitious for their intellects to create a situation characterized by fear and uncertainty. No man was guaranteed a livelihood, no leader's life was safe from assassination, no coin was worth its face value. Roman commanders rebelled and ruled their territories like emperors. The entire known world was racked with argument and religious upheaval. Christianity struggled to survive against Stoicism and Neoplatonism. But like a rule of history, the most persecuted of the three—Christianity—survived. And then came Constantine.

It seemed that history appointed Constantine to arrest the disintegration of the empire. First he ended the persecution and guaranteed Christians, who would not submit to the idea of a divine emperor, legal status within the empire. He even allowed them the same tax-free status given those of other religions. His second great move was to decide to move the capital of the empire from Rome, which was the scene of plot and counterplot. He considered Jerusalem, Sardica, and Thessaloníki. He even thought of Troy. Then, as if by some divine intervention, he chose a small trading town and its surrounding area. It was on an incredibly strategic site jutting into the Sea of Marmara. The town became known as Constantinople, and it grew to be the capital of Byzantium.

Anstice saw Byzantium as the heir of the Roman Empire as well as the first Christian nation. Constantinople embodied all its varied history and embraced its present. It was a city faithful to its classical roots and its Christian beliefs. At the base of the statue of Athena were baskets said to have held the bread Christ fed his disciples, and thus were the old and the new wedded.

Greek philosophy was discussed at court. Homer was read

and studied, yet missionaries were sent forth to seek converts to Christianity, and hundreds of monasteries were supported even though political advice was sought from mystics and thousands believed in other religions. But all too soon in the history of the world the bouquet would again be dropped, and when it was retrieved, the flowers would yet again be rearranged.

Anstice stared down the road as he walked beside his cart. Leandra was asleep on her bedroll, lulled by the steady motion of the cart and weary from a substantial meal of goat's milk, cheese, and ripe red tomatoes. In the distance, and made more dazzling by a lingering sunset, lay Constantinople. Its buildings rose solid from the ground. Gone were the tents of the desert and the adobe houses of Antioch. Gone were the thatched roofs of the countless villages they had passed through. Here was a city! A city of churches and palaces, of rich homes and bazaars, a city of hospitals and theaters and of circuses and prisons.

There were two theaters, over one hundred and fifty public baths, five granaries and eight aqueducts. There were fourteen great churches, fourteen palaces, and nearly five thousand houses of sufficient size to be recorded.

Yes, it was a magnificent city, a perfect city in which to rear Leandra. The immortals had chosen well. There was much to do; time would pass quickly.

A.D. 503
Constantinople

The house was simple, consisting of one large room in which they lived and a second in which he worked. Like all neighborhoods in Constantinople, this one was mixed. There were houses that were owned by the rich—mansions of many rooms with stone fronts and inner courtyards, houses of the middle class, which usually consisted of three or four rooms, and houses such as his—houses that belonged to artisans, who were a class by themselves.

There were many children with whom Leandra could play

when she was not studying, and Anstice marveled at the normalcy of her life, while at the same time never forgetting the reality of her being.

Knowledge was the key to all, but knowledge was not to be misused. The immortals might have provided him with vast wealth, enabling Leandra and him to live in a stone house with a wall that faced the street and an impressive inner courtyard. Instead, he was provided with a modest and consistent income. Customers seemed to seek him out, and he was paid well by them and recommended to their friends. From silver he fashioned jewelry and precious furnishings such as candle holders and bowls of glistening beauty. The fees he received for his artistry paid for a small house, bought their clothing, and provided them with food. Time not spent working was spent tutoring Leandra.

Leandra was an extraordinary child. She could be a child, a normal five-year-old who played with spoons in the sand or who made patterns from the string she held between her hands. Other children liked her, they did not detect the difference that existed between them. Yet when she studied she was like a sponge, absorbing everything, remembering all. Her green eyes were hypnotic, her intensity both admirable and frightening. Even at three she had asked questions that belied her age, just as her memory for the answers mocked it. The movements of the sun, the moon, and the stars fascinated her as they fascinated all immortals. She saw the patterns and understood the changes, she knew the signs that were written in the sky during each of the seasons, she understood the effect of the heavens on the lives of mortals.

Leandra understood herself to be born under the sign of the lion, and she knew she was high in that sign, a powerful lioness who would one day roar as well as purr.

Anstice sighed as he watched her trace the orbit of the sun with her small finger—her adolescent years would be turbulent and filled with the heat of youthful passion. He smiled slightly and thanked heaven he was an old man, an intermediary.

Leandra would make young men suffer—she would create a

longing in their loins and a burning heat in their brains. And when she coupled, it would be with fiery passion that would enchant her mortal mate.

Ah, how well he understood what she would do to those whom she enchanted; that was, after all, how he became an intermediary. Yes, long ago he had mated with one of them, he had been privileged to know a kind of pleasure few mortals ever experienced, and once felt, never forgot. His thoughts momentarily traveled back over the years to those days when he had known Zenobia as a mortal.

Her radiance had held him spellbound even though in the beginning there had been much tension between them and she had seemingly rejected all his awkward youthful advances.

Then, when he least expected it, she yielded to him. It was like taking a fiery ball, it was possession of sheer energy. Theirs was a battle of carnal hunger and ethereal bliss into which he entered enthusiastically and emerged exhausted. She was a snake when she wrapped herself around him, she was a kitten when she curled into his sleeping form. She was wild and furious in her lovemaking with exploring lips and smoldering, anxious kisses. She was divine in every sense of the word, and she was the only woman he had ever wanted. He remembered her now through the fog of time as if it were yesterday, and he knew the man Leandra would choose would be as lucky as he. Those with whom the immortals slept knew rapture beyond all earthly pleasures—an ecstasy so intense, it defied description in mortal terms.

He understood that by being an intermediary he would earn the right to join Zenobia for eternity, and so when she was taken from him, he was reconciled only by the knowledge that they would once again be one.

"What are you thinking, Grandfather?" Leandra did not turn away from her chart of the heavens. She knew his mind though she did not always understand his thoughts.

"Of things you will understand later," Anstice replied.

"Always later," the little girl sighed, and he knew that for the moment the woman inside her had retreated and the child had returned.

"Time will pass quickly for you, my child."

"And then I shall ride a white horse with a golden bridle."

Anstice nodded. She had mentioned the horse before. It was one of her dreams, one of the visions in which her future was foretold. But it was her dream, not his, and he assumed some things were to be kept from him. He accepted the mystery willingly.

"I want to go to the circus," she suddenly said.

He frowned. The only children who attended the circus were those who were born into it. It was a place of adult entertainment unsuitable to children. "You are too young," he answered.

"Then I must be taken to the home of the bear keeper. He trains bears for the circus and for the Hippodrome."

Anstice studied her expression. Her request was made calmly, clearly. He knew it was instruction given to her in her sleep. "Do you know why?" he asked.

"I must come to know Theodora," Leandra answered. "My future, the future of Byzantium, lies with her. She is the daughter of the bear keeper, who trains bears for both the circus and the Hippodrome."

Anstice could not conceal his surprise. How could a bear keeper's daughter hold the key to the future of the empire? He inhaled deeply and let out his breath slowly. That he could not answer this question was precisely what separated him from the immortals. Still, he knew he must not hesitate.

"If you must meet her, then I shall see to it," he promised.

Leandra smiled. "Soon," she said. "We must go soon."

Anstice fairly shuddered at the thought of the circus. It, like the entertainments performed between the chariot races held in the Hippodrome, could be cruel and violent.

Condemned men wrestling with wild animals for their lives was one of the popular entertainments before and between races, as were spectacles in which exotic creatures killed one another. Somehow, in spite of the dancing bears and seductive women

who also appeared, there was always cruelty, a brutality Anstice
himself did not enjoy in the least.

Nearly all Constantinople desired to go to the Hippodrome,
but every weekend thousands were turned away. There was
never enough room even though the seats had been placed closer
together, and there were continual attempts to enlarge its capacity to accommodate the crowds.

It seemed to Anstice that the inhumanity of mass entertainments had increased, as though people could be truly distracted
from their daily lives only by acts of violence. It also seemed
to him that the escalating savagery could be laid at the door of
fierce competition between various groups seeking to influence
the emperor.

The chariot races were arranged by two powerful groups, the
Greens and the Blues. These were the two most important citizen groups in the entire empire and were known as *demes*—the
people, or factions. Each faction supported its own entries into
the chariot races, and each arranged for the entertainments between races. These factions had existed since Roman times, but
here in Byzantium they were most powerful and acted as a sort
of local militia. Each faction had its own leader, or *demarch*.
Beneath the leader there existed a hierarchy of employees and
ceremonial positions. Each faction had treasurers, notaries, ar-
chivists, poets, musicians, painters, sculptors, charioteers, and
circus performers as well as stable hands and animal trainers.

In addition to arranging the activities at the Hippodrome, the
factions also arranged processions and formed the emperor's
escort. They wore special clothes—cloaks and shoes in the style
of the barbarian Huns with tunics that had wide, billowing
sleeves drawn tightly at the wrist. They wore their hair close-
cropped in the front and long in the back. It was through the
factions that popular feelings were expressed. On the day of the
races in the Hippodrome, the Blues sat to the right of the imperial box while the Greens sat to the left. It was during the
interval following the fourth chariot race that the entertainments
were provided, though Anstice did not consider many of them
entertaining.

Again Anstice glanced at Leandra. Could she offer him no further clues? He shook his head. First he would have to discover the names of all the bear keepers who had daughters named Theodora, which was, unfortunately, a common name. Then he would have to find out if this particular keeper worked for the Greens or the Blues.

"I shall do the best I can," he finally said.

Leandra turned toward him. "I think you must find her very soon."

Semira, wife of Acacius, was a practical woman in all but one aspect of her personality. Her generosity, which grew out of the fact that she was a native of Antioch, caused her much difficulty. In her homeland, a place far less harried than Constantinople, she had been taught hospitality. Hence, when visited, she always offered refreshment and she found it hard to turn a blind eye to someone in need. She was always short of money, and food was never plentiful in her cupboard because she gave too much away.

Acacius was driven mad by his wife's nature. The blind man who called daily was fed, but his own dinner was often sparse. Added to that was the distressing fact that Semira had given birth to three daughters and no sons, and now she could have no more children.

Acacius pondered his fate. His pay as keeper of the bears for the Greens disappeared almost immediately. There was nothing left for savings, and Acacius was tormented by thoughts of what would happen to him and Semira in their old age. What indeed would become of their three lovely daughters? In his heart he knew the answer. Comito, Theodora, and Anastasia would become actresses and he and Semira would live in poverty, supported only by the meager leftovers of their daughters' pay. His future filled him with foreboding, and he had grown morose and distracted with each passing year.

It was unfair, he thought as he walked toward the cages in which his bears were kept. It was grossly unfair that after a life of hard work he should have to see his daughters ill-dressed and his wife fretful. It was unfair that this morning—the very day he was to be paid—he should come to work with a partially empty stomach because the tea was gone and there were only crusts of bread for his breakfast.

He muttered as he entered the caged area. His bears were better fed than he.

"She gives the last of our tea to a blind man," he muttered. "She gives him soft bread and even some fruit. I should take over the finances myself. I should not leave her with any money at all. She simply does not know how to handle it."

His three bears watched him, their small eyes concentrated on his mouth, their ears listening for his tone—for some command.

Acacius was so distracted, he forgot himself. He forgot the creatures he trained were, in fact, wild and unpredictable. He forgot they were stronger than he.

He forgot and turned his back on Kleio, a monstrously large bear whose affection for him was boundless. When he turned again, he found her behind him, her breath hot on his neck. She had approached him silently, on padded paws.

He stood stark still, but it mattered not. Kleio reached out for him, and with one giant step toward him embraced him with all her great strength.

Acacius hardly had the breath to shriek, so sudden was the crushing hug given him by the giant Kleio. His lungs were crushed, his breath squeezed out of him in one burst of ursine emotion.

It was two hours later that Semira found him. She stood staring into the cage blankly. The two other bears were on their stools, as if waiting for their trainer to spring into action. Kleio stood guard over Acacius's lifeless form, her giant paw resting on his shoulders.

Semira closed her eyes to block out the scene. To think. The vision of her three daughters danced before her. They wore beautiful dresses and their hair was bound in garlands of ribbons and flowers. They danced out of her vision and were replaced by the large, hairy form of Clement, a wrestler who grew too old to wrestle. Yes, Clement would make an excellent animal trainer and no doubt an excellent father for her three daughters. A replacement for Acacius was needed at once. As she hurried off to summon help, Semira knew she had no time to waste. Before Acacius was even removed from the bear cage she had hit upon a solution to her problem. The solution was clear. She must marry Clement and she must convince the Greens, who had employed Acacius, to hire Clement in his place.

She paused momentarily to assess her reflection in a piece of glass. Yes, she was still desirable, and now she owned three bears to boot. How could Clement, a bachelor, refuse her?

Anstice stood outside the small house and watched as the crowd gathered. Everyone was talking about the tragedy. "The bear keeper is dead, crushed by one of his own bears," it was whispered over and over. On each telling of the story to a newcomer, the bear grew larger, the keeper more vulnerable, the event more spectacular.

"What a pity," he heard a woman intone. "And with three daughters to support. Whatever will become of them? Whatever will become of his wife?"

Anstice moved closer. "Are you a friend of the bear keeper?" he asked, leaning toward the woman.

"A neighbor," the woman replied. Then she added for good measure, "They are circus people, so I suppose they will survive."

"You said there were daughters," he pressed. "Do you know their names?"

The woman frowned and held her chin reflectively. "One is called Comito and one is called—ah, yes, Theodora. The third—"

"It is enough," Anstice said, restraining her with his hand. "I seek Theodora and her mother."

"I can only imagine how distraught the poor woman is," the neighbor said, pointing off toward a modest white house. "But you had better hurry. With no one to support them, they will soon be thrown out of their house by the Greens."

Anstice nodded and headed off toward the house. He hated to intrude on anyone's grief, but he knew he must find Theodora so he could arrange for a meeting between her and Leandra. Though, as he approached the house, he had not the foggiest idea what he was going to say.

The little girl who came to the door appeared to be ten or eleven years old. "We are a household in mourning," she said in response to his greeting.

"I have heard of your tragedy," Anstice said. "Do you have a sister named Theodora?"

"Yes, she is with my mother, who will not be disturbed. I was told to send you away. I was told to send away everyone save Clement."

"Is Clement your uncle?"

She shook her head. "No, he is the unmarried man who cleans the animal cages."

Anstice smiled ever so slightly. It seemed clear that the bear keeper's wife did not intend to remain a widow for long. But he could not blame her; a woman with three daughters to support was not in an enviable position. "Are you the eldest daughter?" he asked.

"Yes. I am Comito."

"Well, Comito, I suspect you and your family will need some money to see you through your period of crisis. I have no desire to intrude on your mother's mourning, so perhaps I can deal with you."

"Perhaps," Comito replied.

"I am Anstice, the silversmith. I am the guardian of a five-year-old child who is very much in need of a companion. If your mother is willing, I will offer a piece of silver a week if Theodora will come and spend several afternoons a week with my ward, Leandra. Here is one silver piece for your trouble. Please convey my offer to your mother. Here are the directions to my house. If it is all satisfactory, you may bring her to my home next Friday afternoon."

Comito took the silver piece and bit upon it to make sure it was real. Then she looked up, smiling. "I am sure it will be satisfactory."

Anstice smiled and bowed slightly. "My condolences to your mother and sisters."

Comito curtsied modestly, a practiced curtsy that revealed she was in training to become an actress. Vaguely he wondered if her younger sister Theodora was also destined for the theater and for all that entailed in Byzantium. It was not an enviable profession since actresses were regarded as prostitutes and the parts they played often subjected them to considerable physical pain and hardship.

Anstice walked briskly toward home. Perhaps this was not the best way for Leandra and Theodora to meet, but somehow it seemed the most straightforward, and Leandra had warned their meeting must be soon.

Two

A.D. 503
Constantinople

Semira adorned herself in a long rust-colored cloak, the hood of which fell in folds down her back. Her dark hair was hidden beneath her best scarf, which was wound about her head in the traditional fashion. The style allowed the ends of the scarf to fall to her shoulders. The wearing of a colorful scarf as a headdress was common among women of her class, while those of the upper classes wore headdresses encrusted with jewels and semiprecious stones. Beneath her robe Semira wore a tunic that fell almost to her knees, and her legs were covered by loose-fitting pantaloons. Her jewelry was unpretentious. It consisted of a single silver chain with a pendant fashioned from striking green malachite, a gemstone taken from the hills of her homeland in Syria. Her earrings, a wedding gift from Acacius the bear keeper were her pride and joy. They were made of delicate silver filigree and shaped in the form of a monkey's torso. Its simian fingers held silver chains, from which dangled a half-moon. Women of her class often collected large quantities of cheap jewelry with which to adorn themselves. But Semira did not approve. She felt it was better to own a few good pieces than a bag full of badly fashioned imitations.

After Comito revealed the nature of the stranger's visit and had given her mother the silver piece, Semira had considered the offer carefully. Of course, she could keep the silver piece and never appear at the door of Anstice the silversmith, but if she had done that, her curiosity would never have been satisfied. Besides, if Theodora came several times a week to act as companion to Anstice's ward, there would be more silver, and in her household Semira always had need of extra money. That was especially true now. And so, all things being equal, she could see no reason why her young daughter should not be hired as a companion for this Leandra, who was, according to Comito, the same age as Theodora. Indeed, as the appointed hour approached, Semira had begun to regard the appearance of Anstice as a good omen, which indeed it was.

Anstice opened the door of his house and bowed before Semira, who was immediately impressed with the elderly gentleman's demeanor and manner of dress. Her eyes roamed the main room, quickly taking in everything. It was extremely neat and clean. Then, as if suddenly remembering why she was there, she turned back to the child who stood behind her. "This is Theodora," she announced.

Theodora stepped forward without further prompting. She smiled and curtsied.

Anstice smiled at the little girl and at the same time made note of the extraordinary impression she made. She was a slight child, thin and pale with a head of dark, rich, thick hair. Her black eyes were the shape of almonds and her mouth was perfectly shaped. He could immediately sense her intelligence and her strength. Young though she was, she knew her own mind. As yet he could not fathom exactly how her destiny was to be fulfilled, but he knew immediately that this child was to become *the* woman to whom Leandra had been sent. Somehow, in some way, this child would grow into the most powerful woman in the known world.

In a moment Leandra appeared. Her strange golden-copper-colored hair was nearly hidden beneath a scarf that was wrapped in a way similar to Semira's. Her green eyes flickered with a wisdom well beyond her age.

Semira stared at her. "I have never seen a child with eyes that color."

Anstice folded his hands. He had always kept Leandra's hair covered in public. It raised too many eyebrows. "Yes, my ward is most unusual. She was born in Antioch—they say she is the granddaughter of a Roman soldier who took a wife from the outer reaches of the empire, from Britannia." In truth Anstice knew little of Leandra's background. After he had taken her, he had spoken to many villagers and he had heard the tale from a woman who claimed to be on intimate terms with the dead mother, a woman named Clementia. Still, the story rang true. Leandra's coloring was unique, and he had read it was the coloring of those who dwelt on that far-off isle they called Britannia.

Semira still paused in the entranceway to the house, but Theodora apparently did not share her mother's hesitation. She went directly to Leandra, who took her hand and led her away into the garden.

Anstice knew that Semira could not have seen what he saw in the eyes of both children. It was unspoken communication—it was remarkable—and he knew it was remarkable because it was fated.

"Everything seems in order," Semira said, looking once again about the modest but clean household. "You seem to be an educated man," she observed. Her eyes had settled on his books and the charts that marked the heavens.

"Learning and teaching are my greatest pleasures."

Semira forced a smile and wondered how anyone could spend their leisure time reading or studying the stars. "But you are not a teacher, you are a silversmith."

"True enough, dear lady. Teaching provides a poor living, while smithing in this much-bejeweled city can be quite lucrative. My profession pays for my pleasures, and I teach only my ward."

"She will be a most fortunate woman. So few woman are learned."

"May I offer you some tea?" Anstice inquired.

"I would be most grateful," Semira replied. She was impressed with his generosity and hospitality. He seemed to have time for the niceties of life, niceties generally absent in Constantinople, niceties she had known in her Syrian home near the sea. "It is so delightful to meet someone who will take time for tea. People here are always busy running about."

Anstice prepared the tea and brought it in silver cups on a small silver tray. "Are you getting on all right?" he inquired.

"I do the best I can. I have hopes. Clement, the cage cleaner, has asked me to become his wife. He will help me with the children, and in return, when they are grown they will support both of us. But in the meantime I must convince the Greens to hire Clement as their bear keeper and trainer, a position held by my late husband. If he does not become a bear keeper, his salary will not be sufficient." She paused to sip some tea. "I do want to thank you. Paying Theodora to be Leandra's companion is a great help in my time of financial need."

"It is my pleasure, dear lady. And will the Greens hire Clement?"

Semira looked down. "I don't know. I have petitioned them, but who knows if they will read a petition from the humble and poverty-stricken widow of a dead bear keeper."

"I feel things will go well for you," Anstice predicted. "You must be patient and let time solve your difficulties."

"Are you a soothsayer as well as a silversmith and teacher?"

Anstice laughed lightly. "Faith, my dear lady. Everyone says they have it, but no one acts as a faithful believer should."

Semira clasped her pendant in one hand and looked down. "I am a believer."

"Good," Anstice returned. He did not ask in what she believed and he did not tell her in what he believed. Mystery was the essence of friendship with a woman such as Semira.

Semira drained her teacup. "I must be going. I shall send

Comito for Theodora in a few hours. Will that be sufficient time for them to be together?"

"I'm certain it will be."

Anstice escorted Semira to the door. He bowed and bid her farewell. She thanked him for the tea and he watched her as she went on her way, eager, no doubt, to return to Clement, and more eager to mend her shattered life.

In the garden Theodora sat on a stone bench with Leandra.

"You seem familiar to me," Theodora said, running her small hands over her tunic. "Have we met before?"

Leandra shook her head. "You are familiar to me as well. I believe we have met in our dreams."

Theodora studied Leandra's face and then she half smiled. She had vivid dreams and she decided Leandra was right. Nor did she think it unusual to have met someone in a dream. Her mother spoke often of dreams and their meanings; everyone she knew believed that dreams foretold happenings of great importance. Her mother had told her that dreams were important to all those who lived in Byzantium and that the emperor himself consulted a dream interpreter, a man of great wisdom, to explain his dreams. "We will be friends," Theodora said.

"Close friends," Leandra confirmed. "You will see me now for several weeks, then you will not see me again for many years. But we will always be friends."

"You're very strange, but I understand you," Theodora said, looking into Leandra's sea-green eyes.

"Listen," Leandra said softly. Her voice lost its childlike quality for a time, and she spoke in words that belied her age.

"Listen carefully. Your mother will marry Clement and the Greens will not give him your father's job."

"They won't?" Theodora looked distressed. "Then what will become of us? We will all starve."

Leandra shook her head. "You and your sisters must go to the Hippodrome and approach the Greens in front of the multitudes. You must beg for your new father to be given the job of your old father."

Theodora's almond eyes glistened. "I can do that," she said confidently. "I am going to be the most famous actress in all of Byzantium. I can go before the multitudes. I am not afraid."

"Now listen even more carefully and remember what I tell you. There will be an accident of sorts and you alone will face a fearful thing. The multitudes will roar. But you must not be afraid. You must stand firm. In the end, your bravery will cause the Blues to adopt you and your family. Clement will be hired to train and keep their bears and your family will not starve."

Theodora's eyes grew wide. "A truly fearful thing?"

Leandra nodded. "But it will not hurt you."

"I am not afraid. I am not afraid of anything."

Leandra took her new friend's hands and squeezed them. "There is a time for fear, but it is not now."

Theodora jumped off the bench. "You have books and charts. Will you teach me what your tutor has taught you?"

"I will," Leandra agreed. "Come, we'll begin now. I shall teach you the signs of the heavens. These you will need to know."

"I was born in August," Theodora said.

Leandra smiled. "So was I."

Semira held on to the side of her dining table for fear of falling over in a dead faint. Before her was an unrolled scroll from someone of the hierarchy who ran the Greens, a secretary no doubt, perhaps someone of even less importance on the bureaucratic scale. She was not worthy of more attention.

In no uncertain terms it rejected her petition and demanded she, her children, and new husband, Clement, vacate the house they had provided for their bear keeper, her late husband.

"No mercy!" Semira wailed. "After all those years that my husband slaved for them! They have no mercy on his wife and small children!" Tears welled in her eyes, and she pounded the table, wept, and then wailed to the unhearing heavens. Her mournful wail was followed by a trill in the manner of the women of her homeland. It was a horrible yet sad noise that seemed to originate from deep inside.

Clement, a huge man, stood by helplessly. He wanted to ask if the refusal of Semira's petition mentioned his present job. Was he to keep it, at least? But Clement could not read, and at the moment he felt Semira was so filled with self-pity, he dare not ask.

Theodora stood poised in the doorway. She had heard enough to know what had happened and she sprang forward, seizing her mother's hands.

"Mother! You must listen to me!"

Semira raised her head toward heaven and again trilled.

Clement covered his ears and winced.

"I have had a dream. You must listen!" Theodora demanded.

Semira looked down at her youngest daughter. Theodora was different from her other children. She was stronger of will and intellect and more mature than either of them had been at her tender age.

Encouraged by her mother's silence, Theodora looked up into her eyes. "You must let us—Comito, Anastasia, and myself—you must let us go to the Hippodrome and plead before the multitudes."

Semira stared at Theodora and wondered if one so young could take leave of her senses. She sounded so entirely adult, yet she was only a baby. "You would never be allowed," she said.

"Comito and I have already spoken with the announcer. He thinks it a wonderful idea, one that will bring tears to the eyes of the multitudes."

Semira was stunned, yet she was so desperate, her mind conjured up the image of her three small daughters begging for mercy in the giant Hippodrome. Well, stranger things had happened. Perhaps the multitudes would demand the Greens help them.

"Who could resist them?" Clement asked. "They are but small, helpless children."

"I have wonderful children," Semira said in a low whisper. "See, they want to help us."

"Then we can do it?" Theodora asked.

"You can only try," Semira answered. "I can see no harm in it."

Theodora bowed and left her mother with Clement. I will not tell her the rest, Theodora thought. If she knew it might be dangerous, if she knew I was to encounter a terrible, fearful thing, she might not have agreed. Theodora congratulated herself. What her mother did not know would not cause her needless worry.

Anstice stood in the long line before the gates of the Hippodrome. He thought for the one-hundredth time that he would not be here were it not for Leandra's pleas. "You must go," she had begged. "You must attend and report everything that happens."

As much as he disliked the cruelty of the Hippodrome, he did not argue. It was not a five-year-old who had asked him, the immortals had ordered him. Yet his mind wandered as he thought of the many more pleasurable things he could be doing on this warm, sunny afternoon.

Constantinople was greatly to Anstice's liking. Much of the city's social life took place on the streets. Friends and neighbors strolled and talked. Sometimes they met in one of the many forums or took refreshment in one of the city's hundreds of cafés or restaurants. Many of the smaller cafés had tables outdoors, where friends sat and played games with numbered cubes while they sipped thick, syrupy tea. On any weekday there were strolling musicians and jugglers in the streets, and there were, as well, many public baths where one could bathe and relax in the calm turquoise waters. There were theaters and ballets, pantomimes and musical shows. To Anstice's way of thinking, there were a hundred things a man might do, yet the Hippodrome remained the most attended. He did not understand why so many men shunned more interesting intellectual pursuits for an afternoon of brutal sport.

But in truth, he knew the answer. In the Hippodrome, each man, no matter how weak, cowardly, or unathletic he might be, could imagine for a few hours that he was a well-muscled chariot driver, a hero to all, the person for whom all Byzantium seemed to cheer. Here, on this ground marked with blood, a man who would never be a hero could find heroes, and for a brief time become that hero in his own imagination.

"Blues!" someone shouted. And the line in which Anstice stood began to move toward the gate. Leandra had asked him to sit on the side of Blues; it was not his choice, nor, he admitted, did he really care where he sat.

Partially because of the force of those pushing behind him, Anstice was propelled through the gate with a horde of Blues. Most of them were dressed in their uniforms, which consisted of long, deep royal blue cloaks, tunics, and the bootlike shoes worn by the Huns. The Greens had a similar costume, but of course their cloaks were a deep forest green.

Anstice was squeezed into a seat in the stands to the right of the imperial box and the rows that had been designated for Blue dignitaries.

After a time, Anstice purchased some salted fish and fruit from a vendor and tried to make himself comfortable on the stone bench. He, like most others, had brought a gaily-colored pillow on which to sit. The races would last most of the day, and he assumed he would be here as long. There was ample time to stretch and eat during the long intervals. In the periods between chariot races, during the entertainments provided by the two sponsoring factions, the Blues and the Greens, vendors walked about selling cheese, olives, and long loaves of bread.

At the end of the fourth race the entertainments began. Today, Anstice had learned, the Blues had brought a giant beast from the west coast of Africa. It had been caught, caged, and brought to the Hippodrome. It was to be let out of its cage to devour some baby piglets.

Amid loud screams, a fanfare provided by trumpets and a

constant weird drumbeat, two cages were carried out, and the doors opened on both. The bearers of the cages ran for the exits, and there safely took refuge.

Just as the crowd began to chant "Come out, monster!" three little girls appeared on the floor of the Hippodrome facing the Greens.

They were all dressed in white with their hair gathered in flowing ribbons. Each wore a garland of fresh flowers, and they curtsied in unison before the stunned crowd.

"These children have come before the Greens to beg that their new father be given the job of bear keeper, a job held by their former father, who was killed by his own bear!"

"Get them out of the arena, they'll be killed!" someone shouted.

Anstice's mouth opened in surprise and horror. The piglets had not yet emerged, but the monster—a huge snake perhaps fifteen feet long and whose fat body was as round as any wheel on a cart—slithered out of his cage onto the sandy surface of the Hippodrome.

The three little girls looked toward the monster, then two of them ran as fast as they could for the exits. The crowd was wild.

The third child stood stock-still, then she turned and walked directly toward the enormous serpent.

Anstice was frozen in his seat, unable to move. The small child, the angelic little girl in garlands of flowers, was none other than Theodora.

All were on their feet now. "She'll be killed! Someone stop her! She'll be devoured by it!"

The huge reptile was coiled now, and its head stood slightly higher than that of the child who approached it.

Theodora kept walking till she reached it. She looked into its face and reached up and stroked its flat head.

Its great forked tongue flicked in and out of its mouth, and that caused a gigantic roar from the crowd, but the snake made no move to devour Theodora. The little girl turned and walked past it till she stood before the stands filled with the Blues. A great roar of approval went up for her.

The emperor, now also on his feet, turned to the Blue de-march on his right. Words were whispered and a messenger was sent. Soon the announcer for the Blues seized the horn. "The Blues will hire the brave little girl's father and see to her family! She is surely the bravest child in all Constantinople!"

The crowd roared its approval.

Theodora curtsied once again and then walked calmly toward the exit just as the first of the piglets escaped its pen. Again the crowd roared. Anstice stood up and made his way out of the stands. He did not need to see piglets devoured by a huge snake. He understood why he had been sent, he understood why this child had been chosen, and for the first time, he began to see how her destiny would be fulfilled.

Even as Anstice pushed his way through the crowds, the child was escorted to the emperor's box for the duration of the entertainments and races. In Anstice's ears the shouts of the crowd still called the name of Theodora. Soon, Anstice thought, Theodora's name would be on the lips of everyone in Constantinople.

The sun disappeared over the rounded golden dome of the Hagia Sophia before it dropped into the Sea of Marmara and disappeared from the far horizon in a blaze of pink and blue. It left behind a sky brighter than usual, a pink-tinged twilight and a shining early-evening star.

From the perfume market on the main road, the pungent aromas of a thousand scents rose on the evening breeze. Anstice sat in his small garden, watching as Leandra built a house of sticks on the grass. Her fingers were agile, and unusually long for those of a child.

"You returned early from the Hippodrome," she said without looking up.

"I believe I served my purpose there."

"Tell me about it."

In as much detail as he could he told the story of what had happened.

"Then, things went as they should have gone," Leandra said, finishing her small structure. "Theodora may continue to come for a month or two, then our lives will separate for a time."

Anstice nodded. "And soon you must begin formal schooling."

Leandra's eyes flickered as she looked up at him. "You will teach me all you know of medicine. Then you will see to it that this is what I am taught."

"Ah," Anstice said. "And what of the white horse?"

"I shall ride him in time, but now I must study."

"You have good hands," he commented.

Leandra held up her hands and studied them, then she let them fall to her sides and she smiled. "You are a fine tutor, and I love you as a father."

He reached out for her. The moments of affection between them were few, but this time Leandra came to him and crawled onto his lap. She looked into his eyes deeply and kissed him tenderly on the cheek. "I am told you will be with your love sooner than you believe."

Anstice frowned. "My work is hardly done. You are a mere child."

"Oh, I did not mean immediately. I just meant sooner."

Anstice was silent. In the five years since he had taken her as a baby from the arms of her dead mother, he had loved her as if she were his own child. It troubled him to think he might have to leave her before she blossomed into the ravishing woman he knew she would become. Still, he was torn. His death meant his return to Zenobia's arms. How the immortals toyed with him! How bittersweet it was to love one of them as a man loves a woman and another as a man loves his daughter.

"Do not torment yourself. What must be will be," she said softly. "You are my father, I shall always love you as such."

Anstice could say nothing. He was a man ruled by the fates, a man chosen.

* * *

A.D. 514
Constantinople

Even in the summer sun Leandra's skin remained pale and soft, her lips like those of a blush pink rose while her eyes were the color of the Bosphorus—a sea-green, deep and mysterious.

She had always been tall, and as she approached twelve, she became awkward and uncoordinated. When her first blood came later that year, so came the changes in her stick-straight figure. Her body took on subtle curves. Her legs were beautiful, with long, shapely calves and slender thighs. Her breasts swelled and her hips rounded. In order not to attract undo attention, she always kept her red-gold curls tucked out of the way and hidden from view beneath her scarf. The days, the months, the years, passed quickly.

Leandra was tutored in medicine. She studied all the remedies taken from plants and animals. She toured Constantinople's hospitals and visited the ill. She saw, she memorized, and she learned.

Anstice had grown old. Old and concerned that he would not live to see Leandra into full adulthood. Constantinople was a wild and wonderful place. It could offer all the stimulation the intellect required, but it could also be an evil city, especially for a young, beautiful woman left alone. It was this that Anstice pondered, and it was this that troubled him most. But each year that went by gave him more hope. Leandra continued to mature, and every day she seemed to grow more radiant.

Anstice sat down at the table and surveyed the feast he had ordered the cook to prepare. "It is a suitable dinner to serve on this the seventeenth anniversary of your birth."

Leandra pushed her long golden-red tresses aside. There was no need for a scarf inside her own home. "I feel older."

"Perhaps because you know more."

"Perhaps because I know who and what I am."

"Well, I not only feel older, my child, I am older."

Leandra reached out and covered his wizened hand with her soft white hand, and her long fingers curled about his. "Zenobia," she whispered. "Think on her, my father, think on her and you will not be afraid of becoming immortal, of leaving this temporal world."

"I am not afraid," he said, again feeling the hypnotic strength of her eyes. And even as he said it he knew the time was close at hand.

"You are too young," he said softly, almost pleadingly.

Leandra shook her head. "The time draws near when I must return to Theodora."

Slowly, and without further words, Anstice ate his meal. Then he obediently allowed Leandra to take him to his divan. He lay down and closed his eyes.

"I shall read to you," Leandra suggested.

Anstice nodded and listened as she opened a book of Greek poetry. She read from the manuscript clearly and slowly. And ever so slowly as she read, Anstice felt himself drifting away until finally he seemed to be floating on top of the room. Below he saw his withered, aged body, and next to him the breathtaking woman Leandra had become. He watched as the aged body on the divan shuddered and then ceased to breathe, he saw Leandra bend to kiss him, and to squeeze his lifeless hand. He saw no more. It was as if the roof of his dwelling opened and he was sucked into a long, dark passage. Then he saw a distant light. He seemed to travel faster than a falling star toward that light, a light that grew brighter and brighter as he drew closer, until he saw Zenobia in all her splendor waiting for him. Zenobia's long, sinuous arms were outstretched, her diaphanous gowns billowing about her perfect body.

He seemed to fly into her arms, and as they embraced he felt himself again young and virile. Anstice the old man had been left behind.

He and Zenobia seemed to be in a palace, and he was acutely aware of the sweet aromas, the circling fog like clouds, the intensity of all his senses.

They were on a bed of clouds traveling to distant stars. Next to him was his beloved Zenobia. She was naked, and when he looked down he saw that he, too, was without clothes. She took him into her arms and he felt once again the softness of her breasts and hardness of her splendid nipples. He felt himself strong and young as they tossed together, lost in an immortal joining that was as ethereal as it was sensual. For here, not only were their bodies joined in wild passionate love, but so, too, were their souls melded into one. He knew her thoughts as she knew his, they felt each other's intense pleasure, and knew of each other's pain.

"I have waited a lifetime," Anstice whispered.

"And I an eternity," she whispered back.

Zenobia moaned in his arms as he sunk deep into her moist, warm depths. Theirs was a love fulfilled forevermore.

Leandra held Anstice's hand tightly. Her own eyes were closed, and in this forced dream she saw it all and felt his pleasure. "Now you, too, are immortal," she whispered as she dropped his hand. "I must let you go," she whispered tearfully.

For nearly an hour Leandra sat still. She recalled all the days of her childhood and all that her earthly father, her special intermediary, had given her. "You chose well, Zenobia," she said aloud.

Her eyes turned to the hourglass and she knew it was time to move on.

Quickly, Leandra gathered her father's wealth and hid it where she had been directed to, in a vault beneath the earth of the garden. She packed her most appropriate clothes and dressed quickly. It was time to find her white horse, and time to join Theodora. Her knowledge of medicine was to be put aside for now. She was in any case too young to be allowed to practice. Now she was to find a new way to earn a living, a way that would keep her in close contact with Theodora.

The theater that was part of the circus was dark, smoky, and filled with the noise of excited men. Well hidden in her cloak,

Leandra watched as Theodora performed the lead role in the play.

It was a popular pantomime in which the husband, having discovered his wife was having an affair, returns home and tortures his wife till he falls exhausted on her and is consumed with brutal desire.

Nearly all plays required the actress to be beaten and bound, though not really hurt. They necessitated stamina, and they demanded that the actress take off all her clothes.

Following the performance, it was the custom for the actress to choose one of her admirers and sleep with him. For this she was paid well, and in addition, she received a portion of all the coins thrown on the stage when first she disrobed or was, in the case of this play, disrobed.

Theodora was truly beautiful. She had masses of dark hair and her skin was white. Her eyes, as they had been when she was a child, were almond-shaped. But there was something else about her, something difficult to describe, since it was more felt than seen.

Though she was slight, Theodora was strong. She was stubborn and she was confident. Her manner won over her audience completely, just as her body seduced them utterly as she was tormented by her supposed husband, who, driven by wrath and jealousy, stripped her of her clothing, hurling it away in a wild rage.

First he undid her scarf and freed her wild mane of hair. The audience of men roared their approval. Next, as she fought and screamed, he yanked off her tunic and then her undergarments till she was bared to the waist. Her perfect white breasts were revealed. They were high and proud with dark, lovely nipples. There were now frantic shrieks from the actress Theodora as the jealous husband began his torments. The audience pelted the stage with coins to show their appreciation.

There were more screams as she was dragged to a nearby post and tied to it, helpless and alone with her tormentor. Next he pulled off her pantaloons, and her whole body was exposed, white and rounded, supple and desirable. The actor picked up the whip and began his mock torture while the actress writhed. It was masterful, the blows looked so real. Finally, panting but still outraged, the actor-husband untied his wife and fell upon her even as she begged for mercy and then for sexual fulfillment.

The audience was on its feet, and hundreds of coins were hurled upon the stage.

"She is the finest actress in all of Constantinople," Leandra heard one man proclaim.

"The finest in all of Byzantium!" another called out.

"No, the finest in the world!"

Leandra fought her way through the crowd and wormed her way through the gathering of men who awaited Theodora. Each one of them wanted to be her lover for the night.

In her dressing room Theodora was draped in a sheer robe that did nothing to hide her bodily charms. The huge guard who pushed back her would-be companions let Leandra slip through.

"Theodora," Leandra said clearly.

Theodora looked at the young woman so securely wrapped in her robes, her eyes locked on Leandra's eyes.

Theodora smiled at Leandra and then looked up at her suitors. "Not tonight! Tonight Theodora has business to see to!" she shouted. "Tonight I am too busy!"

There were groans from the waiting crowd. "Leave us!" she ordered, then to the bodyguard, "get them out of here."

In moments the door was closed and Leandra and Theodora were alone and face-to-face.

"I cannot believe my eyes," Theodora said.

"I was not sure you would remember me."

"I do not forget my friends."

"It's been many years and we were but children."

Theodora sank onto her divan. "We were never really children," she intoned.

Leandra did not argue. She sat down beside Theodora. "My guardian is dead. I have need of a job."

"You want to become an actress? You are alluring enough, though I might grow jealous of your beauty."

Leandra smiled. "No, I want to become a rider in the circus."

"Can you ride?" Theodora asked in surprise.

"I do not know, I have never ridden." She did not say that she had ridden in her dreams. She did not reveal the fact that she knew she could do what she was fated to do. How could she explain she had primordial knowledge, knowledge gained when she rode on Pegasus as he sprang toward the constellation that now bore his name? No, not even to Theodora could she confess she had ridden a winged white horse among the stars.

Theodora laughed lightly. "You are quite as unbelievable today as you were twelve years ago."

"But you believed me then."

"And I believe you now. I will take you to Erastus, the horse trainer. I will see that you are given a trial. Why must you join the circus when you are learned?"

"I must be near you. And the time to use my knowledge has not yet come."

Theodora took Leandra's hand. "Do you see the future?"

Leandra smiled. "Theodora, you *are* the future. I must guide you."

Was it her own ego getting the best of her? Did she believe Leandra because she wanted to believe her? Theodora wasn't at all sure, but she was sure she was destined for better than the theater. "Very well," Theodora said slowly. "And you may come and live at my house."

"I shall be pleased," Leandra said. Vaguely she wondered if it would always be this easy. Did mortals sometimes fail to take the advice of their advisers? Theodora was headstrong, and fates or no fates, she had a mind of her own.

"We'll go now, Leandra. We'll have a late supper together and you will tell me what you have been studying all these years."

"And you will tell me about the theater and the circus. You will tell me about your loves and your interests."

"Don't you know, my little soothsayer?"

"No, I see imperfectly. My dreams are not always realistic."

"Well, let us go. Let us know each other better."

* * *

In their corral the vain circus horses moved freely. They were pampered animals, well cared for and well fed. Erastus, their keeper, was a tall, lean man. He had a strangely horsey face, and shaggy hair like an unkempt mane. It was his exceptionally long nose that gave rise to his equine appearance, and people joked that he had been among his horses far too long.

Erastus walked around Leandra in a wide circle. "You have the body of a rider," he acknowledged, "but, of course, our riders must also be acrobats. You must stand on your head while riding, you must do tricks. The horses are trained to be steady, but it takes practice, and to be honest, nearly all our riders begin their training when they are very young."

Was she to say she had ridden Pegasus to the constellations? No, she could say nothing really. She had to convince him to give her a trial. "I will need no training," she answered.

"Everyone needs training. Being pretty is not enough, this requires skill."

"Let me show you what I can do," she suggested.

He held his chin in his hand and assessed her. "You do have the body for the costumes—is your hair long?"

Leandra shook her head. "My hair will always be hidden."

"It is not the custom."

"It is my custom."

"She is my friend," Theodora put in. "Give her a try? What have you to lose? If one rider has hidden hair, it will be unusual, it will lend mystery to your presentation. Give her a try. We've brought a costume and everything."

Erastus muttered into his hand, which still covered his chin and mouth. "All right," he allowed. "But I take no responsibility if she falls, is that understood?"

"Quite," Leandra answered. "Where may I change my clothes?"

Erastus pointed off to an exit that led out of the arena. "Over there, and be quick. I haven't all day for amateurs."

Theodora grabbed her hand. "Come along, Leandra. I'll help you."

The costume they had brought was green and studded with silver and gold. It fit tightly and gave the illusion of being transparent, though in fact it was merely lined with flesh-colored fabric. It covered her from toe to neck, and around her head she wore a silver scarf that covered her fiery hair. The color of the costume was the same as her eyes, and with Theodora's expertise in makeup they quickly made her eyes seem huge and luminous, and her lips as pink as roses.

"You are indeed unique," Theodora whispered. "Even Erastus cannot deny you. You will bring down the house."

Together they walked back to where the horses were kept. Erastus stood by with a coal-black stallion, and as he saw her approach, his eyes grew large with surprise. Her costume hid nothing! She was ravishing.

"He will not do," Leandra said, looking at the stallion. "I must ride a white one."

"I have only one white horse. I must keep him separated. He is not a good horse. He likes no one. We may have to get rid of him. Last week the girl who rode him fell and broke her leg. No, he is here only awaiting a buyer."

"I must see him."

Erastus expelled his breath and shook his head. "He is out back in the corral, but he won't let you ride him."

Leandra hastened to the corral. She smiled when she saw the horse.

Then she hurried back to Erastus. "I must ride him," Leandra insisted. "He is the only pure white horse." He was for her and she for him. It had been decided long ago.

Erastus looked from Theodora's firm expression into Leandra's green eyes. He shrugged. "I'm not responsible if he throws you."

Leandra smiled and Erastus brought the horse. He threw a blanket over her to serve as saddle, and then he offered Leandra his clasped hands to climb up.

Skillfully, as if she had been doing it all her life, Leandra mounted the steed. She leaned over and stroked him gently, and then she whispered in his twitching ear. "You are for me. I am for you."

Then, as she had imagined it, she gently prodded the horse and he began to trot around the arena.

"She has ridden before," Erastus muttered. "It is quite clear to me, she is most experienced."

Theodora said nothing.

On the second pass around the arena, Leandra gracefully stood up. She balanced herself with ease even as the horse continued to trot. When she approached Theodora and Erastus, Leandra bent over and lifted one leg like a dancer. Her balance never faltered.

"Amazing," Erastus whispered in awe. "It is as if she is one with the animal!"

"She is amazing," Theodora agreed. In her heart she knew she was bound to Leandra as Leandra was bound to her, and that trouble would come between them only if they fell in love with the same man.

Next Leandra stood on her head, her legs perfectly straight. It seemed to her as if she had been riding this magnificent creature all her life.

When at last she bade her beautiful white horse to stop, she jumped down and did a wonderful series of cartwheels.

"Bravo!" Erastus shouted. "You're hired! You're most certainly hired."

Leandra thanked him and went directly to the horse. She rubbed his long nose and he nuzzled her and bent his head. "Ah, Pegasus," she whispered. "We meet again."

Until then she had not realized that animals could also be immortal.

Three

The crowd of Blue supporters that filled the stands on the right side of the emperor's box at the Hippodrome was on its feet, cheering with one voice as the two remaining chariots in the day's feature race rounded the second turn in the track. A great swirl of dust rose up as both drivers urged their horses on to still greater speeds.

To the left of the emperor's box the crowd of Green supporters also stood and shouted, but their shouts were angry and reflected their disappointment and frustration.

On the track below, the two adversaries, Alexander of Ravenna and Clarius of Brusa, were only inches apart. This race was a battle royal between two talented charioteers as well as between two very different men, men whose rivalry extended beyond the sport of chariot racing, men who in truth did not like each other in the slightest.

Alexander of Ravenna wore a blue cape, and his charioteer's helmet was adorned with a blue plume. Beneath his breastplate he wore a short blue tunic. His long, muscular legs were bare, as were his strong arms, and on his feet he wore leather sandals with iron clasps.

Alexander had prodded his horses forward till their heads were even with those of the horses that drew the chariot of

Clarius, who, since he drove for the Greens, wore green plumes and a green tunic.

Alexander was a tall and powerfully built young man. He was well over six feet, a height inherited from his ancestors, whose origins could be traced to the Ostrogoths who inhabited the valleys of the Alps to the north of Ravenna. The Ostrogoths were the eastern division of the Gothic peoples, some of whom had interbred with the Huns to the north. Clues to Alexander's mixed origins could be found in his deep blue eyes, straight black hair, and fair skin, skin now bronzed by the Mediterranean sun. Alexander's well-developed muscles bulged with the strength of an athlete whose freedom and future depended on his training, skill, and ultimate performance.

Again Alexander cracked his whip, but he did not hit his horses. Nonetheless, they sprang forward, again performing for this man who refrained from beating them. Alexander knew his horses well. He worked with them constantly, talked to them, urged them on.

Suddenly, and accompanied by a roar from the crowd, the creatures pulled out in front, and forcing their great hearts, leapt forward, leaving Clarius and his steeds inhaling their dust.

Alexander crossed the finish line to thunderous shouts from the Blues and wails and curses from the Greens. He allowed his animals to continue on for one slower-paced circle of the arena before bringing them to a halt before the emperor's box.

Only now that the wind was no longer in his ears could he hear the adulation of the Blues, who chanted with one voice, "Alexander! Alexander! Alexander!"

The emperor, Justin I, clad in white robes and resplendent with gold chains, was on his feet. He tossed down a bag of coins to Alexander.

"Alexander of Ravenna!" the voice of the announcer bellowed to the crowd, who repeated the name and then began the chant anew. "Alexander! Alexander!"

Alexander rose and bowed to the crowd.

"Does the brave charioteer care to petition the emperor for a favor?" the announcer called out. It was the custom. To the victor came favors—especially today, when Clarius, who had long been famous as the greatest chariot driver in the history of the Greens, had been defeated by a man whom many would consider a barbarian upstart. Not that the word barbarian was in much use these days. Justin, the childless emperor, had adopted a boy who was his nephew, a boy whose father was a barbarian.

"I ask for my freedom! I ask to become a free citizen of Constantinople and to serve my emperor!" Alexander shouted back.

Once again cheers filled the air. "Grant him his freedom!" the Blues shouted. "Make him an honored citizen!"

The old emperor stood and held up his hand for silence. "I shall do better," he shouted. But he did not shout loudly enough, and his words had to be repeated by a professional announcer whose thunderous voice could be heard by all. "I will grant him freedom and citizenship! I will also grant him a rank in my Royal Guard!"

Again the crowd roared. Alexander dropped to his knees and closed his eyes. The noise was loud, the dust dense, his heart full. How many years had he worked to achieve this moment? How long had he yearned for this moment when he was free? He had been captured when he was a mere boy of fifteen, now he was a man of twenty-five. A free man from this day forward.

He took off his helmet, which bore the Blue plume. His brow was beaded with perspiration. He bent again, this time lower, and from above hundreds of brightly colored, sweet-smelling flowers rained down on him.

"Such a handsome man," the empress whispered. Her aged eyes had settled on his thick, dark hair, which in the sunlight had a deep reddish hue, and his handsome, chiseled profile. "He could be a Roman god come to life," she said, smiling. "Oh, and look how strong his legs . . ." Her voice drifted off and her face flushed slightly.

The old emperor said nothing. He was just as accustomed to his wife's amorous daydreams as he was to her lecherous real-life affairs. He cared not. Justin was old and knew his life was almost over. Ever since he could remember, his wife, Euphemia, had been looking at younger men lustfully, complaining about younger women and their shallowness, and nagging him constantly to post more young and virile men to her personal guard. Euphemia had many vices, and indeed her only virtue—at least as far as he could ascertain—was her ability to give him soothing massages. Indeed, now that he ached from head to toe, it was a virtue he valued more and more with each passing day. Euphemia's hands were strong, her fingers long, and her knowledge innate. She could ease his arthritic torment and make him feel young again. It was for that reason and that reason alone that he put up with her. "Alexander is a superb driver," Justin muttered.

"Invite him to the palace," Euphemia urged. Her voice was syrupy, filled with anticipation.

But Justin shook his head. He would not indulge her. "Coin, freedom, and an appointment in the guard is enough," he replied. Then he turned to his nephew, who was no longer a boy but a man in his thirties. "It *is* a sufficient reward, is it not?"

Justinian nodded. "I will go and meet this Alexander. I would like him for my personal guard."

Justin did not look up, he merely pulled his robes around himself. "He would be a good choice for your guard," he acknowledged. "A very good choice indeed. Of course, it would deprive the Blues of a fine charioteer."

"The fame, and indeed often, the very life of a charioteer is short. I would prefer to see this Alexander live longer and prosper. He's worked hard to succeed," Justinian said, rubbing his smooth chin.

"Then speak with him," Justin said with a motion of his hand. Unspoken between them, but understood by them both, was Justinian's agreement to keep the desirable Alexander away from the wanton Euphemia, who might well order him to her boudoir and demand favors of him. Justin felt no jealousy, but he deemed Euphemia's entourage of young studs quite large enough. They were, after all, an expense to the palace, since Euphemia took it upon herself to feed and clothe them as well as provide them with young women who would stimulate them sufficiently before they came to her bed.

Justin turned to the professional announcer. "Let the next race begin," he commanded.

The announcement was made, and Alexander rose. Bowing, he left the arena. He was happy beyond words and decided immediately to go to the theater to celebrate. Yes, a night of entertainment was in order. He had something to celebrate.

In the dressing rooms Alexander met Clarius.

He was not tall like Alexander, though he was strong. Clarius was a bear of a man, squat yet muscular. His hair was short, black, and curly. His teeth were uneven, and his eyes dark and feral. He spoke crudely, and he called Alexander a barbarian. Clarius considered himself superior because he had been born well within the empire, was a citizen, and was free. He considered Alexander an unworthy opponent, an upstart, a man born to an inferior race.

Alexander did not care for Clarius because he treated his horses badly, and Alexander believed that Clarius had a cruel streak that made him most untrustworthy.

"Off drinking to celebrate your victory?" Clarius asked without real interest. Not having been detained by the crowd, Clarius had already discarded his breastplate and donned his robes.

"No, to the theater," Alexander returned.

"I'm surprised you enjoy the theater," Clarius commented.

Alexander avoided taking the bait. Clarius's comment was laden with prejudice. He did not seem to think that anyone from the valleys of the Alps could be cultured enough to enjoy theater. But it mattered not. He felt far too good to allow Clarius to rile him, especially tonight.

Instead, he turned his back and began to change his clothes. He heard Clarius mutter to himself, then Clarius left, deciding to say no more.

Alexander sat with Lucian, who was one of his few friends and who, though now free, had also been captured during one

of the many wars between the Ostrogoths and the soldiers of
the empire. Lucian, too, was an athlete, though not a charioteer.
He was a runner, a jumper, and a shot-putter. He was a partici-
pant in the games and a champion in the decathlon, a ten-event
contest that included running, jumping over hurdles, javelin and
discus throws, shot put, and high and long jumping. But the
games were not as popular as the chariot races, and Lucian was
not as famous as Alexander.

Both sat in absolute silence as the pantomime was performed
and as Theodora, the most famous actress in the circus, was
stripped slowly of her garments and stood helpless before her
tormentor.

"She's stunning," Lucian whispered to his companion. "Look
at her breasts, they're perfect."

Alexander felt his mouth dry. Theodora was indeed beautiful
and desirable. She projected a vulnerable quality that he felt
irresistible, and yet she also projected a kind of inner strength.

And her acting was superb. Her suffering seemed so real, and
when the moment came that her stage husband ravished her,
she dissolved into a passionate pleasure that was projected to
all in the audience.

Beside him, Lucian breathed hard and Alexander nudged him
and laughed. "Better to wait for the real thing," he admonished.
"This is clearly too much excitement for you."

Lucian blushed. "For me there will be no real thing. Theodora
would not sleep with me; I am no hero."

"Perhaps she'll sleep with *me,*" Alexander suggested with a
wink. "Today, and today only, my name is known throughout
the city because I defeated Clarius. Tomorrow I will again return
to the ranks of the unknown."

Lucian laughed. "Even the citizens of Constantinople are not
that fickle. You'll remain famous until you're defeated."

"Unless I give up racing for some other profession."

Lucian raised his brow. "Has some opportunity presented
itself?"

"I'm not sure. But I've been summoned to the palace by the
emperor's nephew, Justinian."

"Ah," Lucian acknowledged. Then he laughed. "Steer clear of Euphemia. Our aged empress compels young men to her bed."

"I shall be sure to avoid her."

"So, will you try to have Theodora for a night?" Lucian asked. "They say she has a different man every night."

Alexander stared at Theodora. He could tell no one that he had never possessed a woman. Men would have laughed at him, women would have shunned him. But it was true. He had been captured young and had begun his training as a charioteer that same year. He worked hard and at first there was no time for women. Then, when there was time, the women available to him were used and spent. They were not lovely courtesans like Theodora, but common prostitutes. And so he had waited.

"If you are going to try, you had better go to her dressing room. The crowd is always large," Lucian advised.

"I'm a hero for a day, should I not have this prize as well?"

"There are less expensive courtesans."

"But are there any more desirable?"

"I suppose not," Lucian muttered.

The stage lights faded and Alexander sprang to his feet. He and other would-be lovers hurried toward the famed actress's dressing room. She would choose one of them for a night of pleasure as she did almost every night.

In her dressing room, which smelled of pungent perfume and was lit only by draped lanterns, Theodora waited for her suitors. She lay on a divan covered with rose brocade. Her shapely legs were bare and visible to the top of her thighs. Her body was draped in loose black robes that clung to the curves of her body. A magnificent mane of dark, curly hair fell down around her shoulders, while her face was lightly powdered and her lips made red with dye. Her luminous dark eyes surveyed each of her suitors, and only after seeing them all would she choose.

"Have them enter one at a time," she instructed her body-guard.

One at a time they came before her. Some gave her money in advance of her decision, while others brought sweets or offered flowers or perfume. At the end of each day there was always a collection of gifts. In her apartment her tables were never without fresh flowers, her bowls never without pomegranates, and her plates never without sweets. Her vast array of admirers also brought seductive clothing and body lotions, stuffed animals, live lizards, and harmless snakes.

Alexander stepped into the room and approached her divan.

Theodora smiled at him, and her dark eyes studied his strong, desirable body. "You're the chariot driver who won today's race," she purred. Internally she shuddered. His arms seemed strong enough to crush her, and immediately she pictured them in bed together.

"I am Alexander of Ravenna."

"What do you offer me?"

Alexander held out a small bag of coin. "This, and all of myself."

"I accept," she whispered. He was quite wonderful, and she saw no further need for deliberations. She pulled the silken cord and her guard appeared. "Send the rest away," she ordered. "And leave us till morning."

"I can scarcely believe my good fortune," he said softly.

"Then come to me," she urged, holding out her slim arms.

Alexander knelt before her and Theodora embraced him. He kissed her red lips and immediately felt his rising passion. Vaguely he wondered what she really expected of him, and immediately he knew this would be no ordinary encounter with a harlot. Theodora had a reputation. She was a love goddess. What better teacher could he have?

As he kissed her, Alexander moved his hands slowly over her silken robe and then, as his lips caressed her long neck, he slipped his hand beneath her black robes in search of her supple skin. His eyes closed as he felt her metal breast-covering, and he sought to loose the silver chains that drew it together in the front. It took little to remove it and slip it away. He held her warm, firm breast—a breast he had seen only from a distance, when she was disrobed onstage. Now he bent to suck on her dark, hard nipple. As he did so, she ran her hand up and down his arm, feeling the ripple of his muscles. She moaned ever so slightly as he sucked a little harder, and then he felt her hands on him, caressing him teasingly.

Theodora shivered. He was huge and hard as bone.

"You will excite me too much," Alexander said, trembling.

Theodora laughed throatily. "I sense I am your first woman. Oh, don't deny it. I will teach you how to satisfy a woman. Lust is not enough." In a second, she wriggled free of him and stood up, pulling her robe back around her. "Come," she whispered.

Silently she led him into an inner sanctum. It was a slightly larger room and its contents surprised him. In one corner, a huge bath gave off a misty steam. He knew that a hot spring ran below this part of the city, because there was a heated public bath not far away. But never had he seen a private bath like this. It looked most enticing, and like everything in Theodora's realm, it smelled of heady perfume.

In the far corner of the room, a huge bed draped in silks stood waiting and a table covered with padding and tightly pulled cloth stood ready for massages. Candelabra provided a subdued light and incense burned in at least two pots.

To his surprise, Theodora bid him to climb on the table. "Let me massage you with essences," she said. "You will know a new kind of pleasure, my young charioteer."

Alexander felt as if he were drugged. He climbed onto the table and looked into her face. "I am not so young. I doubt there is any difference in our ages."

She did not tell him she was younger. "But there is a world of difference in our sexual experience," she returned.

"You will make me want no other woman."

Theodora laughed. "That would be too bad. I am not available for long-term relationships with poor men. No, you will want others. I shall simply turn you into a real lover. Tonight you will come to know what women want."

"It is a lesson I shall enjoy."

Alexander closed his eyes as he felt her begin to massage his

naked back with the perfumed oil. Small though they were, her
hands were magnificently strong. She began at his shoulders
and worked down his back, over each arm and shoulder, then
over his hard buttocks and down his legs. She worked silently
and warned him not to speak, but only to feel her soft touch
and visualize her naked and working over him.

After a time she told him to turn over, and when he did, he
felt a sensation he had never known before. Her caresses were
intimate and stimulating beyond description. They grew in intensity, warm and moist, rhythmic and sensual. He strived not
to reach fulfillment, but he could not contain himself. His whole
body flushed as he came like a fountain.

Theodora laughed lightly. "Do not tell me you did not enjoy
it."

"I wanted to be with you in the bed," he said after a moment.

"And we will be—should erotic pleasure be rushed?"

He shook his head and realized only then that she intended
much more, and that the zenith of their pleasure was yet to
come.

"Now you will massage me," she said. "In the same way,
and you shall be slow. Torture me sweetly, my young lover."

Alexander climbed off the table and Theodora disrobed and
replaced him. For a moment he looked at her slender body and
rounded bottom. Even with the most desirable parts of her body
hidden from view, she was exciting.

He took the pungent oils as directed and began their application. Her skin was soft and pliable, and she moaned slightly
under the movement of his hands as her hips surged up and
down slowly.

When he turned her over and massaged her breasts, her skin
began to glow with pleasure. "Yes," she whispered. "You learn
quickly."

When at last he lowered his lips to her most sensitive area,
she responded with undulant movements that once again caused
him to feel excitement. He wanted to carry her to the bed, but
she insisted he finish. In moments he saw her shudder and

shake. It was an incredible experience to see a woman thus, and to feel his own power to give such pleasure.

After a time, Theodora's eyes flickered open. "Carry me to the bath," she suggested.

In the warm, steaming waters they touched and kissed. Her body wrapped around him like a snake as they played sensually with each other until again he felt himself desiring fulfillment, and until she groaned in his arms, eager and begging for him.

He carried her from the bath to the bed, where their wet bodies were finally united as one. He remained still inside her, not allowing himself to move as she clawed at him in her excitement. Then he finally began to move. She cried out, and unable to resist longer, they both shuddered and completed the act.

Then in the hazy light he looked down on her. Her hair was damp with perspiration and her wet body glistened in the candlelight. She was absolutely beautiful—rounded, exotic, knowledgeable and a teacher of lovemaking. Yet Alexander felt empty. Something was missing from this encounter, something he could not define. It was like a chariot race perfectly run and yet with no joy in the victory. Alexander bent and kissed her cheek. He felt a tenderness toward her—he had been her pupil, she his teacher. Yes, that was it, he realized. He was physically satisfied and spiritually wanting. He could make love to Theodora, but he could not love her. She was not the woman for whom he was destined.

Justinian, nephew of the emperor, half reclined on a divan as Vincent, his faithful servant, poured the bloodred wine.

"Please, sit down," Justinian asked, gesturing to a pile of nearby cushions. "There is no need for formality yet, Alexander."

Alexander felt remarkably at ease in the presence of Justinian even though Justinian was ten years his senior. He supposed he felt at ease because Justinian's origins were humble even if he was the nephew of the emperor and his "adopted" son and heir. Moreover, Justinian was easygoing and friendly.

"I am but a common charioteer," Alexander reminded Justinian.

"A charioteer yes, common no. Now, please sit down. I cannot stand bowing and scraping, nor can I stand having someone hover over me."

He waved his hand in slight irritation, and Vincent bowed and left the room.

"As if when the goblets are empty we cannot pour our own wine," Justinian muttered.

"You don't like your servant?"

Justinian laughed. "Vincent is good enough, but like all the eunuchs in the palace, he relishes in palace gossip. He'll know the substance of our conversation soon enough, no need to hurry matters by allowing him to hover."

Alexander watched as Vincent departed, an ever so slight pout on his face. He silently thanked heaven that such a fate had not befallen him. Certainly as a prisoner it well could have been his fate, though most palace eunuchs had been sold as boys by the poor parents of the conquered. Those who became eunuchs later in life were usually criminals who had received the lifelong punishment of castration. No, it was unusual for prisoners of war to be castrated. Certainly, he reasoned, it was equally unusual for the royal family to employ criminals. No, it was much more likely that the eunuch who had just departed was sold as a child and reared to his position of servant-adviser. Sometimes, as was the case in Persia, eunuchs were employed guarding the wives and mistresses of the rulers. But he did not think that was the case here, since the emperor had only one wife.

"One has to be careful," Justinian confided. "Otherwise gossip comes to rule the palace, and the first thing you know wild stories are flying here and there."

Alexander made no comment.

Justinian laughed again. "You're tactful. I thought you would say that wild stories are already told of the Empress Euphemia.

Every eunuch in the palace has a story about her. The pity is, most are true."

"I have heard a few," Alexander confessed.

"Only a few? What a surprise. She takes young men to her bed, and if they cannot perform for her, she threatens them. But it is just that. Nothing ever happens to them. After all, a man should not be punished for being unable to perform a miracle."

Alexander only smiled.

"Drink some of your wine, my friend. I did not bring you here to discuss the empress or her sexual appetites. I invited you here to ask you to join my personal guard."

"I am honored," Alexander replied.

"Does that mean you will?"

"Yes, I accept with gratitude."

"Good, prepare to move into the palace. I welcome you. It will be nice to have another 'barbarian' around."

Alexander grinned. The young nephew of the emperor knew how the establishment spoke of him. And it was true that Justinian, too, had been born in the provinces—provinces populated by those whom the cultivated citizenry of Constantinople called barbarians.

"I shall serve you with all my loyalty," Alexander promised.

"I can ask for no more. Have more wine and tell me how you celebrated your victory."

Alexander began his tale. But he did not mention the name of Theodora. He believed that a lady's name, even that of as famed a courtesan as Theodora, should be protected. So he spoke only of a beautiful and erotic actress, a woman skilled in matters sexual.

Leandra luxuriated in the steaming bath located in Theodora's apartment. Her ravishing mane of red-gold hair was, as usual, hidden beneath her scarves, but her lithe young body was nude as she rested, eyes closed, in the bath.

Nearby, at a dressing table covered with aromatic perfumes and imported cosmetics, Theodora applied her facial makeup.

"You should have seen him! He was quite the most handsome man to grace my bed in months!"

"Was this Alexander an equally good lover?"

"He was eager to learn and so he became both lover and pupil. But I certainly don't mind. It is a certain guarantee that one gets what one desires."

Leandra smiled though she did not open her eyes. "What did you desire?"

"A long encounter with at least three fulfillments. I wanted to be ravished and tortured slowly and sweetly by knowing hands."

"So, are you in love?"

Theodora sighed deeply. "I could easily fall in love with this man. But he is not rich. I do not allow myself indulgences—especially the indulgence of falling in love with a poor man."

Leandra said nothing. Theodora would be more than rich—but the time was not yet right to reveal her destiny.

"I hear the circus is having a special royal performance tomorrow."

"Yes, for the emperor and empress, for Justinian and for his guard and the entire royal household."

"Will you ride?"

"Yes. That's why I must relax now. Tomorrow will be a hectic day."

"I've heard that Alexander has joined young Justinian's guard. You may have the opportunity to meet him. Remember, I saw him first, and though I cannot fall in love with him, I may still want to make love with him."

"I shall remember that you have staked your claim," Leandra replied. In truth, she had coupled with no one. But it was a secret she kept from Theodora. All the men she encountered wanted her, but she did not respond. And yet she admitted to desire. She felt her wantonness in her dreams, and in her dreams and only in her dreams did she know satisfaction. In those dreams, a man whose face was unknown to her made love to her in all ways possible, and she responded in kind, always awakening in a sweat, shaking and crying to him for more. But dreams were dreams and realities were realities. Her reality was to prepare Theodora. She pushed her dreams away.

"I wonder if Justinian or the emperor will ever attend the theater," Theodora mused. Her mind filled immediately with the joy royal accolades and expensive gifts could bring.

Leandra still revealed nothing, but neither did she abandon the idea. "I suppose you could give a royal performance sometime."

"You are my personal oracle. Don't you know?"

"I know your destiny is to be powerful. But I also know that matters must unfold gradually."

"Ah, Leandra. You are my friend, my joy, and my frustration."

"I'm sorry."

Theodora smiled. "You need not be sorry."

Leandra pulled herself from the soothing waters of the bath. "I must see to my own toiletry and I must let you prepare for tonight's performance."

"As if I had forgotten how to scream and shriek."

Leandra wrapped her voluptuous form in a towel, and then she began to dress. She, too, had to apply makeup and she, too, had to dress herself in her costume. Then, unlike Theodora, she had to prepare Pegasus for his performance. The great white steed who knew her mind as well as she had to be brushed and groomed. Then before hundreds of circus-goers she and Pegasus would perform. As they circled the great arena, they were one.

"Good luck," Leandra said as she departed.

"And the same to you," Theodora replied.

Alexander looked around the stands that faced the great arena. The royal entourage was, naturally, more than a mere retinue. In a box draped with purple banners trimmed in gold, the Empress Euphemia sat next to the old emperor, Justin. To one side, Justinian sat with his guard, Alexander among them. Below the royal box sat the palace staff, and the rest of the stands were filled with soldiers and their women. Opposite the royal box was the box that held the generals. This performance,

Justin had proclaimed, was being held in honor of Belisarius, the empire's leading general. It was to be a night of pageantry and feasting. Belisarius was victorious. All Byzantium was to celebrate.

The first act to fill the arena was a parade of elephants that walked around the great arena, each one holding the tail of the one preceding with his trunk. Each elephant was draped with a different-colored cloth trimmed in shimmering silver, and each was ridden by a woman adorned only in transparent veils that fell about the lower body from a silver belt.

The second act featured trained dogs jumping through hoops of fire, and the third act consisted of jugglers and acrobats. Then the arena was made empty and the crowd was urged to silence as the music of twenty flutes floated on the air and the sweet smell of perfume drifted upward from a hundred sticks of burning incense.

Then from the side of the arena the great white horse Pegasus burst forth. He circled the arena alone, draped in green and gold, a sea-green feather atop his noble head.

From the other side of the arena, a woman who seemed for all the world to be a dancer appeared. She twirled toward the center of the arena, leaping and pirouetting every few steps till she reached the center. She wore no skirts or tunic, she had no robe. She was clad from neck to toe in a skin-tight costume of green and silver. Her hair was concealed beneath a flowing scarf, her slippers were silver, and her legs long and shapely. Her costume hid nothing of her admirable figure, yet she was a total mystery. The crowd applauded loudly when she reached the center of the arena.

The great white horse galloped up to her at breakneck speed. He galloped so quickly that it appeared he might trample the slight figure in green. But when he reached her he dipped his long nose in a nod, then dropped his front legs, bowing before her. The crowd roared again and the announcer called out, "The magnificent Leandra!"

The gorgeous, mysterious Leandra mounted her steed, then stood atop him.

"Quite extraordinary," Justinian whispered.

But Alexander was in a trance. He wanted to reach out to her, he wanted more than anything to unwind her scarf and reveal her obscured mane of hair. Had he really thought Theodora the most beautiful woman he had ever seen? There was no comparison!

His mind immediately began to play tricks on him. He remembered in detail his whole experience with Theodora, but in his dreamy recollection the object of his lovemaking changed. It was not Theodora at all! It was this exquisite creature in green and silver, this Leandra the circus rider—a woman of some fame, a woman admired for her skill and aloofness.

Then, to excited cries and shrieks of delight, Leandra stood on one foot, her left leg extended straight out as she slowly bent down to touch her toe with her fingers. It was remarkable! It was as if she and her magnificent horse were one.

"Bravo!" Alexander shouted. But his voice was lost among thousands of others.

He sank back down in his seat and was immediately again in his daydream. He was in the hot bath with this Leandra instead of with Theodora. He could imagine her white, silken body as it turned pink from the warm waters of the bath and tense from his movements on her desirable flesh. He could all but feel her breath against him as she encircled his member with her small, strong hands. He saw them in his mind's eye, entangled and struggling in heated passion—he could almost feel her lips on his lips. His eyes were fastened on her reality, his thoughts on his dream, and his loins virtually ached for her as if he had been enchanted from the first moment she appeared.

"You seem quite smitten," Justinian whispered.

Alexander had to struggle to find his voice, to appear normal. "She is remarkable," he managed to say.

Leandra was doing a handstand now, and the audience erupted into cheers and applause. Slowly, ever so slowly, she returned to the position of a normal rider, and then she and the white horse galloped to the center of the arena. As the horse bowed, Leandra slipped from the saddle and fell to her knees before her adoring audience.

"Go backstage and meet her," Justinian suggested as he nudged Alexander in the ribs. "Say with whom you visit the circus, and ask for her favors. Indeed, if you wish, invite her for a late supper at the palace. She is your enchantress, but I should not mind meeting her."

Alexander did not hesitate for a moment. He stood up and hurried away, down the stone steps and around the arena till he came to the exit through which the performers disappeared.

Two guards stopped him, but when they saw who it was, and when he told them he was with Justinian, they let him pass.

To his surprise, he was not directed to a lavish dressing room, but, rather, to the stable. There, in a small corral, was the white horse, and there, brushing his mane, was Leandra.

"I am Alexander of Ravenna," he said clearly.

Leandra turned from the horse and looked at him. When she lifted her eyes, he saw what he had not seen before. He saw their color. They were intense and unusual. They were the color of the Aegean, a sea green. He felt drawn to their depths.

"Am I supposed to know your name?" she asked. He was handsome and unusual-looking, she thought. But he was young, and like all immature men, he was too sure of himself and took things for granted. The way he smiled, the way he carried himself—he seemed conceited to her.

"I am champion of the chariot races, now a member of Justinian's guard."

Leandra's lips parted, half in surprise. This was the man who had possessed Theodora last night! Indeed, Theodora had sung his praises half the morning and entertained her with graphic details of their lovemaking.

"You're ravishing," he said, stepping closer to her. "I want you. Come to the palace, let me lavish you with gifts and show you my admiration."

Leandra stepped away and actually laughed. Her laughter filled the air, but then she turned and looked into his eyes. She stopped laughing. "I live with Theodora, the actress," Leandra said. "I spent the morning listening to the details of your love-making. Yes, Theodora praises your 'talents.'"

Alexander smiled broadly. Was she, also, a courtesan? But of course she was! All actresses and circus performers were courtesans. Surely she considered it a recommendation that he had performed so well with her friend Theodora. He ignored her previous laughter and the fact that she had sounded so sarcastic. He felt emboldened. "Then you will know I can satisfy you," he said, leaning over and whispering into her ear.

He was unprepared for the hard slap she delivered to his cheek. "You're conceited and quite absurd!" she said, narrowing her green eyes and looking into his angrily. "I do not sell my body or give it to just anyone."

For a moment Alexander looked at her. No woman had ever hit him. None had ever dared. He reached out and seized her small wrist, pulling her roughly toward him. His other arm encircled her tiny waist, and he held her close enough and tight enough that he could feel the outline of her perfect body against him. She was powerless to stop him. And who would pay the slightest bit of attention to the fact that one of Justinian's guards had forced himself on a circus performer.

He bent and pressed his lips to hers. She struggled against him and refused to open her lips. When she shook loose of his mouth, she hissed at him, "Let me go!"

"Ah, so spirited. I could take you now, here."

"You would rape me?" She stared into his eyes.

But there was no terror in those green eyes, only surprise. Her expressive eyebrows were arched, and he felt almost weak as she looked at him. Suddenly he felt ashamed and he felt his face flush. What was he thinking? She was captivating and desirable, but courtesan or no, he could never force her.

"No," he said sheepishly, "but surely you sell your favors as the others do."

"I just told you, I do not," Leandra replied somewhat coldly.

"But you live with Theodora. She is a love goddess, the most famous courtesan in all of Constantinople."

"Theodora does as she wishes. I do as I wish."

He was surprised by her independence, and more astounded by her rejection of him.

"Are you going to tell me you are a virgin still?"

Leandra drew herself up haughtily. "I am not going to tell you anything."

With that she leapt over the fence and onto Pegasus. She turned the horse away, out of the corral and into the darkness of the night. In moments they were galloping along the shore, under the bright stars and full moon. White-tipped black waves caressed the hard-packed sand beneath Pegasus's hooves.

But even as she rode, Leandra pictured this Alexander. He was arrogant and his arrogance had angered her. He had been with Theodora, and that, too, infuriated her. No, it enraged her that he wanted both of them. But he was so attractive. Theodora had described his maleness well, and now she had felt that maleness against her, felt the outline of his sword, felt the strength in his arms, experienced the softness of his lips and his hot breath. Theodora's descriptions filled her head, and suddenly she felt sensations she had not known before, the pangs of desire, feelings she had till this very moment assumed were not for her. She drew Pegasus in, and they both stood motionless, two majestic silhouettes against the moon.

"I am ruled by my dreams, Pegasus. What am I to do?"

The horse shook his head and she leaned over and patted him gently. "Is this Alexander a good man?" she asked.

Again Pegasus nodded.

"Oh," Leandra said a bit regretfully. She sighed as she turned the horse's reins and headed home. "Perhaps I shall have a dream tonight," she said aloud. But her dreams did not come on request, and seldom were they about herself.

Four

As Leandra entered the main salon of the apartment she shared with Theodora, she rubbed her eyes against the morning sun that flooded in through the windows. When she looked about, she saw that the salon was ablaze with color and filled with the aromatic scent of exotic flowers. Every table, every corner—virtually every bit of floor space—was filled with blossoms! She had to walk sideways to avoid the baskets that held them.

"Aren't they lovely!" Theodora's happy, melodic voice rang out. "They're so beautiful! I've never had anyone send me so many flowers!"

Leandra smiled at her confidante. Theodora was draped in a sheer white robe held only with a single golden cord. Her thick hair was gathered up and pulled back, leaving her small, expressive face framed by dark curls. She was reclining on her divan, in an imitation of the famed statue of Aphrodite.

"Where have all these flowers come from?" Leandra asked. She instantly thought of Alexander. But surely he had not had them sent—former chariot drivers, even those in Justinian's Royal Guard, did not make enough money to lavish flowers on Theodora.

"From my most ardent suitor! Isn't it wonderful? Never have I known a man so generous! And the flowers are not all! He has given me jewels as well—jewels and something even more important."

Leandra felt a pang of apprehension. No dreams had come to her. Why was there no forewarning of this nameless ardent suitor? "Are these from Alexander?" she asked, knowing in her heart they were not.

"Good heavens, no!" Theodora laughed. "Alexander is a fine lover! A very fine lover! But he is poor. He could never afford such gifts as these, nor can I afford to waste my time on pure enjoyment. No, I fear I shall not be able to be with Alexander again."

Leandra felt a sudden wave of relief and wondered why. Perhaps, she admitted to herself, she had wanted to believe Alexander's declaration to her. Perhaps she was vain enough to want to accept the unlikely idea that he had been smitten with her on first sight.

Leandra smiled. "Only yesterday you pronounced Alexander the best lover you had ever had. Now you tell me he is too poor."

"Sexual pleasure is one thing, station and security in this uncertain world is quite another. You have always counseled me wisely, surely you know I'm right."

Leandra felt trapped. She counseled Theodora on the basis of her dreams, and there had been no dreams. Was she to advise Theodora in any case? And even if she were to counsel Theodora, could she give her advice on the matter of Alexander? She thought for a moment. "Theodora, can you also enjoy this new suitor, this man with station who offers security?"

"Oh, but of course! It is only a matter of degree!"

Leandra nodded. "Then tell me about him."

"It's Hecebolus!" Theodora sang out.

"Hecebolus!" Leandra repeated in surprise. "He's nothing but a self-important merchant from Tyre!"

"Ah, but a rich merchant. A patrician! And soon he will be governor of Pentapolis. He has received a royal appointment! And let me add that he is also a fine lover. Of course, I was seeing him long before I met Alexander. And then, just last night, he asked me to accompany him when he takes up his post in Pentapolis."

"Pentapolis?" Leandra asked. Not that she didn't know where it was—it was, in fact, not far from Tyre. But it was certainly far from Constantinople, where she knew Theodora's destiny lay. What was she to do?

"Yes, yes!" Theodora bubbled. "Don't you see? This life of mine is going to change! Hecebolus is going to make me his only mistress! He is going to take me to Pentapolis to be the mistress of his household! I shall be a courtesan no more! I shall be a lady. And he has hinted that we may even be wed."

Leandra felt dumbstruck. She had no instruction, no idea what to say or to do. All she knew was that Theodora's ultimate destiny was here in Constantinople. She was to heal the people and reform the laws of the empire. She was destined, and now that destiny suddenly seemed in question. And she knew she was to remain with Theodora.

"Of course, I'll take you with me," Theodora said instantly. "You need not even ask—I know you will go nowhere without your beloved horse. So there is nothing for us to do but to take him too."

Leandra lowered her eyes. Without her dreams that foretold events, she did not know what to say. "Theodora, I do implore you to think about this plan. Hecebolus is a strange man and Pentapolis is far from Constantinople."

"I have thought about it all my life! I have dreamed of escaping the theater, of being a person of station—of commanding a household. A governor has stature, and I will be more than an actress. This is my real chance to better myself, Leandra."

Leandra felt defeated. If Theodora went to Pentapolis, she would have to go as well. She tried to ask herself why she felt so upset, why she minded. Had she unwittingly grown accustomed to the cheers of the circus crowd? Or was it something else? Even someone else? She forced the thought from her mind. Perhaps this was all part of the plan, conceivably it was meant to be. But still, she felt empty inside and somehow remorseful. The image of Alexander suddenly filled her thoughts. For one moment she felt a terrible regret that they would now not come to know each other, and the next moment she chastised herself, reminding herself of his arrogance and of his passion with Theodora. And yet . . . and yet she could not seem to erase his face from her mind or the feeling of his lips on hers from her memory.

"You are lost in thought," Theodora said.

Leandra forced a smile. "If you are set on this course of action, I have many things I must do."

Leandra turned her thoughts to the burial place of Anstice and to the silver he had instructed her to hide. She must bid the grave of Anstice farewell, and as if directed, she knew she must now retrieve the silver.

Alexander sat in the stands of the circus. Tonight Justinian was not with him, and so there was no royal box as there had been the previous night during the special performance. Tonight he was a commoner, a mere spectator, a man drawn to this place as if by a magnet, though he knew it was no magnet, it was the woman Leandra.

He could not forget the face of Leandra, who rode the white stallion. He could not forget the feelings she evoked within him. He ached for her, but not in the physical sense alone. The physical need was there, but thoughts of her had haunted him throughout the night and during all his waking hours. It was far more than physical longing. Something else had happened when he kissed her. He had felt a meeting of minds, a melting together of thoughts. He had felt an awareness he could not even describe, sensations he suspected he would feel again only with this woman.

"Leandra the Amazing!" the announcer shouted. "In her last performance!"

The crowd roared as Leandra appeared, and yet Alexander hardly heard them. All he heard were the words "In her last performance."

What did it mean? He felt stunned, and yet he could do nothing but wait for her performance to end.

After a moment he could stand it no longer. He left his seat and hurried away toward the exit, determined to wait below, near the corral in which her horse was kept. That way, he reasoned, he could see her immediately after her act ended.

The time passed more slowly than he ever imagined it could. He listened to the roars of the crowd and counted the minutes. Finally, after what seemed an eternity, she appeared, walking slowly and holding the reins of the white horse.

Leandra saw him and stopped. Her eyes met his evenly. "You returned tonight as well?"

"To see you," he said, taking a step toward her.

"For the last time," she said, looking away from his blue eyes, which seemed to see through her.

"What does that mean?" he asked. "I do not understand. What is all this about a last performance, and why am I seeing you for the last time?"

"It means I am going away. It means that I will no longer ride in the circus. It means I shall return to my vocation in life."

"What might that be?"

"I am the daughter of a learned man. I have studied medicine. I am going away, and I shall use my time away to study further."

"You can't leave! I have not yet had the opportunity to—"

"You are not to have any opportunity," she said, forcing herself to sound detached and cold. "There are things I must do, and nothing can interfere."

"Why are you going? Why can't you do whatever you must here in Constantinople?"

"I must stay with Theodora."

"Do you love Theodora?"

She knew immediately what he meant and shook her head. "Like a sister," she emphasized. "It is my destiny to look after her."

"Not so, my beautiful lady. Your destiny is with me."

"You are too sure of yourself," she retorted. "I must go."

He drew in his breath and continued to stare at her. "I shall wait for you. But if you do not return, then I shall find you."

Leandra turned away, not wanting him to see her regret, not

wanting to betray anything or to encourage him in any way. "Do as you wish," she said. "I cannot stop you."

Again, and before he could say anything more, she had mounted the white horse and was off once again on her midnight ride along the sandy shore.

It was August and the sun burned ferociously at midday. It glistened off the rounded dome of St. Irene and shimmered off the tiles of the great Hagia Sophia.

Leandra examined the vessel in which they would sail across the sea to the Syrian coast. It bobbed in the sparkling blue-green waters of the Bosphorus, while above them Constantinople spread out, disappearing into the hills. She took one long look, and then went below deck with Theodora.

Hecebolus stood on deck, waiting for the anchor to be hauled in and for the mighty oars to be dropped into the water.

"Governor," he said aloud. This appointment was like a dream come true. He was already wealthy, but as governor he would become wealthier yet, and he would garner respect as well. He relished in his position. After all, being a governor was rather like being a king. He would live in a palace. He would have a guard. He could demand payment from others.

Hecebolus was a man of two natures. On the surface he was polite and even thoughtful. He dressed well and wore a fashionable beard, which he kept short and well groomed. He was a man who had money, who knew how to save money, and who knew how to use money. But beneath his calm exterior, Hecebolus was not polite, thoughtful, or even kind. He wanted Theodora as a man wants possessions. She was desirable and sought after in Constantinople even though she was an actress and thus a harlot. Since others wanted her, he vowed to obtain her. He used his money to acquire her and then immediately began to regret what he had spent.

Still, he admitted that she was a woman who brought him

intense bodily pleasure, and so he vowed to take her to Penta-polis and over the years—as long as he found her entertain-ing—extract his money's worth from her.

Having decided this, his thoughts settled on Leandra, Theo-dora's companion. What did an actress need with a companion? And what indeed did a companion need with a horse? He grim-aced. They would cost a pretty penny to keep, so he decided he would not keep them. After all, as soon as they began their journey, he was in charge. Theodora would have no means of leaving him so he could do as he pleased. Yes, that was the solution. At the earliest opportunity he would put Leandra and her horse ashore. If the girl had wits, she might make it back to Constantinople; if she did not, she and her horse would per-ish. For a moment he thought of keeping the horse, but it was said that no one but the girl could ride the beast. He returned his thoughts to the cost of feeding it. No, he would rid himself of both of them.

It was a strangely gray day when the vessel on which they all traveled dropped anchor at Smyrna on the coast of Cappado-cia. Leandra, her hair as always wrapped securely in a long scarf, and dressed in flowing robes, made her way across the deck. She felt troubled and apprehensive, even more apprehen-sive than she had on the day their journey began. What could Hecebolus want with her? Since the voyage had begun, she had tried to avoid him and to seek out Theodora only when Hece-bolus was busy with other matters. But it did not matter what she did. It seemed clear to her that Hecebolus resented her.

He was dressed in a blue tunic and was standing by the ship's rail, stroking his beard with one hand.

"You summoned me?" Leandra asked as she drew near to him.

He turned and looked at her. His gaze was cold, appraising.

"You're an attractive woman," he muttered, "but I sense you are far from pliable; indeed, I sense you would cause me much difficulty."

Leandra wondered how to answer him. Had she not avoided him? Thus far, she had certainly not caused him trouble of any kind. "It is not my intention to cause you any trouble," she returned.

"Intent or no, I have no thought of taking you all the way to Pentapolis."

Leandra opened her mouth to protest, but Hecebolus went on before she could say anything.

"I am setting you and your horse ashore here," he told her unemotionally.

Leandra felt paralyzed. She was now a great distance from Constantinople—moreover, she knew it was Theodora's wish that she stay with her.

"I do not understand," Leandra finally managed to say.

"There is little to understand. I do not like your influence on Theodora. I do not intend to keep two mistresses and a horse. Actually, I would keep the horse and set you ashore alone, but the beast seems untamed and quite useless. I recall it being said that you and you alone could ride him."

"Yes. He allows only me to ride him," Leandra said defensively.

"So you can ride him back to Constantinople."

"Have you told Theodora what you are doing?"

Hecebolus actually laughed. "She is locked in her cabin. She has no say in this matter. I am to be governor of Pentapolis, and since we left Constantinople I have been master of this vessel. No, dear lady, I have no need to tell anyone of my plans. As for Theodora, she can be kept under lock and key till she feels cooperative."

Leandra stared at Hecebolus. He was a dangerous man, a man who did not keep his word, a man who could not be trusted. Why had she not been warned about him?

Not that she hadn't had her own feelings of foreboding, but there had been no foretelling dreams. Now what was she to do? It seemed there was nothing she could do except accept matters as they were and wait for direction.

"The planks are laid, you and your horse may leave now. I've had your things packed for you."

Leandra looked at the servant who approached with a bundle, and at Pegasus, who had been set ashore already and awaited her dockside, pawing his left hoof into the sand. She sought Hecebolus's eyes. "You must be careful," she warned. "Theodora is destined for power and will make a bad enemy."

Hecebolus laughed heartily and slapped his side. "Ride to Constantinople, bitch! Hecebolus fears no mere woman!"

Leandra took her bundle from the frightened servant and climbed down the plank onto the dock. She mounted Pegasus and guided him away. She would not give Hecebolus the satisfaction of looking back or of seeing her distress.

Hidden all day by massive dark clouds, the sun set, leaving a prolonged purple twilight. "We are alone in a strange land, Pegasus," Leandra whispered as she guided her horse across the plain of Cappadocia. It was an eerie place, and its few inhabitants seemed to hover between heaven and hell.

Was it going to rain? She glanced heavenward at the rapidly swirling clouds, then again at her surroundings. The trees were all small and leafless, quite unlike the lush olive groves of Antioch or the forest around Constantinople. This was a ghostly place where craggy rocks rose from the barren ground as if vomited up from deep within the earth. They were like misshapen statues on the landscape.

Most of the rocks were honeycombed with caves and grottoes and inside, like layers of human insects, the ascetics of Byzantium, the holy monks who had given up all of life's pleasures, lived out their existence in self-imposed silence and poverty. In starvation they had eaten the leaves from the bushes and in thirst they drank their own urine. They were hollow-eyed men, bearded and unkempt.

Leandra moved carefully through this landscape of human sacrifice. She was respectful of the silence. Just as dusk was sweeping over the plain and the mild breeze caused the brittle branches of naked brush to rustle like skeleton bones, she found an empty cave in which to take shelter. She hoped it did rain. She and Pegasus needed water.

She led Pegasus inside, and there shared what bread she had with her faithful horse. Then, weary and worried, she lay down and closed her eyes in sleep.

In her dream she saw the landscape of Cappadocia as if she were still riding through it. Then a voice penetrated her dream. "Do not worry," it told her. "Theodora must come of age by herself. She must be tested and you cannot assist. It is fated. You must dress as a man for protection and tomorrow you must begin your journey across the Aegean Sea to Salonika. There you will wait for Theodora, who will come. Together you will then return to Constantinople."

The voice faded and suddenly the face of Hecebolus appeared. "Beware," she heard the voice say, "evil wears many masks." Hecebolus's face contorted, and out of the distortion appeared a new face, a face she had never seen before. It was the face of a man with a pointed chin, a beard less well groomed than that worn by Hecebolus, and close-cropped curly hair. "Evil," her dream voice warned. "Beware of evil."

The dream voice receded and grew faint. The landscape of Cappadocia became obscured in a dream fog, and for a moment there were no dreams.

Then Alexander appeared before her. He was naked and glistening in the firelight, and he stood above her, looking down, his eyes hungry for her, his arms held out toward her.

"I cannot, I am destined," she whispered.

"My loins ache for you, my beloved."

He knelt by her side, and before all else unbound her hair, which tumbled out over her milk-white shoulders.

She felt his hot breath on her neck as he kissed her hair, running it through his fingers as if it were spun gold. "It's more beautiful than anything I have ever seen," he breathed in her ear.

She in turn ran her hands over his skin, feeling wonderfully protected in his strong arms. His hands were like hot irons on her cool flesh as he moved them seductively over her body. His lips kissed hers and she felt him undoing the knot that tied her robes. His hands were magic, warming her, thrilling her. His fingers undid her golden girdle and then released her from it, leaving her body white and naked in the flickering light of a fire. His lips touched her breasts and sucked so gently, she felt her own loins on fire in longing. He touched one nipple and nursed the other, and as Leandra moaned she felt a sudden, wonderful throbbing release.

Still feeling the pulsating joy, she blinked open her eyes and shivered as the predawn light filled the cave. She shook involuntarily and felt her mouth dry as she sat up and drew her blanket around her. Nearby, Pegasus slept without dreams.

How could a dream be so vivid? How could one know such pleasure from a dream? And why of Alexander? Was she destined to love him? Had her first dream been her command and her second dream her own? She felt confused and yet exhilarated as she lay back down and curled herself into a ball. Was that perhaps what lovemaking was really like? She closed her eyes, hoping to recapture her dream, hoping to feel the intense pleasure once again, but it was gone.

Far away, in the royal palace of Justin, Alexander lay on his pallet and stared at the dark ceiling as he breathed heavily, still relishing the sensuality of his erotic and fulfilling dream, a dream in which he had possessed the compelling Leandra. Her wild red-gold hair had felt like the finest silk, her skin like velvet, her lips had tasted like ambrosia. Her perfectly formed breasts had throbbed when he drew their pink nipples into his mouth and then, lost in her moist depths, he felt himself explode with pleasure.

It was a miracle, this dream pleasure. No seed was ever spilt, yet it seemed so real. He had known such dreams before, but never any as intense as this one, or as seemingly real.

Alexander clenched his fists. "Let her be sent back to me," he said aloud into the darkness. "Please let her return."

* * *

Leandra arose early, and doing as she was bid, dressed herself as a man. How fortunate that the servant had packed a robe with a hood. She put it on and closed it with a cord. Then she mounted Pegasus. They rode in the early morning light toward the Aegean.

Once there, Leandra guided Pegasus along the rocky coast. Salonika lay across the sea and to the north. At noon they came to a small village and Leandra bought food with the silver she had hidden in bags around her waist beneath her loose-fitting clothes and which she now carried hidden beneath the blanket that covered Pegasus's back.

She watered Pegasus and fed him as well. Then she boldly approached the master of a vessel that had put in to port.

"Where do you travel?" she inquired, trying to deepen her voice.

"To the island of Chios and then westward to Athens."

"How long a journey to Athens?" she asked.

"Four days."

"My horse and I would like to go with you. I have money and I can buy provisions."

The captain of the vessel eyed her suspiciously. "Are you an escaped criminal?"

Leandra shook her head. "A mere performer trying to get to Salonika."

"Salonika is a long ride from Athens."

Leandra smiled. "So it is, but it is at least on the right side of the ocean. Will you take us with you for a fee?"

"Two pieces of silver," he muttered. "Have you that much?"

"That is a lot," Leandra said, thinking she could bargain.

"Not so much. A horse takes up much room. I cannot take as much cargo, therefore I must charge more."

What he said made sense, and so Leandra agreed. She paid him the silver and she and Pegasus boarded the vessel. It would take her many weeks to reach Salonika. And it was a completely strange place to her. What was she to do while she was there?

* * *

Theodora wandered about the lush garden of the Governor's Palace. For months she had known luxury she had not known before. During the years of her childhood, food had always been in short supply and clothing was passed on from one child to the next. As a young actress her daily needs had been met by her lovers . . . now she was alone. Since that morning when Hecebolus had locked her up below deck and sent Leandra away, she had been treated like a pampered slave.

Breakfast was brought in the morning, supper in the early afternoon, and then a repast of fruit and goat's cheese in the early evening. Her bed was soft, her clothes erotically designed and beautifully made, her toiletry seen to by a maid. She was given perfumes for her body and she was allowed to wear fine jewels.

"All my needs are met," Theodora said aloud to no one. "But none is really met," she added as tears filled her dark eyes. Never before in her entire life had she cried, never before had she felt insecure, weak, and alone. Never before had she been afraid. But she felt all of those emotions now.

Hecebolus was cruel beyond words. He gave her everything and nothing. Material needs were met and she was made to submit to his physical needs on demand. The palace, its gardens, and its pool were hers to enjoy. But she was not allowed out beyond the gates, she had no friends, and when he came to her Hecebolus was mean and abusive.

Theodora sniffed as the tears that had filled her eyes began to run down her cheeks. She was so utterly alone, and now she felt alone and helpless. Abstractedly, she ran her hand over her full stomach. It was beginning to swell with the child she carried, Hecebolus's child, a child that would make her unattractive to the man on whom she now depended for sustenance.

Whatever was she to do if he turned her out? In Constantinople she had friends to whom she could turn. She knew where to find food when times were difficult, she knew where to turn.

But here in Pentapolis she knew no one, she did not, in fact, have the slightest idea what the city actually looked like.

"My sweet, you spend far too long each day lost in thought." Hecebolus approached her from behind. His voice was sarcastic and she wondered if she was even allowed to *think* now, to escape into her memories.

Theodora turned toward him and saw the menacing flash in his dark eyes just as she had heard the nastiness in his voice when he spoke.

"What should I be doing?" she asked, trying to muster the confidence she felt she had lost.

"Perhaps exercising to see if you can bring back your fine figure."

He sounded angry as he rounded the bench to face her. He reached down, and taking her hands, pulled her to her feet and into his arms. His mouth sought hers roughly, and he dug his long, hard fingers into her arms.

"Let me go," Theodora whispered. "You're hurting me."

"Look at you!" he suddenly shouted. "Look how fat you're getting!"

Theodora met his dark eyes. There was no use trying to deny it now. He would soon realize she was pregnant, and perhaps when he knew she was carrying his child he would treat her better. "I am with child," she said softly. "Your child."

His expression took an instant to contort, then he slapped her across the face as hard as he could and she fell back down upon the bench, her lips parted in terror.

"How should I know it is my child? You're a harlot! For all I know it could be the gardener's child! Wretched woman! Bitch! I will keep you here no longer. Get out of my house! Get out of my sight!"

Theodora shivered uncontrollably. He was casting her out with only the clothes on her back! She was not even wearing any jewelry, nor did she have a cloak! And she was with child! What was to become of her?

He pulled her down the garden path, past the flowing bushes all the way to the gate that guarded the palace grounds.

"What of your child?" Theodora asked. "Take pity on your own child!"

"I've had enough of you!" He opened the gate and threw her out.

Theodora stumbled and landed on the dusty street. "You're a monster!" she cried out.

He threw a coin after her. Terrified, Theodora picked it up. One silver coin would not take her far; still, she clung to it and with his curses ringing in her ears she hurried away. For the first time in her life Theodora admitted knowing fear.

Salonika lay on the west side of the Chalcidice peninsula at the head of a bay on the Gulf of Thermaikós. Like all great port cities Leandra had passed through, this one also rose from the sea and covered the foothills of higher mountains, in this particular case, Mt. Khortiátis.

"Salonika," Leandra said aloud. She smiled to herself. Anstice had told her about this city. "Founded long ago, and named for a sister of Alexander the Great. The Romans made this place the capital of their province of Macedonia." She patted Pegasus. "Ah, Pegasus, you may rest here. But I do not know for how long.

"Oh, dear," she whispered, wrapping her cloak around her and pulling down its hood. In the distance, coming down the dusty road, there appeared to be a procession marching toward her. All those marching were dressed in ragged gray robes, and as they drew closer, a low, mournful dirge could be heard.

"They seem to be monks," she said, guiding Pegasus to the side of the road. There, by the side of a great tree, Leandra watched as the men marched by. She fought to control herself because the sight was horrendous and the stench almost overpowering. The men beneath the cloaks were filthy and ragged. Their skin clung to their bones and they appeared as living skeletons. In their midst were wagons filled with decaying bodies. They pulled and pushed the wagons and continued their lament.

Then, as if noticing her for the first time, one of their number
pointed at her and yelled, "Salonika is dying! It's the plague!
Beware!" Others followed suit, but Leandra could not move.
Instead, she sat stock-still, waiting for the grim bearers of the
dead to pass by. Then, when the last of the procession had gone,
she continued down the road toward the doomed city. "We must
see if we can help," she said with determination.

Outside the walled city, Leandra drew Pegasus to a halt and
dismounted near a grove of small trees on which grew a round,
firm edible fruit known all over Byzantium as the orange. She
looked around and saw that the orchard was untended. Usually
she would have asked permission, but as no one was about, and
as she assumed, many had fled in the wake of the plague, she
tethered Pegasus and then picked half a dozen of the fruit.

Leandra carefully peeled all the fruit she picked, then she
built a small fire from dry twigs and in her only small pot,
purchased at a bazaar, she cooked the peel of the fruit together
with its seeds. She ate the sweet pulp. When it had boiled for
a long while and the skin was soft, she removed it from the fire
and waited for it to cool. Then she applied the mixture to her
body from head to toe. It was sticky, but it did not smell bad.
Long, long ago Anstice had taught her to do this in order to
avoid the plague were it about. She did it now because she well
recalled how they had once passed through a plague-ridden area
and been spared. Whatever the reason, this mixture seemed to
protect one.

When she was finished, Leandra led Pegasus through the
gates and into the city.

Crude crosses marked the doors of the houses occupied by
the ill, and everywhere fires seemed to be smoldering. Many
believed that smoke kept the disease away, others burned their
clothes or the clothes of those who had fallen ill and those who
had died. Those who were not yet ill barricaded themselves in
their houses and prayed for the unpredictable curse to pass them
by. Yet the plague knew no door that prevented it from enter-
ing—it was a silent, ghostly killer that struck both good and
bad, young and old, male and female.

Still, Leandra was not afraid. She went directly to the hospital and offered herself. "I have studied medicine," she told the doctor, who was weary and frightened. He invited her to help. "I have no time to test you," he muttered. "But time will tell me if you are competent."

Leandra began working among the ill and dying immediately. She bathed the victims and lanced the hideous swellings found beneath their arms and more commonly on their groins. This she had been taught to do and she well knew that this was the critical state of the illness.

If the victims survived the lancing and the removal of the poisons, she covered them lightly and waited to see if their fevers would break or if they would go mad and die. It was a fearful death, though she was well aware that she felt no fear.

A servant brought her food and she was given a room in which to sleep. Days went by, and Leandra worked each day until she was too tired to stand. She worked till her arms and legs ached, her only relief found in sleep, which brought her dreams. Her dreams carried her away from Salonika and the death that haunted it. Her dreams carried her to a beautiful house by the sea and into the arms of Alexander, a man she hardly knew in reality but with whom she had become intimate in her dreams.

Days and nights blended and time passed quickly.

Theodora's long dark hair was bound in a single braid and wrapped in a swirl around her head. She was dressed in a lovely, seductive gown made with silver threads, but her gown was not visible, nor was it as lovely as the day she had adorned it. Over her gown she wore a dark monk's robe and on her feet she wore simple sandals. She had been wearing this gown and expensive slippers when Hecebolus ejected her from his house. In the first few hours she had traded the slippers for the cloak and the silver coin for more practical sandals and some food for her journey.

She walked along the path that ran parallel to the rugged Mediterranean shore, her eyes fastened on the distant horizon in spite of the fact that her shapely legs ached and her small feet had vicious blisters.

Hecebolus was a monster. He had beaten her and threatened her and she had vowed to run away no matter what happened. But he had thrown her out before she could leave him. She had left empty-handed, without even a loaf of bread to sustain her. He had sent her away with only one silver coin.

Now, seven days later, she was well beyond the city and Hecebolus's reach. But it was a hostile world, a world in which she knew she must be very careful. This was not Constantinople, where she knew how to obtain food from the fruit sellers when the market was closing or where she knew people who would help her. This was an alien land filled with alien people. Wearily, Theodora pushed one foot in front of another. "I must get home," she vowed.

The glorious warm sun seemed to fall all too rapidly into the sea, and with its disappearance came a cool breeze that penetrated her thin clothing and made Theodora shiver.

She had run out of bread some days before and since then had eaten only wild berries and drunk only water from springs. In spite of her pregnancy, she was now thinner than she had been, and she felt the cold more easily.

As daylight faded, Theodora climbed toward what looked like a cave. She hated the darkness beneath the ground but she knew she could sleep in the entrance and still be relatively sheltered.

She clawed her way up the rocks and then, to her complete surprise, she saw a wizened old man. He extended his hand toward her. "Come, daughter," he whispered. "Let me help you."

The old man wore a robe not unlike her own, and around his neck was a heavy wooden cross. Theodora took his hand and let him assist her, then she sunk to the ground in the entrance-way of the cave, hungry and exhausted.

She did not ask, but she was eternally grateful when he pressed a skin to her lips and she was able to drink the water mixed with wine. It warmed her insides and she ceased shivering. "Thank you," she whispered.

"Here, daughter, you're hungry."

He held out a loaf of bread, and Theodora took it, eating as if she had never eaten before. She frowned slightly. It was wrong to be suspicious of those trying to help you; still, her confidence was shaken by her experience with Hecebolus.

"Who are you?" she asked.

"Peter," came his clear answer.

"You are most kind to help me."

Peter smiled at her enigmatically. "It is you, my daughter, who are destined to help me—or perhaps I should say us."

Theodora wanted to study Peter's face, but the darkness shielded him from her. Yet his words had a ring of familiarity, and she realized they sounded somehow like those words so often spoken by Leandra. But his voice, where had she heard such a voice? Yes, that was it! Peter's voice reminded her of Leandra's guardian, who had died many years before. She remembered his voice from her childhood. Was all this talk of her destiny real? Things Leandra had said returned to her, and a chill passed through her whole body—each time her life had reached a crisis, someone intervened. It truly was as if she were guided by some unseen hand.

"Where do you travel?" Peter asked.

"To Constantinople," she replied.

"You're with child."

"Yes. It makes me doubly fearful."

"You must not be fearful. I will take you to a place where you will have your child. A place where you must study and learn, a place where you will give yourself to a greater being."

His words were so mysterious, yet somehow she felt comfortable and she also felt a certain faith in this man.

"When the child is born, I will take you to Salonika, and there you will meet your friend."

"Leandra?"

"If that is your friend, yes. You will journey to Constantinople and there you will find your purpose."

Theodora swallowed the rest of her bread. Peter shuffled off and returned with a bowl of hot soup. She ate it gratefully, feeling her strength return with each mouthful.

When she finished, weariness filled her, yet somehow so did contentment. For the first time in many days she knew she was not afraid.

Five

A.D. 518
Outside Salonika

It was midafternoon, and a cool breeze swept off the Aegean, rustling the dusty green leaves of the olive trees that lined the dirt road to Salonika.

Peter drew his cart to a halt near an artesian well. "The city gates are ahead, Theodora. I have brought you as far as I can."

Theodora wore a white robe that fell to her ankles, and her hair was hidden beneath a billowing white scarf. Over the past months her skin had returned to its normal healthy color, and her figure, while still slim, now had its former curves. The greatest change, however, was to be seen in Theodora's face. Her expression had taken on a new tranquility, though her dark eyes still burned with a sense of purpose and self-confidence.

"Am I never to see you again?" she asked as she touched Peter's wrinkled old hand.

"Not in this world," he replied. "But you no longer need me. You have your new faith to sustain you. You know what must be done. Opportunities will arise, and you will know how to make use of them."

Opportunities? She could scarcely think what possible opportunities could arise that would give her the power to stop the religious fighting, to alter the laws of the land, and to perform charitable acts for the citizenry as Peter bade her to do.

Peter was a good man, though sometimes she thought he spoke in riddles.

Yet she could not deny that she had changed, that she wanted to do the things he spoke of, that she now understood matters about which she had never thought before.

"I promise to seize any chance I am given. I will do everything I can." It was all she could promise, and indeed all he seemed to want her to promise. He had not asked her to change in any way. He had simply led her and urged her to think of others.

For many months she had lived in a holy colony, and when her child had been born, she had given it over to the women of the colony for safekeeping. In the long months before the birth of her daughter, and for some time after, she had studied. In a way her studies seemed a continuation of what she had learned as a child in Leandra's house.

"I am still unsure of what you want from me," Theodora said, seeking out Peter's kind old eyes.

"No more than I believe you want from yourself. You will know what to do when the chance is given. But beware of temptation. Each of us is tempted. Not once, but many times."

Theodora whispered, "Yes." She now recognized her affair with Hecebolus as wrong, and while she had always known she had gone with him only to better herself, she accepted Peter's belief that Hecebolus had been one of her temptations—a person set in her path to draw her away from what Peter told her were those good deeds she must do for her people. So she believed and she did not believe. She believed she had found a new faith and a new peace of mind. She believed she could begin a new life. But she could not accept Peter's insistence that she would one day rule all of Byzantium, that she would have the power to change the law.

"Go and seek your friend."

"Salonika is a large place."

"Go to the hospital that serves the poor. There, I believe, you will find your friend. She is a respected doctor."

Theodora expressed no surprise at Peter's revelation. She

knew that Leandra had studied medicine. Indeed, it had bewildered her when Leandra gave up her medical studies to ride Pegasus in the circus.

Peter climbed down from the wagon and helped Theodora alight. "Go in peace, Theodora. Remember, though you do not understand all, you are destined to do important work."

Theodora picked up the bundle that contained all her worldly belongings. She kissed Peter's bearded cheek and she began her walk toward the city gates. In her heart she knew it was a walk toward her future, even if she did not know exactly how long a walk it would be.

Leandra moved from one bed pallet to another, reveling in her work, yet tired of waiting. In recent weeks her dreams had once again left her. She dreamed neither of Alexander nor of Theodora.

"Leandra—it is really you!"

At the sound of her name, Leandra looked up, her eyes traveling the length of the long room to the white-clad figure that stood framed in the doorway at the far end.

Even though her hair was hidden and her manner of dress unusually modest, Leandra knew it was Theodora. She ran toward her, and the two women embraced.

"I feared I would never see you again," Theodora said, adding quickly, "I've been so worried about you."

"And I about you. But this is not a healthy place, Theodora. These people are ill. I can leave now, since someone will arrive soon to take over my duties. Come, let us walk and talk. You must tell me everything." Leandra smiled and turned toward a peg in the wall which held her cloak.

"There is not so much to tell . . . at least not that I understand. I'm afraid my experiences are both real and mystical."

"Then begin your story when we were separated."

"Hecebolus did a terribly cruel thing when he set you ashore, but you must believe me, I did not know. He locked me up."

"That I knew."

Tears fill Theodora's eyes. "When I complained, he beat me. Then later he told me you would be all right, that I should stop worrying. Then he threatened me again. Hecebolus turned out to be unpredictable. Sometimes he would fawn over me, at other times he would fly into a rage and beat me.

"All the time I lived with him I had everything and nothing. When I became pregnant, he cast me out without anything save the dress I was wearing and one silver coin. He gave me nothing, neither clothes nor jewels. He did not even allow me to take the possessions I had brought with me. Never in my entire life had I been so alone, so frightened, as when I stood alone in the dusty road beyond the gate of his palace."

Leandra felt tears in her eyes. As they walked, she put her arm around Theodora. "Come, let's sit here. Finish your story."

"I walked for days and days without food. I think I was near death when I met a man named Peter. He took me to a holy place and the women there nursed me back to health. I had a child—Hecebolus's child, for whom they are caring. A few months ago Peter said we must be on our way, so we began our journey here. Peter seemed to know where to find you. He even knew you were working in the hospital."

"Peter seems to have been a man of great insight."

"I am fortunate to have met him."

Leandra nodded silently. "The hospital here provides me with sleeping quarters, food, and a small stipend. But I sense my time here is growing short. I feel we must return to Constantinople as quickly as possible."

"Yes, Peter said my destiny is there, and that I must go and seek it." Theodora shook her head. "I don't understand all of what Peter told me. I don't know how I'm to influence the future. Peter, you, your guardian, Anstice—do you know what my destiny is? Do you know how I am to influence the future?"

"No. I know only that you will."

"I cannot return to acting," Theodora told her. "Peter did not say that, it is I who know in my heart that I could not act again. Something in me has changed. I know I will love again, but when I do, I shall love only one man."

Leandra patted her hand. "We will find a way to make a living in Constantinople. We'll leave as soon as we can find a ship that sails from Salonika to Constantinople. I have enough money saved to pay our fares."

"And Pegasus?"

"Oh, he is still with me. I would not part with him."

Theodora smiled. "Then we need not enter Constantinople on foot."

Leandra laughed. "I am sure Pegasus will be proud to have us ride him into the city."

A.D. 520
Constantinople

Justinian, heir to the throne and nephew of the emperor Justin, strode out into the sunlight, where the Royal Guard awaited in full dress.

A member of the guard stepped forward and handed Justinian's servant his russet and deep red cloak with its jeweled collar. The servant ceremoniously draped it over his master's tunic. Although he was his uncle's most trusted adviser, and he was influential in all his uncle's decisions, Justinian did not yet wear the royal purple.

In today's procession Justinian was to carry a long spear and sit in his sedan chair, which was to be carried by twelve bearers, high above the crowd so the people of Constantinople could see him.

Justinian indicated his readiness, and then gingerly climbed up and onto the chair. It was draped in royal purple and bejeweled with hundreds of tiny gems that had been sewn onto the cloth.

He took his seat and held his spear at his side, leaving his other hand free to wave at the populace, who by now would be lining the winding road that led from the Imperial Palace to the Golden Gate, Constantinople's most impressive landward entrance. The road he would first follow paralleled the Triumphal Way, allowing him to leave the city and reenter through the

Golden Gate, continue down the Triumphal Way and end his procession at the Hippodrome.

The citizens of Constantinople would stand beneath the olive and cypress trees, singing hymns as Justinian passed them. Justinian acknowledged that at times like this he felt lonely—he looked about quickly, and then for the fourth time in as many days reminded himself that Alexander, who had been dispatched to the front, had not yet returned.

It was always a dilemma. In Alexander he had at long last found a man he could trust, a companion who did not lie to protect his own position. At the same time, such a man was needed to serve in a military capacity. And so, as always, he had been torn as to whether or not he should keep his trusted friend at his side or send him off to take charge of an important campaign. In the end, the needs of the empire won, and Alexander was sent off for a period of some months.

Justinian leaned back and readied himself as the litter was lifted aloft. It was a lovely day, an almost perfect day for a procession.

The road led out of town and then turned north toward the Golden Gate. Justinian peered into the distance, squinting into the bright sunlight. Ahead on the road, and headed for the Golden Gate from the opposite direction, there was a huge white horse and atop it two riders, both clearly women.

"Clear the road for the emperor!" one of his guards shouted.

Justinian stood up and raised his spear. "No!" he shouted. "I will see these women! Halt the procession!"

The guard drew his contingent of soldiers to a reluctant halt. "Totally irregular!" he muttered under his breath.

Justinian beckoned his litter drawn nearer. The white horse had stopped.

Pegasus, well trained, dropped down at Leandra's gentle and unseen gesture. He appeared to bow before Justinian.

Justinian stared. "My word," he whispered. "It's the horse

from the circus. I remember seeing it—oh, it must have been at least three—maybe four years ago."

Leandra bowed her head, wondering if he would perchance remember her. If he did, he said nothing.

"Who are you? You with the long, dark hair."

As Leandra's mane of golden-red curls was hidden, she knew immediately that Justinian was speaking to Theodora.

"Theodora, a woman formerly of this city. I am returning home from a long pilgrimage."

Justinian rubbed his chin. "Theodora." He repeated her name even as he stared at her shamelessly.

"This is my friend, Leandra, who is a physician."

"Ah," Justinian said, his eyes never leaving Theodora's eyes.

Although more than fifty guards surrounded them and a hundred or so citizens who had gathered at the Golden Gate milled about, fascinated by this unforeseen event, it was as if Theodora and Justinian were alone as they stared at each other.

Leandra shivered. She could feel the magnetism between them, and she knew instantly that Justinian, who would one day be emperor of all Byzantium, was the very man who would be instrumental in the fulfillment of Theodora's destiny.

"Follow my litter!" Justinian ordered. "I will take you to the palace, and there we will dine. I will know you better, Theodora."

"And my friend?"

"Ah, but of course. Every court should have several physicians."

With those words Justinian gave the signal and the procession continued onward.

Leandra looked about, her eyes wide with wonderment. As a child she had seen the Imperial Palace many times, but she had never guessed what lay inside its thick walls. It was an incredible place filled with unbelievable beauty. Everywhere she looked, blazing mosaics were offset with white marble. Spacious rooms led to pavilions and terraces, and they in turn melted into gardens with fountains, fish ponds, and turquoise bathing pools. All about there were life-size statues of exotic animals.

The room to which she and Theodora were taken seemed to be half inside and half outside. It was furnished with divans and piles of multicolored pillows. Sheer cloths of varied colors hung from the walls and moved sensuously in the breeze. Beyond a wall of lush plants, four stairs led to an outdoor terrace that contained a large though shallow tiled pool that was decorated in startling mosaics depicting the heavens.

Leandra said nothing to Theodora. It was as if they both understood the significance of the meeting that had occurred earlier in front of the Golden Gate.

Justinian and his entourage swept into the room, and as before, Leandra felt the magic when Justinian's eyes met those of Theodora. But her feeling of joy and happiness faded quickly when she looked beyond Justinian and saw a man with a sharp, pointed beard, small, dark eyes, and close-cropped curly hair. Leandra steadied herself by grasping the side of a chair and commanded herself to be still and not betray her foreknowledge or fear. This man was not the man of her dreams, but of her nightmares.

"Let me see to details first," Justinian said. "Leandra, this is Cyril of Varna, a renowned physician. I am sure you will enjoy touring the royal hospital with him. I have instructed him to find a place for you among the physicians."

Everything in her wanted to decline, but she could not. It was fated. This man was evil, and together they would do battle for Theodora's soul.

But this was not a dream. She could not accuse him. She would have to pretend until he revealed himself to her through some action.

"She is my personal physician. I shall not have her stolen away, even by the nephew of my emperor," Theodora said.

Justinian laughed. "Steal her away? No, it is you I shall steal. She can remain your physician because you will remain near the palace."

A collective gasp was heard among the servants and Justinian's advisers. But when Justinian faced them, their eyes turned instantly downward.

Justinian continued to look at his huddle of advisers. "Too sudden?" he asked. "Do not ask me to explain, I do not understand myself. All I know is that the first moment I laid eyes on this woman, I knew I would make her my wife."

This time the gasp was more audible, and Justinian turned toward his chief adviser, who was shaking his head. "Why do you shake your head?" Justinian asked sharply.

"Justinian, forgive me. But it is against the law for a member of the royal family to marry a woman who was once an actress."

"And how do you know she was an actress."

"I remember her. She was famous. And actresses are—well, you can't—it is simply against the law."

Justinian roared, and his laughter echoed off the walls as he shouted, "Then when the time comes, I shall change the law!"

A silence fell over the assembled and Justinian waved his hand. "Begone!" he said. "Begone! Leave me to know this angel, Theodora."

Cyril of Varna bowed deeply and indicated that Leandra should follow him. She turned away, but just as they left the room, she glanced back. Theodora and Justinian were standing together, communicating silently as they waited for privacy. Between them was an attraction of mind and body that could not be denied. As apprehensive as she felt about Cyril, she knew that a part of her work was done. Theodora was ready to help her people, and Justinian appeared ready to put her in a position to do so.

From a distant room, the sweet music of a lyre drifted on the warm summer air. The royal bed was round and covered with a rainbow of sheer silks and a profusion of lovely fat pillows. Against these Theodora lay, Justinian's head in her lap.

"I quite like unhurried lovemaking," he said. "It is not as if you will leave me, nor I you."

Theodora said nothing. Her eyes were closed and she held

his hand, concentrating on its warmth and on the feelings that were aroused within her. Never in her entire life had she known such feelings. Never had she felt such loyalty. This man she would follow even if he were poor. This man she would be faithful to for the rest of her life.

Justinian's fingers toyed with Theodora's hair, which had now grown out, and hung nearly to her waist. "I have searched long for you. I have seen your face in my dreams, felt your warm flesh in the early morning hours. You are my love, it is for you I have been waiting."

She squeezed his hand to let him know it was the same for her. All the other men, all of her past life, was nothing. It meant nothing.

It was as if the moment she saw him, she was incarnated anew. Yet that was not the case. All her experiences, all the poverty and sadness she had seen on her journey to this moment weighed heavily on her mind. She would help Justinian to understand what she had seen. He was her love and he would one day rule Byzantium.

"I bring you my love, but I also want to help you to know the people—our people. You will be the most beloved emperor of all time. Your good works will be spoken of throughout the empire. We will be one in word, thought, and deed."

"We are one," Justinian said. "And we will do much if I become emperor."

"You *will* become emperor," she said.

"Ah, my love. It is not yours to promise. There are forces that work against me."

"We will overcome them," she said confidently.

"I could talk with you forever, you are the most intelligent and compassionate of women. But now I want not just to love you, but to make love to you."

Justinian slipped his hand inside her white Grecian-style gown and held her sweet breast tenderly before he set about creating in her an unbearable fire that would make her cry out for him and then surrender to him anew.

His fingers sought her nipple and he rolled it gently, then more urgently as his own desire grew with hers.

"Your hands are strong," she whispered.

"And your breasts are soft and perfect. I want to kiss them and ignite the fire within you. Open your gown to me, Theodora."

Slowly she undid the cord of her dress and moved away from him so that his head was no longer on her lap, but rather, he was on his side, propped up on one elbow, watching her.

Theodora parted her dress and revealed herself to him.

He smiled and whispered, "Bring your sweet breasts to my lips, my love."

She lay down on her side, facing him, and lifted her own breast, bringing it close to his lips so he could caress it.

He toyed with her till she fell on her back, her eyes closed, her mouth slightly parted, her body tingling and trembling. His lips seemed everywhere, devouring her with warm kisses while his hands explored her. She shivered in his arms and begged him to join with her, but he only went on kissing her till she twisted against him and their limbs were entwined.

He slithered down in the bed, kissing her till he touched her so intimately, and yet so pleasurably, she cried out.

"Oh, please come to me," she begged. Her skin was warm and she was flushed all over, her breath was short, and she knew herself ready.

As Justinian joined with her, tears filled her eyes. As actress and harlot she had known hundreds of men, but a miracle had occurred. She was like a virgin in this man's arms. She was his and his alone, and he awakened in her a deep and spiritual pleasure she had known with no other.

"This was meant to be," she heard him say, and he lifted her to him. "You will one day be my empress—you are already my soul mate."

She moved fitfully and he lay still, relishing her, adoring her till he could contain his own desire no longer. Just as his seed spilled into her, she cried out again, and he knew they were tumbling into the abyss of pleasure together.

* * *

Cyril of Varna marched down the torchlit corridor with long, purposeful strides. He cast an ominous shadow in the flickering light. His face was grim, his jaw set as he considered his new problems and how to solve them.

This was the older part of the palace, the wing in which the elderly emperor Justin and his empress Euphemia lived.

Even though Justin ruled supreme in the eyes of the Senate and the people, it was clear to Cyril that the old man was ill and that he allowed his nephew Justinian to rule in fact. Equally as bad was that when Justin finally died, Euphemia would lose what small influence she still retained, and he would have to court Justinian's favor on his own.

He reached Euphemia's door and knocked loudly. She called out for him to enter, and he walked directly over to her as she lay on her ornate bed.

"Ah, my doctor!" she said, smiling slyly. "Have you come to examine me?" She lifted her painted brows.

It was her game, and he knew exactly what she meant by "examine."

Cyril's eyes passed over her quickly. She was a thin woman with angular hips and a tiny waist. Her breasts, though now somewhat withered, were still well shaped. Euphemia was old but still desirous. She was fully cognizant of what made her happy, just as she was still able to grasp the meaning of palace politics and react against any threat to her personally or to the influence she wielded.

"You must do something about the day's events," Cyril said, ignoring her flirtatious question entirely.

"What events? Here, sit down, tell me what you're talking about."

She patted the bed next to her and he sat down. "Do not pretend with me, my lady. I know you too well. You are informed of everything that goes on within the palace walls."

Euphemia smiled. "I suppose you are talking about Justinian and the actress with whom he returned to the palace."

"Yes, about that."

"Justinian is young. Surely he is entitled to pleasure himself."

"He's going to marry her, and one day he will make her empress."

"First he must become emperor!" Euphemia burst into peals of high-pitched laughter, and she laughed until she felt Cyril's hand on her. He pinched her breast painfully hard, and she screamed half in pain and half in delight that he had chosen that way to silence her.

"Oh," she groaned, and immediately flung herself on her back and opened her robe just enough to reveal one breast.

Cyril leaned over her. "Listen to me!" His dark eyes fastened on her, and Euphemia stared back at him wide-eyed. "This is serious, more serious than your need for pleasuring."

"He can't marry her, there's a law—" Euphemia replied.

"He will change the law."

"What do you want me to do?"

"I want you to do two things. I want you to forbid this marriage so that Justinian will be forced to keep Theodora as his mistress rather than make her his wife, and I want you to get rid of this woman Leandra. I do not fully understand it, but Theodora gains strength from this woman—this woman must either be sent from court or she must die."

"Leandra." Euphemia smiled. "Death is so extreme, and it is always suspicious in one so young."

"Accidents can happen," Cyril muttered.

"Accidents are even more suspicious. They cause talk of conspiracy, and this court is vulnerable to such talk. We do not want a Persian ruler imposed upon us—then there would be no control."

"Then she must be sent from court."

"I will think on it," Euphemia promised.

"You will do something about it!" he ordered.

Euphemia wiggled ever so slightly, ran her tongue around her lips, and touched Cyril's hand imploringly. "And will you do something about me?" She looked into his blazing dark eyes.

He was not the most handsome man in court, but he was the only one who was not afraid of her. He was commanding, and that made her want him even more.

Cyril looked at her for a moment and then slipped his hand beneath her robe. "I suppose I will," he replied, knowing full well that she was a slave to her pleasures and that he, in spite of being a eunuch, could satisfy her better than any man in court.

Leandra tossed in her sleep. She was walking by the water—on the docks and looking out on the Bosphorus. All around her a low fog swirled, and behind her, the skyline of Constantinople spread out. Constantine's Forum rose above the city walls, the dome of St. Irene and the Hagia Sophia were rounded and glimmering, and the curve of the great Hippodrome could just be discerned. In her sleep she shivered in terror. The normally sparkling blue waters of the Bosphorus were dark and bodies floated on the surface—bloated bodies.

Leandra looked down, and all around her were rats. Some were dead, others were dying. "Plague—plague," she whispered. Then her eyes snapped open and she sat upright and pulled the blanket around her. Was this one of her foretelling dreams? Was this a message? Or was this only a result of having been in Salonika?

She leaned back against the pillows on her bed. Did this mean that the plague was coming to Constantinople? Was Theodora threatened? No, no. By all accounts the plague had stopped spreading, and moved no farther toward them.

She closed her eyes, and though she did not wish to have this dream again, she wished for clarification of its meaning. She sank into thought—surely this was the reason she had been trained in medicine. It may even have been the reason she was taken to Salonika. Now that she reflected on it, it seemed to fit. Theodora might be threatened by the plague and she must find a way to protect her. And what was Cyril's role? She shivered.

Cyril had been sent to stop her. He was from the evil side—it could be the only explanation for her feelings toward him.

Tomorrow, she thought. Tomorrow she would take steps to begin her task of finding a way to protect Theodora from the plague. In the meantime she would advise her, to do as she did—to wash often and to rub her body in the oils extracted from the skin of oranges. Yes, she would ask Theodora to have Justinian provide a laboratory for her so that she might study and experiment, and she decided she would also ask for Saul, the most famous doctor in all Byzantium, to be brought to Constantinople.

For another hour she lay awake in the darkness, then she once again fell into sleep—a deep and dreamless sleep.

When Leandra opened her eyes it was because of the noises she heard. There was shouting outside the palace, and inside, the sound of servants scurrying here and there.

She pulled herself out of bed and wrapped her robe around herself. Just as she automatically covered her body, she covered her hair, hiding it beneath her long scarf. Theodora had once asked about her hair, and she had explained that it was an odd color and so, rather than draw attention to herself, she always wrapped it up and hid it away. No, it was not always wise for a person, especially a woman, to stand out so. There were ignorant people and stories and tales by the hundreds that spoke of red-haired witches. So she did not publicly reveal her hair. Discretion was surely the easier way.

Leandra poked her head out of the door and stopped a passing servant. "What's all the noise and excitement about?"

"It's Alexander! He's returning from the front, victorious! He's to pass through the Golden Gate at high noon and march to the palace for his reward."

"Alexander." She repeated the name, aware that hearing it stirred something inside her. But there were thousands with that name. "Who is this Alexander?"

The servant looked surprised by her question. "He was once

a famous charioteer, then he became a member of Justinian's guard. He was sent to the front, and now he returns victorious with riches and many captives. Everyone had heard of him!"

She leaned against the wall—it *was* the same Alexander! It *was* the man she knew in her dreams intimately but not at all in reality. Ever since he had come to her at the circus she had dreamed of him—but what did she really know of him? Only that in real life he seemed arrogant and far too sure of himself.

"Domina, domina," the servant girl called out as she scurried down the hall toward Leandra. *"Domina,* Theodora wants you to ready yourself and come to the main salon. The emperor, his nephew Justinian, and Theodora will greet Alexander, and you are to be there, too."

Leandra frowned slightly. She had intended asking for an audience today herself, but now it seemed she would have to wait. She turned back toward her room, and vaguely she wondered if Alexander would remember her. He had declared his love for her when he had seen her only from afar. But of course that was not love, it was pure lust. No, she thought almost sadly, he would not remember her; by this time he had certainly found another. As for her dreams of him—she had long ago decided they were her own and based on a certain loneliness to which she admitted.

But what of Theodora? Would he remember her?

She went to the closet and looked at the gowns that hung there. Vaguely she wondered whose gowns they had been. Perhaps some of them had belonged to Euphemia when she was younger, or perhaps they belonged to a mistress long gone. They were, in any case, all quite lovely, and all seemed to fit her well.

Leandra sorted through them and settled on a pale green gown that hung from two gold clasps on each shoulder. It fell in graceful folds, clinging to her body. She slipped her feet into gold sandals and then rewrapped her hair in a pale green scarf that fell to her waist and blended with the folds of her gown.

Leandra stood up and studied her reflection in the mirror, then she left her rooms and walked toward the arcade that was the throne room.

Six

The Imperial Palace complex had no less than seven royal residences, each one separate and yet connected by a series of pavilions, fountains, gardens, terraces, and ponds. It was a place of unparalleled beauty and tranquility, lush with tropical flowers and vegetation, rich in fine statuary, and made even more colorful by the blazing mosaics that decorated every surface.

The royal grounds were also a place of great activity and creativity. Some twenty thousand citizens lived and worked inside the walls of the palace grounds. The artisans in the palace workshops manufactured dyes, silks, jewelry, and high-grade weaponry among other items. In addition to artisans, priests, civil servants, guards, and courtiers, even a few selected entertainers, lived in quarters that were built next to the walls.

The throne room of the Palace of Constantine was a huge gallery with archways and columns. It was here that Justin held court, though these days the ailing older emperor did not often appear, and when he did, he rarely spoke. Instead, he sent his nephew, who read his messages and met with the people.

But on this occasion Justin appeared, dressed in his royal purple robes and holding his scepter. He sat next to his empress, Euphemia, whose bejeweled golden tiara twinkled in the torchlight. Her face was a mask revealing no emotion. Her makeup was applied with great skill to disguise her age, just as her clothes were designed to cover the flaws in her body caused by time. In addition to her tiara, she wore an abundance of jewels, which seemed to weigh down her small body.

Justinian sat on a lesser throne to one side, while Theodora, dressed in an exquisite form-fitting red gown with jewels sewn into its fabric, sat at Justinian's feet on the marble steps. When he spoke, Theodora's adoring eyes never left Justinian's face. She watched him intently, lovingly.

Behind the emperor was his guard, and all around the royal arcade were those who had been summoned to attend. Leandra sat just below Theodora, the folds of her green gown modestly drawn about her, her hair, as always, hidden beneath the flowing silks of a scarf.

Then, from down the long corridor that led to the throne room, the sound of trumpets blared, heralding the return of the hero, Alexander.

Twenty men entered carrying ten chests. These were set down before Justin and opened, revealing a treasure trove of jewels, cloth woven with gold, and fine artifacts.

As each chest was opened, there were loud, enthusiastic cheers from the spectators. When the last trunk was opened and the cheering had stopped, Alexander entered alone and bowed deeply to his emperor.

"I bring tribute from the defeated," Alexander said, looking up. But even as he looked at Justin, he had caught sight of the two women sitting below Justinian. He knew them both instantly, though it was Leandra who held his eyes. She seemed more appealing than the first time he had seen her, more desirable, more mysterious. But how and why had she come to sit at the feet of Justinian? For a moment he feared Justinian had taken them both as mistresses. He forced that thought away and looked at Justin.

In spite of his advanced age, Justin saw the look in Alexander's eyes, and he smiled ever so slightly even though he stuck to the formality of the matter at hand.

"I accept this tribute," Justin said, raising his hand a few inches. "I commend you for your heroism. Choose your reward, Alexander! Choose anything it is my power to grant!"

Alexander looked at Justinian and then made a gesture indicating Leandra. "I choose this woman as my wife," he said, and there was a gasp of surprise from those assembled.

Leandra's mouth opened in sheer shock. She had expected him to approach her later, she had expected him to try to court her once again, but she had not expected this! How could he do such a thing? Worse yet, Justin could not refuse him. She was to become his reward! Her independent spirit railed at the very thought. She looked imploringly at Justinian. "No! Please, I cannot! I am a physician, I must stay here and study."

Justinian looked at her and then at Theodora. But no matter how imploring their expressions, he had no say in the matter now.

"Are you certain, Alexander?"

"Yes," Alexander returned.

"Then I must grant your wish. This woman Leandra is to be your wife."

"No, I must study," Leandra repeated softly. For the moment the fact that she was being forced into marriage with a man she knew only in her dreams became secondary. It faded in the face of her need to protect Theodora, to fulfill her mission! She had been told to study, to try to find a cure for the plague that would come to threaten all Byzantium. She had been reared for this purpose, reborn to enable Theodora to rule and perform important deeds. Had the fates forsaken her? Was this Alexander her temptation? Her enemy? No, it was Cyril's face that haunted her nightmares.

Suddenly Euphemia stood up. "Emperor, you have it in your power to make all things possible." The eyes of the assembled all turned toward Euphemia, whose voice was syrupy and sweet. "Send the brave and daring Alexander to govern Jerusalem, and then this woman, who is to be his wife, and who says she must study medicine, can learn from Saul of Jerusalem, who I hear is the most knowledgeable of all doctors."

Leandra's mouth went dry and her lips parted in silent protest.

Justin clapped his hands. "A fine solution, Euphemia! A fine solution!"

Leandra closed her eyes. What was happening? It was as if she had been cast into a whirlpool and was being spun around and around. Wasn't she destined to remain here with Theodora?

"It is done!" Justin proclaimed. "Go now and be married, Alexander. Then you and your bride can travel to Jerusalem aboard the royal yacht."

Leandra reached out for Theodora's hand. "I do not want to leave you," she whispered.

Theodora smiled and nodded. "It is as it should be. You will return when I need you."

Leandra studied Theodora's expression and her head filled with questions. Had she also been given a dream? Had Theodora not objected to what had just happened because it had been foretold to her? Why had there been no foretelling dream that told she would be forced into marriage? She turned and looked at Alexander. How dare he demand her as his reward! How dare the immortals allow this to happen!

Alexander strode to her side and looked down at her. He extended his hand. "Come," he said with maddening calm.

Leandra shook him loose and stood up. "I will go with you because I must," she whispered. "But know this, I am not Justin's to give away."

Alexander only smiled at her. She had been his in a hundred dreams. Tonight she would be his in reality.

Euphemia lowered her long false eyelashes and half smiled at Cyril, who stood nearby. "You see, you worried needlessly. The solution to your problem turned out to be quite simple."

In the half-light, Euphemia, a master of illusion, looked almost young. And now she looked triumphant, too, because she believed she had pleased him.

"I'm not sure this is a solution," Cyril said coldly.

"But of course it is! Mind you, she seemed no threat to me, but you said you wanted her sent from court. Now she will be going to Jerusalem. It is far away, she'll have no influence on Theodora there."

"But she will return, and when she returns she will have more influence. She'll be a master of her art."

"You worry too much about the future," Euphemia laughed. "Perhaps by then Justinian will have tired of this actress. You cannot know what will happen."

Cyril did not return her smile or comment. Even Euphemia could not know the truth—could not know that he saw the pattern of future events. He knew what would happen if he were successful in his mission, and he knew what would happen if Leandra were successful in hers. Now what he had to accomplish would be infinitely more difficult. He thought of telling Euphemia of just how short her future would be, but he did not. He turned away instead. Perhaps in the coming months he could dislodge Theodora from her position of influence. Perhaps there were still choices to be made, acts that he could undertake.

Theodora poured the wine and sat down opposite Leandra. "Please, have some drink. It will make you feel better."

"I am confused," Leandra admitted. "Have you had a dream? How do you know I will return when I am needed?"

"No, I have not had a foretelling dream. I just know you will. Leandra, I am not the woman I once was. I am stronger now. I know I shall live to do what I must."

"I feel I should be with you."

"No, you must go to Jerusalem. You will study with Saul. I feel strongly that this is right."

Leandra looked at Theodora and tears filled her eyes. "We have been together so long."

"And you have taught me much, but you must trust me this time. It is all right. Besides, it is time you married. It is time you knew some pleasure."

"I fear it."

"Have you never known a man before?" Theodora's eyes widened. "That's it, isn't it? As I think of it, I never knew you to have a lover."

Leandra nodded. "I am a virgin."

"You will enjoy lovemaking."

"Maybe, maybe not. I resent him claiming me as a prize. I have a mind of my own."

"Ah, I know," Theodora said, laughing lightly. "Alexander is a good man, Leandra. I think he really cares for you. If you give the past any thought, put it aside. I did not love Alexander nor he me. From the moment he saw you, he loved you—just as Justinian and I love. It is as if nothing came before."

"Alexander professes his love, but he doesn't really know me."

"Perhaps he does—in a way we can't explain. He told me he dreams of you."

Did he dream of her as she dreamed of him? Her face flushed at the thought.

Theodora patted her friend's hand. "I think this might be a good match."

"I should be here with you."

"No. You should go to Jerusalem and study. Here, I will make you a promise. I promise that if I need you, I will send the fastest messenger in all Byzantium to summon you."

"You must summon me if the plague should start once again to spread."

"I promise. Dear Leandra, go in peace. I have found true love and I can only hope it will come to you as well."

"These chambers are to my liking," Alexander said as he looked about. It was a room with high ceilings and colorful wall mosaics. A large bed covered with cushions stood in one corner. Across the wide expanse of the room there was a steaming pool in which to bathe, a pool with turquoise water and a bubbling fountain.

Leandra stood by one of the great stone pillars. Her body was as tense as that of a cat ready to spring. Her emotions warred with one another, each one fighting for attention, each one chasing the other away. One moment she wanted to live her dreams, another she was filled with anger at having been given to this man as a reward, and yet another moment she was filled with mortal terror, a terror that sprang from the fact that she had never been with a man, save in her dreams.

"You're completely dressed," he said, taking off his tunic and tossing it on the divan with maddening casualness. "Even your hair is hidden from me. You know, I yearn to see your hair, to see you with it free and flowing like the mane of that beautiful horse you rode. Yes, your hair is a tempting secret."

"Pegasus. We must take him with us. You must promise me," she said suddenly.

Alexander saw the sudden panic in her eyes. "Ah, you still have him. But of course I would not leave him behind. Now, lady, back to the matter at hand."

"Are you going to force me?" she asked.

"You're my wife—given to me by the emperor. I am going to love you and take care of you."

"I do not require your care. I asked, are you going to force me?"

He took two long strides and was next to her. His broad, naked chest glistened in the torchlight. The muscular ripples in his arms seemed even larger now, stronger than before. He towered over her, and the maleness of him seemed somehow to envelop her, holding her still, as if chains bound her.

"I shall reveal your secrets," he whispered, suddenly grasping her scarf. "I shall see your hair now."

Leandra protested and tried to move away, but as she did so, her scarf unwound and her long red-gold hair, tightly tied behind her head, was revealed.

"It's extraordinary!" he breathed. "Like spun gold in the sunlight!" He immediately undid the tie and her magnificent hair splayed outward, covering her back and shoulders.

"No!" She moved again, but he had seized her hair, and he caught his hand up in it and pulled her back toward him.

"Yes," he said, holding her close and looking into her green eyes. "You know a wife's duty and you know a wife can be punished for not performing that duty."

"You would not!"

"It would be a great pity. I should not like to have you beaten." A smile curled around his lips, a teasing smile. He pulled her still closer and kissed her lips hard. Her body was tense, and her breath came in short gasps as his large hands moved downward toward her buttocks.

"Your body is wonderful," he breathed. "Lithe and full of unexpected curves. I have seen you in the circus, I know what you can do."

Her face flushed, and with one swift movement he undid her robe and pushed it aside to reveal her breasts. Her whole body felt as if it were on fire.

He simply stared at her, his eyes filled with lust, his mouth half open.

"No." She shuddered as he touched her nipples and rolled them gently till they were like hard stones. She was hot and cold simultaneously. She wanted to run, but she could not move. She felt wanton and repelled all at once. She shivered again, this time feeling an unexpected dampness between her legs. What was happening to her?

He held her fast with one strong arm, and she could not help twisting as he touched her. The reality was far superior to her dream, and she was overcome by sensations as his lips sought to suck one breast.

He lifted her and carried her to the bed. He looked down into her face. Her eyes were large and luminous, her glorious hair was spread out across the cushions. He was filled with desire as his hand moved across her body, down to her thighs, and then slipped between her long, lovely legs. When he touched her in the hidden crevice, she winced and looked at him wide-eyed.

"Please don't hurt me," she pleaded, and it was then, for the first time, he realized the unthinkable. This companion of Constantinople's most famous harlot, this incredibly beautiful woman, who had performed in the circus, was in fact a virgin!

"You have never had a man before?" he asked, seeking to confirm his theory.

"Yes," she murmured. "And I'm afraid," she answered honestly.

"Then I shall do my best not to hurt you."

She opened her mouth to protest yet again, but it was no use. This, too, must have been ordained, and it mattered not what she wanted.

He said nothing more, but he moved his hand away from her entranceway and returned to her breasts. He kissed them and sucked them, occasionally moving his hand over her, occasionally kissing her lips and her ears. Gradually, he felt her begin to relax, even to respond to his movements.

He moved down in the bed and kissed and caressed her feet. Then he gently rubbed her legs, and then her thighs. Then he returned to her breasts, kissing and rubbing her nipples, while now and again moving his hand across her mound of Venus, and then seeking her center of extreme pleasure.

Her body was heated, and he knew she was aroused, yet still a little frightened.

Leandra closed her eyes and gave in to the sensations she felt. There was no fighting the feelings that surged through her whole body. It was the sweetest of tortures. His hands, his lips, were everywhere. He gently rubbed one nipple and sucked the other till she moaned, feeling a need she could not describe as a new sort of tension built inside her, not a tension brought on by apprehension, but a tension brought on by desire. He moved his mouth down her body, kissing and caressing her. He kissed her navel, then slowly he descended.

Leandra groaned loudly as he flicked his tongue over her most sensitive area, touching her just enough, yet leaving her each time she came close to the feeling she had known in her dreams. At the same time, his fingers still caressed her nipples. She tossed and tried to press against him, and again she felt moisture between her legs.

His fingers played where his mouth had just caressed her, and again he drew her nipple into his mouth even as his powerful leg pushed her legs apart and she felt him strong like a sword against her thigh.

Suddenly he was above her, his maleness playing at her entranceway. He gently moved the tip of himself inside her and then sunk more deeply even as she emitted a gasp of pain.

His hand caressed her damp forehead and his lips kissed her even as he lay still, yet joined to her. It was an incredible feeling this, a feeling he had with no other woman. It wasn't just that his organ lay inside her, it wasn't just that they were joined, it wasn't that she was a virgin. It was something else—it was as if at this moment his mind joined hers in a mutual pleasure, as if he knew everything she felt and she knew everything he felt. For a moment he was a traveler among the stars, looking down on himself, seeing and enjoying his pleasure at the same time.

He kissed her damp breasts again. As he did, she began to move beneath him as if reaching for something. Her arms were around him, her legs twisted around his body. He, too, began slow movements. He sucked harder on her breast and she writhed in his arms, panting and clawing his back, struggling against him in pleasurable torment, crying out for him even as he shook violently above her.

Simultaneously, she shuddered in a new and wondrous pleasure as suddenly she tumbled into a throbbing release that was divine pleasure. It was so much better than her dream! She throbbed inside and out, her whole body shaking, her heart beating wildly with this newfound earthly pleasure.

For a long while they lay still and silent, and then he lifted her off the bed and carried her to the steaming pool.

"I am no sooner finished with you than I want you again," he said, setting her down in the pool. "You are the most beautiful creature I have ever seen."

She said nothing, but she stood still while he looked at her. Her long hair was damp and curled around her breasts, her skin as white as mountain snow, her nipples pink and hard, her breasts full yet shapely.

His loins ached for her even as he relived their recent coupling. He tried to remember, tried to define what he had felt. What was it? What happened when he took her? It was an amazing feeling, a feeling of being one with the entire universe, yet knowing he was joined only to her. At that moment he knew one thing for certain. He would never want another woman. Ever.

"I love you," he said, looking down on her.

Leandra looked into his eyes. How could she fight these sensations, these raging emotions he aroused in her, the intense pleasure she felt when she was in his arms?

"You should not have demanded me as your reward," she replied.

"You were all I wanted."

"Then you should have waited for me to come to you."

He pulled her into his arms again. "Would you have come?"

She let out her breath. "I don't know."

He kissed her neck, and as he did so, he let his hands drop to feel her bare buttocks beneath the water. "I could not wait."

She looked down and saw that he was again strong. She stared at him. It had hurt, but the pleasure was far greater than the pain. He said nothing, but suddenly he lifted her as if she were a feather, and she wrapped herself around him, allowing him to penetrate her as she did so.

He carried her to the nearby cushions and lay her down. They looked into each other's faces as he moved slowly in and out. At the same time he held both her nipples.

The sensations she felt were even more incredible this time because this time there was no pain and he was deeply inside her. He was slow, so slow she screamed for him to fulfill her. But he did not. Instead, he withdrew from her. He moved down her body, kissing her, and then his mouth reached her pleasure spot. His tongue moved across it, arousing her to a fever pitch. Her entire body glowed, she was in the grip of sheer wanton passion as he brought her to a long, throbbing release.

But he did not leave her for long.

"I have given you satisfaction, but have not yet taken my own," he whispered as once again he began to move his hands on her flesh. This time he rubbed her with scented oils, lingering over her breasts and between her legs. His fingers explored her inner recesses, and she once again groaned as she felt the fire magically rekindled and her desire growing in the embers of her most recent ascent to bliss.

Just as he rolled her on her back she saw his member strong and ready. He lifted her so that she was on her knees, and he entered her from behind while his fingers caressed her hanging breasts and burning-hot nipples. One hand slid down the curve of her belly and grasped her center of pleasure. Again she felt herself wanting release, wanting to tumble into that pulsating abyss of sheer rapture.

In moments she could stand it no longer. Again her skin was tingled and her flesh was searing. She felt him shudder too, just as she began her ascent toward unbounded joy. They collapsed together on the cushions, panting.

For a long while they curled in each other's arms, then he lifted her and carried her to the bed. He crawled in beside her and drew the covers over them.

"You learn quickly, my little virgin," he whispered in her ear.

Leandra lay against him. Her emotions still warred, but her body was at peace. Tomorrow they would leave for Jerusalem.

Leandra followed Alexander as he climbed the hill to the Temple of the Jews. She wore a long dress that fit loosely so that air might enter its folds. It was far hotter here in Jerusalem than in Constantinople, where the sea was directly adjacent to the great city. Here they were just far enough inland that there was little relief in the way of cool breezes.

Yet there were compensations. The desert heat was dry and the smell of the trees pleasant. It was a land of sand and oases and this was the largest oasis, so large, a great and ancient city had sprung up here, a city that reached back into antiquity.

Fourteen hundred years before the birth of Christ, the Egyptians had ruled here, then the Philistines and the Arabians, who were followed by the Assyrians and Persians. Then Alexander the Great had conquered all, and after that it fell to his heir, General Ptolemy, to rule Jerusalem as part of Egypt. Egyptian rule lasted till the Roman conquest.

Three hundred and forty-five years after Christ's birth, Constantine was made sole emperor of Rome. He embraced the Christian religion. To celebrate his faith, he built a church called the Dome of the Rock in the center of Jerusalem. It was not the only church he built, but it was the most impressive and it could be seen from anywhere in the city.

"This way," Alexander said, holding out his hand.

Leandra let him help her over the craggy rocks. He wore a tunic that fell just above his knees, a metal belt around his waist from which his sword hung, and an iron shield on his chest. His legs and arms were bare, and he perspired in the morning sunlight. Unlike other men, he did not wear a burnoose to protect him from the sun, nor did he choose the long, cool robes worn by most. Instead, he dressed in Roman garb. They had arrived in Jerusalem only two short weeks before, but already the ever-burning sun had turned Alexander's skin olive, and his dark hair had deep red highlights.

Leandra, unlike her husband, had to guard her skin against the sun. She covered her hair, and wore long dresses with full long sleeves in spite of the heat.

"Here we are." He smiled. "Come sit in the shade. I shall send the guards for some refreshment."

Leandra gladly moved beneath the roof, which was supported by graceful columns. They were on the terrace of a crumbling ruin near the Jewish temple.

"I think I should like some refreshment," she replied. She wondered if her eyes revealed her admiration. It was hard not to look at Alexander's body and be unimpressed by his strength, or forget what lay beneath his tunic. She was angered by his blatant demand for her to be his reward, but she admitted to herself that he had given her joy beyond all her expectations. Nor, she thought, did he tire easily. Most important, he treated her well and was even tender. He treated her as if he truly loved her.

"Here, sit here. I shall order a hammock brought."

He indicated a place on the stone. "I'm not tired," she answered truthfully.

They had walked from the palace where he ruled. But of course they had not walked alone. Guards surrounded and followed them at a discreet distance. Servants hovered, waiting for some command.

"There," he said with a sweeping gesture. "What do you think?"

Leandra looked out across the rising plain toward the mount. The earth was sandy, the trees green, the buildings white, and the spires of the many churches were multicolored. Toward the top the trees grew thicker.

"It's the Mount of Olives," he said. "This doctor you must learn from lives there. I have sent a messenger to summon him to the palace."

"Thank you."

"I don't know why you must study. I can give you anything you desire."

"To study is what I desire," she replied.

He stepped closer to her, and she could feel his breath on her neck as he bent to kiss her. "It is not all you desire."

She said nothing, but stood up and turned to walk by the edge of the terrace. "Why have you brought me here?"

"It's pleasant. The view is nice. I thought I would order a litter to carry us to the top of the mount and there we will dine."

"I do not want a litter. It's far too warm."

He grinned. "I forget. Then we shall ride."

He shouted, and a guard appeared from the nearby trees. "Bring Pegasus and my own steed. We shall ride to the Mount of Olives. And order a fine meal brought to us. With wine!"

He turned back to her and slipped his hand around her waist, pulling her closer to him. He was behind her as they both looked out toward the distant hills.

Leandra stood rigid, wondering if the guards were watching. "Please," she whispered as she turned slightly to look into his face. His eyes were twinkling mischievously, and his smile was slightly off center.

She jumped as she felt his hand slide inside her dress, through the folds.

"Someone will see," she protested.

"You are my wife. I enjoy your sensual reactions. And if anyone watches, they will be most jealous," he answered back as his hand slid downward, and then he moved slowly over her, his fingers parting the soft down of her mound as he sought her.

She groaned and squirmed against him. But he persisted till all she could do was lean against him, her breath coming heavily as he toyed with her. She fought desperately to look as if nothing were happening to her, but in seconds she was lost in ecstatic anguish as her throbbing release began and a moan of satisfaction escaped her lips.

She gasped for breath and pulled away from him. "You're horrible," she said, her face still red and her breath still short.

"You enjoyed it."

"What if someone saw?"

"Did I remove your clothes?"

She pressed her lips together and ran to the end of the terrace. In the distance she could see the groom bringing the horses. Dear heaven, she asked herself, will he want me to pleasure him after we've eaten?

Within the hour they were atop the mountain and a table was set up in front of a gaily colored tent. They were brought roasted chicken and fresh greens. They drank a wonderful red wine and ate goat's cheese.

Alexander lay on a piece of woven cloth that was spread out for his comfort and convenience since the ground beneath the olive trees was dry and only sparsely covered with grass.

Leandra sat beside him, her eyes searching the trees and rocks of the rugged landscape. She felt a lack of privacy, knowing that soldiers always guarded them when they left the safety of the palace. Surely their invisible escort could see them well enough, even though she could not see them.

Alexander placed his hand on her back and moved it slowly back and forth, his fingers dancing on the thin material of her gown.

The memory of her recent pleasuring surged through her, and almost immediately she felt herself damp and desirous, wishing for more intimate caresses in spite of the ever-watching eyes of the guards.

A slight pleasure-filled moan escaped her lips as Alexander pressed her closer to him and once again slipped his hand through the folds of her gown, this time feeling her breasts, which seemed to throb with anticipation at his furtive touch.

"Your face is flushed," he whispered.

"I know the guard is watching."

The words escaped her lips just as his fingers closed on her hard nipple, pulling it gently and sending waves of heated wantonness through her entire body.

She shivered, wanting and not wanting, filled with passion yet keenly aware of her own embarrassment. "Please," she whispered even as he continued to taunt her.

He half sat up and whispered into her ear. "Go then to the tent, my love." He kissed her neck, and his hot breath caused another wave of craving to surge through her.

Quickly she pulled herself up, and on standing felt almost dizzy. She hurried into the tent, hidden from all viewers by the purple silk of the tent's sides. Gratefully, she collapsed on the multicolored satin cushions.

"Is this better?" Alexander waited for only a moment before joining her.

She looked up at him as he stood at the entrance of the tent, holding the wine bottle and two glasses.

"They shall still know," she said, though she knew it was a protest without conviction. She wanted him to make love to her.

He smiled and laughed gently. "And every man can then envy me."

He poured a glass of wine and handed it to her.

"If I drink more, I shall be light-headed."

"And even more urgent in your lovemaking."

She sipped a little. "Aren't you having any?"

He smiled. "I shall drink it from your breasts, making it even sweeter."

His words carried a promise, and she shuddered.

He lowered himself beside her and his hands were again beneath her gown, his fingers gently pulling her nipples even as his leg forced hers apart.

Her breath came in short gasps as memories of past lovemaking filled her head. She was hardly aware of his pushing her dress aside, of his lips sucking on her now-hard nipple.

She felt the wine as it touched her flesh, and his warm, prodding tongue as he licked it from her skin, lightly touching areas of incredible sensitivity.

His large hands slipped beneath her buttocks and lifted her to meet his manhood, which seemed even larger than before as he rubbed it against her hidden place of pleasure and teased her with unbearably slow movements as she felt the tension building within her.

She was like a dancer on a tightrope—waiting to fall, waiting for release. She cried out and writhed beneath him. He let her drop slightly, then again lifted her hips. He controlled her utterly, and she gasped when his lips returned to her throbbing breasts.

Again he teased the magical center of her pleasure, and then he entered her, filled her, and continued to press against her as he moved within her, slowly, till she felt the unbearable pressure and then the glorious throbbing release as she shook in his arms and he reared above her, lost in their mutual pleasure.

"You are the only woman I shall ever love," he whispered as he fell beside her.

She curled beside him, tired and feeling a deep pleasure that defied description.

Saul was a tall, thin man with dark skin and thick black curly hair that covered his head and most of his face. He had a long nose, a high forehead, and black eyes. Dressed in his white robes, and wearing a white burnoose, Leandra thought he looked like many other men in this part of the world. Saul's most extraordinary feature was his hands. They were thin and he had long fingers. They were exceptionally graceful hands, yet at the same time strong hands. They were the hands of a healer, and Leandra felt his power and intellect as soon as she met him.

"What you ask is highly unusual," Saul concluded.

Saul was partially reclining on a long divan while eating fruit. Clearly he enjoyed being in the palace, having someone serve him. Nonetheless, Leandra knew him by his reputation. He was said to be a selfless man who tended rich and poor alike.

"I am not asking," she replied. "I am making a proposal, one I hope you will not refuse. I have studied medicine for many years. I tended plague victims at Salonika. I am not the wife of an official who is merely seeking to entertain herself. I am a doctor and I want to learn more. You are reputed to be the finest doctor in all Byzantium."

"But to move here—"

"It is not necessary, but I would be lying if I told you it were not the most convenient solution. I suggest building a hospital adjacent to this palace."

"I do not serve only the rich," he said, scowling ever so slightly. "Besides, they do not suffer from the most interesting diseases. As a student, you will realize that for study purposes a variety of diseases is necessary. I would be a poor doctor if I learned to treat only the illnesses brought on by overconsumption."

"The poor will be allowed to use this hospital just as they will be allowed to use the new hospital being built by Theodora in Constantinople."

"If you will make this public, I will accept your proposal. But let it be understood that it matters not to me that you are the wife of the governor. I will expect you to work hard."

Leandra smiled. "I give you my word."

"And I shall stand behind her word," Alexander said, emerging from the corridor:

"It is then agreed," Saul said, bowing.

"I shall send a wagon to fetch your belongings, and construction shall begin immediately. First we can convert a part of the west wing of the palace to serve till the new hospital is built," Alexander said.

"You are most kind." Saul bowed deeply and then turned toward Leandra. "Good day," he said without kissing her hand.

When he had left, Alexander turned to her. "Are you happy now?"

"Yes," she answered. "Now I can pursue my studies."

Seven

A.D. 526
Jerusalem

Leandra studied the body of the young boy. His skin was gray, his dead eyes hollow. Beneath his arms were large, hard swellings—the buboes of the sort she had come to know so well in Salonika. Usually such swelling occurred on the groin, but often, as was the case with this one, it was under one of his arms. Sometimes she saw similar swellings when the patient had syphilis, but those usually disappeared on their own, only to return much later, when the patient was aged.

Leandra made notes in her notebook. At onset the disease produced intolerance to light, pain in the back and limbs, high fever, vomiting, and sometimes giddiness. Then the glands began to swell. After that the ill usually hemorrhaged and blood trickled from the mouth and nose and there was much mental confusion. Death was sometimes, though not always, preceded by a burst of energy, a short period during which the patient seemed to return to normal. Occasionally the patient would rise up out of bed and do the so-called dance of death. In such cases the patient would turn in circles wildly, suddenly collapse, and die.

Saul saw her and came across the room. His face, never laughing, was even more serious than usual. He said nothing, but picked up the boy's arm, looked at the swelling, and then dropped it.

"Plague," he said under his breath. "I hear the rats are dying in Sheol—Hell."

Sheol—or Hell—was an area outside the city where refuse was left. Much of it was taken by birds and rats, what remained smoked or burned slowly, giving off noxious odors. It was a strange and weird place of low fogs, smoldering fire, and odd sounds. Mothers who grew exasperated with their children threatened them with Sheol—"Be good or you will go to Sheol," they admonished. And lately, the wretched place had become the metaphoric threat of preachers who berated people for living sinfully and told them they would burn eternally in Sheol if they did not mend their ways.

"When rats die, plague follows. It has to do with rats," he suggested.

Leandra bit her lip. She had been working and studying for over five years now—the time had flown by, and though she knew she had learned much, that which she yearned to know the most remained a secret. "Yes, of course. The rats always die first. But why?" Leandra asked.

For a long while an idea had been incubating in her mind. She decided to reveal her thoughts now, wondering what Saul would say. She was confident, because where the matter of the plague was concerned, he knew little more than she or any other doctor about its cause or prevention. In the matter of treating it, Saul had been successful on some occasions. He believed in lancing the buboes and allowing the poison to drain out of them. In some cases his patients recovered, as had some of hers when she tried lancing the buboes on her patients in Salonika. But then, some recovered in any case and without any medical intervention save the application of tepid water and alcohol to cool the skin.

"You are thinking about something," Saul guessed. "You are a talented doctor, Leandra, do not be shy."

"You did not always think so."

"I was afraid you wanted to study as an amusement. I know

now that your reasons were more serious. Please, feel free to share your hypothesis with me. I shall not laugh."

"I have noticed two things," she ventured to say. "The first is that those who bathe with regularity are not so prone to plague, and the second is that both men and rats have fleas."

"These are keen observations, ones I have made myself. But this does not explain how—"

"The fleas bite both man and vermin," Leandra added quickly.

"But how can such a tiny bite cause such an illness," Saul asked, raising his shaggy brows.

"I do not think the bites themselves are the cause, but perhaps it is how it is spread. My mentor always bade me bathe with regularity and use a potion made from the skins of oranges. I have noted that this concoction prevents the fleas from living on my person. I have treated plague and not become ill."

Saul's lips were pressed together as he nodded thoughtfully. Then he said slowly, "I, too, use a potion something like the one you describe. I found reference to it in Greek texts. While your hypothesis might well explain some things, I do think we must consider the size of the bite. It is but tiny. How can so much poison be carried by such a small creature?"

"I do not know. I know only that a bite made by larger creatures can cause much difficulty."

"Ah, but that is understandable."

"Who is to say these tiny creatures do not carry something in their mouths that is too small to be seen?"

Saul frowned deeply. "We cannot know for we cannot see."

"Yes, that is the difficulty. All life is on a scale of size. We know the elephant to be the largest on that scale, Saul. We know the tiny red mite to be among the smallest. But what if there are other creatures, what if there are things so small, we cannot see them? What if it is these creatures that carry plague?"

"It is fanciful to entertain such thoughts," Saul said.

"This disease is too deadly not to explore all possibilities," she insisted.

Saul nodded his agreement, but clearly he did not know how

to proceed. "We can only care for those who have it," he finally admitted.

Leandra did not argue. Saul had taught her much, and perhaps more important, he had led her to important texts. She had read the carefully preserved notes of Galen, a Roman physician. But Galen, who treated the gladiators, was primarily a surgeon who garnered knowledge because he was allowed to dissect those who died. She believed in the Roman writings and dedication to sanitation, and she believed, as many of Rome's wisest doctors did, that there was a relationship between places and disease. They knew swamps to be unhealthy and clean water to be vitally important. They had built sewage systems and aqueducts, public baths, and instituted a health service that codified health laws. Water was inspected for purity, impure foodstuffs were destroyed, they even regulated brothels. The Roman army had conquered because its enemies contracted plague and died.

Now many Christians said that illness was due to sin, and many important health measures and purification systems developed by the Romans were neglected and were falling into disuse and disrepair. Some radicals wanted the public hospitals closed, wanted doctors banned from practice and the public medical service abolished.

Still, doctors persisted. The old texts were preserved. Galen was studied because he understood the human body as no other doctor understood it. Aristotle and other Greeks were read because they had compiled a vast array of pharmacological references. Most important were the works of Hippocrates and his followers.

Saul was a reader of texts and a gatherer of information. It was why she had wanted to study under his tutelage.

But now she knew she had surpassed him. His mind was not agile enough to take the next steps—he could not imagine what he could not see, and yet he was devout. He could accept an entity greater than man as part of his faith, but he could not accept an entity so tiny it could not be seen. Still, a voice within her counseled that it was not yet time to leave.

Saul was again rubbing his chin and looking down his long,

narrow nose. "It can't hurt to let us suggest more bathing and
the use of the citron potion," he suggested.

Leandra nodded. It was his way of trying to tell her he appreciated her work. She pulled the cover over the dead body.
"It will have to be burned," she said. "There are few cases now,
but I fear there will be more."

In flowing robes, with her mane of red-gold hair tumbling
loose over her shoulders, Leandra entered her bedchamber to
find Alexander already there and relaxing in the great sunken
tub of hot water.

He leaned back, his eyes closed. Leandra stopped and looked
at him. For nearly five years they had been married, and for all
that time they had shared each other's bodies and slept entwined.
Yet she still fought him because he had claimed her as a prize
rather than allowing her to come of her own free will. And never
had she told him how much she really loved him. But then, she
reminded herself, he had never apologized for claiming her as
he did.

Moreover, she thought as she looked at his naked body beneath the water, he always commanded her sexually. When he
took her, it was without her consent, though she admitted to
herself that it was always pleasurable and that in reality there
was no time when she would have refused him.

She smiled ever so slightly. He did have a most magnificent
body. His chest was so broad and so firm. His legs and arms
bulged with muscles, and his member, even at rest, was large.
She shivered slightly, thinking of their assignations. Was there
no position in which he had not taken her? And he loved to
pleasure her, often doing so when it was not possible for him
to have her—as it had been that day on the Mount of Olives,
when first they had come to Jerusalem.

Once on the way to a celebration he had teased her into quivering tremors of delight beneath her silken dress as they rode
in an enclosed litter. He was, she silently admitted, a lover to
whom she was totally addicted. Now, looking at him, she knew

she felt more. Her feelings for him had grown so that now she thought beyond their lovemaking. She knew she would stay with him forever, though she had not yet told him of her feelings, or that she really loved him.

You are a good man, she thought as she watched him. She knew he cared for those whom he governed and was just.

His deep blue eyes opened. They were like bottomless pools that drew her toward him.

"How long have you been there?" he asked.

"Only a few seconds."

"Disrobe and join me. The water is lovely and this new oil smells like a thousand orange blossoms."

Slowly, and knowing that she was doing it slowly for his benefit, Leandra discarded her clothing. First her flowing robe, then her golden sandals. Next she unhooked her golden girdle and slipped out of her long white dress.

He stared at her with hunger in his eyes when she touched her breasts and then ran her hands down her sides and smiled at him.

"You taunt me," he said, as his eyes commanded her to his side.

Leandra stared at him. His manhood had grown and was now filled with blood. Yet beneath the clear water, it was slightly distorted in shape. She continued looking at him, her mind racing. On the one hand, her own desire was pulsating through her, on the other, an idea grew—something so simple she had not seen it before.

"Come, I can wait to touch you no longer."

She slipped into the water and his hands were immediately on her, caressing her and pulling her closer.

"Is something the matter?" he asked. "For a moment I saw a strange look on your face."

"You will make me fevered with passion and I might forget—you must remind me of my thought when morning comes. You must remind me that water distorts."

He laughed lightly and at the same time took her buttocks in his hands and drew her close. "I shall remind you if you promise not to be distracted."

She groaned as his instrument of pleasure touched her most sensitive place. She continued moaning as he rubbed it against her till her face flushed with heat and her nipples, as yet untouched, hardened to glorious perfection even as her breasts floated high in the water.

He pulled her closer and moved inside her slowly, ever so slowly, as he took her nipple in his mouth. She wrapped her legs around him and they were fully joined beneath the water. The base of his sex was against her, his lips were everywhere, and sensations ruled her as once again they both tumbled into throbbing bliss.

They held each other for a long while, and then he began washing her and she washed him as well.

"You're different tonight," he said, looking into her green eyes.

She did not answer, but only smiled.

"I must go to Caesarea tomorrow," he told her. "I shall be gone for at least five days and four nights. Do you wish to come?"

Leandra touched his face with her hand. "I would like to come, but I must stay in the hospital. We've had cases of plague. I fear it may get worse."

"You cannot stop the plague."

"I must be here nevertheless. I must try to learn more and more about it. It is my mission."

"I do not pretend to understand your dedication to this, but I admire it. Of course you can remain here, Leandra. But know that I will miss you."

She did not say the words that were in her heart, but she did kiss his lips tenderly.

"And shall I still remind you that water distorts?" he asked, looking amused.

"No. I shall remember."

* * *

Leandra sat before a long table and contemplated her good fortune. Alexander's position was such that she could afford to hire learned scribes to copy that which she did not have time to copy. Three she had set to work reproducing the journals of Galen, while four others worked on Greek texts. This enabled her to see to her own journals in which she wrote all her observations.

She sat at her desk, her own journal to one side, while she read a text hitherto unknown to her, a text written not by a doctor or a pharmacologist, but by an astronomer, one Claudius Ptolemy.

It was a treatise on optics in which he discussed in detail the phenomena of magnification and refraction as related to certain lenses and to glass spheres filled with water. A little chill passed through her. A chill of discovery, as if one of the many missing pieces to a puzzle had been discovered. But it was, she acknowledged, only a tiny piece. It proved only that small things could be made to seem larger, but thus far nothing totally invisible to the naked eye had been revealed.

She completed her notes, certain that this information, and perhaps other information on optics available from astronomers, might help reveal secrets in medicine.

Leandra closed her book and looked up as she heard the door to her chamber open.

"I'm returned from Caesarea," Alexander informed her.

"I am glad you've returned," she said, walking toward him. He looked tired, but then, the road to Caesarea was hot and dusty.

"I have thought of you constantly," he said, studying her. "But I'm not well, Leandra. My head is pounding. The sun was too bright and too hot."

Leandra looked up at him with concern. His face was flushed, and he looked drawn and tired. There were deep lines under his eyes. Alexander was a strong man, and it startled her to see him look this way after only a few days. She lifted her hand to his brow and shook her head. "You're burning with fever," she whispered. "I insist you go to bed immediately."

He grinned. "I do not often refuse a request from you to go to bed, but I've been away and I have things to see to."

"Joke with me if you will, but you also need your rest. You are ill, and I want you to rest."

"I promise I shall come and rest as soon as I've caught up. Now you return to your studies and then ready yourself for me. I'll come in a few hours."

She forced a smile. Alexander was a zealous worker and Justin could not have appointed anyone who would have worked harder. There were disputes to be heard and decisions to be made. Alexander usually saw to all his obligations promptly, but of course he had been gone, so he was now behind.

"The physician's husband has no care," she said, looking into his eyes. "What will people say if you become truly ill?"

"They will say I was stubborn and would not submit to your sweet nursing."

"There is no doubt you are stubborn."

He forced a smile, wiped his brow, and then left her.

Reluctantly, Leandra returned to her reading.

An hour had passed when Leandra heard a great commotion beyond the doors of her chambers. She quickly covered her hair and donned a robe. Then she hurried out into the passageway, only to encounter a number of men carrying Alexander.

"He fell unconscious from his chair during a judgment," one of them said.

"Shall we summon Saul the physician?" another asked.

"I am a physician, as you well know. But do summon Saul. I shall want his opinion as well."

"Yes, *Dominia,*" they answered in near unison.

"Put him on the bed," Leandra instructed.

They did as they were told, and then she dismissed them all, leaving instructions for Saul to be brought as soon as he arrived.

She knelt by Alexander's side. His body was burning up. She went once again to the door. She ordered cold wet cloths be brought to her, and in moments a virtual army of servants appeared carrying the cloths.

Leandra carefully removed his clothing and then pressed the cloths to his body. But even as she did so, waves of apprehension passed over her. Alexander's words returned to her. He complained of the hot sun and bright light. He had been burning with fever then, yet he seemed abnormally cheerful. His fever, his complaints of light, even his appearance, spoke of only one thing. The dreaded plague.

Her heart pounded. He was unconscious and he might never really regain his senses. She was suddenly overcome with fear, which she seldom felt—fear and a terrible regret.

"You can't leave me," she said, putting her head on his great chest. "I won't let you leave me. I haven't had the time to tell you things—Alexander, I love you as I could never love another. You are my mate for all time, I know it." Tears rolled down her pale cheeks, and she touched his face with her hand. "I shall give all of myself to you if you just get well. Oh, my darling, my beloved, how often have I wanted to tell you this in the past months? It is I who am stubborn, I who am too filled with pride. I didn't want you to take me as a prize, but that doesn't mean I didn't want you—"

She ran her hand through his damp hair. He was beginning to perspire now. And he was beginning to shake as well.

"Leandra?"

She looked up and saw Saul framed in the entrance. She beckoned him in and he walked toward her.

Saul did not ask why she had summoned him. He simply began his examination. His expression was emotionless, though, as always, serious. Then in a somber voice he spoke. "I fear it is plague," he said.

Leandra could only nod. It was as if her voice were stuck in her throat.

"He's a strong man," Saul noted. "He can fight this disease better than many other of its victims."

"I want to believe you're right," she said weakly.

"Do you want him removed to the hospital, Leandra? Or will you care for him here?"

"Here, I want to take care of him myself."

"Be sure to burn his clothes."

"I already have. I cast them into the fire myself."

"All I can advise is that you not let him become dehydrated. As a physician, you know that water is the most important of the body's needs. I believe the perspiration carries poisons out of the body, cleansing it."

Or perhaps, Leandra thought silently, fever was merely the reaction of the body to poison. Perhaps if the blood were heated high enough, it killed the disease. Saul would truly laugh if he knew what she had come to believe, even though she was certain she was on the right path. But if she knew for certain that the disease was not caused by poisons but rather by some organism too small to be seen by the naked eye, what difference would it make? Only if she could find something that would kill the organism and not kill Alexander would her hypothesis prove valuable. And there was no time now. He had the disease and she could do nothing but treat his symptoms.

"I shall leave you now, Leandra. If Alexander and his men brought this with him from Caesarea, we will have many more cases. I shall have to go and prepare for them."

"Thank you for coming," Leandra said as she turned back toward Alexander.

Saul walked away, paused in the entrance for a moment, wished her good luck, and then left.

"Oh, my darling," Leandra whispered as her tears fell on Alexander. She again bathed him, then crawled into the bed beside him. It was an odd sensation. He was so large and such a powerful man, yet he lay shaking in her arms, his body racked with illness.

In a few hours she got up, bathed his body again, and tried to give him fluids. She examined him carefully, waiting for the buboes to form.

As the sun set over the golden-capped Dome of the Rock, the swelling began to grow beneath Alexander's right arm.

Leandra watched it, waiting till she deemed the time right. Then, at midnight, she lanced the bubo, cleansed the wound, and again bathed his heated body.

All the while her thoughts were on the pharmacology of Aristotle and Hippocrates. The Great Library in Jerusalem was filled with texts on the pharmacology of the region and of other regions, as well as those texts deemed classical. She had delved into all of them. If this disease were caused by an unseen organism, what might kill it? She thought and thought. Then she remembered that in one of the Greek texts she had read of a certain kind of mushroom. It had been chopped and pounded into a liquid. It had been used to treat a dreadful infection and it had worked. Dreamily, she wondered if ingesting such a thing might kill the organism she believed caused the plague. But perhaps it was among those mushrooms that could not be eaten. Then again, perhaps it was its poisonous quality that killed the organism.

"Leandra—"

Alexander's voice startled her and she grasped his hand. "Do you know me?" she said, leaning over.

"Of course, you are my beloved."

His voice was raspy, and he was still swollen under his arms and on his neck. His groin area was also swollen. Yet somehow he seemed stronger. Was this the energy that preceded death in so many cases?

"You must tell me how you feel," she prodded, leaning close.

"Weak—but still I want you. Still I love you."

She kissed his cheek, unaware that her own tears ran down her face.

"In my dreams I heard you tell me you loved me. I heard you pledge yourself to me."

"It was no dream. I've been a stupid, stubborn woman. I do love you. I love you more than life itself."

A slight smile crept around the corner of his mouth. "I have waited long to hear you say you love me."

Leandra squeezed his hand. "Forevermore," she whispered. "Oh, please get well, I need you so."

He patted her hand. "Stay with me."

"I shall not leave your side," Leandra promised.

And again she crawled in beside him to hold him to her. He enfolded her in his arms, and for a long while they both slept. He will live, she thought. He will survive.

Cyril crept along the corridor, his black robe flowing behind him. He stopped at Euphemia's bedroom as he always did, paused for a moment, and then entered without knocking.

He moved to her side and looked down at her. A feeling of cold filled him. Euphemia, on her bed of scarlet silk, lay silent. Her eyes, as if made of glass, stared at the ceiling, her painted lips parted.

As if he could not believe it, Cyril shook her. But Euphemia did not awaken. He cursed her silently. Euphemia was dead! She was the only obstacle that stood between Justinian and Theodora's marriage!

He closed his eyes, and in a moment planned his strategy. He hurried away without summoning anyone. Euphemia's servants would come soon enough. It was now important only that he reach Justinian.

Down the torchlit corridors—through the silent throne room, and beyond. He came to the emperor's private quarters and hoped that Theodora would be there.

"I must see the emperor," he said, stopping at the door.

The guard lowered his spear.

"Is he alone?"

The guard shrugged.

"Tell the emperor that Cyril of Varna must see him. It is a medical matter." It wasn't, of course, though he would make up one to suit the occasion.

In moments the guard returned and Cyril was ushered into Justinian's chambers. At first he thought Theodora was not about.

Cyril bowed deeply. "Sire."

Justinian smiled. Cyril was full of fine flourishes, none of which Justinian desired to be directed toward him save on public occasions. "The hour is late, I am surprised to see you."

"I come on a matter of medical prudence. I have heard of cases of the plague to the south. I should like to post guards at the city gates to make certain that all those who enter are healthy."

Justinian looked at Cyril and frowned ever so slightly. This did indeed seem a matter that could have waited till morning. Still, he and Theodora had not begun anything they could not finish during the night. She had stepped behind the curtains because they both felt it prudent. "If you think it necessary, and indeed if it would help curtail the plague, I should be happy to issue a proclamation to that effect."

Cyril nodded in satisfaction. Ah, it was far better than he had even dared hope. His eyes had seen the movement behind the curtains, and the toe of one little slipper peeking out.

"There is one other matter," Cyril said softly. "It is a personal matter. I would like permission from you to speak my mind."

"Permission granted," Justinian said. He sighed inwardly and wondered how long Cyril would be. Personally he found Cyril a trifle boring.

"Justin is quite ill, and the Empress Euphemia elderly. I believe you should marry Theodora and make her your empress."

Justinian looked at Cyril seriously. "I'm sure you know that Euphemia would never approve such a marriage."

"The people would approve. Their approval is more important," Cyril suggested.

Justinian nodded. "I am most surprised to hear you say this. Do you approve?"

"But of course! Theodora is beautiful, intelligent, and of the people. She will be a wonderful empress."

Justinian smiled. "I think so as well, and I will consider your suggestion."

"It is all I can ask," Cyril said as he once again bowed deeply. "I shall say good night now."

"Good night," Justinian said. Cyril left immediately, and

when the doors had closed behind him, Theodora stepped out from behind the curtains.

She walked to Justinian's side and knelt before him. "Cyril surprises me."

"And me," Justinian said. "I thought he was Euphemia's man in the palace."

"Perhaps not," Theodora replied. Then she looked up at Justinian. "I hate interruptions."

"Then take up where you left off."

She smiled and reached within his robes. Kneeling in front of him, she began kissing him. He groaned as her lovely mouth enclosed him, and his hands flew awkwardly to her breasts as she aroused him beyond all control.

"You are divine," he murmured.

The cry "Euphemia is dead" rang through the corridors of the palace. By noon, when the artisans were half done with their workday, there was no one in all Constantinople who did not know that Empress Euphemia had died in her sleep and that her consort, Justin, was old, confined to his bed, and also dying.

"The time is now," Justinian told Theodora. "I have ruled for my uncle, but I have not been ordained or proclaimed emperor. The news from Persia is excellent, there are no impediments to our marriage. We shall be married quietly this afternoon and then tomorrow morning I shall go before the Senate and ask to be crowned."

Theodora hugged Justinian tightly. She was sure no one would object. She was of the people and had their love. Justin liked her too, although his feelings toward her mattered little. The poor old man was helpless in his sickbed.

The proclamation, the crowning, and the marriage took place on Easter, April 10, 527. It took place in the Sancta Sophia.

"It is perfect," Justinian whispered in Theodora's ear. "We shall do it quickly, without stirring up the political factions that

ran the Hippodrome or allowing time for public debate. The
patriarch knows that our marriage and my being crowned will
aid the faith and prevent rioting in the city."

Theodora stood by his side. How different this was from her
stage career! In moments this chamber in the Sancta Sophia
would be filled with the illustrious members of the Senate.
Within the hour Justinian would be crowned.

A troop of mounted archers preceded the procession. In addition to their bows and arrows, they carried short broadswords,
a sling, and a mace. They wore helmets, carried an oval shield
bearing the colors of their regiment, and wore a vest of scale
armor over their summer linen tunics.

Trumpets blasted a fanfare as the wealthy members of the
Senate bloc entered. Children, preselected for such occasions,
scattered flowers before the prominent. The elderly senators,
adorned in Roman white robes and wearing a crown of olive
leaves as had been the Roman custom for over five hundred
years, entered the chamber one by one and took their seats.

When all were seated, Justinian took the diadem, and the
senators all rose in silent approval.

While they stood, a servant brought the purple robe and held
it out. The oldest senator, a man of nearly ninety years, came
forward and stood by the side of the servant who held the robe.
He then took the purple robe in his bony, quivering hands and
held it out while Justinian slipped into it. Then another servant
appeared with the scarlet half-boots. The senator took these too,
and he knelt before Justinian and helped him into them. When
the boots were on, two servants were obliged to help the frail
old man to his feet. Then a third servant brought the golden
scepter on a plush scarlet pillow. The patriarch stepped forward
and took the scepter. He presented it to Justinian with a flourish.

Justinian then sat down and yet another servant came bearing
the crown. The patriarch took it, too, and then said a prayer.
Bowing, he placed the crown on Justinian's head and backed
away.

"Long live the emperor!" the patriarch announced loudly.

Then, as all stood, came the unified cry, "Long live the emperor, long live Justinian!"

Justinian looked down. At his feet Theodora lay prone on the steps to the diadem, as was the custom. He touched her lightly, and took her hand, bidding her to kneel before him.

She did so, and from her position could see only the small bare feet of the servant child who bore her crown.

First, a woman knelt beside her and helped her adorn a special belt. Then the flaming woven jewels of the empire were placed on her head, throat, shoulders, and around her tiny waist. Finally, her own jeweled crown.

"I crown thee empress of all Byzantium," Justinian whispered as he touched her lightly with his scepter. Then he extended his hand and bade her sit beside him.

Hardly had she taken her seat when runners were sent from the grounds of the Imperial Palace throughout the city.

"Justinian reigns! Theodora reigns!" they all cried.

Cyril looked at the new rulers with his small, feral eyes. He felt quite at ease. They trusted him and he saw for himself a place of importance in the scheme of things.

It was the last day of July. Justin lay in his bed, his pain eased by drugs that dimmed the mind as well as the senses. It was all that could be done. Cyril watched as life slowly fled the old man. One by one his systems turned off, and when Cyril knelt close, he could smell the humor of death on Justin's breath. At noon Justin expired, and Cyril made the announcement to the emperor and empress.

"I fear I am the bearer of bad news," Cyril said as he bowed before Justinian.

"Is it my uncle?" Justinian guessed.

"Yes. He is at rest now."

Justinian nodded. In his own heart he was glad. Justin had suffered greatly. It was good that his suffering was ended.

"You have tended him well," Justinian said. "You will remain on as court physician, Cyril. Does that suit you?"

"Indeed, I am honored."

"Good. Now I shall summon the populace to the Sancta Sophia."

In the morning, on the first day of August 527, the faithful filled the Sancta Sophia to overflowing. Justinian and Theodora walked slowly down the aisle while the faithful parted to let them pass. Justinian took his seat next to the altar. It was a beautiful ivory throne, carved by a master. Across from him Theodora took her throne. Her slender body shimmered as the flames from a thousand candles glimmered in the facets of her jewels.

Thousands cried together, "Justinian, thou wilt conquer. Ever august! God will aid thee! Long live our Augustus! Long live our Augusta!"

Theodora looked out on the multitude of people. Not even in the circus had she heard such applause. Her heart was filled with love for Justinian and with this glimpse of splendor.

"The people love you," Justinian whispered.

Theodora smiled and thought of all she wanted to do. "I shall earn that love," she answered back.

First and foremost, she had promises to keep to Peter. She would build new hospitals, homes for the aged, a home for unwed mothers, and she would settle the raging religious disputes. These were her priorities, but she also had a score to settle, one she knew she could not forget. Hecebolus would soon be relieved of his duties, stripped of his wealth, and returned to Constantinople. She had no intention of killing him, but instead she contemplated a punishment to suit his crime. She smiled and decided it would be suitable if he spent the rest of his life tending her garden.

Cyril looked at the miniature palace with cleverly disguised disdain. It was a splendid building with many apartments, each of which had a bedchamber, a small saloon, and a cooking area. It was all built around a beautiful shaded courtyard, a courtyard filled with things made by the artisans for children. There were wooden animals for them to ride and climb on, swings suspended from great pieces of wood, and even a small pond with toy boats. Constantinople was known for its parks, but this one was newer than the others and was designed for children.

"I confess I am mystified by this place," he said to Justinian and Theodora as they showed him through it. "There are so many chambers, each one self-contained. And all these things for children—I am at a loss, what is it all for?"

Theodora turned toward him. Her dark eyes danced with happiness. "It is a home for women and children," she announced proudly.

"For women with children and no husbands?" He raised a brow.

"Not all women who have children have husbands. Moreover, many husbands are killed. Such women now must live with relatives and those without relatives who can afford to take them in must beg on the street. The streets are not suitable. Here women can learn to weave, or study some other art or trade. They can live in safety and so can their children."

"Next you will tell me you are building a home for actresses," Cyril said, hardly bothering to disguise his disgust.

"I am, but not here," came Theodora's swift reply. "And two more hospitals, Cyril. There are not enough."

He wanted to ask why these children could not be taken away from their mothers, placed in orphanages till they were seven or so, and then sold to the weaving factories as had been the custom for so long. It would certainly save the state much money. But he was speechless. "What will people say?" he finally asked.

"The people love her," Justinian answered.

Theodora looked quickly at Cyril. A wave of discomfort passed over her. She tolerated Cyril because she believed him to be loyal. But she did not entirely trust him. Still, he was a favorite of Justinian's, and he was the court physician.

"I suppose they would," Cyril said slowly. Then he smiled. "You are the most generous empress the empire has ever known." He swallowed his last words, wanting only to leap across the space between them and strangle her. It was one thing to espouse Christianity, it was quite another to behave in a Christlike way. It could mean only higher taxes. Worse yet, Justinian allowed her to do anything she wished. Euphemia had been right. Theodora was too close to Justinian, and she allowed no one else to become close. She was not only his empress, but his closest adviser.

It is I who must assume that role, Cyril thought. How else could the downfall of Justinian occur? How else could Persia come to rule Constantinople and all of Byzantium? But it was Theodora who had advised her husband to send General Belisarius to fight Persia, and Belisarius had been victorious. Perhaps, Cyril's Persian friends had mused, a victory at court would be far more efficient than a victory on the battlefield. He had agreed, and now this was his mission. Justinian was to become a mere figurehead. Toward that end, he now realized Theodora must be killed. But how?

He smiled at her. "You are an inspiration, Empress!" He bowed and Justinian glowed.

Soon I will kill her, Cyril thought. But I must think on just how to best accomplish this.

Eight

A.D. 530
Jerusalem

Leandra sniffed the hot, dry air of Jerusalem and basked in its warmth. Jerusalem was in many ways a healthful place, where fruits grew year-round, and during the winter months cool breezes blew softly during the night.

It was a fascinating city with narrow streets and underground bazaars filled with people from all over the world. The coal-black faces of African traders from the land of the Ashanti mingled with the pale white faces of European pilgrims. The desert men wore stark white robes with colorful sashes, and they carried sharp, curved swords at their sides, while pilgrims from the far-flung edges of the Byzantine Empire dressed in long robes, tunics, or the cloaks that denoted they lived a monastic life. Yes, Jerusalem was a crossroads just as Constantinople was a crossroads. But it was more than just a center of trade or government. It was the home of great religions.

Jerusalem was a city of good and evil, a city where different religious groups fought one another for supremacy, and where various sects within religions argued over the words of the great prophet. It was a land of contradictions, where men fought to the death in defense of their own form of holiness. The fighting upset Leandra, since all the religions as well as all the sects were doctrinally opposed to war.

"I can change nothing, but am a queen in my own garden," Leandra said aloud. She stood up and brushed herself off. All around her were herbs and plants that she had nurtured and grown. From them she produced medicines.

Still, she had not been able to grow what she tried so desperately to grow, a specific kind of mykes. This she attributed to the fact that it was far too dry. All observers had noted that most varieties of mycota grew in damp places. Perhaps, she thought, it would grow for her in Constantinople, or maybe she could have it grown in some valley near a river, where tall trees would provide shade and the river the needed dampness.

"Dominia! Dominia!" Her servant ran into the garden. "There is a special messenger from Emperor Justinian himself! He has just arrived aboard the royal yacht."

Leandra stood up and brushed herself off. She hurriedly removed the apron which she used for gardening, adjusted her long scarf, and went inside.

In the central room, Alexander sat reading a long scroll. Next to him stood a royal messenger dressed in purple robes.

"My wife, Leandra," Alexander said, introducing her.

"Leandra, this is Horatio. He has been sent by the emperor and he has a message for you."

Leandra bowed slightly. Her eyes studied Alexander's face in the hope that she would see a clue in his expression. She smiled to herself, thinking that while she saw no clue, she did see her husband fully restored to good health. As she had every day for the last two years, she thanked all the powers of the universe for his recovery. She considered it a miracle.

"Perhaps you should read this yourself," he said, handing her the scroll with a sly smile.

Again she suppressed a smile. Alexander's eyes were on Horatio, who looked appropriately surprised. Alexander loved to tease people, to let it be known that he had married an educated woman, a woman who could herself read and did not depend on his good offices to tell her everything.

Carefully Leandra unrolled the scroll and read the words written by Justinian.

My dear Leandra,

*My mind is clouded with worry. My beloved Theodora
seems to grow weaker by the day and I fear for her life.
Cyril, the court physician, is at a loss—and I myself do
not know what should be done. Theodora insists she wants
you. She bids you return with Alexander to Constantinople immediately. I will do anything and everything my
beloved requests. The royal yacht and the fastest oarsmen
in the empire are at your disposal. Please hasten to Constantinople.*

There followed the flourish that was Justinian's signature,
and the royal seal.

"We will set sail in the morning," Alexander said.

Leandra shook her head. "All our goods can follow save
Pegasus. We should set sail within the hour. I shall gather my
medicines and a few clothes."

Alexander nodded his head. "You're right. There is no time
to lose."

Cyril fled the palace and hurried through the streets of Constantinople. "A curse on her," he muttered darkly as he thought
of Theodora. She had not died fast enough. In his caution to
make her disease appear normal, he had failed to give her sufficient poison. Now, in all likelihood, her friend, a master physician who had studied with Saul, would discover what he had
done. He was finished at the palace, a price would be put on
his head.

Why hadn't Justinian told him sooner that he sent for Leandra! That he should learn today was intolerable! A curse on all
of them!

He reached the door of Hadas, who lived in a poor, densely
populated section of the city. From the outside, his dwelling
was a miserable place. Cyril banged on the great wooden door,
his anger taken out on its decaying wood.

The old woman who opened the door looked nothing less

than annoyed. She was dressed in an ugly brown dress, her greasy hair pulled back, and she smelled as if she hadn't bathed in a year. "I've come to see Hadas," he said.

"Hadas does not receive company on Tuesdays."

"I must see him. I must see him immediately. Go and tell him Cyril of Varna is here!"

"He sees no one on Tuesdays."

"Get him, you old crone, or I shall run you through!" He touched his sword lightly and put his foot in the door so she could not close it.

She stepped aside to let him in. "Wait here," she muttered, and then stomped off, cursing under her breath. "Son of a harlot, eater of shit."

Cyril shook with frustrated anger. He would have killed her as if she were a cockroach had the circumstances been different. Instead, she wandered off, and he was left in this pigsty of a room, surrounded by filth and inhaling foul odors.

He waited, tapping his foot. His anger and fear grew by the moment. Finally the woman reappeared. "Follow that hall," she said, fluttering her hand in midair to direct him.

Cyril walked down the long hallway and passed into a well-lit courtyard. The foul odors were gone, and in their place were the sweet smells of flowers. There, in the middle of the courtyard sat Hadas. His skin was brown from the sun, and he smiled as if nothing in the entire world mattered.

"Ah, Cyril. Do sit down. I shall have refreshment brought."

"How can you live in such a hovel? Surely it is not necessary."

"It is necessary to hide oneself, to appear to be what one is not. Of course I do not live in that place you just passed through. I live over there."

He pointed to a door on the far side of the courtyard. "Who is that horrible woman?"

"Someone who keeps away those whom I do not wish to see. Of course, when I heard it was you, I told her to let you come in in spite of the fact that it is Tuesday, and more important, in spite of the fact that you were told never to come here."

"I had no choice."

"I'm sure you didn't."

"That woman, Theodora's friend, has been summoned by Justinian. She's on her way back from Jerusalem. She will discover what I've done!"

Hadas inhaled deeply and then expelled his breath loudly, as if performing some sort of exercise. "Just what do you expect me to do?"

"To stop her! She arrives by royal yacht. She is due at any moment!"

"Ah, and you somehow expect me to stop her from landing. You're absurd! The basin is full of ships commanded by loyal sailors and soldiers. She'll be protected from all sides. There is no way to stop her, no way at all."

"She will discover what I've done to the empress."

"No doubt she will."

"But you must do something."

"We will all do something. But we shall not do it immediately. You have failed, Cyril. Were I a less generous man, I would kill you. Pull yourself together, or else you will become so dangerous for me that I shall have to do just that."

"What do you plan to do?"

"When the time is exactly right, we will foment a riot and proclaim a new emperor. In the meantime, you will lay low so your special talents can be used later."

"But there will be a price on my head! They will be looking for me!"

"We shall see that you are hidden. When the time is right, when we have taken over, I shall let you kill this Leandra personally. If you like, you may also kill the empress."

Cyril smiled. The thought of killing them both almost restored his good humor, even if he knew Hadas to be a man who seldom kept his word. Yet Hadas represented the wishes of a vast empire—an empire Cyril had decided to ally himself with only a few months before. It was Hadas who encouraged him to kill Theodora. She was seen to be too strong and too intelligent. He had tried, and now he had failed. But there was another plan in place, and when the Persians ruled, he was certain he would be elevated.

"What should I do now?" he asked.

"Get a horse and go to the mountains. Go to the village of Adrianople and ask for the home of Craven. He will hide you. You only have to wait."

Cyril thought for a moment. Yes, Leandra would be landing just now. There was time before she could make a diagnosis of Theodora. He would go back to the palace, pack a few things, and take a horse from the royal stables. He would be off, and no one would be the wiser. By the time his deed was discovered, he would be in Adrianople.

The royal yacht moored at the dock just below the palace walls. On any given day, twenty or more gaily painted pleasure craft would be at anchor in the basin, their colored flags fluttering in the breeze beneath Constantinople's blue sky. When the royal yacht had been away, there were hundreds who came to meet it, to throw flowers, and to offer good wishes.

But such was not the case today. The only familiar sight was the blue sky. Today there were no flags, no crowds, no festivities. Constantinople was a city in mourning, their beloved empress Theodora was ill, and rumors of her impending death spread through the marketplace like fire, sending the entire population into a pall. Apprehension dominated all discussion. Could Justinian be strong without her? Surely in his mourning he would be deeply weakened and the Persians would once again pose a threat. Was the prosperity the city now enjoyed to end? Was decency toward the poor to become a thing of the past?

Leandra looked up. Above, the great palace walls rose from the water's edge, its terraced gardens aflame with flowers and small shrubs. She stepped ashore and waited for Pegasus to be brought. She looked up at the steep palace walls, and in spite of her fears for Theodora, she felt good to be home, to have her feet planted in Constantinople. Beyond these walls was the city in which she had been reared. There were memories here, things she did not want to forget.

"Come, Theodora waits," Alexander said, taking her arm.

Leandra turned to the royal guard and handed him Pegasus's bridle. "Please take him to the stables," she asked. "See that he is watered, fed, and exercised."

Pegasus was led away, and the captain of the guard turned to them. "Come," he said, beckoning them to follow.

Leandra and Alexander were escorted through the lower gates of the palace walls. There were three gates in all, just as there were three sets of thick walls. This palace, with its commanding view of the entire city and the great chain that guarded the Bosphorus, was built for siege.

Leandra and Alexander were escorted through a maze of tunnels and up endless winding stairs until they were in Justinian's chambers.

"Thank God! You are here even before I anticipated." Justinian left his throne to greet them. His face was drawn and there were dark lines under his eyes.

"Where is Theodora?" Leandra asked impatiently.

"In our bedchamber. Cyril, the court physician, looks after her, but he says there is nothing he can do."

A deep chill ran through Leandra as all her suspicions about Cyril coalesced into the single thought that he was dangerous. Why had she not received instruction in a dream? Had she been deserted? No, that was not it, she told herself. She had been educated and prepared; she was now left to find her own solutions. Theodora was not dead yet, and she had been summoned.

Leandra did not wait to be dismissed or further instructed, she hurried through the thick doors and into Theodora's chamber. There, in the middle of a huge bed, lay Theodora's tiny form. Her unusually pale small face was made even smaller by the fact that her magnificent black hair was splayed out around her.

Leandra went directly to her bed and sat down on the edge of it. She took Theodora's small hand in hers.

"I am dying," Theodora whispered. "And I have not finished my work, Leandra. I have not finished the reforms—"

Leandra put her hand to Theodora's forehead. It was not feverish. "I will not let you die," Leandra said with determination. She could hardly say, I have not been told yet that it is time for you to die.

"I asked Justinian to send for you. But I don't know what you can do that Cyril has not done. He gives me potions and medicines, but nothing seems to help. I am so weak, I cannot stand."

"I must examine you," Leandra said firmly. "Myself."

Theodora nodded, and as if even the thought were exhausting, she fell back against the pillows.

Leandra's hands moved over Theodora's body. She lifted her arms, examined her skin, and noted that there was scaling of the skin on her extremities. Yet her facial complexion was white and flawless—too flawless. Leandra made notes.

"Tell me about your symptoms," Leandra urged.

Theodora shook her head. "I'm tired, so tired. And sometimes confused, though just at this moment I do not feel so bad."

"When did you last receive medication from Cyril?"

"Yesterday—morning I think, though sometimes my days and nights seem to blend into one."

"Does he usually come more often?"

"Yes, three times a day."

Leandra nodded. Cyril had not come to tell her about Theodora—where could he be? More important, why was he not present? They were silent questions, but her suspicions grew with each of them as well as with the observations she made during her examination.

Leandra again took Theodora's hand. She held it and then looked at her fingers. Across her lovely long nails were white streaks. In surprise, Leandra dropped Theodora's hand.

"Arsenic," she said in a whisper. "My heaven, my dear Theodora, you are being poisoned!"

"Poisoned?" Theodora said in amazement. Her eyes were huge, and she blinked as if she were unsure of what Leandra meant.

"You shall have no more of Cyril's potions!" Leandra said angrily.

"What will become of me?" Theodora's eyes were wide with fright.

"I think you will recover if you receive no more arsenic. You should begin to regain your strength within the week." With that she pulled on the cord above the bed, and in seconds the servant appeared. "Send Justinian and Alexander in immediately," she said.

Leandra stood up and whirled around when she heard them enter the room. "Theodora has been given arsenic. She has been poisoned."

"Poisoned!" Justinian's voice echoed through the bedchamber like the roar of a wounded animal. Then, as if he could not believe it, he said, "But we eat the same food."

"You do not take the same medicines," Leandra said evenly.

There was a moment of hesitation as Justinian digested the meaning of her accusation. Then he leaned toward her. "Cyril?"

"I can only guess. Perhaps he did not act alone. Perhaps there is some sort of conspiracy. Why is he not here?"

Justinian looked bewildered. "I have not seen him—not since the news of your impending arrival."

"Issue an arrest order for Cyril," Alexander advised.

"I should punish all the servants!" Justinian bellowed.

"No," Leandra quickly said, touching his shoulder gently. "I do not think that Theodora would want you to punish the innocent because of what one man may have done alone."

"Arrest Cyril and let it be known that an investigation is under way," Alexander suggested. "Offer rewards for information. Perhaps someone will come forward."

Justinian was fairly shaking with rage. His face flushed, and he bit his lower lip.

"Listen to Alexander," Theodora implored. Her voice was small and weak, but clearly knowledge of her ailment was giving her strength. "Alexander has the cooler head. Put him in charge of this investigation."

Justinian nodded and dropped to his knees beside Theodora's

bed. "I should never have forgiven myself if anything had happened to you."

"Leandra says I will recover."

"And so you shall."

"Leandra, you will care for her, won't you?"

"I shall stay with her till she is well."

Alexander ordered Cyril arrested and he ordered equipment to be brought so that food could be prepared in chambers by Leandra, who insisted Theodora must eat much bread and many eggs to absorb the poisons in her system.

Then, in keeping with his original idea, Alexander let it be known that there was to be an investigation and that rewards were to be offered.

That night Leandra lay in her bed, staring at the ceiling, praying for a dream that might offer her some further explanation of all that was happening. But sleep would not come, only a feeling of foreboding coupled with a deep sadness.

It was midnight when she and Alexander were roused from their sleep by a pounding on the door. "We must all take care until the full truth of this conspiracy to kill the empress is understood," he warned Leandra. So, sword in hand, Alexander opened the great door.

But it was no conspirator who knocked. There, in the corridor, and illuminated only by the torchlight outside on the walls, was the head of the royal stables and the captain of the guard.

"What brings you so late at night?" Alexander asked, sheathing his sword.

"A tragedy," the head of the stables said.

Leandra leapt from her bed and flung on her robe. She stood behind her husband, trembling—the name of her beloved horse was already on her lips.

"The great white horse that belongs to your wife has been killed," he said, trying to see beyond Alexander to Leandra.

"Oh, no, no—" Tears filled Leandra's green eyes, and she fell to her knees, sobbing. Not her wonderful Pegasus!

"It has been reported that Cyril of Varna is responsible. Apparently he tried to take the white horse, but it would be ridden by no one save your wife. In anger Cyril slew the white horse."

"I shall have this Cyril's head on my sword," Alexander vowed. It was not a boastful vow. He loved Pegasus as she did, and his voice was low and menacing.

"Double the guard, and see that more swift horsemen are sent in pursuit of this devil."

They left, and the door swung shut. Alexander bolted it.

What could he say or do to comfort Leandra? He lifted her to their bed and held her tightly as she sobbed against him.

"You do not know," she whispered. "I loved him so much. We rode the heavens together. We rode to the stars."

He kissed her tenderly. "I do know how you loved him."

"I love you more. Oh, please, be careful, Alexander. I could not bear to lose you. This man is a monster, he is from the dark side."

"The dark side?"

"He is evil. I am here to combat his evil, to protect Theodora so she can fulfill her destiny of settling these religious arguments and help Justinian formulate changes in the law."

He held her, trying to understand her words. When she spoke of riding to the stars on Pegasus, he had thought she meant it metaphorically. But now he wondered.

"We once spoke of our dreams of each other," he said carefully, "and you have often spoken of your destiny and Theodora's—"

"I was sent," Leandra said. "I am reborn, I am told things in my dreams."

"The future?"

She shook her head. "The precise future is for no mortal to know. I am told only certain things—I am shown the way. But I can neither bend others to my will nor prevent mortals from taking the wrong path."

"Are you—"

"I believe I am, though I am in this life as mortal as you. But I knew Pegasus—I have known him for all eternity."

Alexander held her close. "That is how long I will love you."

"And I you," she whispered.

December came with its cold winds from the mountains. But apart from the wind and occasional rain, Constantinople was temperate and the days were warm and most often sunny.

Theodora returned to herself. She gained a little weight, though she remained slender. Her dark hair once again began to shine, her skin returned to normal, and her energy returned tenfold.

On December first, Justinian summoned Leandra.

The great hall was strewn with sweet-smelling herbs, and Leandra wore a russet gown encrusted with jewels, and a golden girdle, given to her by a grateful emperor. Her mane of fiery hair was secured beneath a long scarf, and her green eyes rested on Justinian.

She knelt before the emperor, Alexander at her side. "You have summoned me, Emperor."

"To reward you. You are a talented physician. I will appoint you court physician unless there is a greater prize you wish to claim."

Leandra lifted her eyes to meet Justinian's. "There are many fine doctors who could serve the court. I could recommend any one of three as exceptional physicians. For myself, there is a greater prize. Long have I sought to study the plague, My Emperor. I beg for a small laboratory here, on the palace grounds. I beg to be able to continue my studies in hope of finding a cure for this dread illness that takes so many before their time."

Justinian looked at Theodora, who nodded, and then he turned back to Leandra. "Your wish is granted. Write me a list of all you require and it shall be seen to."

"Thank you," Leandra murmured.

Then Leandra and Alexander moved away from the throne and joined the other spectators.

Justinian tapped his scepter. "I am fortunate among men. I have an empress of unusual intelligence and political acumen. Henceforth, each piece of imperial legislation is to be given to her to study and to adjust. She is to receive foreign envoys and answer all correspondence with foreign powers. Never before has a woman been charged with such duties, but I know of no one who could better perform these tasks. And she will further make reforms important to the people."

Leandra's eyes studied those in the throne room. Nearly all seemed happy, but a few surely doubted Theodora's ability.

"This is her destiny," Leandra whispered to Alexander. "The destiny of which I have so often spoken."

"Hers and yours. The emperor summons us to a private supper," he whispered back into her ear.

Within the hour they were all four in the private imperial suite. Theodora insisted supper be served on the terrace, where the sounds of strolling singers could be heard from below. When they were alone they were four old friends, and the formalities of court were replaced by easy conversation.

"She has more brains than any man in the Senate," Justinian told Alexander. Then with a wink he added, "These women are an untapped resource."

"Yes, they are, and a pleasurable resource at that," Alexander joked. But all was not well, to which Alexander could attest. Rumors filled the streets, rumors that Cyril, although long gone from Constantinople, had organized some kind of revolt, a revolt that would overthrow Justinian and Theodora and threaten all the progress that had been made.

"You laugh, make jokes, and look confident, but in your eyes I see worry," Justinian guessed.

"Yes. It is the young men and women who shave their heads and dress like Huns. They are causing more and more difficulty within the city. They are brutal without cause, common criminals who roam the city streets in gangs attacking young and old alike, carrying weapons that should be carried only by soldiers."

"A leftover from days gone by," Justinian said. They both knew full well that for many years the Blues and Greens had run the competitions in the city, and that for a long while they had been armed and guarded the walls and gates of the city. But then Constantinople grew, and now it was well policed so the Blue and Green factions were no longer needed to guard the walls and gates. Nonetheless, some of the Blues and Greens were still armed and claimed the right to remain armed in spite of the changing times. After a time it was their children who took up the dress of the Huns and carried the forbidden and dangerous knife-swords under their mantles. They robbed their victims of clothing and gold brooches and whatever else they carried.

"Dissatisfied youth, displaced men of the factions, and clever political enemies like Cyril and his ilk are a potent combination. Sunday will be a telling day," Alexander warned as he looked into the small fire that had been lit to ward off the evening dampness.

"You believe matters are coming to a head?" Justinian asked, leaning close.

Alexander nodded. "When I left, it was dangerous in Caesarea and even more dangerous in Antioch. The time is coming, we will be tested here in Constantinople."

"You two shall be lost in politics no longer," Theodora announced as she and Leandra came out onto the terrace.

"Never have two men been distracted by two lovelier women," Justinian replied. "But the truth is, a truly intelligent conversation cannot be had without you."

"I should hope not," Theodora said.

Theodora led the way to the table, followed by Justinian, who sat next to her. When they were both seated, Leandra and Alexander sat down side by side. Behind them, a line of servants bore their supper on silver trays.

"There appears to be far more than we can eat," Alexander said, laughing.

"Then indulge yourself. Sample everything."

Justinian poured them each a glass of wine. "Tell me, Leandra, why is your hair always hidden? I know it's a personal question, but curiosity has finally overcome me."

"Because there are many ignorant people," Theodora answered for her friend. "Leandra's hair is the color of fire. Her ancestors were born in the far north of the land of the Anglos, and many of the people of that land have flaming red-gold hair. But it is a rare color here, and the superstitious would say she was of the devil."

"Ah," Justinian said, sipping his wine. "So your hair is a pleasure for only your husband to savor."

Leandra smiled shyly. "It is better that way."

"Let us drink to the future," Theodora said, lifting her glass.

"To the future," Justinian agreed.

Leandra lifted her glass, and so did Alexander, but she sensed her husband's disquiet. "What troubles you?" she asked when they had all finished the toast.

"I wish for the same future as all of you. But I fear revolution. There is no respect for authority among these groups who arm themselves and who so frequently attack the innocent in the streets."

Theodora nodded. "Alexander has a sense for the mood of the people. I am afraid I share his feelings of foreboding."

"What would you have me do?" Justinian asked.

"Let us be sure that the generals and the army can reach the palace in case of difficulty. Let us have a full meeting of the leadership and make certain the army is alerted to all dangers."

"I will arrange it immediately," Justinian promised.

Almost as Alexander had predicted, the trouble started on Sunday, just before the Ides of January and during the opening of the Games at the Hippodrome.

Justinian was rushed from the royal box under guard even as the two orators—one from the Blue faction and one from the Green faction, hurled insults at each other and roused the crowd to hysteria. By late afternoon the crowds spilled out onto the streets and vicious rioting began.

Justinian tried to go to the races on Monday as if nothing had happened. But again violence erupted, this time threefold. The mobs were clearly being led, and when the prison was burned, they were joined by those criminals who had escaped.

Mobs roamed the streets as the terrible fires spread. They all cried out the watchword of the circus, "Nika! Nika!—Victory! Victory!"

By Wednesday the palace complex was cut off. Alexander and Mundus, the commander of the Herule barbarians, went out to hear the demands of the rebels.

Theodora opened the Daphne Palace to the wounded, and there Leandra's and Theodora's women tended those brought in from the streets.

Alexander returned and went directly to Justinian. "There is no doubt that this is a revolt to overthrow you and to replace you with one of the nephews of Anastasius. I know Cyril is behind this, it is a Persian ploy. They have organized and perhaps paid the criminal youth gangs—Justinian, action must be taken."

"Summon the court and Theodora," Justinian replied. He looked tired, and Alexander tried to fathom what was in his heart.

The trumpets blared and all the court appeared. None among them looked confident or unafraid. Save one.

Even Alexander was stunned by Theodora. She came dressed in full regalia and carried herself as if nothing were amiss. She stood tall beside Justinian, her hand enfolded in his. Her resolve radiated throughout the hall. She seemed to have the power of the sun, and she stood strong at Justinian's right side.

But for as strong as Theodora appeared, Alexander was taken aback by Justinian. He looked tired. He looked as if he wanted nothing more than to go away with his wife.

"I have considered everything," Justinian began. "I will step down to end the violence. I will return to Macedonia."

The entire assembled group stood in absolute silence. They were stunned by his words even though they knew he was tired and that he hated bloodshed.

"No!" Theodora's voice rang out clearly and all eyes turned

to her. "You may step down, but I will never leave. Once you have adorned the royal purple mantle of this throne, there is no turning back, there can be no stepping down. If need be, they will bury me in these robes, but I will not desert my people to the rabble or to the sly hand of the Persian infiltrators!"

The room was absolutely silent. "Tell Belisarius and Mundus to quell this riot as they quelled the ambitions of the Persians on our borders," Theodora said.

"So much killing," Justinian said sadly.

"There will be more if this rabble comes to power. There will be more killing if Byzantium falls to the Persians! We have no choice other than to remain. We must protect this empire. Flight is inexpedient, even if it brings safety."

Then she turned to her husband and spoke directly to him. "We are all born into the light and must all one day face the darkness of death, but for an emperor to become a fugitive, a wanted man, is not something that can be endured. We could easily find safety in flight—there is the sea! There are ships! But this is not the way. We wear the purple, we must wear it to our graves."

Justinian turned toward her, and before all he cupped her tiny face in his hands. "You give me strength," he said softly. Then he turned to his generals. "Do what you must."

The fighting continued for days. Ground was held, but still the rioting continued. Then on Friday night the crowds once again streamed into the Hippodrome to proclaim their new emperor, Hypatius, nephew of Anastasius.

The roar of the crowd brought Alexander, Belisarius, and Mundus to the top of the palace, from which vantage point they could look down on the Hippodrome.

"That's a sight to behold," Alexander said as a smile crossed his face.

Belisarius laughed. "Such a crowd should make us tremble, but look at them. My God, all of our enemies have crowded themselves in one place, a place with narrow, wretched exits."

"We must go now," Mundus said evenly. "We must give them no time to disperse."

The three hurried away to join their men, to give instructions, to give the final orders that would quell the rebellion and restore order.

In the Daphne Palace, Leandra walked among the wounded, giving what instruction she could to the multitude of women who came to help. "So much killing," she said to Theodora. "If only they hadn't chosen to follow Cyril."

Theodora's dark eyes were filled with tears. "We live in a cruel world."

"It is your destiny to make it less so," Leandra reminded her. They both knew what had happened. The rebels had been trapped in the Hippodrome just as they had crowned their own emperor. Thousands had been killed when the loyal generals had their men block the exits, killing the rioters as they attempted to stream out of the Hippodrome for a victory parade.

After their victory, the man who would have been emperor was executed. Once victory was assured, Justinian granted amnesty to all those who had taken part in the uprising. The factions were dead, and to a large extent the criminal element had been killed in the rebellion.

"I shall give my house for a hospital," Theodora promised. "I shall work tirelessly to bring education to the masses."

"The law is most important," Leandra stressed. "You and Justinian will be known as the lawgivers."

"You have my word. I shall follow your advice."

Leandra nodded. She felt confident that things were going as they should. No dreams had come to her. No further instructions had been given.

"A feast to celebrate our victory," Justinian said as he waved his arm about, pointing to the couches. "Take your seats. Tonight I offer a banquet for my loyal generals and brave empress."

The evening's festivities were being held in a large hall on the palace grounds known as the Tribunal of the Nineteen Couches. As had been done for hundreds of years now, the feast was served while the diners reclined on couches and enjoyed varied entertainments in the Roman style.

Theodora wore a royal purple gown that fell from gold clasps at her shoulders. Its fabric was encrusted with jewels. Her gold earrings were long and intricate and studded with stones.

Leandra and Alexander took their places on one of the couches. Leandra was dressed lavishly in a green gown with encrusted jewels. It was a gift from Theodora.

Both generals were present with their wives and so were a selection of supportive senators and civil servants, most of whom were eunuchs.

Greek dancing was performed during the first course, game hens were prepared in fruits and covered in a plum sauce. Next came ornate breads made in swirling designs around eggs. Next lamb and goat were served, followed by an array of salted fish, dried meats, baked beans, greens, watermelons, lemons, and oranges. Each of the twelve courses was accompanied by more entertainment. The finale was a troop of Hindu jugglers.

Leandra's eyes fell on one of the eunuchs. And that reminded her of Cyril, who was himself a eunuch. Most doctors were eunuchs, since only eunuchs and women physicians like herself could treat the women of the realm.

"For an evening of such wonderful entertainment, you looked distressed," Alexander said, taking her hand. He had grown to sense her moods, almost to read her mind.

"I was just thinking that Cyril is still at large. The danger has not entirely passed."

He squeezed her hand. "I know."

Nine

A warm evening breeze blew off the Bosphorus as Leandra made her way from her laboratory on the edge of the royal gardens to the quarters she shared with her husband, Alexander.

She passed through a small side gate that was partially overgrown with lush flowered vines. The aroma from the garden was heady, and she inhaled deeply, relishing in nature's perfumes.

Beyond the gate, she followed a narrow cobblestone path that wound past the high east wall of the palace. Next she passed through a second gate, which led upward to another level. Beyond that she went through an archway and entered a maze of torchlit corridors that led to their private quarters—in reality a small self-contained apartment that opened onto one of the many terraces in the Boucoleon Palace, which overlooked the imperial yacht basin.

Their quarters were among the most favored, since therapeutic hot water was fed directly from a hot spring beneath the palace. The main room contained the pool, a small cooking area, plants, and couches for reclining. Beyond the main room was the bedchamber, which contained their clothes chest, a large bed, and dressing table. The remaining room was a small bathroom lined with colorful tiles. There was an airtight toilet from which waste was removed several times each day, and water burbled up into a basin for washing. Like all of the city, clean water to the many rooms of the palace and to central distribution points was provided by a network of aqueducts.

Windows that could be covered with heavy drapes in case of inclement weather allowed daylight to enter along the side of their chambers that faced the terrace garden. At night, and in the other rooms, light was provided by oil lamps.

Beyond, on the terrace that overlooked the water, there were lush flowers, statues, and graceful birdbaths. Drinking water was carried in jugs and food was usually bought in one of several markets within the palace grounds. Mills and ovens were communal, and one day a week a member of the family or a servant, depending on one's class, went to the bakery and made the bread for the week. Wine was brewed communally as well, and the aged jugs distributed when new jugs were committed to fermentation.

Leandra paused before the door and then opened it. She was surprised to see Alexander relaxing in their steaming hot pool.

"You've returned earlier than usual," he observed.

"Frustration," she whispered. "I can no longer work today—I can't find the answers, and yet I know I am close."

His eyes caressed her. "Join me," he requested. "Let me watch you undress, let me touch you to reassure myself you're real."

The look in his eyes made her skin glow, and almost immediately she felt herself grow desirous of his knowing touch.

She did not answer him, but just silently began disrobing. First she discarded her golden girdle, then her golden sandals. Slowly she lifted off her dress, which was, like most of her clothing, designed in the old Grecian style. Next she removed her slips and last her scarf, liberating her red-gold hair.

"Let me drink in your beauty," he said as his eyes devoured her. Her snow-white breasts, with their high pink nipples, never ceased to arouse him. She was perfectly formed with long, shapely legs, a tiny waist, and full, rounded hips and buttocks. And age did not seem to change her. She was as beautiful now as when he had first possessed her thirteen years before. Her wild, beautiful hair was her crowning glory, and it was matched only by the red-gold down that formed a perfect triangle over her mound of Venus.

"Come to me." He held out his hand and Leandra gracefully slid into the water and allowed him to wrap her in his muscular arms.

She leaned against his chest, letting the disappointments of her day drain away. "I know I am close," she said, shaking her head. "If only I could see what I cannot see."

"You speak in riddles."

"I meant I am sure life exists that cannot be seen with the naked eye. If I could but see it, I could solve this problem."

"Are you certain this life exists?"

"Oh, yes. Think about it carefully, Alexander. Take an infected wound."

"I've seen enough of those."

"The infection grows—you have seen it grow."

"Yes, as it eats the healthy flesh."

"And then if we use maggots, they eat the growing rot, but only the growing rot. I am convinced that this rot, this infection, is caused by something alive but unseen. Something that eats and can be eaten."

He laughed softly and smiled at her. "Is this a new definition of life, that which eats and can be eaten?"

"Perhaps," she replied, laughing at herself.

Then she saw his face grow more serious. "Leandra, why do you work so hard to find this cure or treatment for plague? What drives you on? What makes you think you can find it?"

His question had been a long time coming, she thought. He loved her so much, he took everything about her on faith.

"I have told you about my mission, you know about me."

"Tell me everything you can."

"I was born during a darkness of the sun, and one year later my mother was killed. I was rescued by a learned man who said he traveled to Antioch to find me because he was so instructed by his dreams. He educated me, and as I grew older, I, too, had these dreams of instruction. I must obey them. Anstice, my mentor, said I was immortal and that he was an intermediary who would become immortal. I know he was chosen, made immortal because of some deed.

"I cannot remember what occurs between my lives, and I have only a fleeting memory of my previous lives. Anstice told me I was reborn every thousand years and that my mission is to assist powerful women. I was sent to help Theodora."

Alexander held her closer and kissed her neck.

"I want to be with you forever."

"Oh, Alexander, I never want to be parted from you either."

"I love you, Leandra."

"And I you."

He bent down and again kissed her neck, then her ears, then he took one of her delicate nipples into his mouth. It was softer than the softest cloth, and her body smelled sweeter than the most expensive perfumes.

He felt her nipples harden as he sucked, and then he felt her legs around his waist just as her arms were around his neck. He lifted her from the water, carrying her to the cushions. He lay down and pulled her on top of him so that her face looked down into his.

Then he moved his hips up to sink into her. "You are like no other woman," he whispered. "When I enter you, it is like being joined to the universe, to a force that gives complete fulfillment."

One hand held her buttocks, and she moved above him while he toyed with her most sensitive area, feeling it as it swelled with anticipation. She lifted her head back, and her lips parted in a cry of release as she shivered above him and he throbbed into her. She fell against him, her damp body shaking with release.

As it happened, extraordinary sensations seized his whole being. A panorama was unfolded before him. They were in heaven and hell, they were together and apart, they were hot and cold, damp and dry. They were fire and water, and then they were traveling as if on a meteorite through the dark cold of space headed for the brightness of a distant shining star.

His breath had been sucked away and he inhaled deeply. They were always fulfilled together, and their lust for each other was unending. But tonight it had been different. Tonight he truly knew she was immortal, and tonight he had been given a taste of life beyond his own mortality.

Leandra opened the door to her laboratory and immediately felt a strange apprehension flood over her. Her eyes darted around, and she knew for certain that someone else had been there, that someone had violated the sanctity of the place. The door was always kept locked, and seldom did she allow anyone inside because of what was kept there. Not only were all her medical texts there, but so were her own notebooks and observations. In addition, she grew special plants and had lately taken to observing certain poisons and fungi as well.

She moved around, taking a mental inventory of how she had left things. Not much had been moved, and as far as she could ascertain, nothing had been taken. But a stranger had been there—she could feel it and she could also feel evil. A shudder ran through her. She shook off her feelings. No one was here now. It was imperative that she continue working.

She paused momentarily to look at the dish in which she deposited the poison pus drawn from a terrible infection. A strange green slime had formed on top of it, and she studied it, noting that the poisonous area had been growing, but had now stopped, almost as if the green slime kept it from increasing in size. She sighed deeply. If only she knew why or how. Try as she might, she could not create a glass that magnified enough for her to see what she was now certain existed.

Carefully, very carefully, she skimmed the slime from the top of the dish and preserved it in one of many small vials she had made by Heraclius the glassblower. Heraclius was a master glassblower, the most famous in all Byzantium. Such men were called *vitrarii,* and were distinguished from others who made decorative glass in molds. Heraclius fashioned vials of several sizes for her and in addition made her glass rods through which to transfer liquids. She had gotten the idea from hollow reeds which, as a child, she had filled with water.

Leandra held the slime up to the light and studied it through the glass. Was it a living mass? Was it poisonous as was the poison it had formed on? She hung the vial on a rack she had the metal worker make for her and again looked at it. Then she looked back at the dish. A small amount of slime remained in it. She carefully removed it and put it down on a flat plate. Then she went to her jars of maggots. With long tweezers she removed one and deposited it onto the slime. The maggot crawled around but made no attempt to eat the slime. "It cannot be rot," she said aloud. A chill ran through her. Was this the answer? What was this slime that grew in rot and yet wasn't rot?

"Dominia! Dominia!" A rapid succession of knocks on her laboratory door lifted Leandra out of her thoughts. She opened the door to Agathias, a palace messenger.

"Justinian bids you to come, *Dominia.* There is plague in the city and he wishes for you to consult with the other doctors."

"Plague . . ." Leandra repeated the word as if she had never heard it before. But in fact her mind was racing, and her only thought was that she had been too slow and was not ready. Her destiny, the message of all her dreams, was that she save Theodora from the plague. But she was not prepared yet. She had yet to find either the real cause or the cure.

"There are as many as forty cases, *Dominia,*" Agathias revealed in a frightened tone.

"By tomorrow there will be three times that number," Leandra said.

"Dominia, what can we do?"

"Rid your house of all vermin. Burn their bodies, do not touch them with your hands. Wash everything and do not allow fleas on your person," she cautioned.

"How is one to avoid them?"

"Use oil of citron from oranges and lemons. Bathe in it, cover yourself with it."

"I shall do as you say, *Dominia*. And I shall also pray."

"Yes," Leandra said softly. "Pray."

Five learned doctors sat around a table with Theodora and Justinian. Leandra joined them, sitting just to the right of the empress.

"How is your research, Leandra?"

"It goes far too slowly," she answered honestly.

"All of you must speak honestly," Theodora said firmly. "We must know the real situation if Constantinople is to be saved from the ravages of plague."

"Phocas, you speak first," Justinian requested.

Phocas ran the hospital for the indigent, which had been built by Theodora. He was an older man with white hair and a white beard. His eyes were kindly and his skin marked by his seventy years.

"We have many cases; it spreads more quickly in the areas of the poor."

"Because their houses are filled with vermin," Leandra said. "I believe plague is in some way carried by rats or fleas."

"We have those in abundant quantity," Gelimer muttered.

"It is already rampant in the prison. Not that it matters if the condemned die of it. They are to die in any case."

Leandra looked at Germanus, who had just spoken. She said nothing, but an idea had occurred to her.

Zooras ignored them all. "We must post guards at the city gates. We must keep the ill out of the city and deal only with those who are already here."

"No," Theodora said strongly. "I will not close out the sick. The only hospitals are here. In any case, if Leandra is right, we will be closing our gates to the wrong species. Who shall kill the rats that enter Constantinople?"

"We do not know if she's right, talented though she is." Zooras knew she was a court favorite. He was a politician as well as a doctor. But she did not like his suggestion either. It echoed action taken by Cyril some time ago, when Constantinople was thought to be threatened.

"I think we can do little except observe high standards of public health. I, too, believe as Leandra does. We should put a bounty on dead rats, and we should urge the populace to bathe and boil their clothes, to rid themselves of fleas."

"It is all that can be done," Leandra agreed.

Justinian nodded. "I shall send out a royal proclamation urging the killing of rats and encouraging additional measures of cleanliness among the people. We cannot stop it, but perhaps we can contain it."

Leandra waited till all the other physicians had gone. "May I speak with you both, Justinian?" she asked.

Theodora smiled. "Of course."

"Long ago I suggested you use oil of citron. But I know it cannot always keep fleas from biting. It is not the answer I seek."

"Are you close to finding an answer?" Justinian asked.

"I could be—or I could still be far away. I have a problem, one which I must speak to you about."

"You have my full attention."

"I have a substance, something I believe may have medicinal value where plague is concerned. But I will never know unless it can be tried on someone who has the plague. But it is dangerous. It could easily kill as well as cure."

"Do you have a suggestion?" Theodora asked.

"The condemned prisoners who have the plague. I could use them—if they live, they might be pardoned by your excellency, if they die—well, they would have been put to death in any case."

"It is a good idea, Justinian," Theodora said. She had placed her hand on his and she looked into his eyes.

Justinian nodded. "I shall have three such men taken to the hospital. You will go there to treat them."

Leandra nodded and in a near-whisper said, "Thank you."

* * *

"You toss in your sleep, Leandra." Alexander stroked her hair in the darkness and drew her close. "What troubles you?"

"My search, my findings—I have a fluid and I have been given permission to try it on condemned men. But I am not sure how to give this fluid. If I let them drink it, its medicinal properties might be destroyed by acids in the stomach. I want to put it into the blood, but how?"

"Perhaps if you lance the buboes, you can insert it then."

"But then I cannot be sure if the liquid cured them or lancing the buboes cured them—it cured you."

"I think they would be cured differently. I was sick and weak for a long, long while."

Leandra snuggled up to him. It was hard to remember those days when he was weak. He was so strong now. "Yes, I remember. And of course you're right. It is probably the only way in any case."

"You will try it, then?"

"I will go to the hospital tomorrow. I must know. I must try it."

"However did you get the ideas you have about all this?" He was propped up in bed on one elbow and he looked into her face. He was well aware of her theories, and the way she explained them, he understood.

"Reading and observation," she answered. "Among my texts I found reference to a Chinese doctor who lived five hundred years ago. He somehow became aware of the mold that grew on soybeans, and he used that mold to cure boils and abscesses. I believe, as he must have, that such molds are living substances that act on other living substances. I believe infections and diseases to be caused by these unseen substances, and I believe the molds to kill them."

"You are a wonder," he acknowledged.

"I have my mold. It is the product of infection. I must now see if it will kill or cure."

Alexander bent and kissed her soft lips. "You are so rare, my darling. I love you. I would test this liquid myself were I ill."

"I pray you never will be ill again," she whispered.

He moved toward her and she responded. His kisses made her forget to mention that she thought her laboratory had been broken into—his kisses made her forget everything.

Leandra watched her three patients carefully. She had lanced their buboes and inserted her concoction, now she only had to wait for the results.

Hours went by, but she dared not leave their sides. She wrote in her notebooks, observing their reactions, their breathing, their heartbeats, and their fevers. Slowly, as if by a miracle, each one's temperature began to return to normal and their breathing eased. She recorded the first break in fever eight hours after the lancing. Her heart filled with joy, and tremors of excitement ran through her whole body. When sixteen hours had passed and she was certain of their recovery, she hurried back to her laboratory. It was dark outside when the guard provided by Justinian delivered her to her laboratory.

"Wake my husband and tell him I have returned," she requested. Then she opened the door and went into her laboratory, immediately going to where she had left her notes. She bent over and lit the oil lamp.

"I've come for you, Leandra."

Her heart jumped and she whirled about and looked up into the face of Cyril, who stepped out of the darkness. He was dressed in black and he seemed taller in the shadows caused by the lamplight.

"What do you want of me?" she asked, trying not to sound afraid.

"You have defeated me at every turn. First you usurped my position at court! Then you saved that whore of an empress, Theodora! Next your wretched husband defeated the revolt! Now I have lost my allies! I have lost everything! But you will not win your last battle, you little bitch! Tell me what you have discovered."

"I'm not sure—I don't know how to tell you." Everything inside her told her to play for time.

"I think you do. Now tell me!" He stepped closer to her and she saw the long blade of his knife glimmering in the light. Was he alone? Her thoughts were not for herself, but for Alexander, who would surely come when the guard awakened him.

"Tell me! What have you found!"

Leandra's lips parted. "A mold," she said. "When inserted into the blood, it seems to cure the plague."

"A mold," he said with disgust. "You dare to lie to me!" He grabbed the end of her scarf and pulled it from her head. "The hair of the devil!" he exclaimed. "That's what you are! A devil!"

"It is not I who am the devil," she replied. "It is you."

He smiled. "Perhaps," he muttered as he grabbed her arm and pulled her toward him.

He drew the long knife and she struggled. Leandra let out a half-scream as Cyril plunged the long, curved knife into her. She gasped and staggered backward as Alexander came storming through the door, his own sword drawn.

Leandra crumpled to the floor, her mouth slightly open, her life's blood draining from her mortal wound.

Alexander was blinded with rage. Cyril's eyes bulged with fear, and he backed up, forgetting the table behind him.

Alexander let out a cry of anguish, then ran Cyril through, pinning him to the table as one might pin an insect. He turned away quickly and knelt by Leandra's side, folding her into his arms.

"My beloved, my beloved!" Tears ran down his cheeks, and she reached up weakly to touch his face.

"I go to Pegasus," she whispered. "Listen, you must listen. There is one vial left. If Theodora becomes ill, her buboes must be lanced and the liquid inserted. Promise me, promise me you will see to this."

"Leandra, you cannot leave me!" he wailed, and held her. She was like a feather in his arms. He kissed her and her lips were cold. He held her and sobbed. Then he smelled the foul odor and saw the flames. Had Cyril not come alone? He picked up Leandra's limp, dead body and the vial she had pointed to, and he carried her from the now-flaming laboratory into the darkness of the night.

Guards came rushing from everywhere. Brigades brought water to put out the flames. Alexander sat on the hillside by the entrance to the royal gardens. The aroma of oleander filled the air even as the smell of smoke was carried away on the wind that blew off the Aegean.

"Leandra, my beloved," he whispered again, running his hand through her ravishing hair. He looked up at the heavens and saw the bright configuration of Orion and a bright shining light move swiftly across the black velvet sky toward that configuration.

"Leandra, Pegasus!" His eyes followed the light. She was an immortal, just as she had said, just as he had believed. "Let me be born again," he whispered, closing his eyes. "Let me love her one more time."

Shrouded in white, Leandra's body lay in state in the throne room of the palace.

Theodora stood by the side of the coffin while Alexander stood across from her on the other side.

Theodora lifted Leandra's cold hand and kissed it tenderly. "Her medicine cured me—it is a miracle."

Alexander himself felt it was nothing less. Theodora had already been stricken even as Leandra was struck down. As he had been instructed, Alexander delivered the vial of medicine and it was administered according to her instructions. Within hours Theodora was up and about.

"She was my friend," Theodora said softly. "My good friend, my confidante, my most trusted adviser. What can I do, Alexander?"

"Urge Justinian to revise the law. End the fighting, live up to the destiny Leandra envisaged for you."

"Of course. It is the only suitable tribute to her."

"I loved her more than life itself." Alexander's eyes once again filled with tears. Even in death she was beautiful. He bent down and kissed her forehead. "It is time to say good-bye," he whispered. "But we will meet again."

Theodora wiped the tears off her own cheek. "I go now to my duties," she said.

Alexander watched her leave, then he closed the coffin and gave the signal for it to be taken away. He knew as he watched it being carried off that he would never remarry, never love another, and until his own time came, would walk alone.

Part II

Ten

August 1, 1505
Paris, France

Father Jacques Renaud was a powerful figure at the Sorbonne, which was intended to be a place of learning but was, instead, a place of strict rules and orthodoxy. He and the others who controlled the Sorbonne vied for power with the crown, were opposed to the blossoming French Renaissance, and to any and all reforms within the church. They were especially opposed to those reforms that would change such lucrative customs—lucrative to them—of paying for dispensations. To Renaud, it seemed a simple matter, kings paid fortunes to annul their marriages and marry anew, peasants paid their pittances to get into heaven by confessing their boring sins and receiving absolution. It all added up.

The reformers were opposed to secret rituals and claimed to want knowledge and the right to participate in their faith, but Father Renaud knew better. What they really wanted, in his mind, was control.

Those who felt as he did had formed a secret society and called themselves the Guardians of the Faith. They wanted the faith shrouded in mystery, a mystery only they were allowed to interpret. Each of them knew that the sole right to interpretation was a strong power. It was not one they intended losing. Each month the twelve leaders who comprised the Guardians of the

Faith gathered to discuss the changing times and to condemn the growing voices of dissent.

The room in which they met was beneath the Sorbonne and had stone walls. It was a dark, dank place, a place without windows, and was lit only by candles. It was a room sometimes used by the inquisitors, a room most did not come to voluntarily.

It was their custom to meet on the first day of the month.

"The Spanish did not go far enough!" Father Jacques Renaud concluded. His voice was deep, sincere, almost hypnotic. His eyes focused on the candle in the middle of the table. He knew he was a man of some charisma who could easily influence others. He shook his head sadly. "The Inquisition did not cut deep enough. Too many were allowed to escape the flames! Now we will have to contend with these so-called reformers, these subversives who would change everything. It brings sadness to my heart. Too many heretics still preach, still have influence, still find adherents."

Renaud had dark, narrow eyes, a sharp, pointed beard, and flat, dark hair. He was the chief secretary for the men who made the decisions at the Sorbonne. He longed to bring a new Inquisition to France, to quell all talk of change with a "cleansing."

"All books that question the authority of the church should be burned!" another of the Guardians said loudly.

"Not just the books," Renaud said firmly. "Their authors as well."

"One must be careful in these matters," another Guardian interjected. "We must not be reckless in the use of power. We must wait until the Crown acts with us. Our king's foreign wars are a disaster."

"It will do no good to petition the Crown now," Renaud hissed. "There is too much turmoil over the Treaty of Blois."

"Then all we can do at present is keep lists. We must keep our eyes open so that when our time comes, the heretics can be eliminated."

There was grumbling and general agreement, then the meeting broke up with each of the Guardians going his own separate way.

Father Renaud shoved his chair backward and with a wave of his hand, took leave of his companions.

He walked up the winding stairs to the street and out into the warm, clear night. He decided to walk alone by the Seine.

He paused on a stone bridge, one of many that crossed the river. His eyes sought the heavens. He was thinking of all the things he had to remember to do, when suddenly he saw the streak of light, the bright bridge that for a moment seemed to link heaven and earth. He felt a sudden coldness as hatred surged through him.

There were those he knew he must destroy, but he had seen the light in the heavens, and now he knew someone had been sent to stop him.

August 1, 1505
Saint Rémy-de-Provence, France

The seeds of France's future were being firmly planted in the present. None knew better than René de Nostradamus that those seeds would grow into monstrous problems for the next generation.

Louis XII ruled France. He fought disastrous foreign wars and had now created a situation that would have repercussions for generations to come.

Forced in childhood to marry Jeanne of France, Louis XII had the marriage annulled as soon as he was crowned. He then married Anne of Brittany, widow of the previous French king, Charles VIII. The marriage reinforced the relationship of the Duchy of Brittany to France, and was by any standards a popular move.

But unsatisfied with this success, Louis then proceeded to lay claim to the Duchy of Milan and the Kingdom of Naples. French troops invaded and fought a long and protracted war, but the previous year France had lost all of Naples. Anne of Brittany then negotiated the Treaty of Blois. The treaty stipulated that Louis XII, her husband, would be recognized as Duke of Milan by Maximilian I, the Hapsburg emperor of the Holy

Roman Empire, if both Milan and Burgundy were left to the future Charles V and his fiancée, Claude of France.

The nobles were outraged, and all France was angry at the thought of losing Burgundy and possibly Brittany as well. Louis wavered; it was said he planned to break the agreement and wed his daughter, Claude, to young Francis, the heir presumptive to the French throne and the son of Louise of Savoy, rather than to Charles, Maximilian's heir.

"Unsettling times indeed," René de Nostradamus said aloud. He was thirty years old and a learned man of modest means. René owned a small farm near Saint Rémy, in the area of France called Provence. There he lived with his wife, Claire.

Provence was, to his thinking, the most beautiful region in all France. Its climate was sheer perfection. It had long, warm summers and a short, mild winter. On occasion, in the spring and fall, a dry cold wind called a mistral would blow across the land. Sometimes it blew quite violently and destroyed crops and wreaked havoc on poorly built structures. But this was a rare occurrence and was the only unfortunate feature of the climate.

Saint Rémy, indeed part of the land he owned, had been touched by history, a history with which René was intimately familiar. Just above the town there was a Roman mausoleum and the ruins of the oldest triumphal arch in all France. It dated from the Augustan period, while the town itself was built on the same site as the Roman town of Glanum, founded in the second century.

Few knew—though he had seen them in his dreams—that beneath the whole area were more extensive ruins. In the field where his cattle grazed, deep beneath the rich earth, the old Roman Forum was buried. The baths, a nymphaeum, a temple, and many houses were interred adjacent to the Forum. He knew these things because his dreams of his past life revealed he had once resided there. If he concentrated, he could recall having walked the streets of Glanum with his beloved Zöe. In those ancient days, in a life he only vaguely remembered, he was known as Valen. But that was a life long gone. In this life he and Zöe had been reborn as René de Nostradamus and Claire

Verdon. They had found each other anew, married, and been directed to live in Saint Rémy.

It was early evening, and René lay on the hillside near his house. On these warm August evenings he liked to lie on the grass and contemplate the universe. He enjoyed thinking of their life between, the life he and Claire had, and would have once again, among the stars. He also liked to think about politics, history, and the circles that made up life.

He lay in the still darkness on the sweet grass and stared at the heavens, traveling in his mind at the speed of light toward distant constellations. It was a pleasant escape from the troubled times in which he lived.

His wife, Claire, sometimes shared this experience with him. But most of the time now, she was busy tending their young son, Michel, who had been born two years before. Like his parents, Michel was immortal, a rare immortal who, when he was grown, would have the gift of future knowledge as well as past experience.

René was watching Orion, when the bright light of a meteorite filled the dark velvet night sky. It appeared as a great bridge of light between heaven and earth, and was so bright and so fast, he was certain it would fall nearby and explode. He covered his ears, as if he expected the sound of an explosion as it crashed into his field. But there was no sound. It was a silent coming, a streak of soundless white light in the night sky. He stood up and shook himself off. It was the sign for which he had been waiting. She had been reborn and he and Claire were to rear her with Michel as if she were their own.

Claire de Nostradamus had just put her son Michel to sleep, when her husband returned. René's normally placid expression was gone and in its place was a look of excitement.

"It is time," he said, bending down and kissing her cheek. "We must go to the Monastery of Saint Rémy."

* * *

Father DuBois was round and fat with a balding head and a ready smile. He opened the door and bade his unexpected visitors to enter the simple reception room. The inside of the monastery of Saint Rémy, which specialized in the making of wine, always had the faint odor of fermenting grapes.

"Ah, what brings you to us at such an unexpected hour," Father DuBois inquired as he lit another candelabrum to better illuminate the room.

"We were out for a ride, and passing your monastery, I was reminded that I have not made a donation since you converted me a year ago. I thought perhaps it was time I came and paid my due."

Father DuBois smiled broadly. "We are always in need."

René withdrew a small satchel from beneath his cloak. "Here are some gold coins to further your work."

Father DuBois quickly opened the satchel and finding five coins, gasped in appreciation. "It is most generous, most generous. It is touching to think that a *converso,* a former Jew, would be so generous."

Then he turned and looked at Claire. "And you, too, fine lady. Most generous."

René took his wife's arm and turned to leave, but Father DuBois put a restraining hand on his arm. "Wait, wait. I have just had a thought, if you have a moment."

"We do," René said.

"Follow me," the good father requested.

He led them down a long corridor and finally into a common room. "Let me pour you both a glass of our vintage."

He quickly opened a bottle and poured three goblets of wine, one for each of them. The monastery at Saint Rémy specialized in table wine rather than the finer wines made in other regions. It was, nonetheless, a hearty wine with a fine flavor.

"You have a small son, do you not?" Father DuBois asked.

"Michel, he is two. Remember, you baptized him shortly after his birth."

"Ah, yes. A fine, healthy baby. Is he well?"

"Quite," Claire replied. "But of course we would like another. A sister for him, I think."

"And you have had difficulty?"

Clair blushed slightly and nodded.

"Good parents rear good children," Father DuBois proclaimed. "And you are generous to the church. I have a suggestion—perhaps I should call it a proposal. I hope you will not be offended, it's just that when I saw you, I thought, 'Perhaps God has provided me with the best solution.' Please do not accept my proposal if you have any hesitation whatsoever."

"I would not," René assured him.

"Well, this very evening a newborn baby was left on the steps of the monastery. A sweet baby, apparently very healthy. A little girl."

"Oh, may I see her?" Claire asked, her warm eyes gleaming.

"Yes. Please, just wait here a moment."

He scurried away and René smiled at Claire. In a moment Father DuBois returned with a basket. In the basket, wrapped tightly in swaddling clothes, was a beautiful child with a tuft of red-gold hair and unusual green eyes.

"We called her Leona," Father DuBois told them. "Because she appears to have been born on the first of August—Leona for the sign of the lion."

"She's precious," Claire said. She touched the tiny baby's face with her finger.

"She seems to sleep very soundly and be a good baby."

"What is your proposition, Father?"

"We are a monastery full of men. We can hardly raise a female child. Ordinarily we would take her to the sisters in Avignon, who would raise her to be a nun within the nunnery, but I am personally against such practices. I think that believers should come to the church and not be reared by them. If you would adopt her, I know she would have a good home. A natural home, far better than being raised by the sisters. You know, they are the order that wears those large hats." He grinned and whispered, "We call them the Holy Geese."

"Oh, René, please—" Claire said. "I will love her as if she were my own."

"The nuns are so strict," Father DuBois added as he took a large sip of wine. "I should feel much better if you took her."

René leaned over the basket and took the baby's finger as he stared into her eyes. For a moment their eyes locked, and it was then that he knew for certain that this was *the* baby.

"We will adopt her," René agreed.

"I know it is for the best," Father DuBois said, steepling his fingers.

Claire picked up the basket. "We should hurry home before she wakes and wants to be fed."

Father DuBois sighed. "Such a small baby. If you cannot find a wet nurse, may I suggest goat's milk. It is what we gave her and she seems to like it."

René suppressed a smile. The child, once of Byzantium, would naturally prefer goat's milk. "We have a goat in lactation," he said. "No need to worry. She will be well looked after and well loved."

"Then I have done my duty," Father DuBois said with a smile.

1523
Saint Rémy-de-Provence, France

Leona braced herself on the large rock and then pulled herself up the final few feet to the summit of the hill where the ruins of the ancient triumphal arch overlooked the village.

Michel, her twenty-year-old brother, leaned over to give her a hand, "Here, let me help."

"Thank you," she answered. She wore the heavy shoes of the peasants called sabots, a long, crudely woven brown skirt, a white blouse, and a leather vest. Her waist-length red-gold hair was braided in a single thick braid that hung down her back, though wisps of hair escaped and curled around her oval face.

Michel had a squarish face, widely separated dark eyes, a patrician nose, and curly dark facial hair trimmed to form a full beard. His seriousness and intellect made him seem older than his twenty years, though he smiled now as he looked at his adopted sister.

"This is the last time we may ever climb this hill together," he said, looking into her extraordinary eyes. For a moment their eyes locked, and they communicated on another plain. Then she broke away and looked down on the valley.

"Coming here has always been one of my favorite pastimes," she said wistfully as she looked out at the village below. "It's so peaceful here. I shall hate to leave."

"I have to leave as well."

"You're going to Avignon and then to Salamanca! The finest university in all of Europe! How can you be sad?"

"I'm not sad. It's that I hate to leave you behind. You should be going, too."

"Women do not go to university. I am fortunate among women that our father had me tutored with you, that I am literate in Latin, French, and Italian. I am fortunate to have studied science with you . . ." Leona's voice trailed off.

"Life at Avignon will be difficult. The monks are strict. You will have far more enjoyment! You're going to court. From all I hear, the sister of the king is also very learned."

"I might not be accepted," Leona said as she sat down on one of the stones that were a part of the ruin.

"You will be accepted. I feel it."

"I hate leaving here, you, our parents, everything—" Tears filled her eyes, and she ran her hand over the surface of the stone.

"Did we come here to weep?" he asked, bending down to cup her chin in his hand. "Leona, you're beautiful and you're intelligent. You are going to practice medicine, too. Your training is as good as mine."

"But when you leave Avignon and Salamanca, yours will be much superior."

"I shall write you and tell you everything I learn. In that way you can learn from me, and add that knowledge to what you have already been taught."

"I shall still miss you and this place."

"Then visit it in your dreams."

Again Leona passed her hand over the smooth stone of the ruin. From it she felt a strange sensation; it made her fingers tingle. "Sometimes when I come here I feel I can hear the people who were once here. It's as if the stones imprison their voices."

"I, too, have those feelings, those sensations."

"Sometimes I feel I have lived before," she said suddenly. Then she looked directly into his eyes. "And I think you may have lived before as well."

He smiled. "Yes, I have always known it. But you must never speak of such things. It's dangerous."

"It is only lately that I have begun to feel that way," she confessed. "And I remember nothing."

Michel spread out the blanket he had been carrying. Then he sat and put down the basket they had brought. "Are we to eat this lunch we brought, or speak of past lives?"

Leona smiled. "We should eat. I promised Mother I would be home in time to ready myself for the duke who will question me before he recommends me to the king's sister."

Michel laughed. "And who is *he* to question? The man has the mind of a toad."

Leona giggled. "You're unkind."

"No, simply truthful." Michel opened a bottle of wine and watched as his sister took out the bread and cheese. "You must be careful at court," he advised as he looked at her seriously. "It can be a dangerous place."

"Why do I feel we shall do nothing but embroider and read Latin? You—you will have the opportunity to dig into medical texts preserved by the Arabs! Oh, Michel, you are so privileged."

"I shall share my knowledge with you. I promise." Her desire to learn was incredible, he thought, looking into her eyes. She was as smart as he, but he knew their destinies were different. Hers was to fight an old evil; his was to see the future devils of mankind. But he could not tell her that, because she was as yet unaware of herself, of what and who she was. It was not usually so, but in this case he knew she had been born with few memories of her past lives. Still, the communication was beginning. If it were not so, she could not have heard the voices that emanated from the stone ruins or felt that she had in fact lived before.

"You've grown thoughtful again," she said, sipping some of the wine he had poured her.

"We are on the edge, my sister. We are just on the cusp. There is a new world across the ocean; its conquest will change this world forever. I think about it often."

"It's too bad the evils of this small part of the earth must be carried to other parts of the earth," she said thoughtfully.

He tore off some bread and handed it to her. "I think we must hurry. If you are late for your introduction to the duke, our parents will be upset."

Leona nodded. Her father had petitioned the duke to seek his help in placing her at court. He seemed eager for her to go, and kept speaking of her destiny. She herself would have been happy here, but apparently that was not to be. In any case, she would not make her parents unhappy. If this is what they wanted, this was what must be.

"Yes," she said, pulling herself up off the ground, "we must go."

Suddenly she turned to him and hugged him. "Promise me if I ever need you, you will come."

"Will you send a message?"

She looked at him mysteriously and her green eyes flickered. "Will I have to send a message?"

He smiled back at her and knew with certainty that the dreams had begun. Her intuitive powers were increasing daily. "I doubt you will," he replied.

The Duke of Avignon was plump with spindly legs. His legs were made even more scrawny in appearance by the fact that he was fully adorned in the royal fashion of the day, tights from toe to mid-hip and above that his stiff, puffed-out tunic with its billowing sleeves and exaggerated fullness.

Leona could not help but think that only the handsomest of men could sport the day's royal garb. Men built like the unfortunate Duke of Avignon succeeded only in looking like eggs on tiny sticks.

Leona glanced at her mother and was relieved to see that even Claire had a bemused twinkle in her eye.

The egg on tiny sticks bowed deeply from the waist and kissed her mother's hand. Then he turned toward Michel.

"How fortunate you are, my dear Nostradamus!" the good duke burbled. "To have a handsome son who is said to be the most talented young physician in all Provence! And to be going to Avignon and then to Salamanca for further study! You must be very proud."

"I am pleased. It is his accomplishment; therefore, I cannot be proud. It is he who should be proud."

"You always were a most modest and tactful man," the duke said. "And you have not changed since last we met."

"I know you have traveled out of your way to come here, Your Excellency. I do appreciate it. I want to present my daughter, Leona Maria de Nostradamus."

The duke now bent and kissed her hand. It was a furtive kiss, and she doubted it would have been so furtive had not her mother, father, and brother been in the room. The duke had a glint in his eye, the kind every young woman recognizes in spite of her lack of experience.

"She is lovely! And such ravishing hair! My goodness, when you wrote me about your daughter who could read and speak four languages, I did not dream she would be a beauty too!"

Leona's fair skin flushed with embarrassment.

"And modest as well. I cannot think that such a vision of loveliness would not be welcomed at court with open arms."

"Marguerite's arms or some wanton male's?" René asked. "My daughter wants to continue her studies and be a companion to the king's learned sister. She does not want to become a mistress to the king or some other member of the court."

The duke laughed. He was essentially a good and fair man. "With your daughter's academic record, I am sure Marguerite will welcome her. The opportunity to be a companion to the king's sister will no doubt be forthcoming. But I cannot guarantee that the men of the court will not make overtures toward her."

Leona continued to look at the floor, knowing full well that eye contact was not wise at this time. "I am sure I can make my position clear."

"I have every confidence you can," he allowed. Then he turned toward her father. "I have spoken to the good Marguerite myself, and I have given her the documents relating to your daughter's education and experience in the local hospital. I am quite certain you will be hearing from her within the month. And now I shall send her a message saying I have met your daughter and she is all and more than I first described."

"You are most kind. Please, let me offer you and your entourage a meal. I know your journey is long, and who knows how long it will be before you are once again among friends."

"I should be most grateful, René. Most grateful. You are so right. The journey is long, and at the end a war awaits. I might not even return."

"Our prayers will follow you."

"Thank you. I wish this would end. I am not a man who enjoys war. I would not even go except that I have been summoned, as have we all."

"The rivalry between the king of France and the ruler of the Empire is well known," René said.

"So I must fight in Italy," the duke said with a sigh. "Well, I fear the emperor is in a better position than is France. We are not a rich nation, but rumor has it that Charles has wealth from the new world. Gold fills his coffers in Madrid."

René said nothing on the subject, though in essence he agreed. "Come," he said, smiling gently, "our repast awaits."

He led the duke and his entourage out behind his villa. There on the vast expanse of lawn overlooking his fields and a small brook, Claire had asked the servants to erect a long wooden table.

"It looks fit for a king!" the duke said gratefully.

The table had carafes filled with rich red wine, loaves of bread, a variety of hard and soft cheeses, a steaming pot of greens and meat, a huge roast, rare and succulent, and finally, a roast pig, done to perfection.

The duke took his seat. "I hope this is not my last such supper." He inhaled. "I do so love the French countryside."

Leona thought how much she, too, loved it, especially here. She looked at her family, and even though she knew Michel would be gone tomorrow and that his leaving would change everything, a part of her still wanted to stay.

"I think you, too, will miss these hills," the duke said to her.

Leona met his eyes for the first time. "Yes," she answered, unable to take her eyes off his. It was as if she could see into the duke's soul—into his future. What she saw frightened her.

It was death.

It was the end of August when the royal messenger arrived.

Leona had been reading upstairs, but when she looked out the window to see why the dogs barked, she saw the horse and then the messenger in his ornate uniform and shiny black boots. She hurriedly put her books away and went downstairs.

Her father handed her the scroll, and she undid it and read it aloud.

"My dear Leona Maria,

I am most pleased to write you this letter. I have heard a great deal about you from the good Duke of Avignon and I have seen your certificates of accomplishment.

As you may have heard, I am a writer. I do require a companion to edit my work, to talk with, and with whom to learn more. I should be pleased if you would consider coming to court to serve as my companion. We are now

at Lyon and, as I am sure you know, the king is in Italy.
Please come as soon as you can.
> *Gratefully,*
> *Marguerite Angoulême, Duchess of Alençon"*

The trip to Lyon was made by coach. They traveled first to Avignon and then straight up the Rhône valley for some one hundred and forty miles. The journey was both exhilarating and exhausting. It took five days to complete.

Like her home, Lyon had once been a Roman city. But it was far more important. It was located at the junction of the great Rhône River and the Saône. One flowed north and south, the other east and west. Augustus Caesar had made it capital of the Gauls, and by the second century it was a commercial crossroads where traders came from as far away as Asia. All this Leona knew from books, but as soon as she arrived she began to feel more than she could have known.

It was like the day among the ruins with her brother when she had touched the rocky remains of the Roman arch and thought she had heard the voices of the past. As soon as she set her feet down, she felt a connection with a time long gone. And although those around her spoke French, the voices she heard were speaking Latin. The return of the sensation mystified and yet somehow frightened her, as did the growing conviction that she had lived before.

"Welcome, my dear!" Marguerite said, holding out both her hands. She was a small woman with a pretty, triangular face and lively eyes.

"You must rest, I know how arduous such a journey can be!"

"I'm really not tired," Leona insisted. "I would tell you if I were. Really, I have spent five days watching the countryside pass by the window of the coach. I need to move about."

"Then let me show you my library and then your room."

"My chaperone will need to rest," Leona said hesitantly, "as she will be returning tomorrow."

"I shall have the servants see to her needs, you need not worry."

Leona followed Marguerite down the long corridor and finally into an incredible library. There were books everywhere, more books than she had ever seen. Some were printed, others were hand copied, and many were stunning illuminated manuscripts with delicate illustrations trimmed with gold ink.

"Oh, it's wonderful!"

"I thought you'd be impressed. You'll be able to carry on with your own studies as well as help me. I really don't require too much help. I confess, I wanted a companion as much to talk with as to assist me. It is so difficult to find a woman of knowledge."

Leona smiled at Marguerite and thought how much she liked her already. Thirteen years separated them in age, but Marguerite, at thirty-one, was certainly not old. "You flatter me."

"I think not. You are young, but wise beyond your years. You are pretty, but you are also intelligent. We will enjoy each other."

"I know we will, madam."

"Leona, let me assure you I will enjoy having you about even when my husband returns. I am serious about my writing and mine, in any case, is a royal marriage, not a union of love."

Leona was surprised at Marguerite's candor. "I'm sorry," she said, not knowing exactly how to respond.

"Oh, dear me! It's all right." She smiled a little slyly. "It does not mean I don't know what love is."

Leona blushed since this comment was impossible to respond to.

Marguerite turned away and returned to their original discussion. "There are many books, and if you desire something, you must let me know. I may be able to get it, or have it copied."

"There are some medical texts I should like."

"Ah, yes—your interest and training in medicine. I forgot momentarily. It has all been arranged. You can work in the royal clinic each morning. Anyone at court who is ill is taken there. That includes members of the household, the servants, and the guards. There are always a few."

"I am looking forward to it."

"You will like life at court, Leona Maria. I am sure of it. But alas, I must warn you, your first test of endurance, patience, and good-natured tolerance is at hand." Marguerite's eyes twinkled.

"I do not quite understand," Leona answered.

"Nor do I expect you to. It is one Father Jacques Renaud from the Sorbonne, keeper of orthodoxy and propagator of narrowmindedness. He has come to visit, so I suggested he be brought to the library, because I happen to know that books make him very nervous."

Leona could not keep from laughing. She had been told much about Marguerite, but she had not been prepared for her rare humor, nor her rebellious spirit.

"I see you, too, like to laugh, and have a sense of humor about those who believe they speak directly to, and for, God. Well, my dear, prepare yourself. Here, we should sit down. No one should meet Father Renaud standing up."

No sooner were they seated and had made themselves comfortable than a tall, slender man was ushered into the room. He wore black robes, and a long silver chain with a cross.

"Madam." He bowed before Marguerite, who held out her hand.

"How nice to see you once again, Father. Let me introduce my companion, Leona Maria. Leona Maria, this is Father Renaud."

Leona let him kiss her hand as well. As he did so, he looked into her eyes. It was as if her blood ran suddenly cold. His small, dark eyes seemed to pierce her, and she felt a distinct pain in her chest as if stabbed by a knife. She gasped and leaned back as sheer nausea surged through her. Never had she felt so repulsed, so fearful, and so intensely alone.

"My dear, are you all right?" Marguerite was on her feet and leaning over Leona.

"I am—I don't know, something just came over me."

"I shall pray for you," Father Renaud mumbled.

"I knew you should have rested. The journey was more tiring than you thought."

"Perhaps you are right. Perhaps I should lie down."

Marguerite rang for the servant, who momentarily appeared. "Please take Leona Maria to her room." Then she turned back. "I shall come and see you later, my dear. Please, do get some rest."

Leona followed the servant. Why had she reacted so? She had never seen this man before in her life. Yet he caused her great apprehension. She could still hear her heart beating. He also caused her real pain. Her chest ached. His eyes—his eyes contained her worst nightmares.

She hardly looked about the room to which she was shown. She noticed only that her bags had been brought. She flung herself across the bed and closed her eyes, praying for the memory of Father Renaud's eyes to go away.

Back in the library, a servant poured tea for Marguerite and Father Renaud.

"I do hope your new companion is not ill."

"It is just the journey," Marguerite said offhandedly.

"Is she learned?"

"She speaks and reads four languages and has studied medicine."

"Medicine. Really? Sometimes too much knowledge is a bad thing."

"And sometimes it is liberating. Tell me, how may I go about getting medical texts, Father?"

"Oh, that's most difficult. You know, most of them are banned. They show how to desecrate the human body. They contain evil things man should not know."

"Perhaps those who study medicine should know these things."

"They are heretical. They are banned."

"I am the sister of the king. No book is banned to me."

He flushed red. "Of course not," he muttered.

Marguerite smiled. "I will make inquiries of others. Please, have some cake."

Father Renaud looked down at the cake. That woman—that girl who was to be Marguerite's companion was trouble. He had sensed it when he kissed her hand, when he had looked into those eyes, eyes that seemed familiar.

"How old is your new companion?" he suddenly asked.

"Eighteen," Marguerite answered.

"Very young for one so learned," he replied even as his mind did the quick calculation. Yes, she would have been born in 1505, the year in which he had seen the light from the heavens make its bridge to the earth. Was she the one? He narrowed his eyes. This new companion of Marguerite's, who was herself of deep concern to him, would bear watching. Perhaps he would even have to consider something more drastic.

"What brought you to Lyon?" Marguerite asked.

"I was just passing through and thought I should pay my respects."

"I see," Marguerite replied. Usually when he came it was to complain about one of her friends, usually Clement Marot, her own personal poet. Marot had caused those who spoke with and for God considerable consternation. Marot was a reformer, though Renaud called him a heretic. Marot was also on his way to Lyon.

"Are you going directly back to Paris?" Marguerite asked hopefully.

"Yes," Renaud answered. "Indeed, now that I have satisfied myself that you are well, I shall, with your permission, take my leave."

Marguerite smiled. "You have my permission."

Renaud stood. He again kissed her hand. He thanked her and then hurried away while Marguerite watched after him, wondering why he had come in the first place.

Eleven

Philip Antonio de Valor was from the proud Spanish province of Castile. He was the son of a wealthy landowner, a teacher, an adventurer, and on this occasion, the emissary of his emperor, Charles V, known to his loyal Spanish subjects as Carlos.

He was a tall man of six feet four inches with thick dark hair and deep blue eyes. His chest was broad, and his arms and legs well muscled. He was an excellent swordsman, a fine shot, and a man of great honor.

The pink dawn gave off a rosy glow in the east, but overhead dark clouds moved westward, propelled by the cold February winds. Philip surveyed the sky and pressed his lips together. He stood on this fateful morning atop a church that looked out on Pavia, a city under siege by the army of Francis I, the French king.

"What manner of man are you?" Philip said aloud to his unseen opponent. He could not say that the King of France was his enemy, for they had never met. The truth was, circumstances and stubbornness on the part of both rulers had made them opponents. Still, he wondered why this Francis, King of France, persisted. Thousands of the mercenaries hired by France had deserted, having tired of this endless siege. Francis's expected reinforcements from Marseilles had been destroyed, and he knew it. Yet there they were, the French led by their king—practically the whole French nobility, waiting, it seemed, to be either killed or taken captive by a superior army.

This war had been going on for four years now. Philip had hoped the French king would tire of it and go home before this day on which he was certain it would end so decisively.

Pavia was a city surrounded by double walls with a park between the two walls. The city itself was like the Trojan horse of yore—filled with well-seasoned troops under the command of General Antonio de Leyva.

Francis's army was camped in a park that surrounded the inner wall, and the king believed he held Pavia under siege. He did not know that beyond the second wall General Pescara, with his imperial troops, was poised for attack.

Poor Francis. He had to maintain the siege of Pavia and withstand the coming attack of General Pescara, whose troops had already begun to break through the walls of the park with battering rams.

Philip shook his head. The imperial forces were clearly superior. The Spanish arquebusiers—those highly trained men who fought with the arquebus, a heavy matchlock gun fired from a support—could mow down oncoming ground troops with deadly efficiency. There were also many battalions of imperial *Landsknechte*—German infantry troops with considerable experience. There was no way Francis could win this day's battle. It was folly to attempt it. Philip sucked in his breath, thinking he would be glad when the carnage was over.

Realizing it was time to go, Philip climbed down from his perch, bid Pavia good morning, and went to join his troops.

Across the rolling park, as the light increased, Francis and his trusted generals could just make out the first movement of Pescara's advancing troops.

The king gave a hand signal to Galiot de Genouillac, the commander of the French artillery who commenced firing the French guns. They shook the ground beneath both armies.

The first line of Spanish arquebusiers scattered amid screams. In the distance, through his glass, Philip could see the terrible destruction caused by the big guns. That first blast of French cannon was unexpected. Pescara gave the signal and his attacking men withdrew behind a knoll.

Philip moved closer to his men on the wall of the city. He watched carefully through his glass. He could not believe his eyes. The French king was at midpoint of the semicircular battle line. He was signaling his men to follow him, to seize the moment to advance.

At that point Philip swore under his breath. The French king was insane. In his conviction that the first blast of his cannon had won the day, he had led his men forward, placing them directly between his own cannons.

Suddenly noise and confusion erupted. There was no more time for observation. Outside the walls the troops began to move; inside they began to pour out of the gates, thus encircling the French troops. He and his men left the wall and swung to the ground to join the fray. Philip mounted his horse and in moments was through the city gates and out onto the battlefield.

Within twenty minutes Francis's army had been cut into six pieces. Philip guided his horse forward cautiously. The King of France was isolated, his troops in disarray.

Suddenly Philip was set upon by a lone fighter, one of Francis's Swiss troops. He fought his way free of his assailant, whose horse reared and sent the poor man flying to the ground.

Philip threaded his way through the smoke, the terrified horses, and the staggering wounded men. The stench of blood filled the air, the smell of gunpowder was all around them, men shrieked in pain.

Again he saw the King of France. He was on the ground, preparing to fight as a circle of commoners with spears drawn moved in on him. Blood trickled from Francis's hand and from a gash across his face. The gay plumes of the monarch's helmet lay trampled in the dust.

"Victoria! Victoria! Victoria!" German and Spanish filled the air as the emperor's troops realized the battle was over.

One lone French nobleman who had fought against France, and with Bourbon, who had allied himself with the emperor, broke through the troops who threatened the king.

Philip galloped to his side. "Hold! This prisoner must be taken alive!" he shouted.

In a moment General Lannoy galloped up. Francis looked up at him in bewilderment and then silently handed him his sword.

"A fresh horse for the king!" Lannoy ordered.

Philip watched as foot soldiers helped the king onto the new horse.

"They're all dead," Francis said half in a whisper. "It's a horrific sight, this slaughter. It's my fault! All my fault!" Tears welled in the French monarch's eyes and Philip looked at him sadly. He seemed to remember the agony of defeat, the degradation of being taken prisoner. Where this odd feeling came from he did not know, since he had never been defeated in battle, yet sadness and sympathy filled him. He reached over and patted the king's arm. "You will fight another day," he mouthed.

Then silently they rode away, the king and a circle of his elite captors.

Philip was ordered by General Alarcon to ride next to the king. He knew they would only spend one more night in Pavia. Then they would head for Madrid.

Francis turned to him. His eyes were wide, his face pale, and his wounds still oozing blood. "I did not plan for defeat," he said hopelessly. "I have no purse, no valet, not even so much as a comb for my hair."

Philip again patted his arm. Then he withdrew his own purse. "Take these hundred ducats as a loan from me."

Francis stared at him. "I couldn't."

"You must, and you must make use of my own valet. A king does not know how to live without such necessities. Please."

"To whom am I indebted?"

"To Philip Antonio de Valor of Castile."

Francis nodded. "Do you know where we are going?"

"First to the monastery of Saint Paul, then to the fortress of Pizzighettone. Then on to Spain."

Francis nodded dejectedly. "I can tell you are a nobleman, a well-educated noble. I shall not forget you, nor the fact that I owe you a debt."

February 1524
Lyon, France

Leona tossed in her bed restlessly and drew the covers ever closer. Outside, the February wind howled. It was a wind laden with dampness, a wind that penetrated the palace at Lyon as it whistled through the crevices and howled around the turrets.

It was not a good winter, Leona thought. The weather had been unusually harsh, the war in Italy raged on, and France was generally in turmoil.

Leona supposed that she was better off than most and should, therefore, be grateful for life's favors. She enjoyed being at court and she adored Marguerite. They had become the closest of friends and confidantes, and Marguerite tried hard to get her every book she requested. Moreover, in the year she had been there, she had nearly mastered Greek, a language Marguerite was studying and which Leona had learned with surprising ease.

In an attempt to once again fall asleep, Leona closed her eyes and buried herself under the covers. Perhaps her dream would return. It was indeed a pleasant dream of sometime past, of someplace distant, and of some love unknown. The place, as far as she could discern, was only of her dreams, but because it was so vivid, she often wondered if it existed in some other reality.

Unlike France, the place of her dreams was always warm, even warmer than the South of France, which, in many other ways, it resembled. In the land of her dreams there were palms, orange trees, and olive groves. There were great buildings and magnificent statuary, and the walls were not gray and covered with tapestries. Instead, they were made of tiles and multicolored frescoes created by artisans. Her dreams were also full of wonderful aromas, aromas she never experienced elsewhere. There were hillsides of magnificent flowers in both the South of France and in her dreams, and both places had white sand and turquoise sea. But the people of her dream were all swarthy skinned and spoke as strangely as they dressed.

Even as she lay below her blankets a chill passed over her as she recalled her most familiar dream. It was of a man unknown. A large, handsome man with a sculptured face and muscles that rippled beneath his tanned skin. But for as much as the subject of her dream appeared to have the strength of a wrestler, he was intelligent, learned, and honest. In her dreams she was joined with him, struggling in the wild ecstasy of lovemaking. In her dreams he tortured her sweetly, caressing her slowly in her most sensitive areas with his lips, exploring her with knowing hands, slowly arousing her till she clawed at her pillow and awoke breathless, hot, and inflamed, as if she had been taken by him. But he was faceless.

Not all her dreams were of lovemaking nor of the pleasant place in the sun with the tiles and the frescoes. Some of them ended in hideous nightmares when a sinister force would enter her dream, unannounced and unbidden. It was a force that had the face of evil, a face that looked into hers and then rose to enormous shadowy proportions to slay her horribly. From these dreams she sometimes awoke in a cold sweat or screaming. These dreams she dreaded.

Her adoptive father, René de Nostradamus, spoke to her often about her dreams. "You and Michel are both special children. You will dream often, and vividly. You must accept your dreams, and when they are instructional, you must follow them."

But thus far her dreams had not been instructional. Rather, she believed them to be of some past life. Michel was different. His dreams instructed him to study medicine and to read all manner of material. Of late he had been given other instructions and he had written her in detail about his new interest.

René de Nostradamus was a *converso,* a Jew who had converted to Christianity. Michel had now dug deep into his fam-

ily's Jewish origins and though such writings were forbidden
by law, he had uncovered and read sacred commentaries of a
mystical nature.

Painstakingly, he had learned to read Hebrew in order to
translate the documents which were collectively called
Cabala—"tradition." But Cabala was, as he confided to her, an
oral tradition. It was necessary for him to find a "guide," someone who would take him through this mystical veil and thus
avoid the dangers inherent in mystical experiences.

Last summer, during the vacation of the harvest season,
Michel left university for a time, and following the instruction
given him in his dreams, had visited Paris. There, deep in the
heart of a slum, he found an old man who knew the Cabala and
agreed to serve as his guide. Michel learned how much more
there was to Cabala than he had found in his documents. He
learned and memorized the unwritten Torah—that which was
revealed through divine revelation.

His most recent letters reflected his intellectual journey. He
now seemed a far different person from the young man she had
known for so long. She knew that in one short year he had
changed a great deal, and that now behind his dark, brooding
eyes there was a world of wisdom. He told her he had learned
to see the future, to understand the present, and to remember a
past life.

He wrote her a letter in which he said, *I think in another life,
you will do the same. I believe you are one of us, Leona.*

Was she? People, places, and experiences reminded her of a
life she believed she had once lived, and she knew for certain
she would always remember the day when she was studying
Greek and read about Leander.

"Leander, Leandra," she whispered. The name meant something to her. Well, she thought, anything was possible.

She repeated the name now and turned on her side and closed
her eyes. Sleep crept up on her, slowly easing over the edges
of her mind and numbing all thought. She had just fallen into
a deep sleep, when she was awakened by the sound of howling
dogs and servants scurrying down the corridors. She sat up in

bed and listened. There was no doubt about it. Someone was pounding on the great door of the castle.

Leona tossed back her covers and slipped her feet into her shoes. She wrapped her warm robe around her and then, using the embers from the fire, lit her candle. She opened her own door and went out into the hall.

From the far end of the long upper hallway she saw the figure of Marguerite hurrying toward her. "Good news does not come in the middle of the night," she said darkly. Behind Marguerite, her mother, Louise of Savoy followed.

Louise of Savoy was the mother of the king and the regent of France in her son's absence. She was still in her forties, having had her children when she was in her teens and having been widowed when only in her twenties.

Louise was a remarkable and awesome woman, though physically delicate. She had a kind, almost ethereal face and a will of steel. *Destiny* was her favorite word, though everyone who knew her was sure she never counted on destiny alone. As she hurried down the hall this night, she seemed to sense what was in store. The Queen Mother's face was tense and filled with fear.

All three hurried down the winding spiral staircase, and as they did so, the servants who surrounded the two messengers parted.

The message they carried was etched on their faces even though they bore a long parchment scroll detailing everything. Both dropped to their knees as soon as they saw the Queen Mother and Marguerite. They blurted out their terrible news by the light of the flickering candles.

"The French army has been destroyed at Pavia. The nobility is shattered," the youngest said.

"Dear madam," the older of the two addressed Marguerite, "your good husband is in flight."

He turned then to Louise of Savoy. "The king is safe, but he is taken prisoner."

"Prisoner?" Louise said in a near whisper. "Is he hurt?"

"He is well, but he is a prisoner."

"Bonnivet?" Marguerite asked anxiously. He was her friend, some said her lover.

"Dead," the messenger replied.

Marguerite paled and grasped the edge of the table.

Louise pulled herself up, assuming her regal stance. "Please stand up," she requested. "This is not ancient Rome. You shall not be punished because you bring terrible news. There is much we must know."

Leona looked at Louise of Savoy with admiration even though she knew that Louise's ambition had unwittingly helped weave the web that now held her son a prisoner. It was she who had urged Louis XII to break his treaty with Maximilian and wed his daughter, Claude, to her son, Francis, instead of to Charles V, Maximilian's grandson. Unfortunately the spider, Charles V, now ruler of the Holy Roman Empire, would hold his prey until he got what he wanted.

"Are you sure he isn't hurt?" Louise asked, leaning toward them.

"His hand was slightly hurt, but it has healed already, madam."

Louise nodded and drew herself up. Only the messengers, the household staff, Marguerite, and she were there to bear witness to Louise's declaration, but she spoke as if to the emperor himself.

"Francis is alive. He is well. He has his honor. These are the essential facts: life, health, and honor. Now we must see that he is freed. I shall write dispatches to all the crown heads of Europe—we must enlist their help. I will write to Ferdinand in Austria, to Margaret in the Netherlands, to de la Marcks, Cleves, Fuelderlands, and the Wurtembergs. Together they must impress their will on Charles. They must all urge Charles to free Francis."

July 1525

Leona walked in the garden. It was July, the warmest of all months. Spring, the season of hope, had come and gone; now the summer sun shined down, but it did nothing to lift the pall that still enveloped the court.

Louise of Savoy was scornful—she felt betrayed by her own friends and relatives. She had implored them to help Francis and received nothing more than prayers and good wishes in return. One of her royal cousins responded. "Your son's captivity is a trial to test your faith." Another told her that "God had ordained it and you must forebear." Still another wrote: "It is dreadful indeed."

"Charles demands too much," Louise wailed. "Francis will never let him have French land."

Leona agreed that the demands were preposterous. Charles V demanded a third of all France and the renunciation of all French claims in Italy. He also wanted certain troublesome nobles restored to their previous positions of influence and demanded Provence be turned over as well.

"Never, never, never!" Louise shrieked.

Leona listened and Marguerite listened too. "It is a hopeless trap," Marguerite confided. "An insolvable problem."

Leona slowed her walking and stopped reviewing the situation at court as she approached the gazebo, flowers entwined its sides. It was a beautiful summer fantasy. Marguerite was there, sitting quietly with her hands folded in her lap.

"Ah, madam, do I disturb you?"

Marguerite smiled. "Of course not. Not you. I came here to spend some time away from my mother. She is so frustrated—it upsets me to see her this way. She blames herself for errors in judgment, but she cannot admit that blame even to herself. Instead, it eats at her soul and makes her ill." Marguerite shook her head. "We should have sued for peace before this nightmare began."

Leona did not comment. She sat down on the steps below Marguerite. "You have had much to bear," she said softly, sympathetically. Her thoughts traveled back a month in time when Alençon, Marguerite's husband, had returned from the battlefront. She knew full well that Marguerite did not love her husband, but Marguerite confided that they had grown fond of each other and that a certain affection existed between them. "It's more than can be said for many a royal marriage," Marguerite confessed.

Alençon arrived home from the battle and was terribly ill. Shortly after he arrived he had a terrible coughing fit. Blood gushed from his mouth and his whole body shook. He was immediately taken to the royal bedchamber and the physicians were summoned together with a priest. Leona, herself a physician, had been allowed to examine him.

Marguerite was beside herself with grief. She wept and wept as poor Alençon's body seemed to be turning itself inside out. Then he sat straight upward in bed and shouted, "I'm coming! I'm coming!" and he fell back down again, glassy eyes staring at the ceiling. Not even Leona knew exactly what had killed him.

"What are you thinking, Leona?" Marguerite's question interrupted her recollection of that terrible morning.

"Pardon me, madam. I was thinking of your husband's death."

"It is too soon for it to leave our minds," Marguerite replied abstractedly. Then, turning back, she added, "Leona, when he died I made myself a solemn vow. I vowed I would go to Spain and see my brother."

Leona nodded. "I think it would be a good idea."

"My mother will not be entirely happy with this decision. I want you to come with me."

"I shall be happy to do so, madam."

Marguerite smiled and reached out for Leona's hand. "I want you to come not as my official companion, but as my friend. You are one of the few people with whom I can communicate— and virtually the only woman. You're intelligent and perceptive, I trust your instincts. Yes, I want you at my side when I venture into enemy territory to meet Charles and try to obtain my brother's release."

"You honor me."

"You honor yourself. Now, I cannot tell you what to expect from Charles, but I can tell you to be cautious with my brother.

He may be a prisoner, but he is also a charmer. He adores beautiful women, and you are among the most beautiful I have ever seen."

Leona felt her face flush with the compliment. She was not vain, but she was, nonetheless, pleased to hear such praise.

"You're modest," Marguerite said. "I want you to know that I also want you at my side because of your knowledge of medicine. Dr. Rabelais tells me you are very talented."

"He is a friend of my brother's."

"So I am told," Marguerite replied.

"Has Madam selected a date for our departure for Spain?" Leona asked.

"In a fortnight. Yes, I think that will give us enough time. Please travel lightly."

"I shall."

Leona headed back toward the palace. In spite of the reason for their journey, she felt buoyed by the prospect of a trip. And to Spain! Perhaps it would turn out to be the warm, sunny locale of her dreams.

September 1525
Madrid

Madrid's Alcazar Prison overlooked arid land through which flowed the Manzanares River. As far as one could see, the river wound like a snake through barren wasteland.

The morning sun streamed through the windows, and particles of dust played in the rays of light that fell on the floor of Francis's cell. But the King of France lay in his bed, his eyes staring at the distant ceiling, his body hot with fever.

Francis's cell was more than one hundred feet off the ground. The window that looked out on the Manzanares was double-barred with iron rods. The walls of the chamber were thick and whitewashed. It was a narrow room with a narrow bed, the view from the window was monotonous, and the four walls had seemed to be closing in and smothering him. Day and night, as if he were a magician who might somehow squeeze through the bars and take flight, he was guarded by a sullen Spanish officer.

Before he had fallen ill, his guards had taken him into the sheltered courtyard below each day. There he was allowed to ride a mule for less than an hour in the warm sunshine and exercise his stiff limbs.

He wondered why they could not have given him a horse. Was he thought to be so great a horseman that he would jump over the high walls and find freedom?

Now that he was ill, he never left this room. Now he saw only the ceiling with its multitude of cracks.

He had written and written. Why would his captor not come to him? He yearned to confront Charles, to make an honorable peace. Not that he would ever accept Charles's demands. They were too much. He decided he would rather die here, in the prison, fester in the rotten tomb. No, he would not yield and give up any part of France.

Francis clenched the side of his bed with white fingers. Five days earlier he had begun to feel the illness creep over him. His eyesight grew blurred, and his body glowed with an unnatural heat.

These were symptoms he knew. The first abscess had appeared some years before, and while its poisons had raged through his body, he had lain in bed and plotted against the greedy emperor. That abscess had broken, and he had grown strong again and pushed the reality of his infection out of his mind. Now he had fallen victim to it again. He was quite certain he had Spanish disease, and he knew it would return again and again, slowly possessing him, slowly taking his health, his power, and eventually his ability to reason.

Two days ago he had crawled into bed, giving in to his illness far more easily than he would ever give in to Charles.

Philip Antonio de Valor knocked loudly on the thick wooden door and undid the chains on his side.

"Who goes?".the guard answered routinely. In a moment he opened a peephole in the door and stared through.

"Philip de Valor. I've been sent by the emperor."

On the other side of the door the guard lifted the great bolt and the heavy door swung open.

"In the future," he said with annoyance, "I think it unnecessary to lock the door on the inside."

"As you command," the surly guard answered. Then he said with a sneer, "It may not be necessary at all. The King of France looks as if he is dying."

Philip took four strides across the room and was at Francis's side. "How long has he been this way?" he barked.

"Two days—maybe three."

"And you just reported it this morning?"

"Yes, well, he is a prisoner." The guard was hardly five feet four inches tall. His skin was dark and sallow, and his hair was greasy. He had a long mustache and a slightly unkempt beard. In order to keep eye contact with Philip, he had to look up, because Philip was the tallest man he had ever seen. At six feet four inches, he seemed a veritable giant.

"Not just a prisoner!" Philip said, narrowing his eyes. "He is the King of France. What manner of dolt are you?" He did not shout because he did not want to wake the king. So he controlled his voice and kept it low and menacing.

"I didn't mean to do anything wrong."

"He is a king. He needs medical attention. He is a prisoner but he is also a hostage. What good is a dead hostage?"

"I—I—" the guard stuttered.

"Get out of here and on your way. Fetch the court physicians."

"Sí, Señor."

He scurried away like a frightened mouse. For a moment Philip looked after him, then he turned to Francis.

He felt the king's brow and saw the swelling on his head. "Can you hear me?" he asked gently.

"Yes. Please—" Francis struggled to focus his eyes. "I know

you," he gasped. "You're the kind Spanish nobleman to whom I owe money."

Philip half smiled. "Please, don't try to talk."

"I want to speak with Charles. Why won't he come to me?" Francis moved his head slightly and winced with pain. "I must speak with Charles."

"I have sent for the physicians. I shall go for the emperor myself."

"Thank you," Francis muttered.

Philip left immediately. He did not lock the door, but left it open. He hurried down the winding staircase only to encounter the doctors on the way up. He paused briefly to give them instructions, then headed for the royal stables.

"I have need of the fastest horse you have," he told the stable keeper.

Like the guard, he was a small man, but unlike the guard, he was reasonably intelligent. "The fastest horse is an untamed beauty—a pure white steed from the mountains of Andalusia."

"And where is this untamed horse?"

"Come, I will show you. He is in the far corral. But I tell you, he has thrown every rider who has attempted to ride him."

Philip followed the stable keeper. Behind the stables, in a large double-fenced corral, was a beautiful pure white horse.

"Magnificent," Philip breathed.

"Magnificent enough for a nobleman such as yourself, but wild and untamed. This horse must be whipped into shape."

"Never should such an animal be whipped," Philip said, looking at the horse, which had stopped circling and stood stock-still on the far side of the corral.

Philip stared at the animal, which stared back. Déjà vu? A wave of nostalgia flooded over him, then a kind of recognition he could not describe. It was a feeling so strange that for a moment it took his breath away.

"Are you all right?" the stable keeper asked.

"Quite all right," Philip responded. Hardly knowing why, he

whistled through his teeth, and the great white horse came over and stood before them, pawing the ground.

"You must have a way with horses," the stable keeper acknowledged. He shook his head. "That horse has never come to anyone before."

Philip looked directly into the animal's big brown eyes. They flickered with a rare intelligence. It was, he thought, almost as if the horse recognized him or had the same feeling toward him as he had toward the horse.

"Get me a saddle," Philip ordered.

"Oh, I couldn't let you ride him. If he throws you, I would be held responsible."

"He won't throw me."

"Well then, he might well kill you with a swift kick when you try to saddle him. He's never been saddled."

"Then high time he was," Philip said, taking the saddle and slinging it on the side of the fence. Then, in spite of the man's protests, he climbed over, dropping to the ground in front of the horse.

He took the saddle and walked around to the left side of the horse. He threw the saddle across the animal, and it pawed the ground.

"Watch out!" the stable keeper warned. But the horse did not kick and Philip tightened the saddle cinch around the horse's girth, slipped the bridle over his head, and gently slid the bit into his mouth. Then he moved to the side of the horse and stroked its long nose. "What shall I call you?"

Then, just out of sight of the stable keeper, he moved to the horse's head and whispered in its ear, "Pegasus? Yes, it is the only name for you."

Oddly, the horse whinnied and nodded its head.

Pegasus—why had he said it? Why had this of all names popped into his head? Stranger yet, why had the horse responded so?

Philip felt a chill, a kind of anticipation. He climbed onto the horse and patted its side. The horse, as if trained by an expert, cantered around the corral.

"I don't believe it!" the stable keeper cried out. "He nearly killed a man yesterday! I don't believe it. He lets you ride him as if he had been ridden forever."

Philip grinned. "I shall take this horse," he said, leaning over to once again stroke it. "And I shall call him Pegasus."

Charles V was hunting near Segovia when Philip caught up with him.

"Ah, you've decided to join me after all," Charles called out.

Philip bowed his head. "My Emperor, I'm sorry. I do not come to join you, but rather I come with news of importance."

Charles V was tall, gaunt, and sharp-featured. His dark eyes looked into those of Philip de Valor.

"The King of France is very ill. He appears to be dying. I summoned the physicians and came directly here."

Charles nodded, though his lips were pressed together.

Charles was not an emperor who lolled about enjoying excesses. He was a stoic man. Self-denial was his code, discipline his motto, the ability to make a quick decision his trademark. He always dressed in black and wore only a single gold pendant with one jewel. "He begs to see you," Philip said.

"Will my visit keep him from dying?"

"If it gives him hope."

Charles frowned ever so slightly. "Then I will go to my brother, the King of France. I cannot allow my most important hostage to die."

October 1525

"Are you looking forward to Madrid?" Marguerite asked.

Leona looked out the window of the coach. "I love to travel. Yes, it's a wonderful opportunity, I'm only sorry your world is so saddened and that this is a journey of necessity rather than of pleasure."

"I'm not sure what I hope to accomplish," Marguerite confided. "Mother has gone to Austria. Somehow I think she will work something out. My mother is a resourceful woman."

"So are you."

"Ah, not as resourceful as you, I suspect."

"Well, as we speak of travel, would you have chosen to visit Madrid?" Marguerite asked as she returned to their former topic of conversation, clearly wanting to distract herself from what she might find when they arrived.

Leona shook her head. "It would not be my first choice. I suppose I still associate it too much with the excesses of the Inquisition."

"Torquemada has been dead for over twenty-five years," Marguerite murmured. "But his evil deeds and tales of terrible torture live on. I fear an inquisition in France. I am afraid for our future. Tell me how you feel about it."

Leona looked directly into Marguerite's eyes. It was not a question Marguerite would have asked had they not been alone. It was in fact a dangerous question, and an honest answer on her part could be even more dangerous. "I hope this is not blasphemy, or heresy either, madam, but I believe the Inquisition to be cruel and filled with man's prejudice rather than God's wishes. I fear it is an act of men who seek control rather than a testament of faith. It is not about God, but about power."

"You speak honestly and I know how hard that must be. It is not an institution that has created trust among us. Yet I must confess I feel as you do."

"It has created quite the opposite of trust," Leona said firmly.

"I believe in God," Marguerite said slowly, "but I also believe our Church is in great need of reform. I will not allow these men, who call themselves Guardians of the Faith, to still the voices of writers, men like Rabelais and Clement Marot. And for as much as I consider the man an intolerable bother, I must protect Calvin as well."

"You are right, madam. Ideas must be protected. The enemies of tolerance are formidable. In the years to come, you must be steadfast if you are to help these men and others like them."

Marguerite smiled. "Then I really cannot marry Charles V."

Leona's brows lifted in sheer surprise. "Were you thinking of doing so?"

Marguerite laughed gently. "Not I. But then, I might have little to say in the matter. As I told you, my mother has gone to Austria. She will seek a way out of this dilemma by royal marriage. She will want me to marry someone of great import, someone who can help France out of this dreary situation. Of course, she might want Francis to marry the infant daughter of the English king. That would make Henry our ally and not our enemy."

"Madam, I have a vision of you marrying only for love. You married Alençon out of duty. Now he is dead and you should be free to marry for love."

Marguerite fingered her black dress. "Are any of us really free?" she asked, looking out the window of the carriage into the distance, and toward Madrid. "No, I will marry whom I must to save France."

The air in the chamber of Alcazar Prison was hot, stifling, and laden with the putrid odor of infection. Candles lit Francis's sallow complexion as he lay upon the bed, his eyes closed with fever, the sheets soaked with salty perspiration from his once-robust body.

"What is it?" Charles said, looking into the eyes of his own chief physician.

"An abscess, sire. It is near the brain. It is no doubt caused by French disease."

Charles made a throaty, guttural sound. Only a fun-loving and totally irresponsible king would die from French disease. Acquiring it showed he had no discipline whatsoever. He congratulated himself. He seldom bedded any woman who was not a virgin, and all the women he took to his royal bedchamber were first pronounced clean, having been examined by his physicians. Francis was a tavern creeper; he was much too careless for a king. Charles leaned over slightly and looked into the eyes of his oblivious captive. "My brother," he said, shaking Francis slightly.

Francis blinked up at him. "You have come," he whispered.

"Yes, I have come." Charles squeezed Francis's hand.

"I will always be your slave," Francis mumbled.

"I do not consider you a slave," Charles answered.

Francis pressed his cracked lips together. His mouth was dry too, and he felt he might choke on the scratchy feeling that threatened to cut off his breath. The image of Charles swayed before him. He was unsure as to whether Charles was real or just a figment of his imagination.

"Am I dreaming?" Francis rasped.

Again Charles squeezed his hand. "I am real. I am not a dream."

Francis extended a furry tongue and licked his lips. "Water," he begged. "Just a little water."

Charles poured some water and held the cup to Francis's lips. "Drink, my brother, drink."

Francis slurped the water. "I beg you to be kind to my children."

"I would not be otherwise," Charles said.

"I'm dying," Francis muttered.

"You will not die. I have sent for the finest physicians of my realm. I will not allow you to die."

"I want peace," Francis said. "If I live to negotiate, I want no intermediaries between us," he gasped. Oh, the light did seem to be strange, he thought. Charles's black cloak seemed to merge with the tapestry of the fleurs-de-lis that covered the wall behind the emperor. His sharp face moved this way and that. It faded and then reappeared. The room was dancing, and he felt nauseated. Then, quite suddenly, his eyes closed and he fell back upon his pillow as darkness closed in all around him.

"Is he dead?" Charles asked, leaning over.

The elder physician shook his head. "He appears to be in a coma."

Charles stood up and backed out of the room, followed by Philip, who had remained quietly by the door.

"If he dies, I'll lose everything I won at Pavia," Charles muttered. "I know his mother, she is unyielding. She would wage war till every soldier in France was dead. Louise of Savoy is unforgiving. The woman nearly killed herself, seeing that he became king. I have no money for the kind of war Louise will wage if Francis dies."

Philip said nothing. He knew it was his duty to listen while Charles worked through problems. He often talked aloud, but in truth, Charles expected no answers.

They reached the bottom of the winding prison stairs just as two women were being ushered in. One was dressed in a rich black gown and appeared to be in mourning. The other wore a plain russet gown. The one in russet was young, and beneath her veil he could see she had long golden-red hair. Her skin was fair and her eyes were the most penetrating green he had ever seen. He felt something strong when he looked at her. He felt drawn to her as he had felt drawn to the elegant white horse.

"Lady Marguerite!" Philip heard his emperor say.

"Charles." Marguerite bowed, and so did his vision. As she curtsied, he could see her ample cleavage beneath her bodice. She was exquisite! Mentally he undressed her and felt himself grow excited at the very thought.

"This is my companion, Leona."

"My pleasure." Charles kissed her hand. "This is Philip de Valor, one of my most valued nobles."

Philip kissed Marguerite's hand, then Leona's. His heart beat wildly and he felt like a child again, tongue-tied and overwhelmed by the emotions that suddenly roared within him.

"I have come to see my brother," Marguerite said softly.

"Oh, please go to him. He is very ill and needs you. I have sent for all the best doctors."

"Leona is very knowledgeable in all medical matters."

"I have sent for physicians."

"I shall let Leona examine him."

Philip could not take his eyes off this exquisite woman. He felt jealous of Francis, who would be examined by her. He imagined her white hands moving over Francis's flesh and he felt another wave of envy. She was incredible. Her lips were full, her eyes like great green pools, her skin pale, soft, and appealing. Her figure was magnificent. She was a rhapsody of curves and angles. She even seemed to wear some kind of wonderful perfume. It was intoxicating and it momentarily blocked out the ordinary prison smells.

"Come," Marguerite said.

"You will join us later for supper?" Charles asked.

Marguerite turned to him. "Yes, if you wish."

Leona forced herself to turn. She followed Marguerite up the winding staircase. Why did she feel as she did? What was happening to her?

Months earlier she had met Father Jacques Renaud and actually felt the pain of a knife when he had looked into her eyes. Now she felt something else. She had wanted to reach out to this Philip! What was she thinking of? The man she had just met looked at her so boldly. He was strong and handsome. But he was the enemy!

Leona moved around the bed, examining Francis, while two of Charles's court physicians looked on suspiciously.

Meanwhile Marguerite took a seat by the bed near her brother. "Tell the emperor I shall require a bed be brought here for me," she requested. "And a more comfortable chair as well. I shall not leave my brother's side until he either dies or recovers."

Leona looked at the learned doctors and saw the distress in their eyes. They were plainly angry, and a voice inside her warned her to appease them.

"I believe he has an abscess near his brain," she said softly. "I am sure this is also your diagnosis."

They looked at each other, and then at her. "Yes," one of them finally said.

"When it bursts it will kill him," the other said matter-of-factly.

Leona said nothing. Near the brain was not *in* the brain. The abscess had just as good a chance of breaking outside the critical area. "I believe there could be some hope," she said cautiously.

"I will do as I am sure you would advise. We will use warm poultices near where the swelling appears. Perhaps the poison can in this way be drawn forward."

Again they looked at each other. Clearly they had intended doing nothing of the sort, but now it seemed like rather a good idea in the absence of any others.

"Yes, I was about to recommend that," the taller of the two said authoritatively.

Leona smiled. "You are such learned gentlemen. I knew you would have already thought of it."

They both smiled. "But the poultices must be very hot," one of them stressed.

Leona smiled and bowed ever so slightly as the doctors left.

Marguerite looked up at her, and as worried as she was about her brother, she smiled warmly at her friend. "I shall keep you in mind when diplomacy is needed," she said.

"It is unwise to ruffle the feathers of a dangerous bird," Leona replied. And she knew it was true. Somewhere she harbored a great suspicion of male physicians, but she did not know why.

Twelve

November 1525

René de Nostradamus walked through the cobbled streets of Saint Rémy. A warm fall breeze swept across the winding river and through the trees, passing through the houses of the villagers and picking up the smell of freshly baked bread.

He came to the village inn and found the temptation of the mouth-watering aromas far too great to resist. He went in and sat down. Térèse, who worked as a tavern maid by night, approached him.

"Refreshment?" she inquired.

"Some fresh bread and old cheese," he requested. "And a glass of red wine."

Térèse bowed slightly and went directly to the kitchen. René smiled at her as she bustled away. In a few minutes she returned with a wooden tray bearing his order. He gave her a few coins and proceeded to eat. It was a lovely day, the wine was tasty, and the bread and cheese just right.

He had risen early and decided to go for a long walk in order to clear his head. The night had brought him unusual dreams, the kind of dreams he had not had for many years. The subject of his dreams had been his children, Leona and Michel.

He thought first of Leona. Leona had grown into a beautiful and talented woman. She was where she had to be, by the side of Marguerite, the king's sister. She was in Spain now, and he prayed she would be safe from the forces that would try to stop her. He pressed his lips together and pictured the face of the man who kept appearing to him—a man with a sharp, pointed beard, small, dark eyes, and closely cut dark hair. René was unclear why he was a danger to Leona, he knew only that he was. He sipped some of his wine and decided to write a letter to her expressing his apprehensions.

René then leaned back and withdrew a wrinkled parchment from his pocket. It was a letter from Michel.

> *I have had strange visions, Father. The past and the future dance before my eyes like an endless panorama. Something new has come into my life, something so compelling, I cannot tear myself away from its mysteries. It arises from my study of the Cabala. I have made the mystic cubes using the divine emanations and the twenty-two letters of the Hebrew alphabet. When I let these cubes fall as they will, past, present, and future are revealed to me. It is as if I have opened a window on time.*

René refolded the letter that had already traveled far. His son had discovered himself and his destiny. He would accomplish much. He had found the code that would open the door to the beyond.

November 1525
Madrid

Leona walked across the open field toward the gate that led into the palace. It was not a long walk, and although she could have ridden, she enjoyed the exercise.

"My lady! You walk too swiftly."

She turned to see the tall, dark noble to whom she had been introduced on arrival, Philip Antonio de Valor.

"I did not know you were trying to catch up," she answered crisply.

"Clearly it is not your pace I complain about. My legs are

long and capable of lengthy strides. It's simply that you should walk more slowly on such a lovely day, my lady. Such days are to be savored and enjoyed."

"Such enjoyment is for those with time. I must spend most of my time at the king's side. When I am able to leave, I have to write letters and fulfill other obligations."

"You are a dedicated woman, far too dedicated for one so beautiful."

His eyes danced merrily and she sensed he was not just flirting with her, but also making fun of her seriousness. "I fail to see what beauty has to do with dedication."

"You are simply too young and far too lovely to be dedicating yourself to a lost cause."

"What lost cause is that?"

"Your king will die. He has been in a coma for fourteen days now."

"As long as my king lives, there is hope for him."

"But certainly not for his kingdom. The emperor Carlos will rule France."

"I think not," Leona retorted in annoyance.

He fell into step with her and she wished she had ridden, for then she could have galloped off and left him. He seemed doubly arrogant to her, conceited in himself and puffed up because his country had won a victory in battle.

"No matter how sick he is, or how sick he becomes, Francis will not be released until he meets the demands set out by the emperor."

"Francis will not give in. You'll see. A peace will be arranged."

"I do know a way," Philip said, taking her arm and leaning closer. His voice was low now, almost conspiratorial.

Leona shook off his arm. "Are you a confidante of the emperor?"

"Perhaps. Were I you, I would be curious to know what other possibilities exist."

"Why aren't you discussing this with Lady Marguerite? She is the king's sister and the daughter of the regent."

"Her mind is too preoccupied."

"Very well, tell me what other ways there might be."

"Charles might release Francis if his children were sent in his place."

"To be reared in a prison! To spend their lives in a tower! My God, I am quite certain he would rather die in prison than send his small sons."

"You react as a woman, and far too quickly—they would not be reared in the prison or in a tower. They would live at court and be well treated."

"I *am* a woman," Leona said tersely. "Frankly, I doubt you are in a position to guarantee their treatment."

"I can," he insisted. They had stopped walking now, and he stood in front of her, looking down into her face. He grinned. "Yes, you are a woman," he said, his mouth twisting in a teasing kind of smile.

Leona had no time to move away, no time to resist. His well-muscled arm encircled her tiny waist and pulled her against his chest. His lips roughly sought hers, moving against them.

"Yes, quite a woman," he said, breathing into her ear.

Leona pushed him away with all her strength. "Let me go!" she shouted. "I am not some tavern maid!"

He stepped back and looked at her. "Are you going to tell me you didn't want me to kiss you?"

"Yes! Stay away from me! The very idea of taking the little princes! It's barbaric and you are a barbarian!"

She whirled around and marched off, her thoughts full of what he had said. She felt so confused, she didn't know how far she had gone before she turned quickly to see if he followed. But he did not. He had disappeared, perhaps to go back to the prison, perhaps to take some shortcut of which she did not know.

She stared ahead, trying to think what she should do. No matter how distasteful his suggestion, she would have to tell Marguerite what this young nobleman had told her. Still, Marguerite had so many things on her mind. She was simply too worried about Francis to be told now, and so Leona decided to tell her at a later date.

* * *

A cool breeze blew across the plain, rustling the shrubbery, awakening the birds. In the dark sky, a thin line of light appeared in the east. It was the first of the sun's rays on the far horizon.

Leona tossed on her back and then opened her eyes. Enough light penetrated her room that she could make out the massive Spanish furniture filling it. She shook her head, trying to recall her dream, which was unusual and far different from those dreams she usually had.

Every other night she slept in this room and Marguerite slept in her brother's chamber in the tower. Then they switched and she slept in Francis's room and Marguerite slept here. In this way one of them was with Francis at all times.

Usually Leona slept until the sun was high in the sky. But not so this morning. She had gotten out of bed to follow the instructions she had been given in her dream. They were detailed in nature.

She hurriedly dressed, took those items she felt she would need, and made her way down the staircase, through the dark, silent corridors and out of the palace by way of the kitchen door.

She hurried across the wet grass toward the stables. She knew where to go and what she would find. She knew how to use what she would find—but what if it didn't work? What if it made the king worse? She decided then and there to administer secretly this "medicine" to which she was being led. "Follow your dreams," her adopted father always told her. "When they are instructional, you must do as you are told."

She silently passed a sleeping stable hand and entered the stables. She moved from stall to stall, till at last she stood before a huge white steed whose soft eyes seemed to blink at her in recognition.

She hesitated for only a moment before she opened the stall and stepped inside. The horse bent his head and nuzzled her, and she smiled and stroked him gently. "You're mine, aren't you?" The great horse nodded and again nuzzled her.

"I am to ride you now. You are to take me to a quiet stream where a special kind of moss grows."

She looked about helplessly and then spied a stool. She climbed up on it and then onto the side of the stall. The horse seemed to know what she wanted and came to her. She climbed onto him, her long skirts riding up. "Please be gentle with me," she whispered. "I do not know how to saddle you, and I do not know how to ride."

She held on to the horse's mane, and the horse moved quietly, slowly, out of the stable. Once outside, the horse moved more quickly, but sensing his rider's ill ease, he made no attempt to trot or run like the wind. Nonetheless, Leona clung to him.

They moved into a grove of trees and down a hill. The horse followed a well-trod path. As they progressed, Leona felt more and more secure on the horse's back, and the stunning animal sensed her growing confidence and moved more quickly.

They left the path and followed a narrower one till finally, just as the sun came up, they stopped by a stream.

Leona guided him to a tree and climbed off onto a low branch from which she swung to the ground.

She moved around quickly till she found the moss-covered tree. She scraped the moss with a tiny knife she had brought with her into a glass vial. She could cork and carry the vial in a special knotted bit of leather around her neck when she rode. It was all as it had been in her dream. For a moment Leona stared at the contents of the vial. It was somewhat slimy, and as she looked at it, she felt she had done this before in another time and another place. She shook her head as if to dispel her thoughts.

Leona secured the vial and was about to climb the tree in order to remount the horse, when she heard the distinct sound of another rider approaching. She looked up wide-eyed as Philip de Valor burst into the grove, his sword drawn. From the look on his face he was as surprised to see her as she was to see him.

"Are you a horse thief as well as a doctor?" he asked.

His face was a mask, and she could not tell if he spoke in humor or if he did indeed believe she had stolen the horse.

"I am a doctor and I borrowed this horse from the royal stables. Is that a crime?"

"It is *my* horse," he said abruptly. "But I am shocked. He has never allowed anyone but me to ride him. You must be an excellent rider."

"I have never ridden before. He was most gentle with me."

"I am glad to hear it even though I feel you should have sought my permission. And you should have saddled him properly. Ladies do not ride as you did."

"It was an emergency," she said truthfully. "I had need of medicine."

"Herbs and incantations, my lady? What kind of doctoring is this? Some would call it witchcraft."

"Those 'some' would be ignorant and ill-informed. Now I must get back. I have work to do."

He smiled and dismounted. Then he took the bridle off the dark horse he had ridden and secured the stirrups. He then slapped the animal on the rump and sent him home. He bridled the white horse and mounted him.

Leona watched disbelievingly. "You're going to leave me here?"

He laughed and bent down. "No, my lady. I wouldn't dream of leaving you in such a dilemma." With that he swooped her up in such a way that she was forced to part her legs and sit in front of him. His arms went around her to take the reins and he clicked his teeth. The great white horse began to move, this time trotting at a good pace.

Leona felt both afraid and exhilarated. His arms were strong and warm and held her tightly. She was close to him, to his broad, strong chest. But she would not let him know. She kept her face impassive and her body rigid and tense.

"I cannot believe he let you ride him," Philip kept saying. "Pegasus is not fond of strangers."

"Pegasus?" The name was so familiar to her that it sent a chill through her. Suddenly she had vision of a star-studded night and the white horse beneath her. She suddenly felt she had traveled to the distant galaxies on this magnificent animal. Just as suddenly, she felt mystified. Where had such an idea come from?

It was the morning of the twenty-fourth day that Francis had lain comatose. Leona had carefully mixed, prepared, and administered her medicine yesterday, before Marguerite returned to take up her watch.

"Good morning, madam," Leona whispered.

"Is he no better?" Marguerite asked.

"I have hopes, madam."

"You should go now, you need fresh air and sunshine."

"I'll be fine, madam. I should like to stay awhile. He has been restless and I sense his condition may be changing."

Marguerite collapsed into the chair. "Twice in two years have I sat by after death's visit. I did penance for dear little Queen Claude and then for Alençon—now this. I do not want Francis to die, he must not die."

Leona put her hand on Marguerite's shoulder. Little Claude, Francis's wife, had died before she had come to the palace to join Marguerite. She was the mother of royal children. She had died in childbirth, an all too common occurrence.

The door to the chamber opened and two of the court physicians entered.

"Has nothing changed?" the elder of the two asked.

Leona was about to answer when Francis let out a loud groan from the bed, startling them all and drawing their attention to him.

Blood suddenly gushed from his nose, and with it came an outpouring of greenish-yellow pus followed by a hideous, tangled snakelike core of poison. For a few seconds it flowed as if it would never stop—it was a fetid, congealed mass that gave off an odor of rot and filled the entire room with a new and more horrid stench.

Marguerite's skin was the color of snow. She sat rigid and

suddenly she retched violently even as tears ran down her face. "He's dying! He's dying! Oh, dear heaven, he's dying!"

"No!" Leona said, seizing Marguerite's slim shoulders. "No, he lives! The abscess has broken outside the brain. He will recover."

"It's a miracle," one of the physicians muttered. "We must make notes in our journals." They both quickly left. Leona suspected they left to escape the horrible smell and the need to clean the patient rather than to make notes.

Marguerite fairly collapsed in her arms, sobbing with relief.

"Please go, madam. I will send for hot water and clean linens. I must make your brother comfortable. He will regain consciousness soon."

Avignon, once home to popes, had the stoic atmosphere of a monastery. Its rooms were narrow cells with only a bed, a writing table, a lamp, and a crucifix. Michel counted himself fortunate. His small cell was one of the few to have a window, and thanks to his father, he had a fine tapestry to hang on one wall. It added color and indeed helped keep out winter's dampness. But it was not winter now. It was summer, and he felt grateful for the thick stone walls that made it cool inside.

He came into his cell and bolted the door behind him. Then he lifted the corner of his mattress and withdrew the mystic cubes.

He laid them out and said a prayer in Ladino, now a forbidden language. It was the language of the Sephardic Jews massacred in Valencia in 1391. Those who were not killed fled Spain for other cities, creating a new diaspora of Sephardic Jews whose recent settlements ringed the Mediterranean from North Africa to Salonika. A few, like the family of his father, had converted. Yet for even those who converted, the remnants of their faith persevered quietly, carefully, secretly passed from generation to generation. He knew what this Ladino prayer meant to him. He knew he would take all the knowledge he could from this wonderful place, but he also knew he would follow the mystic Jewish teachings of the Cabala.

When Michel finished his prayer, he let the cubes slip from his hands and fall onto his writing desk. He studied them intently, reading their message.

It was a strange message about Leona.

It told him that a mortal had been given immortality because he once helped an immortal—but his gift of immortality was conditional upon his deeds in this lifetime.

That was the substance of the message he read from his cubes. Was he to do something about this? Was he to tell her? No, that did not seem evident. Perhaps he was simply to know so that he could reassure her at some time. Yes, that seemed right.

Perhaps, he would be given further information later—either by way of the mystic cubes or while he slept.

Again he prayed, and again he cast the cubes.

This time the message was troubling. The king would send his sons to Spain. Intolerance would rise in France and there would be more corruption in the Church.

He stared at the cubes and thought he should write to Leona. She would not like this forecast for the little princes, but she had to know.

Philip slipped from Pegasus with Leona, whom he had held close. The grass all around them was soft and fresh, the nearby stream bubbled with cold, clear water and the flowers had an intoxicating aroma, a heady odor that seemed to drug the senses, heightening rather than diminishing touch, smell, sight, and sound.

Leona was dressed in yards of diaphanous light green veils. Her ravishing red-gold hair fell to her buttocks, like a wealth of tumbling rose gold. Her green eyes were glazed with adoration, hot with desire, gentle yet mocking.

He held her and felt her curves with his hands. He cupped her rounded buttocks in his hands, kissed her neck, her hair, her eyelids. She responded, rubbing against him, kissing him back, moving her small hands across his bare chest and through his dark hair.

Then he folded back her veils and revealed her perfect white breasts, their pink, rosy tips already hard, excited by the promise of his mouth.

He reached out and covered her nipple, sucking on it till she moaned in his arms and pushed herself against him. It was torture to feel her wriggle so against him, to know the warm, moist depths of her secret places awaited him.

He moved his lips downward even as he lowered her to the soft velvet grass, where the dew sparkled like diamonds next to her white skin. An expanse of her shapely thigh was revealed as she lifted one leg and wrapped it around him, holding him to her, teasing him with her nearness, her furtive touches, her quick, darting kisses.

Then he slowly removed another veil, revealing more of her white skin. His fingers caressed one breast, his lips the other as she writhed now, begging him to come to her.

He slid down her body till his lips and tongue could caress her intimately, seeking the folds of that hidden rose, kissing the rose as she groaned in delight and twisted in passion.

She was damp with readiness, her breath came in short pants, her skin glowed with excitement, and he parted her lovely long white legs to enter her, to ravish her with all of him.

And then Philip's eyes opened to the darkness of his room. He wiped the perspiration off his brow and sat up, still shaking with the reality of his imagined possession.

He looked down. His own member was full and still throbbed with excitement. He fell back against the pillows and stared up at the ceiling. Many such dreams had come to him, but in the past they were shadowy and without substance. This dream had substance, and for the first time, the woman of his dreams had a face. Leona was real! At that moment he knew he loved her and perhaps had loved her before. In her eyes there was familiarity—and then there was Pegasus. He knew

him, too. Philip was certain of it. Philip shook with his own
revelation.

January 1526

Charles V sat at the head of a long table in the dining hall.

Marguerite looked around and felt depressed by her surroundings. This was a stoic palace compared with a palace or
château in France. Lyon was wonderful, Fontainebleau magnificent—each had exquisite decoration, art, paintings, and tapestries of great value. The main salons had carpets, and at a royal
dinner there was always a white cloth, fine silver, the best china.
Flowers graced every table, strolling players filled the rooms
with music.

But not so here in Madrid. In spite of all the wealth of Mexico, in spite of a treasury filled with gold, in spite of treasures
so valuable they could not be assessed, the palace was furnished
badly, the tables set poorly, the walls bare except for heavy
crosses and religious paintings.

This room, the main dining salon, was certainly a case in
point. The massive table was dark, as was the great credenza.
The serving dishes were pottery, the plates and silver were utterly plain. One great tapestry hung on the far wall behind the
head of the table, but its colors were dull.

Marguerite could not understand it. All the churches in Spain
were ornate while French churches were stoic, at least compared
with those in Spain. Here it was the palace that echoed denial,
self-discipline, all the traits for which the current emperor was
best known. Here the churches were overburdened with gold.

Tonight Charles wore his traditional black garb. It was
adorned only with a single heavy chain and a silver cross. His
nobles were also attired conservatively, though none as conservatively as he. The ladies of the court also seemed to have a
love of black, though they wore lace and some wore roses and
other flowers.

Marguerite sat on Charles's right while Leona sat next to her
and across from Philip de Valor. It was not where she would

have chosen to sit, but she had no say in the matter. Marguerite wore black because she was still in mourning for her husband. But Leona wore a pale green gown, which caused her to stand out among the others who dressed with such austerity.

The servants passed among the diners, silently filling the wine goblets. Chicken had been the fare that evening and it was succulent in a sauce made with white wine.

"Your brother seems quite well now, madam."

"He is gaining strength each day," Marguerite replied. Her conversations with Charles were few, but she always felt as if she were playing a game of cat and mouse.

"Then I feel it is time for you to return to France?"

"I have been thinking that myself," Marguerite said, looking into his dark eyes. It was quite impossible to know what he was thinking, though she was sure he would be glad to get rid of her.

"Your mother is a most active woman. I believe she has visited most of the crown heads of Europe trying to come upon an acceptable compromise."

"France wants peace and we want our king returned."

"I have made my demands, dear lady. Your brother chooses to ignore them."

"He cannot accept them."

"There is one other possibility," he said, leaning toward her.

Marguerite steeled herself. A few days ago, Leona had told her what such a proposition might be.

"I might consider taking the eldest boys in his place. Of course, they will be reared at court."

"It is too cruel."

Charles's eyes narrowed. "Their mother—the woman who ought to have been my queen—is dead. It's not as if they would be ripped from Claude's arms."

His sudden display of bitterness stabbed at Marguerite. "Yes, their mother is dead and they need the security of home and family," she murmured, wanting to avoid his deep-seated anger.

"It is, nonetheless, my last offer. Of course, I might be persuaded to throw in a small bonus. Something for Francis that would soothe your conniving mother."

"You must speak clearly. I do not like these games."

"Bourbon is loyal to me but a traitor to France. He is engaged to my sister, Eleanor. I might consider giving Eleanor to Francis instead."

"Thus betraying him as he has betrayed France," Marguerite concluded. This small bonus frightened her. It was possible that Francis might see in this offer the opportunity to salvage a sliver of his own honor. He hated Bourbon and he would like to get even. But she did not say anything except "The price of the children is too high. I feel my brother would never give in to this."

"Nonetheless, dear lady, I am sending Philip home with you. Should your brother decide to acquiesce into my demands, then Philip will escort the children back to Madrid."

"It is unnecessary," Marguerite snapped.

"No, it is very necessary. Besides, you will need an escort to return home safely."

"We came with only a small guard; we can return the same way."

"Madam, this is my kingdom. You shall leave it in the manner I prescribe."

Leona could feel Marguerite bristle at this suggestion. Indeed, Marguerite bristled at her whole conversation with the self-possessed Charles. She was an intelligent woman and he treated her as he might treat an illiterate, empty-headed lady of the court. But Marguerite was wise. She hid her reactions behind an impassive expression and maintained a direct attitude. She buried her hostilities for the sake of her brother.

"Will your 'escorts' be ready to leave day after tomorrow?" she asked pointedly.

Charles smiled and lifted his glass. "They will leave at any time you find suitable."

Marguerite put her napkin in her lap and looked at Leona. "You must try the sauce, my dear. It is quite tart."

Leona looked at Marguerite and thought what admiration she

had for this woman. She could so easily have been angry and
raged at the emperor. No doubt he hoped she would lose her
regal bearing so he could laugh about the spoiled, overeducated,
and emotional women of the French court. No, it made him more
sullen to realize that Marguerite, like her mother, Louise of Savoy, was stronger than most men of the realm. They were strong
enough to be taunted and survive with their dignity in tact.

"I shall enjoy seeing Paris," Philip said, drawing Leona's attention away from Marguerite. "Or will you go to another palace?"

"Lyon," Marguerite replied. "We will return to Lyon."

"Then I shall look forward to Lyon."

Leona could not even look at him. They were going to be
together for weeks now! How could she avoid him? Would he
persist in his flirtation with her? She felt trapped.

She looked down at the table and studied the grains in the
fine wood. It seemed as if fate were throwing them together.
She took a deep breath. If only he weren't Spanish! If only he
didn't do the bidding of Charles, whose dark personality exuded
a harshness she felt dimmed the spirit. The man had no com-
passion. How could he? He wanted the young princes to be
taken to Spain and raised by Charles!

April 1526

The plan was to travel the one hundred and fifty miles from
Madrid to the seaside town of Castellón de la Plana and from
there to take a vessel to Montpellier. From Montpellier they
would travel up the Rhône valley to Lyon, stopping along the
way at Nimes, Avignon, Orange, Valence, and Vienne. It was a
more arduous trip returning than it had been coming. On the
journey to Madrid they had been able to travel swiftly down
the Rhône to the sea by ship. Returning, they would travel up
the Rhône valley by coach. It was, in all, a journey that would
take nearly a month and a half, since it was difficult to travel
more than fifteen to twenty miles a day.

As they left, Leona thanked heaven it was early spring. There would be time to reach Lyon well before the heat of summer. As an added bonus, they would be traveling just as life burst forth.

They left early in the morning. A royal coach carried Marguerite and Leona while behind them the Spanish guard of twenty troops was led by Philip de Valor. In front of them their own guard of ten was led by the handsome General Guilbert de Mercier.

The royal party and its Spanish escort traveled down the valley of the Mijares, edging closer to Castellón de la Plana and the coast of the Balearic Sea each day.

The trip from Madrid had been a strain, just as the trip from the sea to Madrid had marked the most difficult part of their previous journey.

"Imagine building one's capital on water which cannot be navigated! Imagine putting it on a plateau in the hottest part of the country." Marguerite shook her head in dismay.

But the weather was not hot now. It was, in fact, close to perfect as they headed for the fertile Mediterranean plain. In the past weeks they had navigated through winding mountain passes, through fertile valleys, and down rivers. Now they had reached the valley of the Mijares, and no doubt tomorrow would be on the shores of the Balearic Sea.

Marguerite had embroidered for part of the morning, then, as she often did, she drifted off into a midmorning nap. Leona had looked out the window for hours—she never tired of the ever-changing countryside, and she sometimes took pen to paper to make sketches of certain areas she wanted to remember.

Leona was indeed staring out toward the river, when the coach clattered to an abrupt halt and the peace of midmorning was completely shattered by gunfire and the shouts of men.

Marguerite's eyes snapped open and her face contorted with fright. "What's happening?"

"Get down on the floor of the coach, my lady." Leona pushed

Marguerite toward the carriage floor, but she herself strained to see out the small window to ascertain what was happening.

The soldiers of their own small guard were outnumbered and engaged in mortal combat with what appeared to be ruffian bandits.

The Spaniards, led by Philip, were also outnumbered and fighting, but they appeared more skilled, and she could see that they were holding their own and inflicting considerable damage on the attackers.

Suddenly the coach jolted forward, throwing her back into her seat with considerable force. Leona screamed as the coach gained momentum. It seemed obvious they were being driven away from the pitched battle with speed. Who was driving? Were the bandits taking the coach because they assumed it to hold a treasure of some sort? Of course it did. Marguerite's rings alone were worth a small fortune.

"We'll be killed!" Marguerite wailed. She was wedged between the two narrow seats on the floor, her sewing basket spilled and her embroidery threads strewn about.

Leona gripped the side of the seat. The coach wheels hit rocks and the bumps were terrible. "At this rate a wheel will come off," she gasped as she struggled not just to hold on, but to climb up and see through the small hatch that allowed those inside to communicate with the coachman.

Abruptly, the coach left the rutted road with a terrible jolt and headed off across the grassland at a rapid pace.

Marguerite groaned again.

Leona struggled and then finally succeeded in opening the hatch.

"Dear heaven," she breathed.

"What is it?" Marguerite said anxiously.

"No one drives! The horses are just running wild!"

"We'll tip over and be killed!" Marguerite cried as she once again managed to cross herself.

Leona forced herself upward. "Madam, I must try to bring us under control."

"It's impossible!"

"I must try." Leona was breathless as she struggled with the opening on top of the coach. She would somehow have to pull herself up and into the driver's seat before she could seize the reins and pull in the horses. In a moment the top gave and Leona, ever agile, struggled upward, forcing herself into position to grab the back of the coachman's seat. She propelled herself up and was finally outside, the wind ripping through her long red-gold hair. The many protruding parts of the carriage tore at her long dress, ripping it to shreds.

She struggled into the seat, panting and grasping the side as the horses continued their wild ride across the plain.

She fought to grasp the reins, but they were loose and she could not reach them.

Frantically, desperately, she turned her head, and in the distance saw the white horse belonging to Philip, the horse to which she felt such a bond, the horse which had let her ride him when Philip assured her he allowed no other save himself to even mount.

"Pegasus," she whispered under her breath, remembering the horse's all too familiar name. "Come to me, Pegasus, hurry."

The horse galloped faster than the wind. Each time she managed to turn, she could see the distance between the runaway coach and Pegasus grow smaller.

Then they were side by side. She saw Philip bend from the saddle and reach the reins. He pulled them in, slowing the runaway carriage and finally bringing it to a halt.

Leona collapsed back against the seat and took a long, deep breath.

Philip dismounted. "Let me help you down," he offered, holding out his arms to her.

There was no choice, and so she let him lift her out of the seat and down onto the soft grass-covered ground. He let her slide the length of his warm body and then, still holding her, he looked into her face and smiled. He pulled the sleeve of her dress up. It was ripped, and she realized then for the first time that the rip exposed the curve of her breast. She blushed deeply even as he held her close.

"You've had a close call," he said.

"Thank you for coming so quickly," she said sincerely as she looked into his face. Then, because she saw the look in his eyes, she broke free and turned toward the coach, pulling open its door. "Madam, are you all right?"

Philip bent down and lifted Marguerite to her feet and out of the coach. "We were attacked by outlaws," he said by way of explanation. "Your horses were whipped. Please, I shall attach my horse and personally drive you back onto the road, where one of my men will drive you onward."

"And our French guardsmen?" Marguerite inquired.

"Many are wounded and some are dead, madam."

Marguerite crossed herself. "We owe you our lives."

"Does this mean I shall be granted a royal wish?"

"Do you have a wish?" Marguerite asked.

"Not at the moment, but if I have one, I shall let you know."

Marguerite smiled. "Please do, though my kingdom is poor and few wishes can be granted."

He bowed from the waist as he opened the door to help her back into the coach. "I would never ask anything which you could not grant," he replied.

Was he flirting with Marguerite? Leona looked at him coldly as he moved to assist her into the carriage.

"And will I be granted a wish from you as well?"

Leona did not smile. "I doubt it," she replied. Then she paused. "Wait." She went to Pegasus and rubbed his nose. "It is you I must thank. You're the swiftest, most beautiful horse in the world." Pegasus nuzzled her. Then she returned and without a word climbed into the coach.

As soon as they began to move, Marguerite patted her gently on the knee. "Do not fight your desire to be nice to that young man quite so hard, my dear."

Leona looked down, knowing her face was flushed.

Father Jacques Renaud paced in front of his fireplace. Even though it was early spring, Paris had grown damp, and then unseasonably quite cold. It was not, however, the cold that caused him to pace. It was anger.

"It was a perfect opportunity!" Renaud raved.

In a chair in front of the fire, Father Normand, one of his fellow Guardians, steepled his fingers and stared at them. "We lost nothing."

"We gained nothing either. It was perfect. When will we get another such opportunity? Never," he muttered, having answered his own question. He had planned it himself and had taken the time to go over all the details many times.

The coach would be attacked just before it reached the sea. Marguerite and her companion would be killed. Naturally the Spanish would be blamed, after all, they were royal visitors traveling under a special amnesty. But his plot had failed because the emperor had given the king's sister an escort which, as it turned out, fought all too well.

"You will think of something else," Normand suggested.

"Not so easily, and what could have been more flawless?" He felt wretched. He hated Marguerite and her simpering adoration of Marot and the other heretics. Louise would not go out of her way to protect them, and Francis was self-centered and spoiled. He was not a man who would intervene. But Marguerite would fight him with her last ounce of strength.

Marguerite was to be reckoned with. She had power, she believed in tolerance and adored Marot and Rabelais. She was even willing to put up with Calvin. She would protect them all.

"You could have her assassinated," Normand suggested.

"Not easily done," Renaud replied. "If this plan had succeeded, it would have looked as if they had been put upon by thieves. They would have been robbed and killed. What could be simpler? But no. Assassination would not be good, especially here in France. Assassinations raise questions about conspiracies."

"What will you do now?" Normand asked.

Renaud shrugged. "I shall have to bide my time."

Thirteen

May 1526

Philip de Valor walked the palace grounds, marveling at their beauty and contemplating France, its king, and the stresses now faced by the monarchy. Francis, King of France, was a very different monarch from Charles, whom he served. Francis was clearly a lover of life and of gaiety, while Charles V was a man of denial, a rigid stoic who rejected his desires to own material possessions.

This palace built by Francis was furnished lavishly and the gardens were lush with color and had well-tended paths. Statuary was abundant, and even the furniture that graced the public rooms of the palace was covered with bright brocades.

Francis was clearly a patron of the arts, a man who relished in the rebirth of ideas and creativity, a man who would do all in his power to light the dark corners of his kingdom. It would not be an easy task. Francis had weaknesses, and enemies who knew how to use those weaknesses. In the short time he had been there, the Guardians of the Faith had petitioned the crown twice to reinstitute the Court of the Inquisition, and twice they had been refused because Marguerite had intervened.

The very thought caused him to grimace. He hoped that Francis, if he were released, would continue to resist the petitions and save France from the brutal and hysterical upheaval that would accompany yet another hunt for heretics.

Such wretched thoughts! He chastised himself for lingering over matters he could not influence. He returned his full attention to his sight-seeing.

He stood and looked down on the junction of the Rhône and Saône rivers and suddenly experienced a sensation he had known before—it was a feeling of familiarity, a feeling that he had stood in this very spot before.

He had known this same déjà vu in Italy when he had traveled to Ravenna. He was so drawn to Ravenna that he remained for many weeks. He could absolutely not understand what had come over him. He seemed to know the countryside like a native, and every place he visited he felt he had seen before.

Toward the end of his visit he had begun to wonder about rebirth. Perhaps he had once lived in Ravenna or visited there. When he walked near the ruins of the Forum Vetus, a different kind of emotion engulfed him. It was a kind of stirring, as if he had seen many such structures before, and in his mind he could imagine how they looked when they were filled with people enjoying some spectacle.

He paused for a moment on the winding path that led through the garden and reminded himself that he was looking for the lady Marguerite. He had been told she and Leona were in the garden. He listened, and floating through the quiet of the afternoon he heard soft voices in the distance. He turned and followed the path that led into an open area beyond the rose garden. In a moment he saw them sitting on a stone bench.

"Ladies," he said as he bowed deeply.

Marguerite looked up from her notebook. "Ah, Philip. Come and join us."

"Are you reading tales?" he inquired. "Have I interrupted?"

"My lady Marguerite is reading me a tale she just finished writing," Leona replied.

"You are not interrupting," Marguerite hastened to interject. She glanced at the lovely Leona and the handsome Philip and thought to herself that youth was most certainly wasted on the young. Clearly Philip was smitten by Leona, and she was deeply attracted to him. Yet, thus far, their frequent encounters were like verbal sparring matches filled with Leona's pride in the strength of womanhood and her love of France, and his absolute maleness and favoritism toward Spain.

"I should not want to interrupt, but I have had some news from Spain and I sought you out to share it with you."

"Please," Marguerite said, gesturing toward the empty lawn chair.

"Your brother is well, my lady. I have it that Charles himself has been to see him. Your brother has let it be known he wants to negotiate."

Leona could see that Marguerite kept her face purposefully impassive but that her small hand trembled. Both of them immediately thought of the children.

"Do you have news of what these negotiations entail?" Marguerite's voice quivered ever so slightly.

"No, madam. Only that they have begun."

"It is good of you to tell me."

He bowed his head but made no move to leave. Leona shifted uneasily, because, as usual, his eyes had come to rest on her. It was as if he could see right through her clothing. Worse yet, when he looked at her so intently, she remembered how his hands had held her, moved across her, pressed her to him. She shifted again, suddenly aware of her own excitement. In the name of heaven, did she really desire this man?

"Madam, you once offered me a royal favor. I should like to ask for it now."

"Ask," Marguerite said.

"Madam, I would have you invite my cousin to court. He is a hero of Pavia."

"A Spanish hero?" Marguerite asked, her well-shaped brows arching.

"No, madam. A French hero. Noble bloodlines make for strange relations. But it is true, he fought on one side and I on the other."

"Who is this royal relation you would have me invite to this court?"

"Henri, Prince of the Kingdom of Navarre and heir to the throne of that small country."

"Henri?" Marguerite laughed gently. "Ah, this is no favor, except perhaps to the ladies of our court. My mother invited him some time ago and rumor has it he will arrive within a few weeks."

"He is your cousin?" Leona asked, feeling surprised. If the ill-fated battle of Pavia had one single hero, then Henri, Prince of Navarre, was that hero. He was twenty-four years old, attractive, and an accomplished scholar as well as a military hero. When he had been captured at Pavia, he had escaped by swinging down from the prison tower on a length of rope. Then, disguised as a peasant, he made his way back to France through enemy lines without being detected. Thus Henri had saved his people a 100,000-crown ransom, and it was said his escape had driven Charles V into a vile fit of temper.

Philip laughed. "Ah, Lady Leona. Not only do you think ill of me, you think ill of all my relatives."

"I do not think ill of you. I simply do not know how you can serve a master who demands children as ransom."

"This war between France and the Holy Roman Empire has caused much grief, it has split families, royal families and commoners alike. It has given rise to terrible suspicions, and it is all for naught."

"As all war is for naught," Marguerite said softly.

Leona looked into his eyes. "I'm sorry if I have misjudged you."

"I still serve Charles. But I could wish his desires were other than what I know them to be."

"Do you know when your cousin arrives?" Marguerite asked, seeking to change the subject.

"He is here now, dear lady. He only awaits an audience."

Marguerite stood up and Leona gathered up her papers. "I shall receive him before supper tonight in the drawing room. Then we shall all feast together to celebrate his bravery."

"Thank you, madam."

"At seven, then?" she asked. "Come, Leona, we have much

to do. This palace has been far too dreary since my brother was taken."

They walked swiftly across the lawn, through the rose garden and by the lily pond which was ringed with classic Greek and Roman statues.

"You may speak now, Leona. The dashing Philip is no longer within earshot," Marguerite murmured. "Dear me, Leona, why do you spar so with him? Can't you see how smitten he is with you?"

"I can see he is lustful."

"I think it is more than that. But you're young, and when you're young, lust is quite common. Personally I think I have been far too prudent."

Leona thought of her most recent dream. In it a courageous young stranger had come for Marguerite. As she understood it, Marguerite would be reluctant to marry this man, but it was made clear that this match was right and necessary and that she was to do everything in her power to convince Marguerite to marry him.

"Perhaps, my lady, the coming of this stranger, Henri, Prince of Navarre, to our court will give you the opportunity to be less prudent. Your period of mourning is over."

Marguerite laughed musically. "Ah, my dear Leona! Prince Henri is nine years younger than I! I've seen women follow him wherever he goes. Oh, dear me, no. Such a match would be—to say the least—painful."

"Painful?"

"Oh, yes. I might fall in love. I should not want to do so and then watch my lover entertain a procession of mistresses. No, my youth is gone, and with it all thoughts of romance. I lost my love at Pavia."

"You do not mean your husband, Alençon, do you?"

"No. I mean Bonnivet. Guillaume Gouffier Seigneur de Bonnivet, grand admiral of France and once my brother's adviser."

Leona's thoughts raced back to that night when the message had come concerning Pavia. She remembered the flickering candles and the stricken look on Marguerite's face. After the messenger had told her about her brother and her husband, she had asked, "And Bonnivet?" The messenger had replied, "Dead."

Poor Marguerite! The rumors about her and Bonnivet were true! Up till then she had thought Marguerite's life had been her brother. She had married Alençon for him. Deep inside, it made her happy to think that Marguerite had known real happiness with Bonnivet. Yet it was bittersweet. Bonnivet was dead and Marguerite was all too ready to accept widowhood as a permanent state.

"I think you have buried your youth too soon," Leona said. Her dream had indicated that Marguerite's future, and it was a future of great importance to France and to the world, would be with this Henri, Prince of Navarre. "Madam, is it a rule that one should know only one love?" she asked.

Marguerite blushed. "I suppose not."

"Then remain open to love, my lady."

Again Marguerite laughed. "Ah, and look who gives advice."

The main dining salon was bathed in candlelight as a bevy of servants presided over a sumptuous buffet. Heavy ornate silver platters held roast capons and hares, pastries of lark and sparrow, rolls of beef marrow, black puddings, lampreys and rice, venison and all manner of birds large and small. On a side table partridges, sliced meats, fish aspics, a roast swan, and stuffed ducks bordered by eels turned inside out faced the pièce de résistance, a huge baked peacock. After cooking, the bird had been artfully covered with mock feathers made of some jellylike substance and its deep blue, green, and gold tail feathers with their haunting eyelike design had been reaffixed. On another table there were greens, fruits and nuts, plates of leeks, beans, and black bread. A variety of wines and mead were served.

"You honor me far more than I deserve," Henri said, kissing Marguerite's hand.

"You are a hero come to our court at a time when both the nation and those of us here need a hero," Marguerite replied.

Henri turned and looked at Philip, who was just to one side of him. "And is my rakish cousin behaving? He is on the wrong side, but I cannot hold it against him."

"Nor I, under the circumstances," Marguerite said. "He saved my life, and the life of my companion, Leona. Now I must face the fact that it is he who will be responsible for my nephews, the royal princes. They are to go to Spain. He is to take them and remain with them as their tutor."

Leona felt shocked to the core. She opened her mouth to say something, but words would not come.

Marguerite smiled and turned to her. "I'm sorry. The message came this afternoon. Francis has signed the treaty. He is coming home."

Philip bowed before her and took her hand. "Lady Leona, Madam Marguerite, this is not the worst fate. I pledge myself to them. I know they will be returned."

"It gives me comfort to know you will be looking after them and not Charles. I sense in you a joie de vivre, Philip de Valor. Perhaps it sounds silly, but I would not want them to grow up under such grim tutelage as Charles himself would offer."

"It's reassuring to know I am trusted."

Leona eased away from them all. She had spent much time with the little princes and the thought of their departure caused tears to come to her eyes. Thus far they had been brought up in the company of women; now they would be brought up by men. By the time she reached the door, she was weeping, tears falling down her cheeks. She turned and ran through the door, down the corridors of the palace and up the winding staircase that led to her quarters.

Leona threw herself across her bed, letting the tears flow unabated. Her thoughts were a jumble. The little princes would be gone—but so would Philip.

She stopped sobbing, surprised by her own thoughts, by the revelation that she would also miss Philip. Even now she fought admitting the truth to herself. But it was there—she dreaded Philip's departure, and she dreaded even more the thought that she might never see him again.

"I have been blind," she whispered.

Then she again turned her face into the pillow and cried as anguish for the young princes mixed with regrets concerning Philip and anger at herself.

Downstairs, the nobility mingled. Philip searched the room twice and still could not find Leona. He sought out Marguerite and found her speaking with the Duke of Flanders. He joined them and after a moment was able to draw her aside.

"Lady, I beg your forgiveness for interrupting, but I cannot find Leona anywhere and I must speak with her."

Marguerite nodded and silently touched his sleeve, drawing him near even as they stepped away from others. "Now, this is a true royal favor," she whispered. "Leona does care for you, I have seen it in her eyes. I saw her leave and I believe she was quite upset. I would guess she has gone to her rooms on the third floor. Follow her, Philip."

"Thank you, dear lady." He waited only an instant, just long enough not to be obvious, then, he, too eased out of the dining hall and down the corridor toward the spiraling staircase. He had one chance to make her understand, to let her know that he loved her. But time was so short! He cursed Charles, who had ordered him home immediately. He cursed his own sense of duty, which would compel him to obey his king's summons. "I ache for you," he whispered to himself as he thought of Leona. He reached the top of the staircase and looked down the corridor. "Don't shut me out," he said, catching his breath. "Love me as I love you." But could he speak the words to her as easily as he spoke them to silence?

He followed Marguerite's directions and then he paused before a great door. Beneath it, a light shined. He pushed open the door and stepped into the room. "Leona?"

It was a huge room lit by a single lamp. Shadows played on the wall. "Leona?"

She appeared in an archway, still wearing the beautiful deep shimmering green silk gown she had been wearing earlier. Her long golden-red hair was caught up in a huge roll, her high, perfect breasts pressed against the material of her bodice as if held unwilling prisoners by the lace. Her eyes were still tear-filled, yet they were also luminous and compelling.

He looked around and saw that this was some kind of ante-room and that beyond the archway was a smaller room, doubt-less her bedchamber.

"Leona, you know I will leave tomorrow. My king wants me to return immediately."

"Your king is cruel beyond all words! They're children! I love them!"

"Then come with me!" He blurted out the words. Taking only five long strides to reach her, he drew her into his arms.

"Come with me, Leona! Be with me always."

He held her tight against him and she felt the outline of his body, the strength of his arms, the power of his being. But it was as if she were struck dumb as her dream turned to reality and his lips sought hers in a long, deep, probing, erotic kiss. His tongue moved inside her mouth as he sought her hungrily. Her resistance melted and she opened her lips to him.

Leona was like a feather in his strong arms; she felt incapable of objecting, of struggling, of anything save allowing this pow-erful man to ravage her. And yet it was what she wanted with every fiber of her being. She could even feel a dampness be-tween her legs, an aching anticipation of what was to come.

"You are the most beautiful of all women." His hand fumbled with her hair and loosened it so it fell over her shoulders.

In that movement she had a deep feeling of being freed, as if in liberating her hidden hair, he was liberating her.

His large but gentle hand brushed away her silk dress, fully baring her shoulders. He lingered there, his lips kissing her flesh till she felt both hot and cold. All the while he held her fast against the wall, his imprint upon her, his blood-filled member like a sword between them, an instrument both frightening and wanted.

Leona succumbed to her own desires, knowing she should have been more guarded, yet somehow it was all as if it had happened before, as if they had loved before. She felt faint in his arms, overcome with a sense of deep passion such as one might have for a lifelong mate.

He pushed the flimsy material of her dress still farther, revealing the curve of her breasts, and again his lips touched her skin, kissing her everywhere as his own breathing grew heavier with the excitement of the moment.

He lifted her and carried her to the bed in her inner sanctum, put her down gently, and stripped himself of his clothing. Leona could not take her eyes off him, from the size of him, or from the glistening perspiration on his skin. He fell down beside her and pushed away the top of her dress. For a long while he looked at her breasts.

"Pink-tipped mounds," he whispered as his lips caressed her erect nipples. With thumb and forefinger he aroused one while his mouth played on the other, drawing it into his mouth, flicking his tongue across it, biting it gently till she squirmed in his arms and pressed herself against him.

Before she was even aware of it, she lay naked in his arms. Naked, vulnerable, and exposed before him. He looked at her and then began to stroke her gently, running his hand between her legs, then parting her ever so slightly to reach that place of supreme pleasure. He eased down and aroused her with forbidden kisses till she felt she would scream with desire. She writhed beneath him, begging him.

But he did nothing save kiss her. Then she felt his fingers exploring, taunting, moving toward her gateway.

"You're a virgin," he said softly, as if this were an unexpected surprise.

She nodded as he eased his forefinger inside her carefully, moving it slowly so as not to hurt her. "Lay easy, my love," he whispered. "You are ready, but it will hurt a little."

She put her arms around him and he touched her gently with the tip of his swollen member, then he returned his lips to her breasts, kissing her nipples and nibbling softly on her till she pushed against him and raised her hips to meet him. He pushed into her as lightly as he could, and she groaned but did not struggle. Then he eased in and out again, kissing her while she moaned, while her skin glowed warm, and while she excreted warm, wet moisteners to ease his passage.

When at last he reached her depths, she returned his kisses and moved against him. Then she let out a small shriek and he felt her throbbing beneath him. Her eyes were closed, her head tossed back, her lips slightly parted.

Hearing and seeing her so enraptured caused him to pulsate into her. Suddenly he felt swept away, felt himself travel across the universe, experiencing incredible unearthly sensations as she clung to him. He shuddered and whispered, "I have known you for an eternity."

Leona was overcome and could only whisper one word. "Yes."

Leona cringed as the crowd shrieked and screamed, "Death to the heretic! Burn him! Burn him!" The poor creature was dragged from a cart across the cobblestones to a huge cross beneath which sticks and dry wood had been piled. He screamed in pain as he was tied to the cross and made horrible inhuman noises as the flames rose around him. "Burn the heretic! Burn the heretic!" rang in her ears as above all hovered the face and eyes of Renaud.

And then the image was gone, lost in a dense fog. Leona saw a castle, a castle she did not recognize. It was half hidden in the mist and behind it snowy mountains rose in the distance. She floated above the castle, and then seemed to be in a village square. There was the face of the same man who had been tied to the stake, but he was safe and no one taunted him. She also saw the face of Dr. Rabelais and of Clement Marot, France's leading poet, as well as the figure of Calvin, the reformer. And she knew that in this palace Marguerite and Henri had given refuge to all those who might have been persecuted in France's own belated inquisition—and she saw, too, a Catholic Church in turmoil, a church gathering to reform itself in the wake of many wrongs. And all was revealed to her—the survival of

France depended on Marguerite, who must remain physically strong in the face of the plague, and mentally and spiritually firm in the face of Church opposition.

Leona sat suddenly upright in bed. She stared into the darkness and then down on the sleeping form of Philip de Valor. Tears filled her eyes as she thought of her adopted father's words: "You are special. You must obey your dreams."

Leona covered her face with her hands and wept silently. When morning came, Philip would ask her to return to Madrid with him and with the royal princes. She could not go. It was clear to her that her place was there with Marguerite. She was to urge Marguerite to marry Henri.

The morning sun played on dew that covered the lawn, causing it to appear diamond-studded. Leona stared down on it, her body numb as if she were in a trance. Beside her, Philip played with strands of her long hair, letting it drop through his fingers again and again.

"I cannot believe you won't come with me," he finally said. "I can't believe you don't love me with the same passion I feel for you."

"I do love you," she said, turning to look into his pain-filled eyes. "I love you, but I cannot come. I must stay here."

"You offer me no explanation save some obligation to keep Marguerite safe. Leona, Marguerite has soldiers to guard her. What can you do?"

"I must urge her to marry Henri and I must help her remain steadfast against the Guardians of the Faith."

"She will marry if she wishes and you cannot make her more steadfast."

"I can. She thinks Henri is too young for her. She is afraid and needs reassurance. She has few others with whom to consult."

"Leona, I want you by my side."

"I cannot, my darling. Nor can I ask you to wait."

"Do you think I could find another like you?"

"I don't know what to think—I—" She turned to him in anguish and threw her arms around his neck. "I do love you. Please try to understand. Please."

He nodded slowly. "Summon me and I shall come," he whispered into her ear. "I do not pretend to grasp your reasons, but I do know we are meant for each other."

He leaned down and kissed her, and she returned the kiss with all the passion and desire he knew she possessed. "I must go now," he whispered. "Lingering with you is torture."

Leona kissed him again and then whirled away, running into her bedroom as tears streamed down her face. She closed her eyes and covered her ears. "Let him be gone quickly," she thought. "Before I weaken and follow."

January 1527
The Palace at Blois

The whole royal party was in movement across the French countryside. Francis I was a new man, a king restored. He wanted gaiety and fun. Seldom did the *maison-du-roi,* the royal household, remain in one palace or château for more than three months. Like a wandering Gypsy tribe, the court was gathered up at the king's whim and moved on.

The Château Chambord, from which the court had just departed, had more than one hundred and seventy rooms and more were being added. But Francis tired of it. Those who knew him well before Pavia and his imprisonment said he was more restless now than he had been before the defeat.

The palace at Blois was his favorite palace, even though it was smaller than the Château Chambord. Francis loved Blois and he decided to take his court there so he might hunt in the royal forest.

The cold January winds chilled the rooms of the palace even though the walls were thick and covered with bright orange and red tapestries. Cold or warm, the palace at Blois was a showcase. The tables were nearly all covered with rich gold cloths, and precious objets d'art were on display everywhere. Many of the rooms had fine carpets, and every room was lit by flaming torches and great fireplaces.

But this day was especially damp and the wind whistled around the corners, shook the fine glass in the upper windows, and caused the hunting hounds to howl relentlessly at the strange sounds created by the cruel winds that also brought cold rain from the dark skies.

In spite of the inclement weather, anyone could see that for Marguerite, sister of the King of France, this was the springtime of her life. Her angular face glowed, her clear eyes danced merrily. Marguerite, Leona knew well, was in the full blush of love, and she was also a woman loved. Ah! But how to convince Marguerite, who refused to admit to the possibility that Henri might love her or that such a marriage was even possible? Yet she must be convinced, Leona thought uneasily. Henri would provide Marguerite with the strength and the means with which to fight the growing corruption in the Church—he would offer refuge to France's intellectuals and he and Marguerite would lead the battle for reform. Leona pressed her lips together. She had written to and invited Dr. Rabelais to court. "You'll be my valuable ally," she told him. "I'm sure that together we can convince Marguerite to marry Henri. She greatly respects you both as a person and as a man of letters."

Much to her surprise, Dr. Rabelais had not only agreed to help her, but had gone to see the king as well. Now, as they all sat together, a mysterious expression filled his face. He eased into a chair by the fire.

"You give off the unmistakable aura of desirability," Dr. Rabelais told Marguerite bluntly. He had traded his cloak for a brandy and he leaned back against the great puffed blue and gold cushions that padded the chair. "It is, you know, a quirk of nature. A woman in love is always irresistible to all men."

Leona said nothing. Dr. Rabelais had all the right words. He did not invent them either. What he said of Marguerite was true, and as miserable as she herself felt, she was glad for Marguerite's happiness. In any case, no matter how it turned out, a visit from the good doctor was always stimulating. He was wonderfully brilliant in all areas of knowledge, and the three of them would discuss literature endlessly.

Marguerite's face was slightly flushed. "If you are talking of Henri, you must remember he is much younger than I. Such a love can simply not exist."

"He makes you younger. Anyway, you're not an old crone. Ah, Leona, it is good you invited me. This woman needs convincing."

"I am nine years older," Marguerite protested.

"Why do you think younger women are so desirable? Younger women are so giddy, frivolous, and more often than not they lack sincerity. They are much too busy looking at themselves in the mirror to know true love with another. I think you are a perfect match. A marriage of honor and virtue, of two fine intellects. Yes, a marriage of minds . . . and, ah, yes, I expect you are both good in bed as well!"

"Marriage! Bed!" Marguerite turned beet red. "We are only friends, Henri and I. You know full well that any marriage of mine will be *made,* not chosen."

Rabelais closed his eyes and held his hands out in front of him in the manner of a blind prophet. "I know it will occur. I see it. I feel it," he announced in a theatrical voice while his expression became one of the mock mystic.

Marguerite laughed. "What spirits prompt you to make such a prediction, Doctor? Have you spoken with an angel, or just had too much brandy? Are your spirits true, or alcoholic?"

Rabelais laughed heartily. "Oh, my dear, angels do not have the inclination to speak with me—if indeed there be such ethereal creatures. Nor have I had too much brandy, not that one *can* have too much brandy."

"Are you, then, in communication with the devil?"

"No, only your brother. He may be a minor devil, albeit a lovable one."

Marguerite suddenly looked more serious. "I do not understand."

"You do not understand? Of course you understand. Your

brother has given your marriage much consideration, and rather than send some strange messenger to tell you the result of his deliberations, he asked that I tell you his decision. What could be simpler?"

Marguerite collapsed back against the cushions. "You are the greatest practical joker in all France, but, if this is a joke, I will not forgive you soon."

"For once, madam, I speak in all seriousness. In any case, you are one person with whom I would not jest concerning so serious a matter."

"Tell me, then, what message do you bring?"

"Your brother invites you to remarry. Too long have you waited. Henri is now King of Navarre, his sister has wed Cesare Borgia. Marrying Henri will be advantageous from any point of view, but it is quite clear to me—to us," he added, glancing at Leona, "that this is also a match made with much enthusiasm."

"How does Henri feel?"

Rabelais laughed. "He loves you! He asked for your hand."

"But my age," Marguerite protested.

"I know you. You love him too much. You're afraid he will tire of you and seek pleasure with others."

Marguerite hid her face in her hands. "I cannot hide my fears from either of you."

"You are fortunate," Leona said quietly. "You have two kinds of love. You are still young enough and beautiful enough to enjoy each other's bodies, you may even have children. And if passion fades, you will still have a marriage of minds. It seems to me this is the best of both worlds."

Marguerite turned to Leona. "You're wise for one so young and so troubled. You should have gone with your love."

Leona turned away. "I could not. But perhaps he will return. My lady, I must have faith. I must have faith and so must you. It is essential that you marry Henri. It is essential for you and for France. Besides, I know you love each other, I see it in your eyes."

"May and December cannot long endure," she said, thinking

of little Claude, the child queen who was cast aside by her brother Francis and who died so sadly.

Rabelais took her hand. "If the sun shines warm in winter, do you hide inside because the calendar tells you to?"

"Your words are full of play."

"You need play. You have lived too long in the shadow of your brother. You have too long done your mother's bidding. It's time you were a queen yourself, because you are already a queen among women. This match will give me great pleasure, as it will unite two liberal minds, two intelligent people."

"Shame! You know the ignorant have grace."

"Grace but no charm, my lady. What will happen to the world if they keep breeding? You, you're special. A fine writer, a brilliant woman. Marry. Give love and intellect a chance. Besides, all France will need you to resist future persecutions."

"As yet there are no persecutions."

"There will be," Leona said softly. "I have heard the lists of the accused are prepared."

Rabelais nodded his agreement. "Watch the faculty at the Sorbonne. Those men have mutilated minds. They would mold the faith to seek revenge and power. Beware of men who speak for God. Marot and I may need to hide beneath your skirts."

Marguerite touched his arm lightly. "I think you overstate the danger, but I know it exists. You and Marot will always be welcome in Navarre."

"I see you have made your decision."

"My decision was never much in doubt," Marguerite said.

Leona smiled and leaned across the space between them to hug Marguerite. "I am glad for you," she whispered. "For you, for France, and for those who may need your protection."

Rabelais dressed in crimson and wore a black velvet hat with a feather. His traditional cape swirled about him dramatically when he moved, and his smile was a wonderful study in the maintenance of the social graces, Leona observed. He was here because of Henri of Navarre, for his friend Marguerite, and for

her. The other guests at this wedding reception held no appeal
for him, and the wedding itself was awash with court gossips,
the chattering ladies who always surrounded Francis, and courtiers whose interests were few and whose views were more often
than not shallow in the extreme.

"You are both sly and well intentioned, Leona," Rabelais whispered in her ear. "First you encourage Henri, then you make
suggestions to Francis, and next you use me as a go-between.
You are so cunning that by the time I arrived, the good king really
believed this marriage was his idea—naturally that was quite
necessary, so I congratulate you on your subtlety."

Leona suppressed a smile. "Are you accusing me of manipu-
lation?"

"In a good cause. I know that you and Michel are unrelated
by blood, but sometimes I wonder. Both of you have a strange
facility for seeing into the future, and you both have remarkable
insights."

"Don't compare me with Michel. He is truly a genius and a
thousand times more insightful than I."

"Were it not heretical to believe in such concepts, I would
say both you and Michel gained this knowledge in a dozen other
lifetimes."

Leona stared into Rabelais's dark eyes. Though he had spoken
his words in jest, they surprised her because it was a thought
that had occurred to her more than once. Certainly Michel believed it. René de Nostradamus, her adoptive father, had told
her a hundred times that she was different. How many times
had she found a new experience familiar? She seemed to have
memories that should not have existed. Even when she had been
studying, there were things she knew but could not have known.
Then there were the images and insights that came in the night
and the power they had over her—a power her adoptive father
had urged her to accept, to follow.

Suddenly she was filled with a desire to speak to her
brother—to confront him with this concept about which they
had spoken only once and which the good doctor had only stumbled on in jest.

"Oh, dear, you look quite thoughtful," Rabelais said.

Leona smiled and forced a small laugh. "Well, perhaps I have lived before. Indeed, perhaps you have lived before. It is not I who writes of a utopia and creates wonderfully impossible people."

"Do you mean my giant, Gargantua?"

"I believe him to be a metaphorical giant."

"See, you are too wise not to have lived before."

At that moment trumpets blasted a salute through the grand reception hall and the babble of several hundred conversations ceased as Francis entered, leading the royal entourage. He was resplendent in his deep red robes with their gold tassels and fine ermine trim. The scent of pungent Oriental incense mingled with the aroma of exotic foods, and a smoky haze floated over the heads of the invited guests.

Francis took his throne on the royal dais and there was another announcement from the trumpets. Henri, King of Navarre, walked slowly into the gallery with his bride, Marguerite, on his arm. She wore a deep rose gown with layers of transparent veils. Her dark, intelligent eyes darted around the room, settling on no one but seeing everyone.

Again the blare of trumpets. The crowd moved to the sides of the hall, and through the entrance nine gaily dressed acrobats tumbled into the room. They were a blur of colors as they flew this way and that, forming human pyramids, then diving from the pinnacle of their own wild structure of bodies and turning over and over in somersaults and cartwheels. They flew from one to another across the room, and each of their antics brought applause from the amazed onlookers. It was as if their bodies were without skeletal structure.

The trumpets again sounded and the acrobats gave way to dancing bears and their keepers, and then jugglers appeared with balls and hoops and gaily colored discs.

Leona watched as Marguerite and Henri sat side by side. She felt a sudden pang of loneliness, a yearning for Philip. She had given in to him so completely, so naturally. And he was among the familiar which she had just acknowledged. Yes, she was sure of it. He had possessed her before that night in her room and nothing so convinced her as her experience with his horse.

She turned, expecting to see Dr. Rabelais still at her side, but he was near the arch that was the entrance to the gallery. He was speaking to a dark-clad messenger. He turned suddenly, and seeing her, hurried over. "This way, my lady, we must speak privately."

Leona had no time to say anything. He guided her away, through the arch, around one of the corners, and down the hallway. They entered a small room.

"You know your way around Blois better than I," she said, smiling. But the smile quickly faded from her face as she saw the look of distress on his. "What is it?"

"Clement Marot. He's been arrested by our own little band of inquisitors at the Sorbonne."

"Father Renaud?" Leona even hated saying his name. Suddenly she felt a terrible pain in her midsection and she clasped her hand over it. In a moment it was gone.

"Are you all right?" Dr. Rabelais asked.

Leona nodded and bit her lip. "We must see that Marot is released immediately."

Rabelais nodded. "If I were not here, I'm sure I would be in jail as well."

"I'll speak to Marguerite right away. She can speak to the king immediately. I'm sure we can get a royal proclamation to release him."

"They'll be furious. They're already furious about that German reformer, Luther, and virtually hysterical about Calvin. They've probably arrested Berquin, who translated Luther's writings."

"Did your message mention him?"

"No, just Marot."

"Come," Leona said firmly. "We must see her now."

Rabelais and Leona hurried toward Marguerite. They spoke with her and Henri for a few moments, then both Marguerite and Henri turned to talk with the king.

After a long conversation Rabelais saw a messenger and

guard officer summoned. Francis looked at Leona and Rabelais and crooked his finger, summoning them to join him, his sister, and Henri.

"I have ordered your friend to be released," Francis promised. "Marguerite will invite him to her court—at least until the gentlemen of the Sorbonne settle down."

Relief flooded through Leona even though she knew there would soon be others who would need refuge. At the same time, her thoughts went to the little princes. According to her most recent dream, the time had come to urge negotiations.

Leona knocked on the great double doors that separated Louise's chambers from the others in the palace. A dark-haired girl opened the door a crack, then, seeing who it was, opened it wider and bowed. "You are expected, madam."

Louise of Savoy was resplendent in a long gown that fell to the floor in generous folds. She wore a stiff lace collar above the collar of her dress. She was seated at her writing desk and she smiled when she saw Leona.

Leona bowed deeply. "Madam."

"Please, my dear. There is no need for such formality."

Leona stood up and smiled. There was a need for formality, and Louise's words meant only that the formalities need not continue. "Are you busy now?" she asked.

"I'm always busy, my dear. But I have not forgotten our appointment, if that's what you mean. Please, sit down and tell me why you asked to see me."

Leona hoped the direct approach would be best. Not entirely direct, of course, but as direct as possible. "Madam, my mind has been very much on the little princes of late."

"And mine, but of course I know you were close to them."

"It has been a long time, madam. Too long."

"Yes, it's frustrating. I don't know what to do. I have tried everything."

"I have had an idea, madam. I would like to ask you to hear me out."

"Of course."

"As you know, the children have been placed in the care of Philip de Valor."

"A good man. I was impressed with him. And I daresay you were, too."

Leona's face flushed. But she was not surprised. There were few secrets in this court. Doubtless someone saw him going to her chambers that night—or leaving the next morning.

"Don't be embarrassed. Were I younger, you would have had competition. He is terribly dashing, and I believe intelligent as well."

"Yes, madam. But my concern is with the princes."

"Of course. Please continue."

"Well, it has been a long time since you and I, and for that matter, Marguerite, have seen the children. I wonder if you should write to the emperor's aunt, Margaret of Austria? You might suggest that the princes visit her, and while they are there that you and Marguerite might be invited as well. I mean, how can Charles refuse to allow them to visit Margaret of Austria?"

"How indeed?" Louise asked.

Leona nodded. "My thought, my very strong thought, is that if Margaret saw you and Marguerite with the princes, she would be struck with the cruelty of this treaty. She has much influence on Charles. He has, after all, made her regent of the Nether-lands. Perhaps you two ladies could work out an agreement. Something more humane than the present treaty."

"You know, my dear, that is a splendid idea. And I do believe that I should ask if this Philip could bring them. Then you could see him as well."

Again Leona blushed. "Oh, madam, that is not the reason I made this suggestion."

Louise laughed. "I know that. But after all, if there is to be a bonus, why not a bonus to you? I like this idea very much. I shall write today."

Leona stood up and bowed again. Then she left the Queen Mother's chamber and the smell of lilacs which always seemed to follow Louise wherever she went.

Philip—she hardly dared to speak his name lest she begin crying. In spite of his frequent letters and his pledges, she wondered if he had remained loyal to her or if he had found another lover. But seeing him, if she did, was an aside. Her dreams had directed her to make these suggestions, and she had followed their instruction.

Renaud paced his rooms, his expression blacker than usual. "The king ordered them released!" he shouted loudly. "We ordered the arrest and he freed them by royal proclamation! It is a slap in the face!"

"It is his sister's doing." Normand did not rise. He never paced, he simply sat and seethed.

"She must die! Her influence with Francis is far too great! And that woman who is her companion must die too!"

"I agree," Normand mumbled, then looking up, he added, "but you said assassination is risky."

"It must look like something else. I must think on this."

"I hear that Louise is going to see Margaret of Austria. If a treaty can be reached, the princes may be returned, and if they are returned, there will most certainly be a ransom to pay."

"Of course, of course," Renaud said impatiently.

"Ah, my dear Renaud, ask yourself who will pay this ransom? Surely not Louise of Savoy? Certainly not Marguerite, Queen of Navarre. I suggest the royal treasury is quite empty, so who might pay it?"

Renaud turned to him and rubbed his chin. "We might—in exchange for, shall we say, leverage?"

"Yes, leverage, enough leverage to overrule Marguerite's objections to arrests."

Renaud frowned. "Even with leverage Marguerite must die."

"When?" Normand asked.

"When the perfect opportunity arises. And it will arise."

Normand shrugged. "We shall have our way in any case."

Fourteen

August 1529
Chateau Cambrai, Northern France

Picardy, Artois, and Flanders, were more often thought of as "the Northern Territories," rather than as a part of France. Two of the three regions, Artois and Flanders, were in dispute. Francis I was their overlord, Charles V, claimed them.

Chateau Cambrai, in the village of Cambrai, on the Escaut River, was small and seldom used. It was, however, close to the Netherlands where Margaret of Austria often held court. Charles V had finally agreed to negotiations, and not surprisingly, since Louise of Savoy was to negotiate for her son, Francis, Charles nominated his aunt, Margaret of Austria to negotiate on behalf of the Empire.

Margaret of Austria, Duchess of Savoy, and Regent of the Netherlands, was forty-nine years old and in less than good health. She was a petite woman with a slender angular face, a sharp chin, a long nose, and bright blue eyes. Her gray hair was hidden beneath a pure white covering like those worn by nuns. When she spoke, Margaret's voice was always a surprise. One expected so small a woman to have a highly feminine tone, but Margaret's voice was crusty and somewhat deep.

Louise of Savoy, mother of the King of France, and once regent of France, was fifty-three. She was a remarkable and awesome woman, a physically delicate creature with the face of an angel and a will of steel. Her small size was in direct contrast with her emotional and mental strength. Her voice was always steady, her eyes never revealed her emotions. Louise, it was said, did not accept destiny, she carved it, bending the very fates to her will. Louise inspired two emotions only—love and hate. No one had neutral feelings toward her, and whether they loved or hated, everyone respected her.

The two ladies had taken chairs opposite each other, while Marguerite, Queen of Navarre, and Leona remained in the background.

"I yearn to see my grandsons," Louise said as she looked at Margaret. When she negotiated with men, she gave nothing of herself emotionally. But Margaret was another woman; Margaret would respond to the reality of a woman's need to see her grandchildren.

"They are here with me, and when we have finished talking, you may spend as much time with them as you like. Indeed, if the negotiations go well, they will no doubt be returned to you."

"That is my most fervent wish."

"Of course, you understand that mine is not the final decision. Your grandsons will have to remain with Charles until the treaty is signed. He must make the decision, and it is he who must send them home to you."

"I understand that. I also know that Charles trusts you more than he does any other person in his realm. Come, Margaret, if you recommend that my grandsons be returned, they will, in all probability, be returned."

Margaret neither denied nor confirmed Louise's statement. "This has been a terrible draining war, Louise."

"And it must end," Louise said firmly. "Both sides are exhausted, please do not pretend otherwise. Neither the empire nor France can continue. We are both short of funds."

"Nor is victory even possible for France since the Genovese navy defected to the empire."

Louise did not allow her facial expression to change. The admission of French weakness was painful to her. As long as the weakness was mutual, she could talk about it. But the defection of the Genovese navy was a blow to France, and Margaret was right, it meant victory was impossible.

"Let us get on with it," Margaret said, leaning forward. "Will Francis renounce his claim to Italy?"

Louise drew in her breath, and then, her lips pressed together, nodded.

"And is he willing to give up his right to be overlord in Flanders and Artois?"

Louise thought of what her son would say. He would not like it, but he would give that right up. "Yes."

Louise knew it was her turn. "Charles will have to renounce his claims on Burgundy," she said without blinking.

"If he does that, there will likely have to be ransom paid for your grandsons—in place of the land."

Louise stiffened like a board, and only after a long silence did she nod again, indicating her acquiescence. "If my son accepts these terms, he will have given up his allies. I wish to demand the possessions of his enemies in return. I want Bourbon's possessions as well as those belonging to the Prince of Orange." She knew as she spoke that her voice was full of venom. Bourbon was a traitor.

Margaret smiled. "Ah, you drive a hard bargain, Louise. But I would protect my son as well, and I, too, would not want my grandchildren reared in a foreign court. So yes, I will forward these terms to Charles with my recommendation that he accept them."

"Is it done?" Marguerite asked.

"Yes. It is done," Margaret replied. "The boys are upstairs with their tutor."

Leona's heart skipped a beat and she was filled with excitement, an unnatural energy. She had known he was here! She had felt it!

This meeting which she had urged had been so long in the making! She had originally suggested it so that the women could get together and, if all went well, settle the main arguments. But Charles would accept nothing less than full-scale peace negotiations. Charles wanted Margaret to negotiate, but she had been ill for months, delaying this meeting until now.

Leona's thoughts raced back to Philip—they had written, but it had been over three years since they had seen each other. Would he still feel the same way? In her dreams he had held her, but these were not dreams she trusted. These, she suspected, were wishful thinking, daydreams as well as night fantasies.

There was no time for her to ponder her own questions. Margaret tugged on a satin length of cord. In a few moments the door to the room swung open and the two young princes came bounding into the room. The oldest was thirteen-year-old Francis, the dauphine. He was a serious and contemplative child. Henri, who was just eleven, looked awed. Nonetheless, when they smiled, it was evident how happy they both were to see the three women with whom they had spent so much of their earlier childhood.

Tears filled Marguerite's eyes. "You were only seven when I last saw you," she said to Henri. Then, reaching out for Francis's shoulder, she added, "And you were only ten. Please, both of you come walk in the garden with your grandmother and me," Marguerite said. "You can visit with Leona later."

Leona looked up and saw Philip beyond the archway, walking slowly toward the door. It was almost as if she had been hit by lightning. She felt rooted to the spot where she stood, unable to move.

The royal ladies were bustling about, preparing to go into the garden of the château to be with the princes.

Philip came in and bowed to Margaret, kissing her hand. He did the same to Louise and Marguerite. Then he turned to her, his blue eyes studying her. He could not have greeted her as she would have liked. There was protocol to be observed.

"Please," he said, holding out his hand. "Come talk with me."

Leona held out her hand and he took it and kissed it. Not as he had kissed the others, but longer. Nor did he grasp her limply, though that was the polite way to take a lady's hand. He gripped her hand hard, as if he had no intention of ever letting her get away again. It was then she realized she had tears in her eyes.

The others walked down the hall and toward the entrance of the château that led to the garden. Leona, feeling almost in a dreamlike state, let Philip lead her out of the chamber and away toward the side entrance of the château.

"When I first knew I would see you again, I was both anxious and fearful," Leona said honestly as they passed out of the château.

A path led into the forest that surrounded the château and Philip held her hand, leading her down the path and through the trees. He squeezed her fingers gently. "I cannot say my emotions were much different. Every day we were parted I was eager to see you. Every day I was afraid that when I found you again, you wouldn't want me."

Leona stopped walking, and he slipped his arm around her waist and looked down into her green eyes—eyes that carried him back, back. He couldn't remember; he only knew her eyes drew him in, that they soothed him, that he felt as if he were floating on air when he looked into their depths.

"I want you," Leona said. Her expression was serious. "When I first met you I felt as if I had been looking for you for a long while. You became the face in all my dreams."

Philip frowned. "I, too, have dreams, Leona. Until I met you, the subject of my dreams was faceless, an entity of love that came over me in the night like an incubus and enveloped me."

"My dreams were the same," she whispered as their fingertips again touched. That touch was startling! It was magnetic, as if their minds and bodies were suddenly fused, yet the past could still not be seen, nor did they truly understand the emotions that surged through both of them.

Philip embraced her and drew her close, running his hands through her red-gold hair, kissing it with his lips, inhaling its sweet aroma. "I have missed you so," he said softly as he kissed her ear, then ran his finger around its edge, sending a chill through her.

Before she could say another word, Philip swept her into his arms and carried her farther into the woods until they came to a hidden stream, a place where the trees gave way to a sheltered spot of soft grass covering the earth.

"I shall loosen your garments here," he breathed into her ear. "I must have you. We must have each other. Each moment of waiting is agony."

Leona shivered as he put her down, making a pillow for her head out of his tunic, which he had pulled off. Beneath his breeches his member was quite visible. It was swollen and hard, and she reached out to touch it, half in wonder, half as an act of love.

He closed his eyes as her hand enclosed him, and then gently stroked him through the material.

His mouth half opened with the enjoyment of her touch, but then he removed her hand and kissed it. "I shall be satisfied too soon," he gasped.

She said nothing, but she understood. Slowly and deliberately he removed her outer garments. Then he delved beneath her laces and pushed them aside to bare one perfect breast.

"I have dreamed of kissing you thusly," he said, touching his lips lightly to her hard, erect pink nipple. His tongue circled her velvet-soft areola, inflaming her still further. In a moment he drew her nipple full into his mouth and sucked strongly, like a hungry child, till she embraced him and wriggled beneath him in sheer delight.

"Touch the other," she whispered as she drew him ever closer.

He kept his lips on one while he exposed the other, his thumb and forefinger caressing her. Then he reared back and looked down on her. She lay both breasts exposed, both nipples hard and pink. Her cheeks were flushed, her mouth slightly open. She looked as if she were lost in that nether world between the pain of deep desire and the pleasure of being readied.

She opened her eyes and looked up at him wonderingly because he had ceased, momentarily, in his sweet torments. He smiled and finished removing her clothing, piece by piece, folding it carefully and laying it aside.

Then he ran his hand slowly across the red-gold triangle of

hair that hid her womanhood. She groaned and raised her hips slightly as he moved his hand between her legs and then played at her entranceway with knowing fingers.

He leaned over and returned his lips to her ears, her long white neck, her beautiful breasts. He sucked and taunted her, he stroked her and kissed her. Three times he brought her to the brink of raging desire.

Her arms embraced him and drew him tightly to her. Her lovely long white legs wrapped about his middle, and she writhed in his arms. Almost crying, she whispered, "Please, fulfill me now. You torment me too long."

He touched her twice in her most sensitive area before he entered her, and he leaned in such a way that he rubbed gently against her as he delved in to her soft, moist, warm depths.

They both moved with tempestuous, turbulent passion, tumbling through the heavens, through the centuries together, joined tightly as they were deeply possessed with the throbbing pleasure of satisfaction both temporal and ethereal.

"We must never be separated again," he said firmly. "You will stay with me until the treaty is duly signed. Then together we will return to the French court with the princes."

Leona nodded, then added, "I must return to Marguerite. I must stay with her till the danger I feel so strongly passes."

"I will stay in France with you until you feel free to leave, Leona." He made the promise because he, too, had a sensation with which he could not argue. Somehow he knew Leona had to be in France, that she, perhaps both of them, were destined to be there. He did not speak to her of his own fears, his strong sense that she herself was in danger.

Margaret of Austria was dressed in a deep-burgundy gown. She wore a headdress of stiff white organza and a simple ruby and diamond necklace. She sat primly in her brocade chair in the reception room with her small hands folded tightly in her lap.

From the hallway, outside the entrance to the room, the ballads of a minstrel could be heard. He sang in a high tenor voice and accompanied himself by strumming on a dulcimer. "I have always loved music," she said to Philip, who sat across from her.

He nodded his agreement.

"I summoned you to tell you what a fine job you have done with the young princes. I am well satisfied that they have been properly tutored."

"Thank you, madam. Am I to return to Spain with them and await the signing of the treaty?"

Margaret waved her hand. "There is no need for that. We will wait here for Charles. As soon as the treaty is signed, you may deliver them to the French court at Versailles."

"Madam, do you know when the emperor will arrive?"

"Not for several weeks."

"Then I should like to request leave to marry the lady Leona."

Margaret looked at him and her expression did not change.

"An attractive, well-educated woman. A good choice for you, Philip. I grant you leave."

"Thank you, madam."

Philip stood up and bowed, then he left to go in search of Leona. He had decided that he would take her to Bruges immediately. He loved the place itself, and he wanted to take her away from the pressures of the royal household.

Outside, a mild breeze swept across the rivers that intersected at Bruges and in the clear sky a full moon rose over the city.

They had been married quietly at a side altar in the Church of Our Lady, the same church in which Philip the Good, Duke of Burgundy, had taken Isabella of Portugal to be his wife in 1468.

"This is one of the most beautiful places I have ever been," Leona said as their small boat glided along the calm waterway. It was propelled by two oarsmen, one fore and one aft.

"They call Bruges the Venice of the North," Philip confided.

"I have never been to Venice," she admitted. "Though I have read of it and would like to go."

"Bruges is an important place of trade," Philip told her. "It has access to the sea, and to the Oostende and Sluis rivers in Holland. All these lovely homes belong to wealthy merchants. And, of course, some are guildhalls."

Leona marveled at the city, which was far cleaner than most French cities. Its houses were neat and gabled. They were set around squares or in rows with narrow streets between. Above the city, ornate church spires rose to meet the sky, while the whole town was enclosed by shallow ramparts.

"Yes, I am quite in love," Leona said softly as she leaned her head on his broad shoulder.

Philip kissed her hair lightly and laughed. "With me or with this place?"

"With both," she confessed.

"Tomorrow we must begin the journey back to Cambrai. Charles will be arriving soon. With luck he'll sign the treaty right away and we can be on our way to Versailles."

Leona smiled. "Yes, I must not be away too long."

He did not ask how long was too long. He leaned over and closed his eyes, kissing her long white neck, then the curve of her ear.

Leona took his hand in hers and then lifted it and kissed his fingers. "I have a confession to make—and you must hear me out."

"A confession? Is it of another love?"

She shook her head quickly. "No. I have known no other man. But when we make love, when we are truly together, locked together, I have the most peculiar desire."

He felt a strange surge of emotion pass through him, as if she were about to speak about an experience he himself had. "What is this desire?" he asked, even though he thought he could almost guess.

"I want to call you by another name, Philip. It is all so odd, perhaps because I have studied history. Perhaps because Philip of Macedonia was the father of Alexander of Macedonia. But I sometimes want to call you Alexander."

"Alexander." He let the name roll off his tongue and was surprised that he seemed accustomed to it. "I have told you I dream of you too, and it seems these experiences we have separately yet together are providential. But I must confess to you, the name you want to call me by seems almost to be my own, even though I know no one by this name. And there is something just as strange. I want to call you Leandra—though I know your name is Leona and Leandra is a name belonging to another language."

Leona touched his cheek with her hand. "Perhaps we are foreordained, perhaps we have lived before. There are other signs. Please do not think me mad if I tell you that ever since I was a small child I have known I was different in some way."

"And your brother?"

"My adoptive brother. He is different as well. He is gifted."

"So are you. You are the most beautiful and delicate woman I have ever known, and yet you possess a powerful intellect and knowledge of all manner of things."

"And you can still love such a creature?"

He laughed and kissed her lips. "It makes you more intriguing and I love you all the more."

"I shall cherish you, Philip—Alexander. Perhaps we can sometimes call each other by these secret names."

He kissed her lips tenderly and slowly. "My Leandra," he whispered. Suddenly it was as if a wonderful peace settled over him. As if he had confessed his deepest secrets and been accepted. Even as he held her, he knew it must be true. They had lived and loved before and both had vague memories of that life.

They had begun traveling directly after their wedding. They stopped at a lovely old château in Roeselari the first night.

"This is an enchanting place," Leona said as she looked up at the high ceiling and breathed the scented air that floated on the night breezes through the extensive gardens and up to this room.

Theirs was more than a sexual encounter, more than mere lovemaking in any mortal sense of the word, Philip thought as he looked at his bride.

They had made love before, but now they were wedded and he sensed from something in a past he could not totally recall that this was to be the melding of spirits, the perfect union of mind, body, and universe, the sublime combination of the spiritual and temporal. The words *Those whom the immortals choose for love are blessed in a way unknown to others* rang in his mind as if spoken by himself in that other life, that life when first he had reached out to this woman, when first he had held her and known her.

In spite of all his rationalizations, all his study, all his grounding in reality, he was willing now to give in to what he had sensed for so long, what he had tried to put aside, what he could no longer ignore—what he remembered, had in fact happened. He had lived before and so had she. He had loved her then, and he loved her now. He accepted this on faith as he looked at her.

Tonight she was no longer his mistress but his wife. Tonight she lay beside him in white laces, her ravishing hair his to unravel, her body his to explore. He knew also that she felt about him as he felt about her. She explored him with the same relish he had for her, and though each knew their own sweet pleasure, they also knew a shared pleasure. And they knew the third element in their union. The third element wed them to the universe, and between them there was a force, a discharge of power, the sort that split the heavens with sudden light during a storm. It was a feeling no other coupling had; it was absolutely unique.

"You're so thoughtful," Leona said as she looked into his face. "What are you pondering?"

"It is only now that I have come to terms with the truth, Leona. You *are* different. Our love *is* different from any other."

She was lying on a bed strewn with rose petals and she was covered in white lace, her hair around her like a halo of light.

He stared into her eyes and felt as though he were diving into cool blue-green waters, as if a spell were being cast over him. He let himself be drawn in, he surrendered to the spell and found the water was as clear beneath as on the surface. Yet it was all softness, and the images that floated before his eyes were fantastic images, dream beings moving effortlessly through the liquid.

He felt her hands on him, cool on his flesh, yet warm when they touched him. She slid her hands the length of his member, letting it rise as her warm fingers caressed it. Somehow he felt detached, yet he could feel intensely, more intensely than he had ever felt before. Somehow he felt he was still in the cool green pool, yet at the same time he was above her, hovering over her, watching her face as her hands wrapped around him, moving on him slowly while the perfume of her body filled his nostrils and the angelic beauty of her face sent him deeper into his trance.

She guided him toward her and then let him come to rest on her golden triangle. He shuddered and then kissed her lips before easing away her laces and revealing her milk-white skin which was flushed with desire.

Her hips rose to him when he caressed her breasts. She moved wonderfully as he teased her entranceway. Their kisses covered each other as they struggled lovingly to prolong their joy and this incredible experience of journeying through soothing waters.

When he entered her it was not as it had been before. It was a sensation of far greater magnitude, and the emotions that accompanied it flooded over him like successive waves on a beach. Then they were tiny creatures, lost in the inner maze of a giant conch shell, holding each other as they journeyed and searched in the dizzying darkness of the passage. He withdrew from her to kiss her anew, to watch her, and yet to journey with her to unknown places, to new levels of consciousness.

When his lips reached that place she cried out and moved against him, clutching him, holding him.

She trembled in his arms as they once again united, their minds, their bodies, their souls forging into one. In those glorious moments they emerged from the labyrinth of the shell and were taken by a soaring eagle as it traveled up, ever upward. Then they tumbled into prolonged ecstasy as they both began a throbbing descent, tumbling through the night sky and past a million stars, clinging to each other, blended into one. For a long time they lay spent in each other's arms, and they knew there were no secrets between them, that somehow all things were possible, and that one day their mutual questions concerning the past would be answered.

Charles V undid his black cape and with a single swirling motion removed it. Next he carefully took off his gloves, then his three-cornered black velvet cap.

Philip bowed before him. "It is good to see you again. Have you had a good trip, sire?"

"Very good. Our black galleons have returned from Mexico filled with silver and gold."

"Spain is the envy of the world."

Charles smiled and then changed the subject. He was not a man to spend time on idle chitchat even with good friends. "I have received dispatches from Margaret with regard to the treaty. I am willing to sign, but the children cannot be released till the money is received."

"It is my understanding that it is being forwarded even as we speak."

"Then as soon as I have confirmation, you may take leave and deliver the princes to France."

"I should be happy to do so, sire. I should also like to take this opportunity to tell you I've been married to Lady Leona."

"Ah, the pretty one with the red-gold hair. Congratulations."

"I wasn't sure you would remember her."

"I am not dead. Of course, I am not Francis either. I do not sleep with all the women in my empire."

Philip grinned. "He has not slept with this one."

"Good. Well, she seems a royal prize to me, and I hold with the introduction of new blood into old bloodlines now and again. The aristocrats interbreed too much. I offer you my best wishes."

"Thank you, sire."

"You have served me well, Philip. It is my duty and my pleasure to reward you with full titles to all your lands in Castile."

Philip bowed and the emperor motioned for him to stand. "I shall go now and rest before dinner. In the meantime I will have a proclamation drawn up. Will you be returning to the French court immediately?"

"As soon as possible."

"That suits me. I have no interest in these royal children save the ransom they bring."

Charles left then, turning abruptly and heading for his chambers. Then, midway up the stairs he turned. "Do you know from whence the money for this ransom comes?"

Philip frowned and Charles continued upstairs. It was a rhetorical question to which neither of them could possibly know the answer. But it was an interesting question, one he thought he would put to Leona.

They walked in the garden and smelled the lush flowers. "I ate too much," Philip confessed. "When the emperor is here, Margaret serves meals that are far too lavish."

"I hardly know why, he eats little."

"She serves many dishes so he will have many choices, I expect," Philip answered, then more seriously, he added, "I've been dying to be alone with you all day. I have a serious question."

"Yes?"

"Do you know from where the money to pay the ransom comes?"

Leona pulled away and looked into his blue eyes. She slowly shook her head. "To my knowledge, there is no such money in the treasury—I have heard it is always empty."

"How about Louise?"

Leona shook her head. "Louise has money in her own coffers, but not that much."

"And Marguerite?"

"Oh, no! She told me that while Henry is frugal, much of his wealth was lost fighting the Italian campaign. No, there is not enough for the ransom Charles demanded."

They neared a stone bench and Philip sat down, pulling her down next to him. "Where then? Could it be from the coffers of the Sorbonne—from the arbitrators of good and evil, from the Guardians of the Faith?"

Leona inhaled as the enormity of his suggestion sank in. The old men who issued orders and who so fought the reformation would never give money without demanding something in return. For years they had fought the liberal tendencies of Francis and especially those of his sister, Marguerite. For years they had watched them release those who were arrested. For years they had watched as tolerance grew toward men like Erasmus and Calvin, and Marot was Marguerite's own court poet!

Then, as though guessing her deepest concerns, he echoed them. "Renaud would never part with so much gold unless he had traded it for power."

"We must return to Versailles quickly," Leona said. "I am very worried."

"We will return as soon as the ransom is delivered," he promised. "Whatever you fear, I fear. I know I am here not simply to love you, but to help you."

"I don't know how we found each other," she whispered. "But I know I would have looked forever."

Again he brushed her soft cheek with his lips. "I too."

Fifteen

September 1529
Versailles

Marguerite and her mother, Louise, returned to the court at Versailles a week after the negotiations were completed. They left Philip and Leona to escort the young princes back to the French court when they were formally released.

As the royal guard wound along the road that led to Versailles, trumpets preceded their entourage. When the coach and the guard arrived outside the entrance to the castle, the entire staff, the full royal guard, and Francis himself were gathered on the stone steps in front of the scaffolding.

Philip nudged Leona gently. "It seems this palace is under construction."

Leona, feeling lighthearted, laughed. "Versailles is always under construction," she replied. "It is more than a palace. It is the king's hobby."

"From the looks of it, it will continue to be a hobby for some time to come."

"The court won't stay here long. I imagine they will return to Chambord or Fontainebleau quite soon."

"All this movement will be a change for me. Charles seldom leaves Madrid."

The coach drew to a halt and the doors were opened. The princes were lifted down by the coachman, and though they had been away nearly four long years, they ran enthusiastically toward their father, who greeted them with joy while the bevy of tutors who would groom them for the future stood by, waiting to meet their young charges.

Their aunt, Marguerite, Queen of Navarre, and their grandmother, Louise of Savoy, who had seen them more recently, hugged and kissed them.

"How cruel the last four years have been," Marguerite cried as she embraced her nephews. "But now you are home."

After all the formalities of state, Francis came alone to the rooms occupied by Philip and Leona.

"I'm told that I am remiss in many things," Francis confessed as he quaffed down a goblet of wine. "But I want to thank you both. You, Philip, for being a good tutor and you, Leona, for being a faithful servant to my sister."

Francis snapped his fingers and a valet appeared with an official from the royal treasury. The official was dressed in bright red, and four heavy silver chains hung from his neck. He deposited a velvet bag and a small chest on the table.

"This is a token of my gratitude," Francis said, indicating the chest to Philip. "And this, my noble friend, is repayment of the debt I owe you from that awful morning in Pavia when you and you alone came forth to help me. Has he told you about it?" Francis asked as he looked at Leona.

Philip's face was red with embarrassment.

"He has never spoken of Pavia at all."

"He is too modest. Your husband is a true gentleman, a rare man, and one of the few left who knows the real meaning of chivalry. He saved my life, and when that was done he saved my honor."

"It is good to know from another what I feel in my heart," Leona answered.

"Yes, my dear Philip," Francis continued. "I was going to give you the gift of land, a place in the French nobility if you had wanted it. But I am told by my sister that you would prefer a monetary reward because you are going to Navarre when she goes."

"You're too generous," Philip said. He did not mention that he was already a man of means with land in Castile. There were many good uses to which this money could be put, he thought.

Francis again snapped his fingers and a servant filled their goblets anew. "To the future!" Francis proclaimed grandly.

They lifted their glasses and toasted with the king. Leona did not ask the question that plagued her most, the question concerning the source of the ransom. She feared she already knew the answer.

When the king took his leave, they sat down to finish their wine. "Is it your wish to leave for Navarre right away?" Philip asked.

Leona shook her head. "Marguerite wants to take her mother and the young princes with her to Touraine when Francis goes to Fontainebleau next week. If you have no objection, we will go with Marguerite and stay with her till she returns to Navarre."

"Of course I have no objection."

"Have you spoken to Marguerite about the source of the ransom?"

Leona shook her head. "Not yet. I know she will be very upset. I was waiting till we knew for certain."

Philip shook his head. "I fear that will be after the persecutions begin."

Leona bit her lip and lifted her hand to her brow. "I am afraid you're right."

Marseilles was a great coastal port, normally teeming with people from France, North Africa, and the rest of Europe. Its harbor was filled with vessels, great galleons with crisp white sails.

At a normal time, men with coal-black skin in full-length white caftans could be seen bartering in hand language with bearded, wizened old men who came with fists full of gold to meet the ships from Morocco or Algiers. At a normal time, women came to the great dockside market to buy fish, bread, meat, cloth, trinkets, and all manner of household goods. At a normal time, children played in the streets, men got drunk on wine, and women leaned from brothel windows, offering themselves for a price.

This was not a normal time.

This was a dark black time. A time when death stalked the streets, came into the houses, hid in the pantries, and visited the most pious of churchgoers. It could be found in the giant cathedral, in the fish market, and in the aching old timbers of the ships in the harbor. This was a time of furry tongues, of strange, violent bouts of madness, of hollow, fearful eyes.

It was a time of sudden death.

Michel de Nostradamus walked through the deserted streets. The whole city carried the stench of death. Everywhere fires smoldered, acrid smoke rising in the air, fumes carrying the smell of filthy clothing, of burning flesh, of dead rats.

Half of Marseilles was dying. The other half hid. As if one could hide from death—as if one could cheat fate.

He had gone into hundreds of houses to examine and treat the dying. Some he knew he had saved, but for hundreds of others it was too late. Filth and pestilence, they traveled together. If only people could be taught to bathe, he thought ruefully. If only the religious zealots would stop killing cats because they believed them to harbor the spirits of witches!

He closed his eyes as he filled with anger. So much had been lost! So much had to be redone.

"I have faith!" he said aloud, looking heavenward.

But still, he felt angry. So much history was lost, so much ignored. The Egyptians, the Greeks, and the Romans had made remarkable medical progress. Even those in Byzantium understood that man was a conduit through which medical knowledge was to pass. Illness was not punishment for sin, it was a state of nature and could be cured. God had given humankind the brains to solve problems and the free will to choose. Too many chose ignorance and called it faith.

As the zealots took hold of the crumbling Byzantine Empire,

all scientific study ceased. The Church decreed the study of dead bodies was a sin. The gift of exploring the human body was denied by those who failed to understand the true meaning of faith.

Even now it was forbidden to study or dissect the dead. Not that it had stopped him or others. He had done it clandestinely; he had unraveled the mysteries of man's internal organs and he had found the human body the greatest of all wonders. It was a world within, a true miracle, a tribute to God. Far from destroying faith, the man who explored such knowledge could only feel greater awe.

In nature all cures existed. But why had those of early Christendom not understood this? It was man who was to find and catalogue these cures, experiment and modify them. He knew he was on the edge of learning more about the molds. The molds he obtained cured the plague if the case was not too far advanced. Indeed, they cured multiple illnesses.

He thought of Leona. His role and hers had only recently been made known to him. It came in dreams; it was confirmed when he threw the mystic cubes.

They *were* immortals, though she did not yet know, nor did she have his memory of the past, or his means of seeing the future. He was to write of the future, to cast the mystic cubes and write of what was to come, a kind of guide to mortals. Leona was to help him by bringing him to court, where he would serve a future queen, a woman he knew would be named Catherine.

In the meantime, Leona was to guide Marguerite and help save the intellectuals of France. And there was another. A strong man who was to love Leona and who had been brought back because of service in a former life. If he served in this life too, he would join the immortals, those special beings who led the spirit world and guided the temporal world by returning to help certain leaders in their fight against darkness and evil. Good or evil? It was mankind's eternal privilege to choose.

In their ethereal guise some would call them immortals, others would say they were angels. In their material form they would be remembered only for the good they did. But there was always blackness. There was always a counterforce. Such a force was gathering now. He could feel it with all his being.

His thoughts again went to Leona. It had been a long while since they had been together. He decided he should see her soon, though it was not yet time for her to fully know about herself. When the time came, he would receive a sign.

Michel reached his horse, which had been tethered near the fountain in the main square. He mounted and prepared to leave the death-ridden city of Marseilles. Tonight he would read the mystic cubes. In the meantime he would try to find out where Francis was currently holding court. Marguerite was there, and that could mean only that Leona was there as well.

Father Charles Renaud sat in judgment. He judged fact from fiction, black from white, right from wrong, sin from virtue, and, on occasion, life from death. He was a dark, cruel man whose evil deeds preceded him like a shadow precedes a figure in the lamplight.

He was tall and gaunt with a long, narrow face. But it was his hands that those who knew him remembered most. He had exceptionally long fingers with strong, yellowed nails that curved under at the end. His eyes were small and his face pitted as if it had been pelted with a thousand small stones.

It was his duty to judge heretics, to set in motion the means of punishment, to see to it that orthodoxy prevailed.

The stone walls of the Sorbonne gave off a musty odor that pervaded the long room lit by torches and candles. The assembled were all dressed in their long black robes and wore their silver chains.

Renaud sat at the head of the table, looking down the two equal rows of devotees and religious scholars.

"Reformers," he sneered. "Thanks to the king's sister, they have far too much power! They gain new adherents every day!"

The others said nothing, but they grunted their agreement.

"Calvin is protected by Marguerite. Rabelais and Marot are

also protected. In the Netherlands, Erasmus influences far too many! Calvin even visits court!"

"What are we to do?" one of the monks on the left side of the long table asked. "If these people are not given over, they cannot be executed."

Father Renaud could not admit his true plans even to these trusted Guardians of the Faith. For years now he had thought of killing Marguerite—but then she married. The situation was doubly complicated. He needed a time when her household was vulnerable, a time when someone else could be blamed. He was ever vigilant. He waited, though none too patiently. But now he had to appease the others, give them something to work on.

"For now the leaders can wait! It is their adherents we must pursue! If fear is instilled in their bones, then this reformation will lose its power."

"We cannot root out everyone—"

"It is not necessary to root out everyone. We have lists made—men and women who write books, people who are wicked and dangerous, people who are subversive about personal and private confession. Everyone who questions the papacy. We must find them! They must see the light through suffering! Pull out their tongues! Disembowel them! They will be burned alive!"

"France has not known such—" another monk began.

"France has been too tolerant! This pastor from Neuchâtel, this Calvin, has released a spring that will be uncontrollable if we do not act!"

A silence filled the room and for a moment Renaud said nothing. He waited only for the meaning of his words to sink in.

"Persecution excites—stories multiply, fear is a tool we must use if we hope to be successful, to survive, to retain our power."

Again silence. Then Renaud said, "Are we agreed?"

"Will the king allow it?" one of the learned men of the Sorbonne asked.

"The king is in our debt. He has no choice."

There was no answer. He smiled to himself. "Bring forth the

heretics. I will judge them. At last we are free to strike. The king will not stop us."

Marguerite, her mother, and the princes, accompanied by a small entourage including Philip and Leona, left early in the morning on the journey to Touraine. They had just reached the village of Gretz, when Louise collapsed.

Leona felt Louise's brow. She was burning with fever and her symptoms seemed to indicate she had plague. She had complained of the bright light, and in the hours before her collapse she had been filled with energy.

"I have so much pain," Louise breathed. "I always have pain though."

"Madam, you should have told me. Where is this pain?"

Louise lifted her arm and touched her breast. "Here, all around. It's terrible. It is like being stabbed with a knife."

Leona carefully undid Louise's undergarments and examined her breasts.

"Your touch is so gentle," Louise murmured.

Leona felt the hard lumps. One extended from the side of the breast to the underarm. These were not the buboes of plague, although Leona thought Louise also had plague. These were tumors, and there seemed no doubt that Louise was in an advanced stage of cancer as well.

"I shall give you some sleeping powder, madam. It will ease your pain and help you to rest."

"Thank you," Louise said.

Leona mixed the powders and lifted Louise's head so she could take the mixture with a little water.

Louise swallowed and then fell back against the cushions. She grasped Leona's hand. "Come closer, my dear. Now, listen carefully. You are a fine doctor, but you are not a master physician like your brother or the court physicians. You must have Marguerite send for the court physicians—though I doubt they know as much as you, it is the politic thing to do. I'm going to die, Leona. Let the court physicians be the ones who tend me.

And summon Father Renaud too. I like him no better than you do, but if he is not notified of my mortal illness, his nose will be dangerously out of joint."

Leona nodded. She understood Louise's concern and appreciated it. Louise understood all the nuances of court politics. Yet she herself felt nothing but danger where Renaud was concerned.

"I'll call the maids to undress you and make you comfortable," she promised as she left Louise's side.

"How is she?" Marguerite asked. She stood just outside the bedroom anxiously.

Leona took her arm and guided her to a nearby chair. "She is very ill, madam. She has plague and she has cancer. She will not survive regardless of treatment. She asks for the court physicians and for Father Renaud."

Marguerite's eyes filled with tears and she nodded. "I shall summon them and go to her immediately."

Renaud read the message written on the parchment. He dismissed the messenger with a wave of his hand, and only when the lad was gone did Renaud smile.

How many years had he tried to plot to kill Marguerite, Queen of Navarre? He could not calculate. Plot after plot had been foiled. There were too many people about, the court was always moving, Marguerite was traveling. No plan had been brought to fruition. But now opportunity had knocked. It was absolutely perfect! Nothing he had ever planned was this safe.

Bless Louise of Savoy! She was so utterly politic. She was deathly ill and she had asked for him to come to her! She wanted to make certain all her fences were mended. He was utterly beside himself with excitement.

He hurried to his rooms and packed a few things, then he immediately sent for a coach to take him to Louise's side. He smiled to himself. She would never recover, her daughter would be killed, and the king would be deprived of all the women who propped him up.

* * *

Marguerite knotted her handkerchief again and again. "I've tried and tried to find Francis," she said distractedly. "But messenger after messenger has returned with undelivered letters."

Louise lay in the center of a massive bed which served only to make her appear smaller and weaker.

"At least my grandsons have been freed," she whispered, turning her head toward her daughter, who had been kept at a distance by the fussing physicians. Louise had been irrational now for many hours, but she suddenly seemed to know what she was saying. "And your brother is to be married again. Perhaps the marriage will bring a real peace."

Marguerite was silent. Louise was speaking of Ellenor, Charles V's sister, to whom Francis would be wed. But not even his mother, Louise, understood the hatred that burned in her son's soul. There could never be peace between him and Charles. And Ellenor would be simply a thorn in his court of flowers. Francis had confided that he hated Ellenor's simpering obedience to Charles, and he had vowed never to touch her when they were married. It was a vow he bragged about. A vow he intended keeping.

Louise trembled and shook violently as the physicians moved in closer.

Leona and Philip stood just beyond the doorway. "The physicians are a sight to behold," Leona whispered.

The physicians wore heavy cotton shirts soaked in seven liquids which were said to have magical qualities. They also wore seven colors reputed to ward off the plague. Over their shirts they wore heavy leather to keep out the bad air. On their noses they wore vinegar-soaked cloths, and their eyes were covered by glasses. Each one also wore a garland of garlic as an added precaution.

Marguerite left the bedroom and came to them. "I am so glad you are both here. I cannot begin to tell you how frightened I am. I fear for my nephews," Marguerite said ever so softly. "What if they get the plague?"

"I think they will not," Leona said. "I have taken precautions to protect them. They've been bathed and doused in oil of citron. I have also given them medicine my brother told me about."

Her face was drawn and tight. "Thank you. There is more. I hear rumors—there have been several horrible public executions in Paris. My brother says he cannot stop them. I am certain it is because the ransom was paid by—"

Leona put her finger to her lips. "We must be careful," she whispered. "The walls have ears, madam. This is a subject about which I intended speaking with you—when it is safe."

"Let us go where it is private," Marguerite replied.

Young Prince Henri, son of Francis, sat on the garden bench and watched his older brother play in the afternoon sunshine.

All around him the flowers seemed brighter than bright just as the sky seemed bluer than blue. It was quiet in this small villa. His grandmother, Louise of Savoy, was deathly ill with plague, and everyone else feared getting it. His aunt was pre-occupied with his grandmother's illness, and everywhere he overheard dark conversations.

He stood up and walked curiously over to the sundial that occupied the center of the garden. He studied it with consider-able fascination. It was divided into twelve equal parts so that one could tell the time of day by the position of the sun's shadow.

Henri was deep in thought when he saw a long shadow, a shadow made by the figure of a man rather than by the sun.

He turned around, his mouth slightly open in surprise.

The man smiled and raised his gloved hand. "Please, young prince, I did not mean to disturb you."

Henri, who was not dressed in royal garb, ran his hand through his hair. "How did you know I was a prince?"

"I guessed. Besides, the town is awash in gossip because the royal entourage has stopped here."

"Because my grandmother is ill. We were unable to continue to Tours."

"Is Marguerite traveling with your mother?"

"Yes, and Lady Leona and Philip, my tutor. But who are you?"

"Michel de Nostradamus, Leona's brother." Michel smiled and touched young Henri's shoulder. "So, you like sundials."

Henri smiled. "Yes, and telescopes as well. But my grandmother told me to put them all away. She does not want anyone to think me heretical."

Michel laughed. "I should think not, though it's true, the good judges of the Sorbonne do not know the difference between heresy and science."

"Those could be dangerous words," Henri said. "Father Renaud from the Sorbonne is on his way here. Marguerite did not want to send for him, but my grandmother insisted."

"Can you take me to my sister?" he asked. "The garden wall was not so daunting, but the royal guard may well be restrictive."

Henri smiled. "How can I be sure you are who you say you are?"

"You can't. But if I am not, the royal guard will have me in the end in any case."

Henri smiled as he looked at the stranger. There was something fascinating about him and Henri could tell he was a very learned man. "Follow me, then," he said, turning from the sundial. "I will take you to your sister."

"And I shall show you how to make a sundial when time permits."

"Michel!" Leona ran into his arms. "Oh, so much has happened. 1 have written you but received no answer."

Michel sat next to her, and he held her hands and looked into her green eyes. "I've been traveling. I have much to tell you, but the telling—all the telling will come later."

"You speak in riddles."

He laughed and squeezed her hands. "And is this silent, patient, and unquestioning man your husband?" He looked at Philip, who sat across the room.

"How did you know? You said you didn't receive my letters."

"I knew, just as you probably knew I was coming."

"I saw you—and I tried to reach you. But no matter, you are here. Yes, this is Philip. We were married in Bruges."

"My heartfelt congratulations. We will celebrate and you will be properly welcomed into our family when all this trouble has passed."

"Yes, Louise has plague and cancer as well. She is very far advanced. I have only taken the precaution of making everyone use oil of citron, as you taught me. And I gave the princes medicine, medicine such as I once gave the king."

"Made of moss?"

"Yes, how did you know?"

"I have been using it myself, that and molds."

"It is best to keep our medicines a secret," Leona suggested.

Michel nodded. "You've done what you could. Will you take me to Louise now?"

"Of course. Marguerite will be glad to see you too."

"And the court physicians?"

"They are like clowns. They have nothing to offer her save their endless arguments about which one of them is right."

Leona stood up and beckoned her brother to follow her. Philip came too, his eyes sharp to irregularities, his mind filled with thought.

Last night he had a foretelling. It was veiled in fog and was unclear. He knew only that his night vision had shown him that evil threatened Leona and perhaps others. So he followed her now, his hand near his sword, his vigilance doubled.

Nostradamus bent to one knee before Marguerite, Queen of Navarre. "My Queen," he said. "It is an honor to kneel before you. Dr. Rabelais and my sister have both told me of your writing, and of all your many and varied talents."

"I have heard much of you as well. My mother is dying. Please, I beg you, make her comfortable."

Nostradamus entered the room and looked at the royal physicians in their absurd clothing. They stared at him resentfully as he walked directly to Louise and felt her fevered brow.

"You're too close," one of the doctors warned. "Look at you, you're not even dressed properly."

Nostradamus looked at them in disdain. "How can you treat a patient you're afraid to approach?"

"We don't know how it travels. But we're certain it has something to do with the air."

"I am well acquainted with the plague, my friends. I am Michel de Nostradamus, and I have just seen this disease kill more than half of Marseilles."

"Well, you shouldn't touch her," another warned. "It may live on the skin."

Nostradamus raised his brow. "Perhaps it travels on the babbling tongues of bad doctors, perhaps even on communion cakes or with unbathed priests."

The doctors' faces reddened with anger, but they said nothing. Nostradamus was well known.

Another person entered the darkened room and took up a position to one side of the bed.

Nostradamus's eyes strayed to the imposing cloaked figure. His hands were folded, and his long, yellowed nails curved under. "That's blasphemy," the man uttered.

"What's blasphemy?" Michel asked.

"What you just said about communion cakes."

"It's common sense," Nostradamus said firmly as he sought to look this man in the eye. But the priest's eyes were hidden.

"I have heard of Nostradamus," one of the physicians said, breaking the tension in the room. "You are a master physician from Montpellier. I've heard you've visited many places where nearly everyone died. I've heard you treat plague and never get it."

Nostradamus acknowledged the physician with only a nod.

He bent over and continued to examine the patient, Louise. She was barely conscious.

Marguerite shuddered. "She is in so much pain."

Nostradamus knelt by Louise's side and held her hand. He then retrieved a liquid from his bag. He held her head gently and told her to drink. She did so laboriously, and then fell back against her pillows with a half smile on her face.

Renaud stared at Nostradamus hatefully. The man was a heretic, another one of those men of ideas protected by Marguerite. He felt his fingers close on his knife as he looked at her. This was not the time, though it was the place. He controlled himself, knowing it would be soon.

Renaud sat in the corner of the small room he had been given in the villa. Yes, the more he thought of it, the more he realized that opportunities such as this were few and far between. Marguerite was his enemy, the enemy he had to rid himself of before full power could be obtained. How fortunate he felt. The means, everything, had fallen into his lap.

Again he thought about it. Francis would be lost without his mother; he would be nothing without Marguerite. Furthermore, the so-called intellects who called for reformation within the church would have no royal allies, no place to hide. It seemed clear to him that Louise's death, his being summoned to this godforsaken little village, even the presence of the "doctor" Nostradamus, could not be better. When he had left Paris he had thought the situation ready-made. Now, because of Nostradamus, it was even better.

In Paris or Versailles he would need accomplices, an elaborate plan, and much time to take care of all the details. A royal murder was difficult to arrange. But there were hardly any guards here. Furthermore, all the players were assembled.

He would kill Marguerite and blame Nostradamus. He would say he saw the doctor coming from her bedroom chambers; he could easily convince people. He would kill Marguerite with the doctor's own scalpel. Darkness, the lack of guards, the strangeness of the villa, would all be his allies. And what a hero he would become! Hero enough to spirit young Francis and his brother away for proper indoctrination.

Renaud smiled to himself.

Yes, it was all perfect.

Leona was in the stable. She patted Pegasus's long white nose and fed him carrots from the garden. Philip was nearby, brushing the horse's tail, grooming him for the journey they would soon take to Navarre.

"You'll like it in Navarre," she told Pegasus. "There are high mountain meadows in which to graze."

The horse nuzzled her affectionately. "He was with us," she said. "Do you remember?"

"I remember no details. But somehow I think you're right."

"I remember no details either, but I know this horse. I have always known him."

"Ah, you two are here," Michel said as he came into the stable.

Pegasus whinnied. "Ah, he knows you too," Leona said as Philip walked around the horse and came to stand by her side.

Michel stroked the horse. "Something is amiss," he said slowly. "I do not like it."

"Renaud," Leona said softly. "He is evil—I shiver whenever he comes near me."

"What could he intend?" Philip asked.

Michel shrugged. "I have tried to think on it. I have no answers." He sensed the evil as Leona did. But suddenly he could not read the mystic cubes. Nor did he dream. He wondered now if he should tell them what he knew of them, but then he decided it was not yet time. The sign had yet to come.

"Louise is dying," Philip said slowly, "but Marguerite has the king's ear and considerable power. If something is wrong, it is surely Marguerite who is in danger. That's what Leona believes."

"If special guards are used, it will alert the culprit. If it is Renaud, he will never be unmasked," Leona added.

"If it is Renaud, the trouble is deep indeed," Michel concluded. "We shall all have to seek refuge in Navarre."

"I will guard the good queen's chambers myself," Philip offered. "You, Michel, you guard the princes."

"None of us should sleep in our beds," Leona suggested. "Let us make bundles out of pillows so it will look as if we are all asleep. I sense the danger is very real. It is as if all my nerves are standing on end."

"We are agreed," Michel said.

Philip and Leona nodded.

"We had better go now. It is not wise to leave things for so long," Michel suggested.

"And we must prepare Marguerite," Leona said.

"My mother is dead," Marguerite said in a near-whisper. "It's hard for me to believe."

"Come, madam," Leona said. "We'll go to your room. I'm sure you want to say your prayers."

"Yes, my prayers. When she is buried, I want to go home to Henri, to Navarre."

Leona led Marguerite to her room and sat her down on the edge of the bed. "Madam, I know you are filled with emotion and very tired, but I ask you to bear with me, to listen."

"Of course. What is it, Leona? You seem so serious."

"I am afraid, madam. I am afraid and I need your help."

It was the darkest of all nights. Clouds hid the stars and the new moon's light was weak and could not be seen.

Renaud waited till it was long past two in the morning, then, dressed in black to match the night, he left his room and stole down the corridors of the villa in search of the doctor's chambers.

He leaned on the latch and opened it carefully. He slipped

into the room and waited. His eyes had become used to the blackness by now, and on the bed he saw the doctor bundled in his blankets. His dark eyes darted around the room, seeking the black leather satchel containing the medical instruments. It was on the trunk at the foot of the bed. Renaud eased himself toward the end of the bed, hardly breathing. His skin tingled as if each nerve had been set in motion. He was certain his heartbeat could be heard in the deadly silence. He reached the satchel and opened the flap cautiously and felt inside. He found the shape he was looking for and carefully lifted the box containing the sharp scalpel. Silently he removed it and temporarily sheathed it where he usually carried his own stiletto. Then he replaced the box, closed the satchel, and slipped out of the room, pulling the door closed behind him.

He moved stealthily down the hall toward Marguerite's door and opened it with the same care he had taken with the doctor's door. He stepped inside and waited to make sure she was asleep. She did not move, so he crept toward the bed and leaned over the sleeping form.

Carefully, he withdrew the scalpel, and holding it tightly he pulled back the covers, ready to grasp her hair, jerk her head back, and slit her throat.

"What!" Renaud gasped in surprise but his utterance hardly escaped his lips when he whirled about, aware he was not alone.

"Enough!" Philip cried as he jumped from behind the heavy drapes, his sword drawn.

Renaud seized the pillow he had thought was Marguerite's head in his free hand and narrowly fended off Philip's thrust. His eyes flashed with hatred as he slashed Philip across his left arm.

Philip sensed the coming blow but could not retreat quickly enough. He winced with pain as he freed his sword from the pillow and struck Renaud in the side of his head, sending him to the floor. Philip scrambled after him. His heart was beating wildly and a vision filled his mind—it was his love, his wife, Leona, and a strange curved knife protruded from her midsection. But it was not Leona! It was Leandra, and suddenly he knew.

"Cyril!" he cried.

Renaud rolled on the floor to his knees and again lashed out at Philip as he approached. He lunged at Philip's face, scalpel flashing.

"You cannot stop me!" he exclaimed. "She must die as before!"

Philip sidestepped the blow. He could not erase the image of Leandra, and blind with fury he ran Renaud through with his sword. Renaud's eyes bulged out, and his throat gurgled as his lifeless form fell in a heap to the floor.

Marguerite emerged from the alcove and covered her mouth with her hands. But she did not scream. She rushed over to Philip.

"He who would have killed you is dead," he said.

Then, realizing the position they were all in, he whispered urgently, "My lady, I urge you to send the guard away. This matter must be kept quiet."

Footsteps filled the hall, and without another question Marguerite went to the door. "I only had a nightmare," she said. "Go away, it is all right. It was just a bad dream."

The guards instantly retreated and Marguerite bolted the door. She hurried to the burning ember and from it lit the candles by her bed.

She looked at the crumpled body of Renaud, the scalpel still held tightly in his right hand. "You were all right; Leona was right. He meant to kill me." Marguerite continued to stare at Renaud. "Now we must all fear for our lives. We have killed the most powerful of priests, an evil man, yet powerful," she breathed.

"Had he killed you, his power would have been increased tenfold," Philip said.

Marguerite nodded. She noticed his bleeding arm. "Your arm, Philip!"

"It's just a flesh wound," he replied as he tore a piece of material from the pillowcase and wrapped it around his arm.

Marguerite helped him tie it on and said, "You are right, no one must know. We cannot call the guard. We must dispose of the body ourselves if France is to be saved terrible religious torment. This, my friend, is the stuff of civil wars."

"Let me get the others," Philip suggested. "We will have to decide what to do." He wondered if she had heard him call Renaud Cyril or if she had understood Renaud's response. Probably not, he decided. What did it mean, this vision he had just had? He could not explain it, yet it had been strong and detailed. More startling yet, Renaud had responded as if he, too, had the same vision and indeed knew who Cyril was.

In a few moments Leona and Michel joined Marguerite and Philip.

Michel examined Renaud and removed the scalpel from his fingers. "I believe he intended blaming me. You have saved two lives, Philip."

"I am most grateful," Marguerite whispered.

"Let us wrap him in sheets and weight the body. The river runs swift this time of year," Leona suggested.

They looked from one to the other and nodded their mutual agreement.

"If you leave by this window, you will have an easy time getting him to the river without being seen. Be grateful the night is so dark," Leona said.

Philip smiled. "Earlier I cursed the darkness."

"No one must ever know of this deed," Marguerite emphasized again.

They all agreed.

June
The Kingdom of Navarre

Leona ran through the field of wildflowers while Pegasus trotted about, tossing his proud head and relishing the warm air.

"It's so lovely here," Leona said as she collapsed beside Philip on the grass.

"Where is Michel?" she asked.

"He's coming. He said he would stop and say good-bye to us."

"I can't believe he's going all the way to Italy."

"To the home of the de'Medicis no less."

"Well, according to you, one day Catherine de'Medici will be queen of France."

"She will learn well from your brother."

"That is his destiny."

"Ah, here he comes now. Over here!" Philip waved.

Michel guided his stallion to where they were. Now was the moment. Last night a shadow had passed in front of the moon. It was the sign for which he had been waiting.

He drew his horse to a halt and slid off. "I'm eager to leave and sad to go."

Leona kissed him on the cheek. "It is your destiny to advise Catherine. Will you return to France?"

"In a few years. You will both stay with Marguerite. Soon the persecutions will end completely and it will once again be safe in France."

"I had hoped they would end when Renaud disappeared, but I know it is not as bad as it would have been had he lived. And of course, many dissidents are here, living in safety."

Michel nodded. "There is always another Renaud. There is always someone prepared to take advantage of people's hatreds and fears just as there is always someone to fight those people. Our light must be cast in the dark corners; truth does not thrive in darkness."

"I wish you well," Philip said, clasping Michel's shoulder.

"You will see me again and again. You will know me forever as you know Leona and Pegasus. Now I can tell you both. You, Philip, were brought back—reborn—conditionally. You passed all earthly tests. You, too, will walk among the stars, my friend."

"We both lived before, didn't we?" Philip asked.

"Yes, in Byzantium. Where you, Leona, had begun working with molds and mushrooms as a cure for infection."

"Yes. As you know, I used a kind of mold on the king when he was ill in Madrid—I was directed to it."

"And I found your ancient notebooks, my sister. They were hidden away and rescued by some crusader who found them interesting. Since then they have been languishing in the medical library at Montpellier. By using them I have developed something similar for plague which, if given in the early stages, seems to help."

"How long have you known about us?" Philip asked.

"For a time. I was told to reveal it to you both when I was given a sign. I have been given that sign."

With that Michel remounted, and with a wave of his hand, rode away.

Leona turned and leaned against Philip. "We are not mad," she said softly.

"Did you think we were?"

"A little, my love. A little."

He drew her into his arms and kissed her deeply. "We'll be together always."

"Time and again," she whispered.

Epilogue

It was July 1566 and Michel de Nostradamus stared through his telescope at the summer sky. Beside him were his journals in which he had just written the final quartet in his guide to the future, a future filled with turmoil and with wonder. The greatest wonder was the promise that all ignorance would be removed, and that all would see with unveiled eyes.

He was sixty-three and felt old, though he knew that in years to come, men would not feel old at sixty-three. He smiled at the heavens. He loved the summer sky; it gave him great pleasure.

He moved his telescope outward and suddenly saw a bright streak across the night sky—clearly, without question, the image was revealed to him. Headed for Orion was the great winged white horse Pegasus, and on it were the two star-crossed lovers who were now to be lovers forevermore.

He let his telescope drop slightly, smiled, and closed his eyes to join them.